# BLUE HOLLOW FALLS

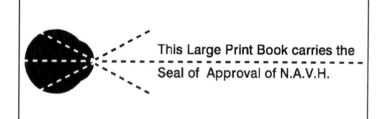

This Large Print Book carries the
Seal of Approval of N.A.V.H.

# BLUE HOLLOW FALLS

## DONNA KAUFFMAN

**KENNEBEC LARGE PRINT**
A part of Gale, a Cengage Company

Farmington Hills, Mich • San Francisco • New York • Waterville, Maine
Meriden, Conn • Mason, Ohio • Chicago

Copyright © 2017 by Donna Kauffman.
Blue Hollow Falls.
Kennebec Large Print, a part of Gale, a Cengage Company.

**ALL RIGHTS RESERVED**
Kennebec Large Print® Superior Collection.
The text of this Large Print edition is unabridged.
Other aspects of the book may vary from the original edition.
Set in 16 pt. Plantin.

LIBRARY OF CONGRESS CIP DATA ON FILE.
CATALOGUING IN PUBLICATION FOR THIS BOOK
IS AVAILABLE FROM THE LIBRARY OF CONGRESS

ISBN-13: 978-1-4328-4289-5 (hardcover)
ISBN-10: 1-4328-4289-7 (hardcover)

Published in 2017 by arrangement with Zebra Books, an imprint of
Kensington Publishing Corp.

Printed in Mexico
1 2 3 4 5 6 7 21 20 19 18 17

*For Mom & Dad*

# CHAPTER ONE

In the span of one hour, twenty-nine-year-old Sunny Goodwin had gained an eighty-five-year-old father (recently deceased), a ten-year-old half sister (very much alive), and a seventy-two-year-old stepmother (possibly immortal). She'd never heard of any of them, much less laid eyes on them. In fact, she would have sworn, with utmost confidence — on a stack of Bibles even — that since the death of her mother eight months ago, she had no living family. Or she could have, if you'd asked her anytime up until about, oh, an hour ago.

Sunny was also the proud new owner of a two-hundred-year-old silk mill. Well, part owner. Along with her new baby sister, step-mama, and someone named Sawyer, who hadn't even bothered to show up to claim his share.

"So," she murmured under her breath, still trying to absorb it all. "That just happened." She stood on the front steps of the Rockfish County courthouse, deep in the heart of Virginia's Blue Ridge Mountains, and took a slow, steadying breath. The tiny town that housed the county seat, charmingly named Turtle Springs, was tucked up into a crook of the winding north fork of the Hawksbill River, which hugged the little burg from the west. The courthouse faced the ancient, timeworn tumble of boulders and thick forest that made up the Blue Ridge Mountains, which rose up right at the edge of town to the east, with only a lone stretch of two-lane country highway separating the two.

Trying to take a moment to get her bearings back, she was instead caught up immediately in her surroundings. She breathed in the crisp scent of the late-September air, lifting her gaze to the rise and fall of the smaller hills that led up into the bigger, taller mountains, whose alternating rounded and pointed peaks marched along the horizon as far as the eye could see. The rich array of colors that all but burst forth from them made it look as if someone had tossed the most beautiful handmade quilt over the entire range, cloaking every ripple, accentuating every fold, in the impossibly rich hues and shades of early autumn. The overall pattern was so stunning, it made her heart fill right up. It was hard to believe she was in the same state she'd grown up in, a mere few hours east of that very spot. Her home in Alexandria was tucked along the far gentler curve of the Potomac, facing the equally majestic peaks and spires of the nation's capital just on the other side of the river.

Tearing her gaze away from the oil painting view, Sunshine Meadow Aquarius Morrison Goodwin stared down at the official legal documents she held in one hand, and the key to the mill dangling from the other. Then she shook her head, a rueful smile curving her lips as she looked up at the wide open sky, her thoughts pushing beyond that gorgeous expanse of aquamarine blue to the heavens beyond. She was sure Daisy Rose Rainbow Love Garcia Goodwin was loving every moment of this. *Thanks, Mama.* She jingled the keys, then curled her fingers around them. *Thanks for the warning.*

Sunny's mother had spent a good part of her younger years out here, though a bit farther down the range, and higher up in the hills. Daisy Rose had been born Deirdre Louise Goodwin, daughter of Chuck Goodwin, who'd run his own contracting business, and Betty Dayton Goodwin who had been Chuck's secretary before they married, and a mother and homemaker from about eight months on after they said their I do's.

Dee Dee, as her mother had been known during her childhood, had grown up in the fifties and sixties and by her twentieth birthday, she'd become a bona fide peace-loving, war-protesting, commune-living, flower child — much to her suburban middle-class parents' bewilderment — and had remained such all of her life. More in spirit than actuality during Sunny's lifetime, but once a free spirit, always a free spirit. The legal name change had come when Dee Dee had turned eighteen. She'd just moved into a hippie commune that specialized in, uh, herbal farming, located about an hour south of Turtle Springs, nestled way up in the higher elevations of the Blue Ridge.

Daisy Rose had explained her chosen nom de plume to her young, inquisitive daughter, saying she'd wanted to honor her flower power culture, the full spectrum of the colors of the universe, the commune's mantra that love conquered all, and, last, but never least, her personal spiritual guide, Jerry Garcia. Yes, the Grateful Dead's own Brother Jerry.

Sunny, unfortunately, had had no say in

hers. It came with the birth certificate. Daisy Rose — and her mama had always been Daisy Rose to everyone, including her daughter, as she was firmly against people being called by titles or labels, no matter how beloved the job itself might be — had explained to her only child that she'd named her daughter to honor the glory of Mother Nature, the celestial alignment of the stars and the moon on the day of her daughter's birth, and, because Daisy Rose had still been grieving his loss some twenty-odd years after his death, her not-so-spiritual, but still mystical and, yes, oh-so-sexy, personal guide, Jim Morrison.

It could have been worse, Sunny had reminded herself. *So many, many times.* Her mother could have been more deeply infatuated with Blue Oyster Cult. Or Engelbert Humperdinck. Their music had also been on rotation during the soundtrack of Sunny's childhood. Her mother's tastes were nothing if not as eclectic as her name.

In Sunny's younger years, usually after a particularly challenging day being tormented by her classmates over her name, she'd promised herself she'd be like her mother and change it the moment she reached legal age. Only, in Sunny's case, she'd be changing it to something as normal and mundane as possible. She'd spent long hours doodling in her school binders, trying this name and that on for size. But the world worked in mysterious ways, and by the time Sunny had reached her eighteenth birthday, the roles of mother and daughter had long since reversed.

Her mother's ongoing health issues had put Sunny in charge of her care, and pretty much everything else, by the time Sunny had hit puberty. And somewhere along the line, Sunny's own eclectic string of names had gone from being fodder for peer group torture to something of a cause célèbre amongst her now older and envious classmates. Yes, envious. They'd all been at the age of trying to figure out who they were, and Sunny had already cornered the market on being unique, no self-realization required.

It hadn't hurt that her closest acquaintances had also met her mother by then and fallen under Daisy Rose's charming, ditzy dreamer, Peter Pan spell. Her friends had adored her mother. In fact, Sunny wasn't too sure that some of her friends hadn't put themselves in her orbit expressly so they, too, could spend time with her infectiously likable mama. Everyone wished their mother was like Daisy Rose. Everyone, that is, except the only one who actually had her for a mother.

Not that Sunny hadn't loved her mother; she had. Deeply, and with all her heart. She wasn't immune to Pan's spell, either. But Sunny knew, in great and sometimes alarming detail, just what the cost was for the person responsible for being . . . well, responsible. A trait Daisy Rose hadn't been blessed with, even in passing. Love might conquer all, but love didn't pay the bills. Or cook the meals. Or clean the house. Or oversee medication dispersal. While simultaneously being the overmedication police.

Sunny had wished, many times, that she could just up and run away from home, from being responsible, or come home to a mom who was normal, or at least more like the other kids' mamas were. But no matter how trying Daisy Rose could be, she'd always had an unflappable faith in things working themselves out for the best, and she'd had a way of making Sunny believe that, too.

Questions about her father, whom Sunny had wasted a fair amount of her youth praying would come rescue them, had always been met with a wave of a heavily beringed hand and a smile . . . and no explanation of who he was, much less where he'd gone.

"You're my miracle baby," Daisy would always say. "A gift from the stars." Daisy Rose proclaimed that the universe had decreed she and Sunny were their own special tribe of two, and wasn't that just grand?

Sunny hadn't always thought so, but her mother was a force of nature whose unending sweetness and perennial optimism would seemingly indicate a doormat type, while in reality, Daisy's ferocious need to believe in all things good had been far more steamroller than pushover. No matter what life handed her, Daisy Rose Rainbow Love Garcia Goodwin had faced it with a smile on her face and a twinkle in her eye. Mother Nature would take care of them. Things were tough, yes, but they had each other, and that made them rich beyond the stars.

Stars were big with Daisy. She'd always claimed she had these mystical powers and would pass along her "revelations" to all of Sunny's friends, who had affectionately called her Mrs. Goodwitch, even though there had never been a Mr. Goodwitch. And the only Mr. Goodwin had been Sunny's grandfather, Chuck, who, along with her grandmother, Betty, had passed on before Sunny had been born.

Sunny knew from her mother's stories that

their sudden, untimely passing in an automobile accident had been the reason Sunny had been born at all. Apparently, her grandmother, Betty, had held out hope that someday Daisy would meet a "normal" guy, fall in love, get married, and somehow morph into the regular, everyday suburban housewife Betty had always hoped she'd be, a daughter she could connect with, have something in common with. She'd be Dee Dee again, give them grandchildren, and through that miracle of birth and raising her own kids, she'd see her free love, flower power, commune living past as just a crazy phase she'd been going through. The immaturity of youth.

Daisy had indeed met her share of men — more than her share, if all of her colorful stories and the trunk full of scrapbooks she'd created were any indication — but Daisy had also always been careful to the point of being a little paranoid about things like sexually transmitted diseases, and unwanted pregnancies. Betty, perhaps, could at least take credit for instilling that bit of wisdom in her daughter. When her parents died so suddenly, so tragically, Daisy's attitude changed somewhat, and she became convinced that she had to bring two souls into the world to somehow make up for the two souls who had departed before their time. Something about life cycles, the universe, and balancing the scales.

At thirty-seven years of age, Daisy had gotten pregnant with Sunny, only it hadn't been an easy pregnancy. The birth, overseen by a midwife who had come by the job title simply by being the one in the commune who had helped deliver the most babies, had been nothing short of harrowing, coming very close to costing Daisy Rose not only the life of her baby, but her own life as well.

Shortly afterward, amongst a host of other postpartum complications, Daisy had had a complete hysterectomy — performed in a hospital, thank God — meaning Sunny's soul would be the only one brought forth to balance the spiritual scales. But even a life-threatening birthing followed by drastic emergency surgery hadn't resolved all of her mother's medical issues. Daisy Rose had never regained full health and her physical limitations were many. Commune living, therefore, hadn't been a wise option for her and her newborn daughter.

Sunny had been forever grateful, more times over than she could count, that one of her mother's free-love, commune-living beaus had been so smitten with her that he'd deeded her his family's empty, unused Old Town Alexandria row house after Sunny's near-tragic birth. He'd renounced city life, but knew it was Daisy's best bet to be as healthy as possible, while giving her daughter a decent chance.

Had it not been for her mother's benefactor, Sunny knew they'd have been forced to find a way to exist in commune living, or a shelter. Or worse. As a child, Sunny had often wondered if that mystery man had been her father — who else would give Daisy a whole, perfectly good house? But when she'd learned from snooping through those copious boxes of mementos and endless piles of journals and scrapbooks that their erstwhile benefactor was close to twenty years her mother's senior, Sunny's adolescent brain had assumed he couldn't be. Too old. Standing on the courthouse steps, she stared down at the papers in her hand once again.

She'd been very wrong.

Doyle Bartholomew Hartwell, eighty-five years old upon his death and eighteen years older than her mother, had, indeed, been Sunny's father.

No point wishing now she'd pushed her mother harder, or pushed her own curiosity further. Both of her parents were gone now.

And what would have been the point in hunting for a man who'd obviously thought enough of her mother to take care of her and their child, but not enough to marry her, much less bother to ever meet his own daughter?

Sunny looked at her name, all five parts, typed in on the line of the deed that said "co-owner." She smiled. Love it or hate it, she'd never changed it. Her own personal tribute to her frustrating, challenging, yet beloved mama. That said, if Sunny were ever of a mind to add to the planet's population, she wouldn't be passing that tribute down to her own progeny.

The heavy, double oak doors to the courthouse were suddenly thrust open behind her, bumping her off balance. She grabbed the handrail to steady herself, and turned to find her brand-new extended family emerging from the big, redbrick building. *I won't need to populate anything,* she thought, still feeling more than a little bewildered by the day's events. *My life just got populated without my even trying.*

"There you are," her newly inherited stepmother said. Addison Pearl Whitaker was another aging hippie, but that was where the comparison to Sunny's own mother began and ended. Where her mother had been all fluttery scarves, flowing gypsy skirts, and love beads, Addie Pearl was more the tie-dyed, oversized T-shirt, faded old green Army shorts, and well-worn leather work boots type. Her gun-metal gray hair was long — very long — and plaited in a single, narrow braid all the way down her back, past her wide waist, to the equally wide, but flat-to-almost non-existent fanny below it. Her face was well-tanned, well-worn, and deeply creased, but her eyes flashed the most peculiar shade of crystalline lavender, which made her look both kind and a bit spooky all at the same time. Her smile, which she flashed naturally and quite often as she spoke, showed two rows of well-maintained, perfectly aligned dentures. She used a walking stick made from a hand carved oak tree branch, though Sunny was fairly certain from the woman's sturdy arms and legs, not to mention her bubbling energy, that she could climb Everest without aid of walking stick or Sherpa. Her posture was a wee bit stooped, but even standing perfectly erect, Sunny figured Addie would top out a good five or six inches shorter than herself, no taller than five-foot-one or two at most.

Addie Pearl, as she'd asked them to call her, was followed out by ten-year-old Bailey

Sutton. Apparently, Doyle had continued to father children out of wedlock all the way into his mid-seventies. At least that they knew of. Only, in Bailey's case, her mother had taken Doyle's support money, dumped her infant daughter into the foster care system, and headed off for parts unknown, never to be heard from again.

Bailey looked tall for her age, thin but in a wiry way, not frail. She had naturally pale skin, freckled cheeks and nose, strikingly bright blue eyes, and a waterfall of straw-berry blond hair — heavy on the strawberry — that hung in rumpled waves down to the middle of her back. She had on old but clean blue jeans, a western-style, teal blue and green plaid shirt buttoned up over a pale yellow T-shirt, and beat-up cowboy boots on her feet. All she was missing was the wide-brimmed cowboy hat, and Sunny didn't doubt she had one tucked away somewhere. Possibly with a horse or three.

Sunny looked behind Bailey, assuming the young girl's caseworker, who'd accompanied Bailey to the legal proceedings, would be stepping out next. Only, the door closed behind Bailey. And stayed closed.

Sunny looked at Addie Pearl. "Where's Miss Jackson?"

Addie shrugged one knobby shoulder, but

the gleam in her ethereally colored eyes was an undeniably satisfied one. "On her way back to where she came from, I guess."

Sunny's eyes widened and she glanced briefly at Bailey. "But — ?"

Addie reached for Bailey's hand, and kindly tugged the girl, who was almost the same height as she was, forward a step. "She has real family now. Doesn't need herself a caseworker, much less that fake family she's been staying with." Addie's voice was a bit rough, which went along with her weathered appearance, and had more than a bit of a Southern twang, which Sunny was coming to realize was the norm in this mountainous part of the state. She supposed if she'd thought about it, that would make sense, but she'd spent her whole life in the metropolitan part of Virginia, which wasn't Southern at all, so the voices she'd heard in the courtroom had momentarily surprised her. There was a bit of a western-mountains lilt to the accent as well.

Sunny looked at Bailey, who hadn't spoken more than the few words necessary inside the courthouse to make it clear she understood what she'd been bequeathed. She knew from the court proceedings that Bailey's most recent foster family owned a farm that ran right along the border of West

Virginia, a few hours northwest of Turtle Springs, but beyond that, Sunny didn't know her history. The young girl met Sunny's gaze easily. Not defensively, but not shyly or uncertainly either. She gave a small shrug in response to Addie's sentiment, but said nothing, apparently unfazed by this latest transition in her life. Sunny wished she was handling the events of the past hour with such easy aplomb.

She glanced down at the papers clutched in Bailey's small hands. And the key to the mill she'd also been given. Sunny had wondered about that. She looked back at Addie Pearl, who hadn't gotten a key, as she'd already owned her part of the mill. It had been part of her divorce settlement from Doyle — whom Addie had referred to in court as D. Bart — over twenty years prior. And if there was a sliver of suspicion in Sunny's expression over possible motives Addie might have for befriending the girl, she wasn't going to apologize for it. Addie was the only one of the three of them who came from Blue Hollow Falls, where the mill was located.

The mill had been only one of many properties Doyle had apparently owned in his lifetime, if not at the time of his death. He'd handed off a number of them over the years. Not only the row house Sunny still lived in, but, as she'd learned from asking Doyle's attorney during the court proceedings, he'd also owned the property the mountain commune had used, the one her mother had lived in from the age of eighteen until she'd given birth to Sunny. According to Addie, Doyle hadn't actually been part of the commune, but he'd enjoyed visiting from time to time, when he wanted to "get away" for a bit. Sunny got the feeling Doyle had been more interested in checking in on his "cash crop," but what did that matter now?

The commune, long since disbanded, had been located close to two hours south and west of Blue Hollow Falls, near the North Carolina border, where the Blue Ridge became the Smoky Mountains. Sunny's inheritance wasn't that far from Turtle Springs, but given the old mountain roads and the steep climb, Addie said it would take her almost an hour to get to it. Blue Hollow Falls was still in Rockfish County, but well up into the Blue Ridge, high above the Hawksbill Valley. Addie described it as deep woods surrounded by high meadow, tucked in along Big Stone Creek, which was the source of the falls that had, in part, given the tiny town its name. She explained how it tumbled over boulders beside the mill, then wound its way down through the steep mountains, before feeding directly into the winding Hawksbill River far below. She'd made the Hollow sound both historic and not a little magical.

Addie had lived in Blue Hollow her entire adult life, and as the only woman to actually ever marry Doyle, one could easily assume she'd have believed the remainder of the mill would be passed down to her.

*Well,* Sunny decided, giving Bailey a brief, but hopefully encouraging smile, *if the old woman thinks she's going to take advantage of a poor orphan girl, she has another think coming.* It hit Sunny in that moment that she, too, was now an orphan. She'd never thought about it like that. However, she was a grown adult. Bailey was a child. A minor. With no one to look out for her best interests, other than a foster family who got a paycheck for housing her and an overburdened caseworker who likely was happy to have one less file stacked on her desk.

"You need a ride?" Addie Pearl wanted to know.

Sunny blinked, realizing Addie was talking to her. "Oh, no, but thank you. I have my own car." Sunny paused, then said, "Ride to where?"

"Blue Hollow Falls." Addie nodded to Sunny's right hand. The one that held the key. "Don't you want a look at your inheritance? You've come out this far."

While Sunny didn't want Addie Pearl to take advantage of Bailey's situation, that didn't mean she wanted to be wrong about the woman's intentions in general. If Addie wanted to take good care of Bailey, and oversee her inheritance in a fair and legal manner, Sunny didn't plan to stand in the way. Personally, she had no need for any part of a two-hundred-year-old, long-defunct silk mill, and she hadn't even begun to wrap her head around what having a ten-year-old half sister might mean. Other than being surprised to know there had actually been silk production in the state of Virginia, or any of the original colonies, for that matter, she wasn't interested in owning a share in the mill.

In fact, she'd already been planning to make Addie Pearl a deal she couldn't refuse. Then Sunny looked at Bailey again, and caught a brief, unguarded moment in which the child looked behind her at the empty space where her caseworker had been, then down at the key and envelope holding the legal papers she had clutched in one hand. Despite having eyes that looked like an old soul lived behind them, she was just a ten-year-old kid. As Sunny had once been, when confronted with the reality that she was going to be caretaker to her mother, and not the other way around.

"Yes," Sunny said, "I guess I should take a look, shouldn't I?" She smiled. "I'll follow you." It was probably a good idea to check it out anyway, if for no other reason than to assess it and come to a fair agreement with Addie on divesting herself of her share. Then, if everything looked kosher, she'd be heading back to Old Town, back to her life. Back to her work as a horticulturist for the U.S. Botanic Garden. Back to that old row house on King Street. The one that seemed impossibly quieter now, without her mother's musical laughter filling the rooms, without her endless chattering to the songbirds who favored, as Daisy Rose had, spending a great deal of their time in the keyhole garden nestled in the tiny, brick-walled backyard.

Sunny had begun that garden as a nine-year-old who'd always had a penchant for digging in the dirt, and she'd continued to build on that scruffy and scraggly early effort, nurturing to life something beautiful for her mother, something that had eventually become her own life's calling. Sunny pictured the padded turquoise chaise her mother had loved, perched under an awning made of beaded scarves, like the throne of a fairy queen. Sunny smiled briefly, sadly. Her mother had been very much that. Maybe Sunny would invite Bailey to come visit. Bring some life and new perspective to the place. *Yes,* she thought, satisfied with the idea, *that might be a very good place to start.*

Sunny followed along behind Addie Pearl's ancient, forest green Subaru in her own little robin's egg blue Mini Cooper, thinking they made a kind of cute little caravan, winding up and up into the hills, deeper and deeper into the mountains. She felt like she was a world apart from her life in the city, finding it hard to believe she was only a few hours away from home. She decided to simply enjoy the seasonal colors and the opportunity the twisty mountain roads gave her to use the lower gears of her zippy little six-speed to their fullest potential. There would be plenty of time to sort through all the new family information and figure out how it would fit in with her life going forward.

Sunny admitted as she drove through Buck's Pass, along the rushing waters of Big Stone Creek, and eventually up into the bucolic idyll of the high pocket meadows and deep forest that housed Blue Hollow Falls proper, that the utter beauty of it all tugged at her soul in ways she couldn't put into words, and made her itch like mad to sink her fingers into the dirt.

The rolling hills and dales of rich, verdant farmland rose up into the dense forest, showcasing an artist's palette of vivid autumnal colors, and disappeared into ancient, rounded mountain peaks. She assumed those peaks were the ones Addie had said were known to the locals as Hawk's Nest Ridge.

It was up in those hills, in the shadow of the ridge's crest that she finally pulled in and came to a stop, parking next to Addie. In front of her sat the Hartwell Silk Mill, her inheritance, along with a good deal of the property that surrounded it. But it wasn't the mill alone that had caught her breath tight in her throat. Compelled, as if being physically pulled from her vehicle by some giant hand, she climbed out of her car, and simply stared. It was, quite literally . . . breathtaking.

She'd had no idea what to expect, but she'd have never imagined this. The mill itself was an old pile, to be sure, but a much bigger one than she'd pictured. Built out of stone and old weathered wood with a paneled tin roof, the building was at least two stories from the front view, possibly three given there was a lower part she couldn't see where the land sloped down around the back. It was set at the top of a steeply sloped crook of Big Stone Creek. The main part of the long front and shorter side walls of the building were paneled in old gray wood, structured like an old warehouse, with rusted metal-framed windows marching along the front. There was a crooked and bent weather vane topping the large cupola at the center of the peak of a tin panel roof that had seen better years. Decades, most likely. There were two stone chimneys that she could see, framing either end of the building, and the bottom part of the front and side wall, and all of the lower part of the back of the building, were built from stone as well. There was a small dirt lot down there, which she could see now was connected by a narrow service road to the upper dirt lot they'd pulled into.

None of that was what had tugged her from her car. No, what made her heart drum inside her chest was the tumbling waterfall that began as a glassy cascade over the boulder-strewn ledge jutting out from the side of the mill, then churned into a froth of white as it tumbled down over huge, waterworn boulders. It rushed on down the mountainside, but not before passing under the giant metal waterwheel that was attached to the far short side of the mill.

The whole of it looked like something out of a vintage, black and white postcard, only it was in full, vivid color, framed by a forest of rainbow-colored trees. Far above the treetops soared a ridge of jutting gray rock, capped by the startling blue sky. She could barely take it all in. Despite the dilapidated state of the mill itself, the beauty of the scene was beyond picturesque. It was truly staggering.

The waterwheel, which appeared to have once been painted red, wasn't functioning, and the property surrounding the centuries-old mill appeared to be long out of use as well, looking overgrown and scrubby. However, once she could pull her attention away from the falls and really look at the place, she immediately realized there was work going on. In fact, a renovation appeared to be underway. Once she adjusted to the thundering roar of the falls, she heard the unmistakable sound of electric saws whining, hammers being pounded against wood, and the lilt of folk music echoing through the much cooler high mountain air.

Before she could turn to Addie, ask her

what was going on with the place — now partly her place — a man strode out of the open, barn-style sliding doors. He gave a short wave and headed across the scrabble of grass and stone toward the lot where they stood.

"That would be Sawyer Hartwell," Addie told Sunny and Bailey as the man approached.

If the mill and its surroundings were a thing of natural beauty, the man now striding toward them fit right into the picture. *Dear Lord, have mercy.*

Sunny had asked Addie about Sawyer back at the courthouse, whether she knew him, knew why he hadn't shown up, and all Addie had said was, "Well, Sawyer isn't much of one for following convention or worrying what other folks think."

So Sunny hadn't known what to expect. She'd figured maybe he was some backwoods hermit type, too stubborn to venture forth, even if it meant he might have inherited something of value. He had the same last name as her father, but that could mean anything. Brother, cousin, who knew? Other than his ownership of the silk mill along with her, Addie, and Bailey, the magistrate had skipped over any other parts of the will that pertained to him since he wasn't there to hear them.

The man was definitely no hermit, back-woods or otherwise.

Sawyer Hartwell was a bigger-than-life, broadly smiling, welcome-everybody kind of guy. Emphasis on the big part. A towering six-five to her heretofore-thought-of-as tall five-foot-eight frame, he had a white slash of a smile that some might describe as cocky but was at the very least boldly confident. That smile was framed by twin, deep set dimples that propped up well-defined cheekbones, all of it topped by a pair of crystal blue eyes that appeared to channel every bit of light in that beautiful sky above directly through them. His dark hair was close cropped, almost military style, which only served to enhance his chiseled . . . everything. He was, in a word, *gorgeous*. As all hell. And then some. *And me with no fan.*

He filled out his filthy white T-shirt in ways that made all of her girl parts wish like hell the two of them weren't possibly related, as he did those equally filthy and beaten-up old jeans that hung on lean, narrow hips. Jeans that slid down just enough in the back as he reached down to pick up a handful of nails that fell out of a hole in his back pocket to show that one of the conventions Sawyer Hartwell apparently flaunted was wearing underwear. *Heaven help us all.*

He gave Addie a quick, one-arm squeeze before turning to her and Bailey, welcoming grin still in place. Sunny quickly jerked her gaze up to his, hoping he hadn't caught her all but ogling him. It wasn't like her to have her head turned so easily. Or at all, really. Maybe it was finding him amidst all the other overwhelming beauty of the place that had her heart skipping a beat or two. Or three. Maybe.

"Hello," he said, his voice deep, silky smooth, and unsurprisingly as perfect as the rest of him. He tipped his head toward Bailey as well. "Nice to meet you both." His open, engaging smile earned him a brief one in return from the young girl, the first Sunny had seen from her. *Handsome men,* Sunny thought wryly, *lethal to a girl at any age.*

He leaned down, gave Addie's weathered cheek a quick peck, then pulled his battered leather and suede work glove off to extend a broad, well-tanned hand to Sunny. "Any friend of Addie's," he said, his smile deepening, making his blue eyes twinkle. Eyes, she realized now, that were the same crystalline blue as Bailey's.

*So,* she thought, *that answered that. Settle*

*right back down,* she schooled her still-galloping hormones, *we're related. Dammit.*

"Meet our one and only Sergeant Angel," Addie said proudly, sliding her arm through his, her lavender eyes full of love and admiration.

The man gave Addie a dry, if affectionate look. "Please," he said with a wry twist to his mouth, then looked back at Sunny, his dusty hand still proffered. "I'm Sawyer. Sawyer Hartwell."

"Hello," she said, giving his broad, warm hand a quick shake that did nothing to quiet the apparently all-too-easily aroused parts of her body. "So . . . you're renovating the old mill?" She asked the question to steer them toward a topic — any topic — that would help get her mind back on track, but also because she wanted to know the answer. How would the work he was doing fit in with the fact that she and Bailey now owned a third of the place? Maybe Sawyer and Addie hadn't thought they'd show up to claim their share? Sunny realized this was maybe going to be a bit more complicated than she'd thought. *Like finding out I have family hasn't complicated things enough.*

Or, upon further consideration, maybe not. If he and Addie were renovating, then perhaps that made Sunny's share all the more lucrative and they'd be that much more eager to buy her out. Of course, that didn't resolve the concern about Bailey's share. But one problem at a time.

At Sawyer's nod, Sunny said, "It looks like the place hasn't been in use for —"

"One hundred and seven years," Addie finished for her. "Last time that wheel worked was nineteen-ten. A few folks have sniffed around it over the ensuing years, a historian here or there, but it's a monument to our beginnings and the one thing D. Bart had left that originated with the first Hartwells to come to this country. He didn't have a sentimental bone in his body, the old coot, and he wasn't much of one for sticking around, but he couldn't — wouldn't — get rid of his birthright. What's ours stays ours. Despite the neglect, it's stood the test of time."

Sunny suspected Addie might have had more than a little to do with why Doyle had held on to the property. And she didn't react to the "what's ours, stays ours" part, but she tucked that bit of information away. *Good to know.* On further observation, Sunny noted that the renovations hadn't just started. Looking down the slope around the back of the place, she could see stacks of lumber, some construction machinery.

So, it appeared they were well underway on at least some part of it. Which meant they'd begun the process before Doyle had passed. Sunny didn't say anything about that, either. Instead she asked, "So, why now?"

Sawyer flashed another grin, making those dimples flash and making her want to fan herself again . . . or something. It was as if he exuded pheromones along with his sweat. *You're related,* her little voice sing-songed.

"I guess I mean for what purpose?" she said, forging on determinedly through the pheromone cloud.

"For the purpose of making my home actually habitable."

That gave Sunny pause. "Your . . . home? You live here? In the mill?"

"I do," he said, happily, proudly even. "If you can call an old cot and a camp stove under a heavily leaking roof living." He let out a short laugh. "But I've survived on a lot less and in a lot worse." He said all this without so much as a hint that she might be a bit troubled by such a pronouncement.

Though why she cared, she didn't know. Because, really, what did it matter? What did any of this matter?

"Why did she call you Sergeant Angel?"

36

This from Bailey.

It was the first sentence she'd spoken, other than *yes, ma'am* or *yes, sir,* since Sunny had first laid eyes on her. Bailey's voice was soft, her accent distinctly Southern, making Sunny wonder how and where she'd spent her young life thus far.

"Don't mind that," Sawyer told Bailey. "You can call me Sawyer."

"He was a master sergeant, actually," Addie began, but a friendly, if direct glance from Sawyer shushed her from going any further.

Addie's responding smile wasn't so much abashed as it was indulgent. It was clear she and Sawyer were close. Very close. The family kind of close. And Sunny had the sudden thought that — could he be — was Addie Pearl his . . . mother? Sawyer appeared to be close to Sunny's own age, maybe a few years older, early thirties at most. So . . . no. More likely Addie — who was at least in her seventies — would be his grandmother. Wouldn't she have mentioned that at the courthouse, though, when Sunny had asked about him? That could explain why Sawyer hadn't felt the need to show up in person.

This new piece of information scrambled around in her brain, along with all the rest, and she tried to quickly figure out, if he was Doyle's grandson, what that would make him to her. Some kind of second cousin? No, wait — *gah* — her nephew? *What?*

"And you two would be . . . ?" Sawyer asked courteously, mercifully interrupting her mental gymnastics. His gaze encompassed both her and Bailey.

And that was the moment Sunny realized he had no idea. He hadn't been hoping she and Bailey wouldn't show up to claim their share of the mill. He hadn't shown up himself because he hadn't thought there was anyone but him and Addie left to claim the mill.

*Oh, boy.*

Addie hadn't looked particularly surprised to see Sunny or Bailey at the proceedings, hadn't seemed upset, or angry, but what did Sunny know about the old woman or her motives? *Nothing. That was what.*

"Sunny," she said to him, skipping over her full name. "Sunny Goodwin. And this is Bailey Sutton." Sunny lifted the key she'd palmed from her pocket.

She noted that Bailey had fished hers out of her pocket as well.

Sunny let the key dangle from her fingertips, and she felt her lips curve a little as Bailey did the same. "She and I have differ-

38

ent mamas, but it turns out Doyle Hartwell was our biological father," Sunny told him. "And now Bailey and I officially own a third of your house."

# CHAPTER TWO

Sawyer felt his smile slip just a tic. It took a lot to catch him off guard, but the pretty brunette and her cute little redheaded sidekick had just managed to do a very fine job of it.

He immediately shot a questioning look at Addie, who merely lifted a knobby shoulder and smiled, utterly unrepentant. That last part didn't surprise him one bit. "Did you know about this?" he asked her, keeping his tone easy, body relaxed, his smile still in place. "Before you left here this morning, I mean?"

"If you're asking if I knew D. Bart fathered other children, well then, yes, of course I did."

At her use of the word *other* Sawyer felt the brunette's gaze laser back to him. So she thought they were related by blood? What had she said her name was? Sunny? Sunny Goodwin. She looked about his age, give or take, and despite how young her sidekick was in comparison, he didn't doubt her claim that Doyle had fathered them both. That wasn't the shocking part. He looked back at Addie. "Whether or not Doyle fathered any progeny isn't what I'm asking. I'm asking if you knew about the will?" He knew he should be having this conversation in private, but at this point, what the hell? They would all know the full story at some point. "Are there —" He broke off, glanced at Bailey. Then again, maybe this wasn't a conversation she needed to be hearing.

"More *progeny*?" Sunny asked, placing emphasis on the last word. "I have no idea. I never met the man. From what I understand, neither has Bailey."

The young girl shook her head, and he was struck at how calmly she was taking all this. Calmer than the adults, it seemed.

"So, you two — ?" he asked.

"Just met today," Sunny finished for him, smiling despite her direct, no-nonsense tone. She didn't seem particularly emotional either, neither pro nor con; she was definitely all business. While Bailey was dressed like she'd just gotten done at the stables, and Addie was dressed, well, like Addie, Sunny had put on a nicely pressed go-to-court city suit, complete with a tailored brown skirt that fell just below the knee, stockings, and sensible brown pumps to match, a smartly tailored tweed jacket over a cream-colored silk blouse, topped off with a pretty teal and green paisley scarf and tasteful gold studs tacked to her earlobes.

Her dark hair was a waterfall of thick waves, made glossier by the afternoon sun and styled to fall neatly just past her shoulders. It was all one length, no bangs, no nonsense, but he guessed that little widow's peak just to one side had something to do with that. She wore little noticeable makeup, which suited her even features just fine. She was pretty enough, but not overtly striking in any particular way. She had nice cheekbones, a square chin that suited her determined air, dark eyebrows, neatly shaped, that matched dark lashes framing eyes the color of whiskey. Really good whiskey, he found himself thinking. So maybe she was striking, if you paid close attention. Her mouth suited the frank nature of her face, lips well defined, but neither full nor thin, with faint brackets lining either end, which could be from excessive frowning, or smiling. The jury was still out on that. Her speech was easy and smooth, but quick and a little clipped, as if she was used to getting things done in an orderly and swift fashion.

He couldn't help it; he smiled. "Not from the country, are you?"

"Alexandria," she said by way of response. "Old Town. And Bailey and I were the only other two named in the will, if that's what you're worried about."

He didn't respond to that. "So, if you just met, where is her — are her —" He broke off, then looked to Bailey. "I'm sorry. You're standing right there. When I was a kid I hated it when people did that to me." He gave her a reassuring smile. Or maybe he was just trying to reassure himself. Because *What the hell, Doyle?*

"Foster care," Bailey said matter-of-factly. She looked up at him, her eyes squinting a little in the sun as her gaze reached his face, but her expression otherwise unreadable. "So, it's just me." She had a sweet, soft, Deep South accent that was completely at odds with her otherwise smooth, seemingly unflappable demeanor.

"But surely you had — ?" He stopped, looked at Sunny, then shifted toward the older woman. "Addison Pearl Whitaker, tell me you didn't just bring a child on up here without telling someone." He didn't make it a question.

For her part, Addie merely dug her cane a

bit more firmly into the gravel and held his gaze squarely with her own. "She's a Hartwell, no matter the last name on her birth certificate. Makes her family." For all that the top of Addie's head came up no higher than the middle of Sawyer's chest, she wasn't the least bit cowed. "And don't go trotting out my full name, sonny boy. I can still apply this cane to your behind, even if I have to swing a little higher these days."

His mouth might have kicked up a little at that, mostly because they both knew it was true, and from the corner of his eye he saw Sunny and Bailey do the same. "And what about her foster family?" He looked at Bailey. "Do they know you're here?" he asked the young girl directly.

"My caseworker knows," Bailey said, again not seeming overly concerned. She wasn't defiant or smug, which told him she was smarter than he'd been at her age. Nor did she strike him as being particularly pliant, which was also a good thing. It was more that she was just used to the shuffle. And wasn't that a sorry statement about the world?

But then, he'd seen parts of the world with kids in situations far sorrier than hers. Still, he admired her evenness. He was sure it had stood her in good stead. Poor kid.

"Good," he told her; then his smile broadened. He crouched down and braced his hands on his thighs so she wouldn't have to squint to look up at him. "I only asked because, well, let's just say Addie Pearl has a reputation for adopting a variety of strays. Most of them of the four-legged variety." He glanced at Addie, who was once again smiling indulgently at him, then back at Bailey. "But there have been a few of the two-legged variety in there as well. Only one other time, though, was that two-legged stray underage." He saw the brunette bristle and automatically put her hand on Bailey's narrow shoulder, but he kept his gaze on Bailey as he finished.

"You?" Bailey asked, not seeming at all intimidated by him. If he could read anything in her expression, it would be curiosity.

He nodded in response.

"How old were you?" Bailey asked, her bright blue eyes glinting with interest for the first time. Now that they were more eye to eye, he noted the freckles hidden under her tanned cheeks. So, she wasn't so fair skinned she couldn't be out in the sun, but she sported the requisite redhead sprinkle across the cheeks and nose nonetheless. He wouldn't say she was a cutie-pie type; her life had made her too cool for that. But there was kidlike spunk mixed in with all that older-than-her-years evenness. He'd bet on it.

"Nine," he told her.

"I just turned ten," she offered. "September third."

"Almost thirty-three," he told her. "November twelfth."

"That makes you a Scorpio. I'm Virgo."

Her comment got an interesting reaction from Sunny, who had already tucked her hand back in the pocket of her jacket, but was now studying the young girl with an unreadable expression on her face.

"I am indeed," he said, looking back at Bailey.

"You lived here since then?" Bailey wanted to know.

"I spent some time overseas working for Uncle Sam, but this has been home base, yes."

"Army, right?"

He nodded, surprised at the guess, then saw her gaze dart to the tattoo of two arrows crossed over a sword on his right bicep. "Yes, ma'am." That didn't answer how she knew that particular symbol belonged to an Army vet. "Did you know someone who served?"

In response, Bailey merely looked past him to the mill, and her nose might have wrinkled the slightest bit. It was the first hint of any kind of opinion she'd allowed him to see. "You lived in there since you were nine? On a cot?"

"No, child," Addie said, answering for him. "He lived with me." Before Sawyer or Bailey could say anything else, Addie smiled and clapped her hands around the knob of her cane, then tapped it decisively into the dirt. "How about it? You two want a closer look at your inheritance?"

Sunny and Bailey both glanced down at the key each held in her respective hand, then shared a brief smile when they caught themselves mirroring each other's actions again. It was Sunny who spoke next. "I'm guessing we don't actually need the key to get in," she said dryly.

The banging of hammers and buzzing of saws had continued unabated while he'd been chatting with them. "At the moment, no." Sawyer realized they would need to have a much more serious talk, figure things out, but for now, there was certainly no harm in letting them see their grand inheritance, such as it was. Hell, one look at the ancient heap in its current state might resolve everything before they even got started.

He turned and motioned for them to follow him. "Careful, the ground is a bit uneven. More rocks than dirt and they can shift or slide." He headed back across the grounds toward the big sliding door he'd emerged from earlier. "Do you know the history of the place?"

"No, I'm afraid I don't," Sunny said, keeping her stride short he noted, so she and Bailey walked side by side, and allowing Addie to keep pace while using her cane over the scrabbly ground. "I didn't know that silk was ever milled in Virginia, or anywhere in the States for that matter. It's not one of the exports or crops I ever learned about in school."

"It was a short-lived experiment," he told them. "Blue Hollow Falls began as a farming community, very early, in the seventeenth century, in fact. These were British colonies then, and they brought mulberry tree seeds and moth eggs with them that had been given to them by the king."

"Moths have eggs?" This came from Bailey.

"More like little pods," he said, deciding that was better than getting into a fertility discussion of any kind with a minor. "These were special moths called *bombyx mori.* They start as silkworms and spin their pods in mulberry trees. It's from those pods that silk is made."

"With babies in them?" Bailey looked disgusted, though he wasn't sure if it was because that was gross, or an insult to living beings.

"No, after they hatch," he said. "The pods are like a chrysalis. Like how caterpillars turn into butterflies," he added, having no actual idea if that was how it worked, but it was close enough for the purposes of history and young ears. "It used to be that the Chinese were the only ones who knew the secret to making silk, but once the news got out, France and Italy started producing, and King James, who was the king of England at the time, decided he wanted in on that business. But the silk moths weren't too keen on the damp and cold weather in England, so he decided to ship them over here, and see what his loyal subjects could do with them."

"So, what happened?" Bailey wanted to know.

He caught Sunny intently listening, too. "It took some time," he said. "After all, they had to grow trees and such. It did work, but because they had to send the pods on big

ships across large oceans, which took forever, eventually the folks here figured out it
would be better if they could just mill the
pods and actually spin the silk right here.
Spinning machinery had improved during
that century-plus span of time, and we'd
become independent from England by then.
That's when this mill came into being." He
paused just outside the big door, sliding it
shut to block some of the construction noise
as he finished his story. "The mill was
initially constructed back in the early
eighteen-hundreds by the first Bartholomew
Hartwell, but soon after that, crops like
tobacco and cotton gained in popularity
because they were a lot easier to grow and
harvest, with cotton in particular being
much easier and cheaper to weave into fiber,
and therefore more immediately profitable.
Eventually, most of the silk trade died out."

"Most?" This came from Sunny.

He nodded. "There are still silk mills
operating in this country today, but the
Hartwell mill shut down around nineteen
ten. And the town here, such as it is, mostly
shut down then, too."

Sunny looked around. "There was a
town?"

"Still is," he answered, smiling, liking that
she was showing some sincere interest, even

if it might make the larger issue at hand more complicated. It was her birthright, too, now. More so than his, truth be told, even if he'd spent most of his life here and she'd just set foot in the place. "You came up and into the Hollow from the north. The town proper is a bit south of here. It's not very big," he added, "but we're a solid community."

"And we've still got mulberry trees around," Addie put in. "Fortunately, the Hartwells had other business interests back then, so they survived the mill closing, though there was a span of time when none of them lived here. The other town properties passed down to family members who, a generation or two later, like the Hartwells, slowly came back up to the Hollow for one reason or another. Usually hardship in their own families. They started farming the land again. Apple trees mostly. But corn, too. And cows, chickens, sheep, and the like. Subsistence farmers, most of them, back then, but shops began opening up again in town to service those folks, and little by little Blue Hollow Falls came back. Different from before, but home to folks who love it up here and appreciate its history, too. A surprising number of them are direct descendants of the first settlers. I was born here, as was my daddy before me, and his daddy before him, and on back. Not an original settler, but close to it."

"Back at the courthouse, when they were reading through the will, it said you were a weaver by occupation," Sunny said. "So, does that mean you weave silk?"

Addie chuckled, shook her head. "No, honey, not that. I do work with fibers though, mostly wool, but some other things mixed in, too. I spin my own fiber, dye it, rack it, bundle it."

"So, you sell the fiber then, or —"

"I do, yes. Got my own website now and everything." At Sunny's lifted eyebrows, Addie cackled a hoarse laugh, and added, "We're backward in some ways, but we can change with the times. Especially if that means we get to keep our way of living. I am a weaver by trade. Rugs mostly. I sell those, too."

"Addie is being modest," Sawyer said, then chuckled. "So unlike her." She gave his booted foot a bop with the bottom of her cane, but he went on, saying, "She's what is known as a master weaver. Her work is incredible. And over the past fifteen years or so, she's convinced a handful of other crafters and makers to relocate up here. We're becoming something of an artisan community. Which brings us to the renovation." He gestured up at the building. "Addie got to thinking that it would make sense if, rather than each crafter being responsible for finding their own way to market their wares to the world beyond the Hollow, maybe they should join forces."

"Well, we've already done that." She extended her hand to Sunny. "Meet the founder and current president of the Bluebird Crafters Guild." Then she let out a cackling laugh and spread her arms. "Such as it is!"

Sunny shook Addie's hand slowly, then looked back up at the mill. "So, you're not restoring this to a functioning mill."

"Oh, no, child," Addie said. "This town doesn't have need of a mill any more now than it did a hundred years ago." She looked up at the building, pride shining in her eyes. "This is going to be an artisan center."

Sunny looked at Sawyer. "I thought you said this was your home."

"For the time being, it is."

"We're envisioning it as a place for the locals to sell their wares," Addie explained, "but also as workshop space, and classroom space. We'd like it to be something of a destination for other artisans, as well as a marketplace for folks to come purchase our creations, see the historic mill, learn a little history, enjoy the local scenery."

Any further discussion on that topic ended when the saws and hammering suddenly ceased, leaving only the music and the sound of the falls filling the air. A moment later, the door was dragged open from the other side and a lanky adolescent stepped out. "Hey, Sawyer," said the boy, his voice soft, but cracking slightly. "Pa says they're ready for you to come help with the support beam." He looked somewhat shyly at the two newcomers and gave them a brief nod, then smiled at Addie Pearl. "Hi, Miss Addie. Thanks for the sandwiches. And the apple. You didn't have to —"

"I know Jacob. That's why I enjoy doing it. Introduce yourself," she said, nodding to Bailey and Sunny.

His cheeks flushed, but he turned, nodded to the two girls. "Jacob McCall," he said, then glancing at Bailey, he added, "Jake. Pleasure to meet you."

"Sunny Goodwin," Sunny replied, smiling at the boy.

"Bailey," said Bailey, when Jake continued looking her way. "Sutton," she added when he didn't say anything, just kept staring. She gestured to the building. "Do you live in there, too?"

Jake looked surprised by the question. "No. We live down in town. Our place is out past the post office."

"Oh."

When nothing else was forthcoming, Jake shuffled his feet, and finally turned to Sawyer. "What should I tell Pa?"

Sawyer looked at his watch. "Tell him we'll get to it tomorrow. He can send everyone home, then you guys can pack up and head out, too." He laid a hand on Jake's skinny shoulder and smiled reassuringly. Jake was a hard worker for a youngster, and stronger than his gangly body would lead one to believe. He was twelve going on thirteen and awkward, which just compounded his tendency to quietness. "It's about that time, anyway." It wasn't quite four o'clock yet, and the truth of it was, Sawyer had hoped to be much further along as they headed toward colder weather. Getting that central support beam up was key to their plan. But then he hadn't been expecting this little family gathering, either. Or the family itself. "I appreciate you helping your father out after school, but I'm sure you've got a pile of homework waiting."

"Yes, sir, I do. I'll tell Pa. See you tomorrow, then." With a brief glance and nod to the three women, he slipped back inside the building.

Sawyer glanced at Sunny and Bailey. "At least now you can get your first look without needing earplugs." A moment later, the music shut off, and he let out a short sigh of relief. Despite the way he was pushing everyone on the renovation, he'd be lying if he said his favorite part of the day wasn't when silence fell once again. After a few very active tours of duty, he'd never take the luxury of peace and quiet for granted again. He turned to usher them inside, and had just opened his mouth to warn the two newcomers to watch their step and their heads, when another head popped out from around the far side of the door.

Actually, Seth's stout beard poked out before the rest of him did. "Will said we're quitting? Are you high, man? We've got the beam all lined up and —" He broke off as he pushed through the door enough to see that Sawyer wasn't alone. "Oh, hey, sorry there, Miss Addie. I didn't see you. How'd it go down at the courthouse? We all legal and legit now?"

Sawyer nudged the door open wider so Seth could see the rest of the group. "Oh, ho! Well, why didn't you tell me we had company?" His smile broadened as he wedged his muscular frame out past Sawyer, then stepped right in front of him, barely missing Sawyer's toes with his clodhopper-sized feet.

Seth stuck his hand out toward Sunny, then realized he was wearing work gloves and pulled one off, wiped his hand on his pant leg and stuck it out again. "Hello there. Seth Brogan. Former platoon buddy turned dog boy to the slave king here. Pleased to meet you."

To her credit, the far more pristinely dressed Sunny took Seth's sweat-stained hand without pause and gave it a decent shake. But then, Seth had that effect on women. Apparently, the neatly trimmed, but abundant beard and the man bun were lady magnets. *Who knew?* Occasionally a man magnet, too. At least from Sawyer's observation. Seth was firmly heterosexual, but he loved attention and therefore welcomed all audience members. It had made him something of a challenge when they'd served together, since their work often required the exact opposite of "look at me!" But Sawyer couldn't ask for a more loyal friend than Seth Brogan. The fact that they'd saved each other's bacon on more than one occasion had forged an unbreakable bond few would understand.

"Your benevolent slave king is giving you

the night off," he told Seth. "Unexpected company," he added, not unkindly. "I'm about to give the grand tour, such as it is. You can head out with the McCalls and the rest of the crew. Go play with your vines and tell Dexter I said hello."

Sawyer noticed that both Sunny and Bailey were watching the byplay between the two men with interest. Sunny's attention was on Seth. *Big surprise.* Bailey's attention, however, had remained firmly on him since Seth had mentioned they'd served together. When she'd recognized the Special Forces tat on his arm, he'd suspected there was a story there. He was still coping with the revelation that these two had a share of his homestead. But that didn't stop him from being curious. About both females.

"Dexter?" Sunny asked. "Dog?"

"Llama," Seth responded.

Her perfectly shaped brows lifted. "You know, now that you say that, I could have sworn I saw a few of them on my drive up the mountain."

"Not mine, I'm across the creek. But it's not as uncommon as you might think."

"Great wool," Addie chimed in.

"There is nothing common about Dexter," Sawyer said. "Speaking of which . . ." He let the sentence trail off and sent a meaningful gaze toward Seth. "We'll jump back in at oh-six-hundred."

"You'll jump in," Seth replied easily. "Count me in about an hour later." He stroked his beard. "Man needs his beauty sleep. And I have chickens to feed." He looked back to Sunny and wiggled his eyebrows. "Need any eggs?"

"I beg your pardon?" she said, clearly more flustered than affronted. A typical reaction to Seth Brogan.

"Get directions to my place from Sawyer. Swing by. That your Cooper?" He nodded, looking past her shoulder to the Mini parked by Addie's Subaru.

"It is."

"Sweet. Trade you a few dozen eggs for a spin."

Sawyer was about to butt in, save the poor woman, but Sunny took care of that herself.

She lifted one of those expressive brows and her lips lifted in a dry smile. "And then you invite me in to see your llama etchings?"

Seth barked out a laugh, but shrugged. "I've never etched a llama. Pretty sure Dex would hate that." He leaned closer. "But I do have some very interesting war . . . uh . . . souvenirs."

Sunny laughed. "I'll just bet you do."

"If it makes you feel any better, you can bring your . . . sister?" he said hopefully, shooting a grin at Bailey.

"No, thanks," Bailey said, answering for herself. "Llamas spit."

All of the adults laughed at that while Sawyer thought he couldn't recall one woman ever shutting Seth down so effectively, much less two. *Bravo, ladies.*

"You've worked with them?" Seth asked the young girl, seeming quite sincere.

"Tolerated them, more like."

This earned a surprised smile from Sunny, who looked like she approved of the girl speaking up.

"Well, if you stick around, you've got to come meet Dex. He'll change your mind."

Bailey said nothing, but her expression made it clear she was doubtful of that ever coming to pass.

"Heck, maybe you can give me some llama pointers."

"Okay, dog boy, enough," Sawyer said, smiling nonetheless.

"That's corporal dog boy," Seth joked, then took a step back, sketched a brief bow to the women, clicked his work-booted heels together, and delivered a crisp salute to Sawyer. He shifted his gaze to Sunny as he turned the salute to a mock phone beside his ear and mouthed, "Call me." With a wink at Bailey and a kiss blown toward Addie, who blushed as if she was a good five decades younger than her actual age, he was gone.

The whirlwind that was Seth Brogan. Sawyer shook his head, smiled. "Sorry. Where were we? Oh, right. Watch your head, and take care where you step. We're still in the tear-down phase."

"You're not tearing it all down, though, right?" Sunny asked, concern and surprise filling her expression.

He couldn't tell if she was upset at the idea he might be razing an historic building, or because he could be leveling her inheritance. "Come inside and see." He shoved at the door, which squealed loudly on the metal tracks.

Both Sunny and Bailey covered their ears at the screeching noise, but followed him inside.

"Whoa," Bailey breathed, barely more than a whisper.

She and Sunny both stopped just inside the big door, which Sawyer shoved closed again behind him. As the afternoon waned toward evening, there were more than a few wild critters who'd be quite happy to share his cot. He knew this because he'd had to evict most of them when he'd come back home after serving Uncle Sam. Not that there still weren't ample entry points, but he didn't have to go hang a welcome sign, either.

"What's that?" Bailey asked, pointing to the hulk of rusted machinery attached to the far wall.

"That's what operates the waterwheel," he told her.

"Does it work?"

"Not yet," he said, with a smile. "The waterwheel generated the power here, once upon a time, but the place was modernized over time. Hard to tell that now it's been gutted. We're still on generator power, but the windows along the front wall up there, along with the skylights, take care of the indoor lighting anyway." He motioned upward, but the two were already glancing up at the metal roof, soaring a full two and a half stories overhead. Parts of it had rusted through here and there, creating unintentional skylights, but there was no point in starting in on repairing them until the infrastructure was shored up.

Sunny walked out toward the middle of the big open space and turned in a slow circle, taking it all in. Scaffolding covered two of the interior walls, and in addition to his small homemade homestead in the far corner, there was construction detritus everywhere. Otherwise, though, it was a cavern at the moment.

"Was it always open like this?" she asked. "Was the machinery that big?"

Sawyer shook his head. "No, there were two floors actually, and a loft. We're in what amounts to the basement. See the line around the perimeter a few feet up?" He pointed up the wall where a stripe showed where the floor joists had been. "Half of this level is underground with a sidewalk out, where we just came in, and the rear walk out there." He pointed to their left, where a series of what were once glass-paned doors lined the center of the long back wall. Most of the glass was long gone, and the empty frames had been covered with plywood. "This is about three-quarters the size of the floor space above — or what will be the floor space when we put it back in — and is built right into the side of the mountain. It was the boiler room when the place was modernized and also where the electrical panels and such were. All that had to be gutted as well, as you can see." He pointed higher up. "The floor above the main floor wasn't a full floor. You can see another line about fifteen feet or so above the first one. That was more of an attic space, sort of loft style storage. It was only about five and a half feet high, so not an actual full floor."

"Are you putting that floor back in, too?" Sunny asked.

He nodded. "That's the plan, but we'll put it in a bit lower since we don't need the overhead space on the main floor here like they did originally. That will create a full second floor. We'd like the main floor to be the marketing area, with workshop space and classroom space upstairs in what was the attic. And this space, or part of it, will still hold all the fuse boxes and water heaters and the like, plus office space for Addie."

"What about you?" Bailey wanted to know. "Where will you live? Down here in the basement?"

"Oh, I have some property up in another part of the Hollow. Closer to Hawk's Nest Ridge." He grinned, and winked at her. "That's my next project. But first things first."

"What part of the mill is original?" Sunny wanted to know.

"What you see, generally speaking. The tin roof was replaced several times, but that tin is a century old. What's left of it, anyway. The stonework has been repaired and shored up over the years, but is original to the building. The plank wood exterior has been replaced as needed over time, so it's varying degrees of old, but what is here is at least —"

"A hundred years old," Sunny echoed. "When were all the machines taken out, or whatever they used to process the silk?"

"The company sold most of it off when they closed, so there wasn't much left. Doyle's ancestors tried to lease the property, but way up here, what was anyone going to do with it? So it was eventually abandoned and left to the elements, which, in turn, did a number on the interior."

"Hence the gutting," she finished.

"Exactly. And that isn't a bad thing, all in all, as it allows us to restructure how the space is used to suit our needs now. The property was already considered historic when it closed down, but the Hartwells at the time, and since, didn't allocate any money to take care of the place. As Addie said, none of them lived in town at that point, so to say the mill had become over-grown and dilapidated is an understate-ment. Doyle's grandfather was the first one to come back in more than a generation. His only son took off, so he was left to raise Doyle himself." Sawyer smiled. "He became smitten with our Miss Addie here, so he stayed on after his grandpa passed on."

"When he and I split up, I knew there was nothing going to keep him here," Addie said, speaking up for the first time, clearly not interested in having her marriage to Doyle Hartwell as a subject of conversation. "So I had him deed part of the place to me, as insurance, I guess. I knew the place was an old heap, and I certainly didn't have the wherewithal to do anything to it, but I couldn't stand the idea of it ending up in the hands of someone who would tear it down or disrespect its heritage. Then it became Sawyer's heritage, too, and I aimed to keep it that way."

Sawyer noticed Sunny's gaze shift to him, then away again, and he wondered what was on her mind.

"Now it's your heritage, too," Addie said to Sunny and Bailey.

"So, where does that put things?" Sunny asked. "I mean, I'm assuming you didn't know Doyle was going to leave his share of it to anyone else, and why would he? But now there are two other part owners. So, before you do anything else to the place, we should probably have a talk about who is responsible for what, right?"

Sawyer worked to keep the smile on his

face open and easy. He could well imagine the surprise Doyle's two daughters had felt in that Turtle Springs courthouse today, but that was nothing compared to what had happened to him. He hadn't even let himself think about it yet, but apparently that was about to change.

"Meaning what?" he asked. "This property might have been historic, but it was also an eyesore and a heap. Everything I've done has only improved it."

"Yes, and that's great. Wonderful, actually. But it raises the value of the property, for one, and therefore the taxes. Then there's the matter of who will be held responsible for the costs and the liability of the structure." She held up her hand when he started to reply. "I'm not being argumentative. I didn't even know this place existed a day ago. I'm only saying that since this has happened, I think we should all sit down, discuss it, and come to some kind of written agreement about who will be responsible for what. I'm just trying to be smart. For all of us." She looked at Bailey, then back at him and Addie.

Addie stepped forward. "I've spoken with Bailey's caseworker about transferring her guardianship from the foster family to me." She looked at Bailey. "It will take some doing, and we still need to go get your things, but we'll sort that all out, I promise."

Bailey looked at the legal envelope and key in her hand, then back at Addie. She nodded, but said nothing.

Addie held up a hand when both Sunny and Sawyer started to speak at the same time. "As for the two of you, just hold on to your horses. Let this old woman have her say. As the only person who was actually married to the old scoundrel, and the one who knew him for more years of his life than anyone else, I think I can be considered the authority on what he might have been thinking when he put all this to paper."

She dug her cane into the dirt floor and turned to Bailey. "I know your life thus far hasn't likely been what any young person would hope for. I also know, if you're like me, you want to know what's what, no beating around the bush. What we all want is family. Whether it's blood or someone who becomes your blood out of love and pure devotion." She cast a look at Sawyer, then looked back at Bailey. "Well, from what I heard today, you've been bounced around your whole life and never got to have either of those things. I'll leave your mama out of it, as I don't know her, but D. Bart should be ashamed of himself for leaving your lot

68

up to fate. That said, you've found your family now. You're a Hartwell by blood, and you belong to Blue Hollow Falls because we take care of our own. I don't know what you think about that, but to my mind, a forever home counts for a lot. I hope that means something to you, but you need to know it means everything to us."

She didn't wait for Bailey to respond, leaving her to think on that. Instead, she turned to Sunny next. "I know you don't know me, or Sawyer, but let me assure you we are not out to do anything nefarious here. I want what's best for Sawyer, yes, but not at the expense or to the detriment of D. Bart's final wishes. Leave it to that man to make a muddle of things, but I can attest that though he had about as much stick-to-it-iveness as a bee does to a single flower, his heart was as big as the moon. Fortunately, so was his wallet. He'd want everyone to just get along, and his way of making that happen was to throw money at it. Or property. Or both. That's how he took care of your mama, or tried to, and I'm only sorry he didn't do more, or that I didn't know about you earlier on, so I could have pushed him to do better. Maybe this was his way of making up for his faults. Not that it does —

I'm just saying what I think was in his heart."

She looked at Sawyer next. "Honey, I know you came back here to do right by what's yours, right by your hometown, by all of us, trying to help everyone out. That has been what you've always done, for so many. If D. Bart showed his love with money and things, you have always shown yours by giving yourself over to doing what's right, to making a difference. I couldn't be more proud of you. By rights, this should be all yours. We both know that. It wouldn't have seemed like any kind of gold mine to anyone else. Just the opposite. Certainly no one else would look at this heap and envision what you have, much less pour his own blood, sweat, and tears into making it a reality. Maybe the old man didn't have faith that you'd come back home, by choice or by fate, so by giving the mill to all three of his own he made sure it would stay in the Hartwell family one way or the other. Maybe he grew sentimental in his old age. Or maybe he did it for me. Probably the latter. Old coot."

"I came home to you, Addie Pearl," Sawyer told her. "As far as I knew, Doyle had no idea where I was, or what I was doing."

"He knew," she said quietly. "He always

70

knew where you were, or at least who you were working for." Then she turned to the other two. "I can't say what he knew about the two of you, or that he kept tabs. We'll never know that, I don't guess. But he hadn't forgotten you, that's clear enough to see now, and in true D. Bart style, I guess he was trying to do the right thing by you both by giving you something." She let out a short chuckle. "Just like him to wait long enough that he could still have an excuse for not doing anything himself, in person, in ways that would truly matter. But that's neither here nor there. He died like he lived, doing things his way, and only his way."

She tucked her cane under her arm, and clapped her hands together so sharply, Bailey and Sunny started, and Sawyer's gaze shifted more tightly to Addie. "So, here's how it will be. This place is the only thing of D. Bart's vast array of possessions, all the rest of which he divested along the way, that belonged to his family, his ancestors, dating all the way back to the beginning. Like it or not, you're what's left of that family. Despite what some might say, I won't live forever. And though I'd like to believe that all three of you would come to care about this place, I might be old, but I'm not senile. And though I do believe in the Lord moving in mysterious ways, I don't believe in fairy tales. So, bottom line, what's important to me is that this place stay with at least one of you going forward. That the history of this place, this town, and what happens to it, continues to matter to someone who will do right by it."

She looked at Sunny. "We already know Sawyer has taken on that mantle, so that takes care of that. If you want out, I will give you a fair market price for your share, as it stands right now, cash on hand. It'll be a far sight more than it would have been worth if he'd kicked the bucket any earlier, that I can tell you." She looked at Bailey. "You're not old enough to decide now, so your share is yours until you're of age. You can decide then what you want to do with whatever it's become at that point. You'll have to trust me to do the right thing with it until then. I have no cause to cheat you and I only want to do what's right by you. Ask anyone you want and they'll vouch for my word. And you can start with Sawyer, who knows better than anybody."

She spared him a look then, and though she was a woman driven by her passions for any number of things, he didn't think he'd ever seen her so serious . . . and maybe, underneath all that, a little scared. This was her legacy, too, after all, or would go on to be, when it was done.

She stamped her cane back on the floor again, gripping the knob as she held their gazes evenly with her own. "So, let's keep this as simple as possible for all involved. We are family. You were his, and he was mine once upon a time. Now he's gone, so I count you as mine. That's all that matters."

There was absolute silence in the room, save for the sound of the wind rustling through the open patches in the ceiling, and the sound of Big Stone Creek rushing over the tumble of boulders that stood just on the other side of the far wall.

Then Sunny cleared her throat, and took a step forward. "What if I don't want to sell out my share? What happens then?"

# CHAPTER THREE

Sunny sat in her car with the engine running, looking at the mill, wondering what in the fresh hell had come over her.

She blamed Addie Pearl. The old woman had proposed a solution that would have made this all so very easy — here's your money, see ya later, bye. And Sunny would have taken her up on that offer. Happily. She wouldn't have even dickered over the price. Heck, she might have even just signed her share over to Bailey, who was the only one of the three of them who appeared to really need financial support. Assuming the mill would be worth something someday, and not a burden to the poor kid.

Then Addie had to go and make that beautiful, impassioned speech about the value of family and how she was sticking by what she considered her family, her responsibility, her heritage, and Sunny was standing there, thinking about her mother, thinking about herself when she was Bailey's age, and how hard she'd thought her life had been. Bailey's had been so very much harder. None of Doyle's three children had apparently had any kind of father, but she'd had her mama, and Sawyer had Addie. What did Bailey have? And they were sisters, for God's sake. *She had a freaking sister!*

Sunny still hadn't had the time or space to really and truly consider that, figure out what it meant to her, or how it even made her feel.

She also had a brother, apparently, although she couldn't even go there yet. Not until she managed to get her head and the rest of her body to understand that they were related. *Related, you hear?*

Sawyer was . . . a lot. In all possible ways. He filled up the space he was in without even trying. He had that kind of natural magnetism and charisma that held every bit of her attention without even trying, and without her permission. She didn't want to be drawn to him, but even standing inside that cavernous, gutted old mill, he'd made her feel . . . stifled. As if there suddenly wasn't enough oxygen to breathe.

*Simmer down, sister!*

Emphasis on the *sister.* Yeah. She was trying. She was sitting in her car, not anywhere near him. Yet she still had the urge to loosen a few buttons, take a few deep breaths. It didn't help that he was an apparent war hero who'd come back to single-handedly rescue his little mountain hometown.

Bottom line, she had no idea what she wanted. Or didn't want. She only knew what she couldn't want. And she was failing at that. Miserably.

All of this felt more than a little surreal. Where she was sitting, what she was contemplating. She felt a little like Alice, right after she'd taken that header down the rabbit hole. Sunny had had no idea what she'd expected when she'd left her nice, safe, predictable life in Old Town that morning, but it had most definitely not been anything like this.

She picked up the legal envelope she'd tossed on the passenger seat and slid the official papers out, the ones that provided proof — in case she doubted it — that her life had just gotten complicated. "Oh, Mama," she murmured, as she read through the exact words that spelled out her inheritance. "Why didn't you tell me about Doyle?"

She missed her mother. In ways big and small, light and dark, heavy and . . . well, heavier. Sunny missed her laughter, her dogged optimism, her endless flights of fancy, her companionship. She didn't miss the work of taking care of Daisy Rose. The feeding, the bathing, the battles over medication, the weary-to-the-bone amount of time, energy, and just plain grit it took, or the toll it had taken on her mind, body, and spirit to do a job she'd been handling every single minute of every single day for as long as she could remember. Even eight months later, she was still quietly stunned as she discovered, almost daily, all the ways she now felt free. Jubilantly, joyously, utterly, overwhelmingly, and yes, guiltily free.

She'd always known that her life had been a lot of work; caring for Daisy Rose had been the cornerstone of every day of that life, from childhood on up. It was the reason she was still single, the reason she buried herself in the USBG greenhouses for far more hours than even her demanding job required. She'd been looking for solace, respite, maybe a teeny, tiny escape to rebuild and restore the energy she would need to get up and do it all over again the next day. Even if she had never let herself think about it that way.

Sunny had still been working her way through adolescence when she'd figured out that if she ever let herself think about her life, or her mother, like a millstone she'd been forced to carry, if she regretted the life she'd been handed, then the burden itself would have swallowed her whole.

No, she'd worked hard to be more like her mother in that regard, to look at the wonder of the world, embrace the joy, dig in the dirt, and celebrate life. And she had done that, too. Every single day.

She missed her mama. But she loved being free. *Loved.* At first, it had felt wrong, like a betrayal. Then she'd realized that if any one person in the whole wide world would want — no, demand — that Sunny embrace her newfound freedom and utterly revel in it, it would have been Daisy Rose Rainbow Love Garcia Goodwin. So . . . Sunny had. Or she'd certainly been making big inroads into doing so. She'd yet to really figure out what she wanted for herself now. What she wanted now that couldn't have let herself want before. What was important to her? Would she date more? Though life with Daisy Rose would have terrified most mere mortal men, it wasn't as if Sunny had lost the love of her life because of her caretaking role. She'd never met someone who'd meant enough to her that that had become an issue.

Was it because she hadn't let herself fall

in love? Had she subconsciously avoided becoming too deeply involved with anyone, because she knew the likely outcome?

She laughed then, and started stuffing the legal papers back in the envelope. "Yeah, then the first guy who really makes your girl parts sit up and pay attention turns out to be your half brother. Ha!" She shook her head, thinking — and not for the first time — that maybe it was like her co-worker and close friend Stevie had been telling her since shortly after Sunny had confided why she couldn't hang out after work or do a girl's weekend on the eastern shore. Stevie had told Sunny that if she couldn't get more help with her mother than a daycare nurse to watch over her while Sunny worked, the least she should do was get herself a good therapist.

Sunny's lips twisted in a dry smile as she fumbled with the pronged closure on the envelope. "And to think, Mama, I believed that after you passed on, the crazy part of my life was all behind me."

A light rap on her car window made Sunny squeal and clamp the legal envelope to her chest, covering her now-galloping heart. She shifted around to find Seth Brogan and his long, manly man beard grinning down at her. She pushed the button to lower her window.

"Sorry," he said, white teeth flashing, making his golden brown eyes dance. "Didn't mean to startle you."

"No worries," she told him, swallowing down the momentary surprise, then taking a short breath to settle her heart rate. "Is something wrong?"

"Wrong?" He looked confused. "No, why? Did something happen?"

"You mean other than finding out I have two siblings and now own a chunk of a centuries-old silk mill?" She smiled. "No, that's been quite enough already."

"Two . . ." Seth trailed off, then looked over the top of her car toward the mill, then back at her. "So, the master sergeant is your big brother?" He hooted and the grin that had been open and friendly before took on a decidedly masculine gleam once again. "Well, hell, I might stand a chance then."

"Stand a — ?" Sunny broke off, shook her head. She couldn't even go there at the moment. "I'm sorry, what was it you wanted?"

"I got halfway home and realized I'd left some tools back here that I'll need for a little project I'm working on at my farm. I just pulled in and noticed you sitting in there, staring out the windshield, and wondered if you'd like to see the rest of the property."

"Oh!" she said, surprised, but pleasantly so. "Well, thank you, that's very kind of you. But I've seen the mill, if that's what you mean."

He shook his head. "There's more to the property than just the building."

"There is?" She looked down at the envelope. There had been a surveyor's plat map included with the papers, but she hadn't really looked at it. According to the magistrate, the surrounding property that came with the mill inheritance was all undeveloped.

She looked back to the mill, to the enormous iron waterwheel. Her gaze shifted to the thundering rush of Big Stone Creek as it tumbled over the boulder ledge, then to the thick forest that encroached on the open area around the mill, then up to the craggy gray stone edifice of Hawk's Nest Ridge, which soared above it in the background. The whole of it tugged at her somewhere deep inside. She attributed it to the pull of nature, to her natural-born desire to dig in the dirt, to her education and training.

"I —" *Want to,* she realized, but didn't say it out loud. She looked down at herself, then glanced out at the sun, which was brushing the tops of the towering pines as it continued its descent toward the skyline. The cool nip in the mountain air was becoming more pronounced and she hadn't brought anything heavier to wear. Not to mention, her sensible pumps weren't exactly designed for hiking. "— appreciate the offer. I do. But I'm not exactly dressed for a stroll through the woods, and it's getting late. I still have to drive back to the city."

He frowned. "You're leaving? You just got here."

"I have to go to work in the morning." Despite her inner disquiet, she found herself smiling up at him. His easy, cheerful manner and puppy dog enthusiasm made it almost impossible not to. Plus, stout beard notwithstanding, he was not at all hard on the eyes. *What's in the water up here, anyway?* "I work in D.C.," she explained. "It would be a bit of a commute from here."

"True that," he said, seeming to take her rejection in stride.

Something told her he didn't let much bother him, but she suspected he wasn't as much of an easy-come-easy-go kind of guy as he might like to put on. Sawyer emanated a kind of throttled intensity all the time, but she imagined there was more to Seth Brogan than met the eye.

"What is it you do in our nation's capital?"

he asked.

"I'm a horticulturalist. I work for the U.S. Botanic Garden in D.C."

His eyes widened a bit at that and his smile spread to a grin. "Plant lady. I like it."

She laughed. "I . . . yep, that's one way to put it." She kind of liked it, too. "Llama guy."

He barked a laugh at that. "I knew I liked you." He laid his palms on the roof of the car, leaned down just a bit so his gaze was more level with hers.

His eyes were a beautiful, deep golden brown, sort of in the same family as hers, but much richer in color. Added to that they managed to twinkle when he grinned despite their deep color. She wondered if there were dimples under that beard and mustache. She'd bet yes. Probably a cleft in that chin, too.

"Maybe they'd understand you taking a sick day, or some leave. I mean, your father did just pass away. My condolences by the way," he added, sounding and looking sincere.

She wondered just how much Seth knew about the situation, then realized that maybe he'd actually known her father. She wasn't sure why that mattered, or even if it mattered. Even so, her curiosity won out.

"Did you know Doyle?" she asked by way of response.

He shook his head. "No, I'm sorry. Never met the man. I'm a new arrival. I've heard some stories, though."

"I bet," she said, more to herself. Then, to him, she added, "I really do appreciate the kind offer, but you've got a llama to feed and I have a drive to make."

He looked disappointed, and she'd be lying if she said it didn't feel kind of nice to have a handsome, charismatic man wishing he could spend more time with her. That he was a handsome, charismatic man she wasn't related to was a definite bonus.

"When will you be back?" He braced his hands on his thighs now, and she couldn't help but note the ripple of shoulder muscles straining impressively against the seams of the zip-up fleece jacket he wore over the long-sleeved, beaten-up T-shirt he'd had on earlier. "The offer to meet Dex and take a little stroll in the woods remains open."

"I appreciate that," she said with a little laugh. "Honestly, though, I don't know what my plans are regarding Blue Hollow Falls," she said, speaking the one truth she knew. Would she be coming back? Or would she just call Addie Pearl and relinquish her share of the mill after all? And what about

Bailey? She shook her head. "Give Dex an extra carrot — or whatever llamas consider a treat — and tell him it's from me." She shifted so she could extend her right hand through the open window. "It was a pleasure meeting you, Seth Brogan."

He looked at her hand, then back to her face, his expression one of exaggerated sorrow. There might have even been a little pout, which drew her attention to his mouth. Framed by that beard, she had to admit it was more than a little sensuous.

"Don't go doing that now," he teased. "Or I'll be tempted to follow up. I'm incorrigible like that." He grinned again. "Fair warning."

She jerked her gaze back to his, realizing he'd caught her staring at his mouth. Now it was her turn to bark out a short laugh. "Right. Warning taken."

He took her hand before she could pull it back inside the car and brushed a quick kiss over her knuckles. His lips were warm, and his beard soft, not bristly. She couldn't say it made her feel all tingly, but it did make her pulse speed up a little. It felt . . . nice. Flattering.

Her thoughts shifted, without permission, to Sawyer. To how he made all sorts of things speed up inside her without even trying. And while Seth was sweet and charming, Sawyer was . . . more. A whole lot more.

*Seriously with that. B-R-O-T-H-E-R. Stencil it on your forehead if you need to. Get a grip.*

Would she even be seeing him again? Which prompted Sunny to wonder if her newfound older sibling was planning on keeping in touch with her. What had Addie's little speech make him think about, or feel?

"I must be slipping," Seth said, jerking her thoughts back to him, to the present.

"Sorry," she said, realizing her thoughts had wandered. To Sawyer. Again. "It's been . . . a day."

Seth was still holding her hand, and he gave it a reassuring squeeze before letting it go. "I can imagine." He straightened then, and reached in the back pocket of his thoroughly disreputable, ancient to the point of disintegrating Army fatigues and took out a rather nice-looking, hand-tooled leather wallet. From it, he extracted a business card, and handed it to her. She wasn't sure which part of that surprised her more. That he had a nice wallet when he looked like he did his clothes shopping at Goodwill? Or that he had a business card.

"Thanks," she said automatically, then glanced down at it. In a casual script, the card was printed with the name of his business, Bluestone & Vine, followed by his name, a post office box address, his phone number, e-mail, and Web site address. She giggled as she read the caption at the bottom of the card. "Home of the Llamarama Label." On the right side of the card, there was a pen and ink sketch of the head of a llama reaching up, as if leaning into the frame of the card, and nibbling on a grape bunch dangling from a vine that wove around the top corner, then through the name of the winery. The card was cream colored, and the paper was textured. The vine and grapes appeared as if they'd been painted with watercolors over the pen and ink. It was both beautiful and whimsical. Kind of like its owner, she thought. Or what she knew of him, anyway. She recalled Sawyer telling him to go play in the vines. Now she knew what that meant. "You're a vintner." She looked back up at him. "Family trade?"

He lifted his hands away from his narrow hips, making his fleece jacket drape flat against what appeared to be a hard set of abs. "What, I don't look like a winemaker?"

His dark blond, sun-streaked hair had partially escaped his man bun, and he was deeply tanned, dusty, and scruffy — kind of a lot in his own way. "I have no idea what a winemaker is supposed to look like," she said.

"Safe answer."

She nodded, her expression sage, despite the smile fighting its way to the corners of her mouth. "So sayeth the plant lady."

He chuckled, then clasped one hand to his heart. "A botanist and a winemaker. We could make beautiful music together, Sunny Goodwin."

She could have corrected him on the job classification, but it wasn't important. "Yes, but then our plants would die of neglect."

He choked on a laugh, clearly caught off guard by her suggestive rejoinder, but delighted by it all the same. "Well, well." He braced his hands on the roof of her car and leaned down once again. "Now you have to call me."

She tucked his card under the strap on her sun visor and started the engine. She looked back at him, but said nothing. He winked, then straightened and propped his hands on his lean hips. *He might be fun,* her little voice prompted. *And you sure could use a little of that. Maybe more than a little.*

"We'll see," was all she said. Unfortunately, whatever fun she might have with Seth Brogan would be all tangled up with the newest complication in her life. Fun yes, but worth it? She wasn't so sure. "Thank you," she told him, quite sincerely.

"For?" he asked, still smiling despite her unwillingness to accept his offer.

"For making the day better."

He nodded. "Any time. If you want to talk, about the mill, about Blue Hollow Falls, your new family, about growing plants . . ." That twinkle shifted to a sexy gleam. "Or neglecting them? Give me a shout."

Sex appeal notwithstanding, Seth struck her as the kind of guy who'd be a good friend. Except for that part where he'd be trying to get her into bed the whole time. And maybe the part where she'd be tempted to let him. Still, true friends were few, and she'd learned that recognizing them when they showed up was important. Key, even. And, despite the way they ribbed each other, or maybe because of it, it appeared Sawyer thought a great deal of him, too. "I will," she told him.

He patted the roof of her car, then stepped back. "Safe travels, plant lady."

She grinned and put her car into gear. "Vine on, llama guy."

He grinned, lifted a hand in a short wave, then shifted it to his ear and made the universal "call me" sign again.

She laughed, thinking if things were different, she might have done just that. She could use a little walk on the wild side. *Or any side,* she thought. She backed out of her spot and did a tricky little three-point turn in the narrow dirt lot, then, not entirely certain she'd ever be coming back out here again, gave the rearview mirror a quick glance. That was when she saw Bailey, standing in the open sliding door to the mill. She wasn't smiling, but she didn't look upset, either.

Without thinking about it, Sunny lowered her car window and stuck her arm out. Lifting her hand as high as she could, she waved as she turned toward the country road that would take her back down the mountain, back to civilization, back to the life she knew. The only one she'd ever known.

Bailey simply stared, so, feeling a little awkward, Sunny pulled her arm back in, rolled up the window, and turned onto the road. It wasn't until she glanced back, one last time, when Bailey probably thought she wasn't looking any longer, that the young girl lifted her hand from her side, just a smidge . . . and waved back.

Sunny almost braked the car right there to turn around, but then Sawyer came out of the mill and stood beside Bailey. He motioned behind the mill toward the woods, and the two of them started off in that direction. Sawyer didn't look her way, and Bailey never looked back. They'd moved on.

*Good,* she told herself. *That's good. Sawyer will be there for her.*

Sunny didn't glance over to where Seth had been standing. Whatever little buzz his attentions had given her was gone now. Instead, she headed back down the mountain, then away from the Blue Ridge, until she couldn't see any hint of the mountains in her rearview mirror. She looked forward to getting back to the city, back to the world she knew. Her world.

She didn't let herself think about the little pang she'd felt, seeing Sawyer and Bailey stroll off together. Without her.

# CHAPTER FOUR

"She's *where?*"

"Hold on," Will called down.

More than a little stewed over this latest development, Sawyer nevertheless waited patiently while Wilson McCall climbed down the scaffolding that braced the interior wall of the mill. He covered the distance from top to bottom as easily as a squirrel running down the side of a tree. Will was tall, with a lean, ropy build that belied his surprising natural strength. He tossed impressive pieces of blue stone around like another person tossed dice. Young Jake took after his father. Both were soft-spoken by nature with a strong work ethic.

A stonemason by trade, Will had initially come in to help assess the condition of the stonework that made up the foundation of the four exterior walls, as well as the boundary walls around the property immediately surrounding the mill. Sawyer had hired the man full-time when it became clear that Will McCall gave new meaning to the term *jack-of-all-trades*. And any fear he'd had that they'd essentially be providing day care by hiring on Will's young son as a laborer and odd jobs guy had been allayed on day one. Jake more than earned his keep, putting in time after school almost every day, or whenever Sawyer had work appropriate to his abilities. Since neither father nor son said much, Sawyer couldn't say he felt he knew them all that well, despite having worked beside them on an almost daily basis since late spring, just before school had let out. What he did know, however, was he liked and admired both McCall men.

If that hadn't been good enough for him, Addie Pearl knew a whole different side of the McCall family. Wilson apparently was quite the fiddle player, and an even more skilled fiddle maker. Sawyer had to take Addie's word on that, as he hadn't been lucky enough to hear the man play, nor had he seen proof of Will's instrument-making skills. Will had quietly declined Addie's persistent urging to bring in one or two of his handcrafted fiddles and mandolins, until Sawyer finally had to tell her to leave the poor man alone.

There was one other piece of Sawyer's

connection to Wilson, but the two men had never spoken of it. Sawyer had done three tours in Iraq, and another two in Afghanistan. He'd seen things, and done things, that most men would find hard to reconcile within themselves. Sawyer had managed to find his way through, and gave thanks and praise every single day for feeling solid, and centered, for being productive and forward thinking. He knew, firsthand, that so very many hadn't been as lucky. He credited having the great good fortune to have served under a commander who had watched, looked, and listened to the men he supervised, stepping in when he saw any sign of the early stages of personal crisis.

Sawyer also credited having a small, but loyal-to-the-core unit of buddies he'd have given his life for, as some of them had, indeed, done for him. Seth Brogan was one of those men. He'd also spent some solid time after his return in the care of several extremely competent therapists, without whose guidance he'd have been lost for sure.

In Wilson, he saw the signs, saw the shadows. He had no idea where Wilson had served, or when, for how long, or even in what branch of the military. But there was no doubt in Sawyer's mind that Wilson had also seen things, and perhaps had been ordered to do things, that no man should ever be asked to bear witness to or carry out. Maybe at some point, the moment would come when they'd speak of it. But until then, Sawyer gave Wilson what he could. Support, friendship, steady work to focus on, and an outlet. Hard physical labor was one way to work through mental distress. Not enough to fix anything long term, not by itself, or so Sawyer had come to realize, but a hell of a lot better than no outlet.

On the positive side, Jake, despite his natural shyness, looked like a happy, healthy, and well-loved young man. Sawyer didn't know the whole story about Jake's mother, other than she'd passed away when he'd been a little tyke. Wilson's mother, Katie McCall, had come to the Hollow after Sawyer had enlisted, so he hadn't met or known the woman, but Addie Pearl had very kind things to say about her. From Addie he knew that she had played some role in the boy's life, helping to raise him, and when she'd passed on, Wilson had inherited her property. Will had moved himself and his young son there full-time shortly afterward. Sawyer had still been overseas at the time.

It seemed like a lot to know about a person, and yet, to Sawyer, who had a knack for getting folks to talk about themselves without seeming to realize how much they were revealing, it seemed he'd barely skimmed the surface. There were deep waters there. But they had time, he thought. And wasn't that a good bit of knowledge to wake up to every morning? He was thankful every day for that truth.

So he waited patiently for Wilson to cross the packed dirt floor. The man wasn't yet forty, maybe four or five years older than Sawyer at most, and he wasn't one for shouting.

"Addie's up in D.C. Thought you knew," Will said, taking a rag from the back pocket of his heavy canvas work pants and wiping the dust and dirt from his face. "She and Bailey headed out around . . . I guess it must have been before nine. I got here at quarter past eight, after dropping Jake off at school. Wasn't much after that."

"What, exactly, did she say?"

"Just that she was taking Bailey on a field trip to our nation's capital. Her words." He lifted a densely muscled shoulder. "I thought maybe she was homeschooling her or something."

*Or something, all right,* Sawyer thought. Addie Pearl was up to one of her tricks, and Sawyer would bet the mill he knew exactly what — or who — that *or something* was going to involve. Sunny Goodwin worked in D.C., or so Addie had told him, despite the fact that he hadn't asked. His personal jury was still out on the woman who was, by law anyway, his stepsister. He'd liked her well enough. She was sharp, smart, and had her wits about her. A good sense of humor lurked there, too, which was a big point in her favor. Helped to balance out that almost too-serious, take-charge side of her.

Although, to be fair, she had been thrown as big a loop as he'd been thrown that day, just from a different angle. She'd asked a few pertinent questions, and had seemed to feel protective of her newly discovered stepsister. He wasn't sure who had been more surprised when she'd asked what would happen if she held on to her share of the mill: Sawyer, Addie, or Sunny herself. Up until that point, every one of his battle-tested instincts told him she was out the moment she could get out.

And he didn't hold that against her, either. She hadn't had a clue about her father, much less that he'd leave her some random property out in the mountains. Along with that avalanche of information had come the fun news that she also happened to have stepsiblings. Oh, joy, right? Bailey hadn't

97

really had a say in how things were going to go, although he was sure if she'd asked to stay with her foster family, Addie would have at least considered it. But Bailey hadn't said a word about wanting to stay where she'd been.

In Sunny's case, however, the reality was that her life was elsewhere. A good life, according to Addie, who'd apparently asked a lot more questions of the young woman than Sawyer had thought to ask. Addie had also found out during the court proceedings that Sunny had recently lost her mother.

So, no, he didn't hold it against her that she'd seemed to flip-flop on what she wanted, nor that she'd headed out shortly after making her surprise announcement. It had to have been a lot to process in one day.

That day had been two weeks ago, however. And he, for one, would like to know what her decision was going to be. She was right in thinking they needed to dot the i's and cross the t's before he went much further with the renovation. What she decided to do with her share was just business to him. The family part? Well, Addie's little speech that day notwithstanding, they weren't family, not really. So, he didn't much care what Sunny wanted to do about that part.

As for Bailey? He liked the kid. And he loved Addie even more for wanting to do the right thing by her. He suspected in time Bailey would come to mean a lot more to him, since they'd be living in the same town and the same woman who'd helped to raise him would now be raising her. Bailey didn't know it yet, but her life had just taken a very, *very,* lucky turn. He had no idea where his would have ended up had it not been for Addison Pearl Whitaker stepping in and doing the same for him. But that also meant her share of the mill wasn't in limbo.

All that was left was tying up the loose end that was Sunny Goodwin. And if he thought that was what had prompted Addie Pearl to head to D.C., he'd have driven her there himself. Unfortunately, he knew Addie too damn well to suppose that was the case. "Did she say how long they'd be gone? Were there overnight bags involved?"

Will frowned. "I didn't think to look. I was already up the scaffolding when she stuck her head in to say they were heading out. Sorry."

Sawyer shook his head. "Nothing to be sorry about. Not your problem."

"What's not his problem?" Seth strolled

in just then, a tray of take-out coffee balanced in one broad hand. A white pastry bag with steam escaping the top and grease soaking through the bottom was clasped in the other. He lifted both. "Whatever it is, I can guaran-damn-tee this will make it better, *cher*." He said that last part in a mock Cajun accent.

Wilson leveled a very serious look at Seth. "Hattie's back?"

"She is." He grinned, proffered a cup, but held the bag back.

"Thank you, Jesus," Wilson murmured, cradling the cup between two broad palms and taking a nice, long sip, the scalding temperature of the coffee be damned. "And there will be life," he added, clearing his throat a few times as the hot liquid went down.

Sawyer took his cup, nodding his thanks. "You can skip showing me what's in that bag, though. The last thing I need right now is a sugar rush."

Seth just grinned. "Don't have to tell me twice." He uncurled the top and let Wilson peek inside the bag. "More for us."

Will groaned in deep appreciation. "God is good."

"Hattie is better," Seth said, chuckling, as Will reached in and pulled out a plump, golden brown beignet, the dusting of sugar coating the surface glinting in the morning sun. He closed his eyes as if in prayer as he sank white teeth into the warm, puffy pastry.

"Damn straight," Will said, around a second bite.

Hattie was Henrietta Beauchamp, who ran Bo's, the only diner in town. She opened at six every morning, seven days a week. Her menu boasted all-day breakfast, a daily lunch special from eleven to two, and supper served from four to six every evening. Closing time was seven-thirty sharp. She'd run the place longer than most folks in Blue Hollow Falls had been alive, but "her people" as she termed them, hailed from Louisiana. As did her cooking. All of it learned at her *mamere*'s knee, as she liked to tell pretty much anyone who'd listen.

She'd recently taken a trip south to attend her great-nephew's wedding and visit family. Likely the last time, given her advanced age, that she'd be able to make such a trip. Privately Sawyer was pretty sure she and Addie would outlive them all, but he'd been happy she'd worked it out to get down there, with the help of her great-granddaughter.

What the whole town, such as it was, hadn't been okay with, was her shutting

101

down Bo's for the duration. As she made clear, she didn't give her recipes out "to nobody." So while she was gone, they'd just have to feed themselves, now, wouldn't they? She'd smiled her partially toothless grin and told them they'd respect her more for it, be more thankful for her on her return. As the collective reverence for Hattie Beauchamp was second only to God, he wasn't sure how much more revered she could be, but folks certainly wouldn't be taking her for granted anytime soon.

"I'm glad she's back, too," Sawyer said. "Her biscuits and gravy are like no other. And if you tell Addie I said that, I'll deny it." They all chuckled and the two other men continued to groan in abject sugar bliss as they polished off the bag. At the last second, Sawyer snagged the bag and wolfed down the final one himself. Maybe he needed a little fortification after all. "Dear Lord, it's almost better than sex," he said on a groan.

Seth did a fake jab to Sawyer's midsection. "Brother, if you think *anything* is better than sex, then you definitely ain't doing it right."

"Don't let Hattie hear you say that." This from Will, which had the other two men bark out a surprised laugh.

"Listen, I need to head out of here for the

day," Sawyer told the two men, hating to miss a day, but knowing damn well it was his only real option. "Will, go ahead and start in on repairing the mortar joints on the exterior lower stone wall." Then he turned to Seth. "Have a go at that wheelhouse. I know you've been dying to get your hands on it."

Seth's eyes gleamed. "Damn straight. But I thought we were continuing on the frame out of those upper-floor joists. That other stuff is extraneous, at least until the important work is done."

"I know, but I have to —"

"It's like he doesn't think we can handle it unless he's here ordering us around," Seth told Will in exaggerated dismay.

Will, who was used to their back-and-forth, but refused to play the straight man, merely shook his head, then took their empty coffee cups and doughnut bag and headed over to dump them in the mortar bucket that doubled as their trash bin.

"I'd love nothing more than coming back to find those pain-in-my-ass boards in place," Sawyer told him. "It's not that. I'm just thinking it might be in all our interest if I clear up a few things with my new, uh, partner before we go any further."

"Ah, yes," Seth said with an appreciative

sigh. "I'm guessing you mean the lovely Miss Sunshine. You heard her whole name, didn't you? All five of them? There she was, all business on the outside, but peace, love, and rock and roll underneath. Now that's just damn sexy." He wiggled his eyebrows. "Perhaps you should give dear old sis a call and ask her to drop on by again. I'll be happy to help you negotiate."

Sawyer just shot him a level look, and completely ignored the sudden protective streak he felt at the thought of Seth doing anything with Sunny. It was one thing to instinctively want to protect Bailey; she was just a kid. But Sawyer was pretty sure if anyone could take care of herself, it was Sunshine Goodwin. In fact, according to Addie, she'd done just that, as well as taken care of her flower child mama, from the time she was around Bailey's age. "What I mean is that Addie Pearl is up in D.C. right now, on a 'field trip' " — he used air quotation marks — "and I think I know who is on her first tour stop."

Seth's suggestive smile fell. "Oh." He winced. "Yeah, an intervention might not be a bad idea."

"Why does it matter?" Will wanted to know, surprising them both by giving an opinion on the matter. When Sawyer and

Seth turned to look at him, he merely shrugged and said, "Looks to me like Miss Goodwin could care less what you do to this place. She came, she saw, she split." He pulled his work gloves from a back pocket and put them on. "It's not like she's going to be upset that her share is worth more, especially seeing as you're not expecting her to chip in on the restoration costs or anything else."

It was a fair point and one Sawyer had been telling himself the past two weeks. "True," he told Will. "But, end of the day, I don't know what she wants or doesn't want. What *I* want is for her to sell her share to me or Addie, or at least give one of us legal control over the decision making for her. Letting it simply sit in limbo like this isn't making me all that comfortable. Apparently Addie is feeling the same."

"But?" Seth prodded, knowing Sawyer well enough to know that wasn't the whole of it.

"Only, I'm afraid Addie is looking for a different resolution than I am, or she'd have discussed it with me, and we'd have moved forward on it together. And she wouldn't have taken Bailey along with her." Sawyer sighed. No, Addie wanted to keep Doyle's newfound offspring in the immediate orbit of his other newfound offspring, and if Sunny wasn't going to initiate contact, she'd take matters into her own hands. "You know Addie, she's all about family, and I suspect she's going to make this one happen whether said family members want it to or not."

"When do you figure you'll be back?" Wilson asked.

"Sometime tonight."

"Lot of driving in one day," he replied. "We can keep on getting on while you're gone, if you need to stay up there a night or two."

"I appreciate that, but I suspect Miss Goodwin will be quite happy to tell us whatever she's decided without a lot of haggling. She didn't strike me as being particularly wishy-washy."

"Truth," Seth agreed, and Sawyer noted the gleam of interest once again.

"Simmer down, big guy," Sawyer told him. "One thing I'm pretty certain about, no matter how she decides to manage her share, is that it will be a way that doesn't require her on-site presence. You saw how fast she lit out of here. She's a city girl."

"I was born in Seattle," Seth reminded him.

"Yes, well, you're also a child of the

leprechauns and wee folk, so we can't go by you."

"If only it were true. My nana Aileen would be so proud," he replied, his grin ever wider when Sawyer just rolled his eyes. "All I know is I saw Sunny sitting out there in her car, and she didn't look like her mind was all that made up."

"According to you, she shot you down right easily enough." This from Will, which made Sawyer choke on yet another surprise laugh. Must be all that sugar.

"If I had time, I'd ask for details," Sawyer said. "But I don't. Which is probably just as well." He pulled his truck keys from his jacket pocket.

"You gonna call Addie and let her know you're coming?" Seth asked. "That might be enough right there to get her to hold off on whatever she's got planned."

Sawyer gave Seth a look. "Again, I ask, have you met Addison Pearl Whitaker?"

Seth chuckled. "Right. Well, we'll be here, keeping it real. It's not like we'll run out of stuff to do. Just let us know if things change. I've got to see a guy about some wine casks later this afternoon, and Will's got something at Jake's school, so —"

"No worries," Sawyer said. "Do what you have to do, I'll check in later. And thanks," he said to Seth, and to Will who was already heading over to where he'd spread his tools out. Will just gave a short wave over his head, and continued on with the work at hand. "I do appreciate it," Sawyer called as he headed out, already mentally reconfiguring the rest of his day. Unfortunately there was no squeezing in a six-hour minimum round trip plus whatever time they all spent chatting over the future of the mill and still getting any significant part of the daily to-do list done. Most of which required daylight, and as fall raced toward winter, those rapidly shortening hours were more in demand than ever.

"Well, sis," he muttered, as he stuck his key in the ignition. "I hope you appreciate the intervention I'm about to mount on your behalf."

# CHAPTER FIVE

"So, you haven't talked to them? Any of them?" Stevie was crouching down, checking the undersides of the glossy green leaves of a recent arrival at USBG's production facility. The *Cinnamomum kotoense* was five feet tall and had the look of an ornamental tree. Currently on the critically endangered list, the species was part of the Care for the Rare program. "It's been, what, two weeks?" she added. "And they haven't called you either? Not even Abbey Road?"

"Addie Pearl," Sunny corrected her, with a wry twist to her lips. "And no, I haven't."

"Nothing from Ringo or Paul, either?"

Sunny spent most of her time working with the endangered orchids that were part of the same program, but she and Stevie often worked together on new arrivals, checking them before introducing them to their specified greenhouses. In this case, the new *Cinnamomum kotoense* plants were on the list to be moved to the conservatory where the public could see them, along with several other endangered and rare species that would be new to public view. She stopped her own examination and straightened. "I'm afraid to ask which one you think is which. And what's with the Beatles references? You're way too young to remember them."

"You knew who I was talking about, and we're the same age."

"Because my mother was the queen of oldies," Sunny said. "Unfortunately, I am a walking encyclopedia of all music from the sixties and seventies." She shot her friend a smile. "Whether I want to be or not."

"The Beatles weren't unfortunate," Stevie said. "They were brilliant. And I have you trumped on the mom deal."

Sunny laughed at that. "Oh, my young padawan, I think not."

Stevie merely arched a brow. "Okay, Obi-Wan. My name? Stevie? It's not short for anything. I'm not a Stephanie, or a Stevanna, or anything lovely and exotic like that. I'm just Stevie." When that didn't make Sunny so much as blink, she said, "You know my folks are musicians. I was named after my mother's favorite group, Fleetwood Mac. She loved Stevie Nicks."

That had Sunny's eyebrows lifting. "We've been working side by side for, what, a year and a half now? How is it I never knew that?"

"I try not to let it come up in conversation. You don't even want to *know* what my middle name is."

Sunny's smile grew. "Only one middle name? Good try, but again, I've got this. In fact, I can pretty much guarantee you that you've finally found the one person on earth who will think your name is downright boring. At least by comparison. But you go right on ahead."

Stevie slid off her thin blue gloves and folded her arms. She was slightly shorter than Sunny, with enviable curves where Sunny had none, skin the color of golden mahogany, beautiful green eyes that were bright and sharp, and a thick head of reddish brown hair that she kept tamed into a bun during work, but that Sunny happened to know sprang into a full, gorgeous afro when all the pins were out of it. Stevie gestured at herself with one hand. "Do I look like a Stevie Nicks to you? Even if I donned the boots and the scarves and had a painfully thin, guitar-playing husband, do you see any Stevie in me? Do you honestly think my mama took one look at me when I was born and thought, *Hey, little Stevie Nicks?*"

Sunny cocked her head to the side. "Little Stevie Wonder, maybe," she deadpanned.

Stevie's eyes went wide but she hooted in laughter. "Oh, no, you didn't. Okay, I see how it is. You must know we're good friends. I can't believe you just said that."

Sunny smiled, knowing they were, indeed, good friends, and thankful for it. "You're going to make me guess your middle name, aren't you?"

"Oh, no, honey. I'm not telling you now."

Sunny pulled off her own gloves and extended her right hand. "Hello, it's a pleasure to meet you. I'm Sunshine Meadow Aquarius Morrison Goodwin."

Stevie goggled. "You are making that right up. Props for creativity though."

"Would you like to see my driver's license?"

Stevie's smile faltered. "You're serious? They got all that on your license?"

Sunny just smiled. "And you think you have it bad filling out paperwork."

"We've worked together for what, a year and a half now, and I'm just now hearing about this?" Stevie parroted back at her.

"I don't like to talk about it," Sunny shot right back. She wiggled her fingers. "So,

cough it up. Stevie . . . Janis? Stevie Grace?"
Her eyes widened and she grinned. "No!
Could it be . . . Stevie Cher?"

"Aretha."

That stopped Sunny. "But . . . isn't your
last name —"

"Franklin? Mmm-hmm," Stevie said. "My
father had a sense of humor. And he'd
already relented on the Stevie part."

Sunny reached out and laid one hand on
Stevie's arm as she pretended to wipe away
a mock tear. "I just want you to know, I have
never felt so close to another human being
in my entire life."

Stevie brushed Sunny's hand off, but she
was laughing, and she gave Sunny's shoulder a quick squeeze before they both got
back to work. "So," she said, as they worked
their way through the specially zoned greenhouse, "you never answered me. Are you
going back to the mountains?"

They were in one of thirty-four greenhouses that made up the largest greenhouse
facility of a public garden in the United
States. The greenhouses were carefully
modulated into sixteen different temperate
zones, depending on the plants they housed.
The production facility held all the plants
that were rotated into and out of the public
conservatory on a seasonal basis, as well as

a significant number that were never on display, but were grown and cared for there as part of any one of a number of different programs. The Care for the Rare program was one of those, but there were others that focused on things like sustainability and conservation.

The orchids under her care were part of a joint collaboration with the Smithsonian Environmental Research Center. It was, in all ways, her dream job. She spent her days tending to some of the most fantastic and amazing plants in existence, and was left largely alone in her happy place. What more could anyone want? *Not a defunct, crumbling silk mill in the middle of nowhere, that's for certain.*

"Earth to Sunshine," Stevie said, then chuckled at herself. "Ha! I like it."

"Show some respect, Aretha," Sunny shot back. They shared a grin, then a laugh.

"So," Stevie prodded. "Have you decided to sell your share? What about your new baby sister? You said you thought about inviting her to come visit you. I think that sounds like a good plan. I can see why you wouldn't want the hassle of that place, or to get tied down again in any way, but if you invited Bailey here, then she can become part of your world. Doesn't mean you have to do the same in return. I bet she'd love to see your place, visit here, or at least tour the conservatory."

Sunny smiled to herself as Stevie chattered away. She knew she'd be in for an earful when she told Stevie about her inheritance, and the basics about the convoluted family tree, but that was precisely why'd she'd told her about it. Sunny had never been good about talking things through out loud. Her mama had done enough talking for both of them, and it wasn't as if Sunny could talk to her own mother about the conflicts she felt because Daisy Rose was at the heart of them. Yet, at the same time, Sunny fiercely protected her mother, so talking about her to someone else seemed like a sort of betrayal. Stevie, on the other hand, had none of those reservations. Quite the opposite. So Sunny let her good friend talk through things for her.

"I don't know," Sunny finally said at length. "I've been thinking about maybe giving my share to Bailey."

Stevie paused, leaf in hand, and looked at Sunny. "That would give her a full third of the place, right?"

Sunny nodded. "I think of the three of us, she's the one who could use whatever boost life could hand her. I don't know if owning a bigger share of our inheritance will be a boon or the proverbial albatross, but Sawyer seemed optimistic about where he thought the renovations would take them, and it's a pretty cool plan, really. So that would surely up the value of her share."

"Don't you worry that giving her more of a share would be too tempting for Abbey Road?"

"Addie Pearl. And what do you mean?"

"Given what I know so far, *Addie* and Sawyer are tight. Like, mom and son tight, to hear you tell it. So, putting her in charge of an even bigger share of the place just seems" — she shrugged — "risky."

"I've thought about that, too," Sunny admitted.

"Of course, if you hold on to your piece, then you still get a say. Which means you can watch out for how Bailey's piece is being managed," Stevie said.

"You're right," Sunny agreed, having had the same thought herself. "It's just . . ." Now she lifted a shoulder.

"Spill it," Stevie demanded, then motioned with her fingers.

Sunny smiled, thankful again for their friendship, even if Stevie wasn't exactly the tea and sympathy sort. Maybe because of that. "Holding on to my share, even if I'm playing more of a monitoring or advisory role, still means staying involved with all of them."

Stevie propped her hands on her hips. "Well, they're your family now whether you want to stay involved directly or not."

"A family I'd never even heard of until two weeks ago. None of us had heard about each other until then. We were doing fine without each other this long."

Stevie clapped her gloved hands several times. "See? Wasn't so hard now, was it? Let it out, sister. Tell me and these plants here how you really feel."

Sunny did the mature thing and stuck her tongue out at her friend, making them both laugh.

"You know, maybe it's not that complicated," Stevie said, going back to work as she talked. "Maybe Addie will do right by the little girl like she promised she'd do. From the sounds of it, Sawyer turned out to be a good guy and she took care of him when he was little." She leaned around the tree she was examining and wiggled her eyebrows. "Damn shame he's related though, from the sounds of him." She smoothed her neatly pinned-up hair. "Maybe you could hook this sister up, though."

Sunny just rolled her eyes, but she was smiling as she continued her own work.

"So maybe you're right and there is nothing to worry about," Stevie went on. "They carry on, and you don't need to do more than check in from time to time. If Addie is cool and Sawyer is sticking around, then it seems like Bailey's life is already way better."

Teasing aside, Sunny really listened to what Stevie was saying. "You're right. It doesn't have to be complicated." But it already felt complicated. Sunny hadn't even had the time to really get used to being free. To finally being able to put her needs, her wants, first. Heck, she didn't even know what those wants and needs were yet.

"Don't do anything rash. This all just happened. Sit back awhile and take it as it comes," Stevie advised. "You have your share. They're not coming after you to invest in the renovation, or anything. So, let them have at it, and go about your business. If things change, then you have the right to change your course of action."

"That's what I've been doing these past few weeks," Sunny said. She looked at her best friend, smiled. "But hearing you say it out loud makes me feel a lot more confident in that choice. I think you're exactly right.

Thank you." She let out a slow breath, and a good deal more stress than even she realized she'd been carrying felt like it was being released from her along with it. No immediate action was due on her part. She could just go on living her life. Her free-to-be-me life.

She laughed, feeling almost a little light-headed as the revelation sank in and took hold. "Nothing has changed, really. Unless I want it to."

Stevie started humming "Let It Go" from the Disney epic *Frozen,* making Sunny snicker. There was no one else in their sector, so Stevie picked up a trowel and used it as a mic, as she went full on Idina Menzel and began to sing the iconic song in earnest. She actually had a pretty good voice — great, even — though Sunny thought better of saying as much to Stevie Aretha, or she'd never hear the end of it. Literally.

Instead, the normally far less demonstrative Sunny, who was a horrible singer, for once in her life really did let it go and added a little performance art as backup. She picked up a spare apron and swirled it over her head as she spun around Stevie, using exaggerated arm movements to match the refrain.

She was just swooping in front of Stevie

119

as she hit a piercing high note when some-one cleared his throat behind them both.

Stevie broke off mid "go" and both she and Sunny swung around in surprise, then stood, well, frozen to the spot.

Sunny found her voice first. "Sawyer?"

"Do they teach you that in horticulture school?" he asked, an amused smile on his handsome face. He cast his gaze around the interior of the greenhouse. "I have to say, it appears to be working."

"You should see how they respond to Motown Week," Stevie quipped, then turned to Sunny so Sawyer couldn't see her face. She let her mouth drop open and shook her hand in front of her as if to say, "Whew!" while mouthing *Oh my God!*

"What — what are you doing here?" Sunny asked him, not risking looking at Stevie a moment longer. She didn't need to be told how drop-dead gorgeous Sawyer was. Apparently, two weeks of thinking about him as her brother hadn't done one lick of good. Then the plastic panels that separated their section of the greenhouse from the rest parted and another head poked through. "Bailey?"

At Bailey's glance upward, Sunny realized she was still holding the apron aloft. She pulled her hand down, and balled the apron up in front of her, pasting a big smile on her face as her brain scrambled to catch up with the rest of her. "Hey! What a surprise." She started to fold her arms, forgot the bundled-up apron, then comically tried to figure out what to do with her hands, finally plopping the apron down on a worktable and propping one on her hip and using the other to smooth back the strands of hair that had escaped the single braid she wore when at work. "What are you guys doing here?"

"Nice Elsa," Bailey said to Stevie as she stepped fully into the space.

"I'm here all week," Stevie said, then did a deep curtsy, complete with theatrical head drop. "Matinee's on Sunday."

Bailey and Sawyer both grinned at that, but then were nudged out of the way when the plastic panels rustled again behind them.

"Looks like I missed the show," Addie Pearl said as she fought her way through the moving panels with her cane. Sawyer held them aside so she could make her way into the hot and humid temperature-controlled space. She took a sweeping look around and beamed. "Well, isn't this something. Can't wait to hear all about it." She looked at a now madly grinning Stevie, who appeared downright tickled pink at this latest turn of events and gave her a big, welcoming smile. "I'm Addie Pearl Whitaker. This here is Bailey, and that's Sawyer. We're Sunny's family. Pleased to meet you."

# CHAPTER SIX

"I'm just sorry you came all this way," Sunny told Addie, as they strolled along the downtown National Mall, past the Air and Space museum, heading toward the Botanic Garden conservatory. "We could have talked over the phone about whatever paperwork needs doing so you can continue moving forward with the renovation. I didn't intend for you to stop the work or anything like that. I didn't realize you were waiting for me."

"It's good to get out, stretch your legs," Addie said by way of reply. She was using her cane, but moving along at such a clip that they all had to hustle to keep up with her. "Besides, Bailey has never seen the Capitol, or any of the monuments. It's a field trip."

Sawyer walked a few paces behind the two women, close enough to hear the conversation, but hanging back just enough so he didn't have to participate in it. Bailey strolled along next to him. He glanced down at the young girl. "This is your first time here?"

She nodded, but otherwise said nothing. She had been pretty quiet since he'd met up with them in the parking lot of the production facility. Fortunately, when Addie had seen that Bo's was open again, they'd stopped and had breakfast before heading out of town. He was surprised Seth hadn't run into them there on his beignet and coffee run. So, Sawyer had been able to catch up with the two just as Addie was trying to talk her way into the production facility, after having already stopped by the conservatory only to find out that Sunny worked at a different location. She hadn't seemed all that surprised to see him, which had only confirmed she was up to something.

Sunny didn't have an office, so there hadn't really been a convenient place to talk privately at the greenhouse complex. Addie wanted to see the Botanic Garden, so Sunny had taken a long lunch break, and they'd caravanned over from Anacostia to the city proper. They'd parked at L'Enfant Plaza, walked down to the Mall, and were now heading down Jefferson toward the conservatory, which sat in the shadow of the

Capitol Building. It was a pretty fall day, clear skies, unseasonably warm temperatures, a light breeze, perfect for an excursion. Except for the part where Addie was the only one who'd actually planned on taking said excursion.

Sunny hadn't seemed exactly excited about the proposition, either, but Sawyer couldn't blame her, given they'd all dropped in completely unannounced. She'd handled it well enough, though, especially where Bailey was concerned. As they'd learned when they'd entered the place, the production facility was only open to the public one day a year, which happened in March, but Sunny had offered to pull a few strings to give them a look at the rare orchids she cared for. She'd taken time with Bailey and Addie both, showing them some of the specific work she was doing to help find new ways to cultivate the critically endangered members of the species.

He'd found it fascinating as well, and while his impression of Sunny was still that she liked others to think she was an all-business sort, her obvious love and passion for her work had shone through the no-nonsense exterior, adding a sincere warmth and earnestness he wouldn't have previously ascribed to her. Of course, the little song and dance skit he'd inadvertently inter-rupted had already forever changed his opinion of her. For the positive. Made him wonder how else she lived up to those five names of hers.

Brogan had gotten that part right, as it turned out. *Damn sexy, indeed.*

Sunny had told them before they'd even left the production facility that she'd de-cided to hold on to her interest in the mill, but wouldn't block Sawyer or Addie from doing whatever they wanted with the place. She'd offered to contact the estate attorney who had helped her with her mother's liv-ing will to get something in writing to that effect, which would protect each of their interests. Addie had told her to do whatever she felt best.

Sawyer had hoped to be right back on the road after that little announcement, but then Addie had come up with her plan to see the Botanic Garden. Which was when Sawyer had known she wasn't done yet.

"Any particular thing you'd like to see?" he asked Bailey as they walked past the Museum of the American Indian. He de-cided since they were here, they might as well take advantage of the visit. *In for a dime, in for a dollar.* He had great respect for the District of Columbia and all it represented.

It was a powerful place to be, and to see. He'd visited the city countless times in his life, and it had never once failed to move him. The domed Capitol Building, stationed as if keeping watch at the head of the table, sat at one end of the National Mall, with the stone edifice of the Washington Monument soaring skyward at the opposite end of the open, parklike area, which was lined on either side by the Smithsonian museums. Then there was the Jefferson Memorial, holding sway over the Tidal Basin with the cherry trees draped around the water's edge like a festive garland each spring, and the Lincoln Memorial, stately and reverent, at the end of the grand reflecting pond. All of it reminded him why he'd given service to his country. This was the foundation of the entire nation, the seat of freedom.

Since Bailey was being more or less dragged around with no say in the matter, he found himself wanting to make this trip meaningful to her in some way. "The Museum of Natural History has everything from dinosaurs to gemstones. Air and Space has lunar modules and —"

"I'm good," Bailey said.

Sawyer glanced down at her, but she was looking straight ahead, glancing here and there, taking it all in. She seemed to be exactly as she'd stated. Good. If she was feeling upset or put out by the field trip, she certainly didn't show it. Conversely, she didn't appear to be all that excited about it, either. She was just . . . good. Going with the flow. He'd noticed she did that a lot, and wondered if that was how she'd learned to hold it together.

He recalled their brief conversation the day they'd first met; he knew there was a sharp, observant, inquisitive brain inside her young head. He wondered if the lesson she'd taken from her life thus far was to basically go along and not rock the boat. He wondered if she let herself want things. Any things. Or if that was just too damn scary, given her life could change at a moment's notice, based on the whims of others. The way it had just two weeks ago. Did she have dreams? Did she want to be something specific when she grew up? Did she dream about being old enough to break free, to be out on her own?

Sawyer had talked to Addie at some length as she'd begun the process of becoming Bailey's legal guardian, so he knew that Bailey wasn't a problem kid. She'd never run away, she'd never been in any kind of legal trouble, or trouble in school. She was a good student, made good grades, never truant, though quiet and not exactly a joiner. In fact, her teachers and her various foster families had always had good things to say about her. The word *shy* had been used more than once, but Sawyer didn't buy that. Bailey had no problem speaking up; she simply chose not to. Her caseworker had told Addie that Bailey's file was one of the thinnest she'd ever seen. Mostly just listing her various residences, beginning and end dates of her time with this family or that. Her being shuffled around the system had always had something to do with the foster family itself, which was common enough, rather than any problem with Bailey.

Sawyer thought about his own childhood, prior to landing with Addie Pearl. He smiled then, thinking maybe Bailey was the smart one after all. He had not been particularly good at going along to get along. His case file would not have been described as thin. He knew what it was like to yearn, to want, to dream. To want something other than what he'd been handed in life. He'd felt all of those things when he'd been her age and had worn every bit of it on his sleeve. And on his tongue. Even after landing with Addie. Once an orphan — whether in fact or by abandonment — always an orphan. At least to some degree. Even when life got better, it was still part of the core truth of the person, and that affected how they looked at things. It couldn't not affect them.

Their similar backgrounds should have made it easier for him to find a conversational toehold, but he felt at a complete loss. So he just respected her silence, watched as she looked around, thinking maybe she'd give a clue if something in particular caught her eye.

In the end, she solved the problem for him. "Have you been to the Wall?" she asked, as they waited at the corner to cross Maryland Avenue.

He knew which wall she meant. "I have," he told her.

She looked up at him then. Her crystalline blue eyes were sober, yet inquisitive. "Do you know anybody on it?"

The Wall she was talking about was the Vietnam Veterans Memorial. A long, sloping granite wall with the names of all who had made the ultimate sacrifice during that war engraved on its long, segmented face. "I do," he told her. "Buddies of mine have their father's names engraved there."

"Army buddies?" she wanted to know.

He nodded, then the crosswalk light turned white and they hoofed it across the busy thoroughfare. She startled him by taking his hand, and for reasons unknown to him, the gesture made his eyes burn. Just a little. She seemed so cool, so together, it was easy to forget she was just a little girl. He curled his big fingers around her far smaller ones, but a quick glance down showed him she wasn't looking up at him. As soon as they got to the sidewalk on the other side, she let go. She didn't seem embarrassed, or, well, anything really. It had been matter of fact, like everything else the young girl did. As if that's just what you do when crossing a busy street. And maybe that's all it had been. Probably. But Sawyer knew it would be a while before he forgot the feel of her small hand in his.

"Would you like to see the Wall?" he asked her, as they neared the old glass conservatory that he now knew, from seeing where Sunny worked, housed only a small part of the U.S. Botanic Garden's collection.

"No," she said, with a quick shake of her head.

"I'm good," they both said at the same time. She glanced up, caught his sardonic wink, and busted out a short trill of giggles. The transformation was a pure delight, causing Addie and Sunny both to look back, big smiles creasing their faces now, too. Bailey was a cute young girl, but far too sober. Seeing her face light up, hearing her laughter, which was surprisingly girly, considering the girl herself was not, lifted his heart. He made a promise to himself to see about getting her to do that more often.

He caught Addie's backward glance at the two of them as they continued on down the walk, noted the satisfied gleam in her eye before she turned her attention forward again. *Ah. So that's the plan, is it?* Addie had introduced them to Sunny's delightful co-worker, Stevie, as family, and apparently that's what she aimed for them to be. And not just in name only.

Sawyer appreciated her intentions, especially where Bailey was concerned, but he also didn't want any false hopes to be built, either by Addie or Bailey. He wasn't going anywhere, and Bailey would learn she could count on him. But it wasn't fair to rook Sunny into anything, or make her feel as if she should contribute something to her newly discovered clan unless she felt personally moved to do so. Coming into a surprise inheritance didn't bind her to anything except having a legal share of that old mill.

Sawyer found himself watching her, the swing of her step, the forthright manner in which she strode down the walkway. She was not a tentative sort, and given what little he knew about her childhood, he imagined she'd never had that luxury. If he found himself curious to know more about her, well, that wasn't entirely surprising now, was it?

They arrived at the conservatory then and Sunny greeted the staffer just inside the door by name. Sawyer was curious how she'd introduce them, but all she said was, "I've got some friends with me today who surprised me with a visit. Can we get them some VIP badges, please? I'm going to take them through the back."

The young man nodded, smiled back, then handed out lanyards to Addie, Bailey, and himself, with badges dangling from the ends that had VIP PASS printed on the front.

Sunny smiled at them in a tour guide kind of way, and said, "If you'll slip those on, I'll give you the grand tour."

He respected her for handling this intrusion into her busy day with aplomb, and for giving Addie, at least, what she wanted. A family day outing. At least in spirit, if not in truth.

"Bailey," she said, motioning to the young girl, "why don't you come on ahead of them so you can see what I'm talking about."

He happened to glance down then, which

was the only reason he caught sight of the young girl start to lift her hand toward his, then press her palm flat to the side of her leg instead, as if willing it to stay there. Sawyer wasn't sure where the instinct came from, but he simply took Bailey's hand in his, as if he did it every day, and said, "We're good."

He was smiling at Sunny as he said it, but he caught the brief upward dart of Bailey's gaze from the corner of his eye, the brief twitch at the corners of her mouth. She also didn't let go of his hand. He gave her hand a little squeeze. She squeezed back.

And that was it. He was a goner.

He didn't know why Bailey had chosen to trust him, but she had. And he knew, firsthand, how monumental that was. He vowed right then to do whatever he had to do so she'd never regret it.

"No worries, then," Sunny said, catching sight of Bailey's hand in his, which made her smile falter for a split instant, then grow wider. "We're already getting ready to set up a few new events for the coming holidays. I can take you back to one of the rooms that is currently off public display, and show you a little of what we do here."

Sawyer was trained to be hyperobservant, so he hadn't missed that little momentary falter, and he couldn't deny he was intrigued by it. It wasn't dismay he'd seen in her eyes, but . . . yearning? Or something like it. Maybe she just missed her mama. Probably that was it. But . . . what if it wasn't? What might Sunny Goodwin want? She'd made it clear she didn't want them. Or so he'd thought. Now he wasn't so sure. He recalled Seth mentioning much the same when he'd come back for his tools and found her still sitting in her car, staring at the mill.

"Can we take pictures?" Addie wanted to know. "I brought my new smart phone with me." She pulled it out of the pants pockets of her faded green khakis and showed it to Bailey with a wink. "We can take a selfie."

That got a wry little smile from Bailey, which she shared with Sawyer in a quick glance upward. He shared her dry smile and lifted a shoulder as if to say, *What are you gonna do?*

"As long as you don't post them on social media, sure," Sunny said.

"Not even Instagram?" Addie wanted to know. At Sawyer's surprised look, she said, "Seth set it up for me."

"Of course he did," Sawyer said sardonically.

"What?" Addie wanted to know. "It's a great way to connect with folks, show 'em what we're doing. He said we could do an upstart campaign even, to help with funding the renovations."

"Kickstart," Sawyer said, chuckling now. "And you don't need to go worrying about that. I told you I've got that covered. You work on getting the guild shored up and agreeing on the plans for how they want to split and share the space, and let me deal with the rest." He looked at Sunny. "Sorry. No social media photos. I swear." He looked at Addie on that last part.

Addie just held her hands up. "Don't worry. I have some self-restraint."

Sawyer chuckled again at that and Sunny smiled along with him. Their gazes caught and held for a moment, and in that split second, he decided, yeah, maybe he did want to get to know her better. She was an intriguing woman with an interesting occupation, interesting life history. She'd worked for what she wanted in life while simultaneously dedicating herself to family. She was clearly passionate about what she did, and enjoyed sharing her passion with others. He had a deep respect for all of that. She was also sharp and observant, like her little half sister, and pretty, too. Had he met her elsewhere under other circumstances, he'd have absolutely been interested.

"Shoot," Sunny said, frowning briefly, and breaking him from thoughts he'd probably be better off not having. "I guess we should have stopped by one of the food trucks and picked up some lunch on the way in."

"I'll go," Sawyer said quickly. Maybe too quickly. "My pass will get me back in, right?"

"Yes, but —"

"Hot dogs okay with everyone?" Suddenly, he decided he needed fresh air. And a little time to reorganize his thoughts. Thoughts that had already been undergoing a major overhaul.

Addie and Bailey nodded. "No relish on mine," Addie said.

Bailey, wrinkling her freckled nose, shook her head in agreement on that.

Sawyer smiled, then looked at Sunny, eyebrows raised. "You're good with that?"

"Sure," she said. "Thanks."

"You're good?" he asked Bailey.

She nodded and let go of his hand, then said, "Extra mustard. And a bottle of water, please."

"You got it," he said with a wink. The kid knew what she wanted. Sawyer would bet that extended to more than hot dog toppings. She'd been pretty decisive in befriending him.

"You know what, why don't I go with you, help you carry," Sunny said. She turned to Addie and Bailey. "You two can go ahead and wander the public exhibits. I'll be happy to answer any questions you have after lunch. Meet us back in here in about twenty to thirty minutes? The lines are long out there around this time."

Sunny didn't give anyone time to dissent, least of all Sawyer. She moved to the door, opened it, and held it open for him to go with her.

*So much for regrouping.* But he wouldn't deny he was perversely happy for the chance to spend a little one-on-one time with her. He nodded at Addie, winked at Bailey, and off they went.

No sooner were they outside the conservatory door than she said, "I'm guessing this little outing wasn't your idea."

*All business. No nonsense.* He had to fight the urge to smile. "Why do you say that?"

"You came in two vehicles."

He smiled. "That's the only reason?"

She stopped at the sidewalk and turned to him. "Bailey clearly trusts you most. She would have ridden with you, but she came with Addie. Her backpack was in Addie's car."

"You'd make a great detective, Miss

138

Goodwin."

Sunny smiled, but continued. "So, I'm betting that means you made the drive up here after they left and caught up with them at some point."

"That would be at the front desk of the production facility," he said with a grin, lifting his hand. "Guilty as charged, ma'am."

Her lips twitched in response. She wasn't upset, simply trying to get the lay of the land. "So this *was* all Addie's idea. I thought so. Why did you come after them? What did you think she was going to do?"

"I didn't know," he answered honestly, surprised by the questioning, but thinking it was smart for them to simply be up front with each other. "All I knew was she had something going on or she'd have told me her plans. Honestly, I don't think she was surprised I followed her up. In fact, I'd say that's exactly what she wanted."

Enlightenment dawned in Sunny's pretty whiskey brown eyes. "Ah. Getting all of us together again, then. One big happy family?"

He nodded. "If Mohammed won't come to the mountain, and all that."

Sunny turned and headed down the sidewalk toward a row of food trucks lining the curb. He fell into step beside her, but said nothing.

"So, what is her big plan?" Sunny asked, as they neared the first in the long line of trucks. It was a pretzel vendor, so they kept on walking. "I mean, as far as I'm concerned, anyway? I told her I'm not going to get in the way of your restoration. I'm assuming you aren't planning to ask me to invest in it?"

"No, I'm not."

She paused again. "You were expecting me to sell my share, weren't you?"

"I was hopeful. It would have simplified things. I was as surprised by all of this as you were."

"Probably more, given the mill is your rightful inheritance. Or should have been. I don't blame you for wanting the rest of it back." She walked on again and he matched her pace. "I thought that's what I was going to do," she said, then glanced up at him. "Sell it to you, I mean. Or Addie."

"But now?"

She shook her head, then lifted a slender shoulder. "I think I should hang on to it. For a bit, anyway." She looked up at him, studied him for a moment, then apparently decided he could hear the rest of her truth. "I'm considering signing my share over to Bailey. She's the only one of us who might really need it down the line." She looked at him again. "That might be an assumption on my part, but since you're bankrolling the renovation and not wanting help with that, I thought it was a safe bet."

"But you're not doing that now," he said, not really making it a question. "Signing it over to her, I mean."

She shook her head, but lifted her hand before he could speak. "It's not a question of trusting Addie Pearl. I mean, I know what she did for you, and my first impression, my instinct, is she wouldn't do anything to negatively impact Bailey. I just . . ." She trailed off, then looked away, apparently not as ready to reveal all as she'd thought.

So he did it for her. "You wanted to keep a hand in. For Bailey, I'm guessing. If you own a share, then you have some legal sway in keeping tabs on how things are going."

She looked a little surprised by his insight. Now he lifted a shoulder. "It's what I would have done in your place."

They joined the end of the line at the hot dog truck. Despite the warmer than usual October day, the ever-present breeze that whipped down the Mall made it feel a bit chilly. She clasped her elbows and folded her arms close to her body, either as a defense against the wind or as a barrier to

141

him, he wasn't sure which. "And you're okay with that?" she asked.

The breeze was whipping those loose tendrils of hair into a dance around her head, occasionally causing them to cling to her cheeks and lashes. He had to work far harder than he liked to admit to keep from reaching out and tucking them out of the way. Not because the errant strands bothered him, but because he wanted an excuse — any excuse — to touch her. "I'd have liked to have heard it from you sooner so we wouldn't be making assumptions," he said frankly, "but yes, I am."

"I was still pondering," she responded. "I hadn't decided yet."

"But you're sure now?"

She nodded and tucked those strands behind her ears before wrapping her arms back around her middle. She seemed entirely unaware of the effect she was having on him, which he counted as a point in his favor. He slid his hands into his pockets anyway, because the fact that there were no tendrils of hair left to tease him hadn't lessened his desire to touch her one whit.

"It was talking to Stevie about it today — my co-worker you met earlier — that really helped to cement the decision," she said. "In fact, I'd just decided to leave things as is when you all came in."

He shot her a grin. "Ah. Hence the little Disney dance routine? Just let it go?"

Her cheeks turned a bit pink, and she seemed surprised that he got the *Frozen* reference. Sawyer placed the blame for that bit of arcane knowledge squarely at Seth Brogan's clodhopper-sized feet. The man had learned to control his damn llama's penchant for being, shall we say, overly amorous by singing Disney tunes to keep the beast happy and in line.

"I especially liked the apron twirling part."

To her credit, she held his gaze easily, pink cheeks and all, and her laugh was purely self-deprecating. "Stevie thinks I have a problem with needing to control every little thing, and she might have a point. But, in my defense, it's a habit I picked up pretty early on. Hard to shake."

"Shake it off," he said, then sang a few bars of the famous Taylor Swift song. He might have done a little hip move, which made the folks in line smile and made her cheeks turn even pinker.

"Something like that, yes," she said, then laughed outright when he added the *"haters"* line, and did another little boogie. "I can see why Bailey likes you," she said.

"You're still embracing your inner ten-year-old."

"There are times when we'd all be better for it," he replied, and tried not to let her see she'd sparked his full attention with that laugh of hers. It was full-bodied and unrestrained, which seemed a bit opposite of the woman he'd seen so far. He liked it, and he liked her even more for it. The line moved up and they stepped forward with it. "I appreciate your concern," he said, "for Bailey's well-being, I mean," he explained when she gave him a blank look. "Addie told me about your mom passing recently. I'm sorry for that. I haven't been through that particular loss, not in the way you have, at any rate, but I've lost other people I've loved. It's never easy."

"No," she said, more soberly, "it's not." Then she offered him a brief smile. "Thank you. That was kind of you to say." She looked at him more directly. "Were you close to Doyle? I mean, Addie made it sound like he wasn't around, but" — she waved a hand, dismissing her question, and looking apologetic — "I should have said this sooner, that I'm sorry for your loss. I am sorry. I do know what it's like and I should have been more sensitive to that when we first met at the mill."

144

"Thank you," he said. "You were handed a lot that day, so it's understandable. I didn't expect condolences. Which, I guess, answers your question. No, we weren't close. In fact, I only saw him sporadically after moving to Blue Hollow Falls and not at all as an adult." Her eyes went wide in surprise, but he pushed on with the rest of what he'd begun to say. "And I only brought up your losing your mom because I can't imagine it was a welcome surprise to find out you had this other family you didn't know about. A possible new burden to deal with. A family who didn't even know they were one until a couple weeks ago."

"In some ways, that makes it easier," she said, surprising him with her candor. "It's not like any of us are stepping into some kind of established tableau where we have to figure out how to fit in. We were all in our own lane already. And, yes, I know you and Addie are family to each other, but —"

"I know what you're saying. Yes, Addie is the closest thing to family I've ever had. She is my family. And I'll admit I wasn't sure what to think about her abrupt decision to bring Bailey home. She did the same for me, so her motives aren't in question," he hurried to add. "But despite appearances to the contrary, Addie isn't going to be around forever. So it was a lot to consider for me, too. She and I have talked about it and she apologized for not really thinking that part through before doing what she thought was right."

"Are you okay with it? I mean, it's done now and Addie is hardly going to dump Bailey back into the foster care system, but —"

"I know Bailey and I will form some kind of relationship. And I know there will be responsibility there, on my part. At least I feel there is."

"I'd say you two are already forging a bond. It's clear she's chosen to put her trust in you, at least to some degree."

He nodded. "I know. And I've been in her shoes, so I know what that means. It's not that I don't want — I mean, I'm open to whatever kind of relationship we form. She's an easy kid to like and my heart naturally goes out to her. We may not be blood related, but Addie has a way of making folks feel like family, even when they otherwise aren't." He grinned. "If Addie has her way, she'll be my little sister in every way that means anything before I even know it's happened." He paused, and he knew then something in his heart had already shifted where Bailey was concerned. "And if I'm being honest, she'd already made a good start." It was only when he looked back at Sunny as the line inched forward again that he noticed she'd gone still.

"Wait," she said, then moved forward to catch up with him. "What do you mean? About not being blood related? We're exactly that."

He chuckled, shook his head. "I wondered about that. I guess the magistrate didn't make it clear, and Addie didn't explain."

She was looking quite perturbed now. "Explain what?"

It was their turn at the food truck, and he could all but feel Sunny vibrating next to him, waiting for his response. He placed his order for himself, Bailey, and Addie, then turned to her. "My treat. What would you like?"

"What? Oh, uh . . ." She turned to stare at the menu.

Now it was his turn to feel a little . . . vibration. She'd been staring at him like . . . well, like she wanted to take a bite out of him. Maybe not in a good way, but . . . to be honest, it sure hadn't felt entirely like the bad way, either. In fact, he really wasn't sure what the electricity that seemed to hum between them was all about. He'd chalked it up to the simmering tensions about their shared inheritance. Now he wasn't so sure.

She gave her order and they shuffled to the side a bit while they waited, allowing the next person in line to order.

"What didn't Addie explain?" she said, enunciating very clearly.

Oddly, her sudden intensity, the blazing directness in those honey gold eyes of hers, only served to ramp up that simmering . . . something. And definitely not in a bad way. *Ratchet it down a few notches there, big guy.*

"We're not related by blood, Sunny. At least, I'm not. To any of you. Doyle adopted me." He lifted his hands. "I don't know why me and not the kids he actually fathered, but —"

"You said Addie took you in," Sunny said. "I'd assumed that was because Doyle didn't stick around, but now I remember you telling Bailey that Addie brought you to Blue Hollow Falls." She lifted her hands, then let them drop. "I'm confused."

"She did. And yes, Doyle Hartwell wasn't exactly the type to stick around, which he didn't in my case, either. I think that's why Addie harassed him about making it legal. She was trying to protect me. I'm sure if she'd known about either of you two, she'd have done the same."

"So, how did you end up there? How did

148

she find you?"

"My mother was one of Doyle's . . ."

Sunny waved her hand as he paused. "Got it. Go on."

"She was living with someone else when I was born. That didn't work out too well. It turned out not to be all that unusual a situation where she was concerned. We moved around. A lot. She wasn't particularly maternal, so there wasn't much supervision for me."

"You were a little kid," Sunny said. "I mean, if you came to Addie at age nine, then —"

"I'm not saying I recall the early, early years as a baby or toddler, of course, but from the age of five until when Addie came and got me . . . yeah, I do remember a good part of those years. I can't assume it was any different really, before that."

"So, how did Addie get involved?"

"My mother finally hooked up with a guy who could support her in the lifestyle she wanted, but he didn't want to be saddled with a kid. So she contacted Doyle, told him I was his kid and he could either come and get me or she'd hire an attorney and sue for child support and joint custody. I don't know how Doyle would have responded to that, but Addie somehow found out and she came and got me."

"Weren't they divorced by then?"

Sawyer nodded. "They'd been divorced a good while at that point, but Addie and Doyle, despite everything, were connected for life in many ways. She was the only one who really knew him, seeing as they'd grown up together. She was younger than him, but —"

"No, I get it. First love and all that."

Sawyer nodded. "Of course, he was gone far more than he was ever around, but he'd communicate with her from time to time, usually when he was experiencing a low point and needed to confide in someone. He came home to the Hollow on occasion, but less and less the older he got. He hadn't come at all from the time I entered middle school until I enlisted, but I know he stopped by a few times while I was gone."

"But you're sure you weren't his?"

Sawyer nodded. "We're sure. Apparently, Doyle told Addie about my mom's threat, so she came to check things out and, apparently once she saw the situation, she didn't ask too many questions. She just got me out of there. Doyle tried to throw money at the problem, but Addie pressed him to do the right thing, which I'm sure he did mostly to quiet her on the matter." He looked at Sunny. "I don't think Addie knew about you, or she'd probably have made some contact on his behalf. And that was way before Bailey."

Sunny waved that off. "My mother had no contact with him after I was born, or I'm sure I'd have either heard about it or read about it in her journals later. She considered him this kind of avenging angel who intervened in her life, then left it just as abruptly, after bestowing on her the gift of me. And, mercifully, our house. She really didn't want or expect anything more. She didn't love him and didn't want or expect him to love her. In her mind, the two of us were like this divine tribe of two." She fluttered a hand, as if at a loss to explain it. "My mother wasn't . . ." She paused, then smiled, a little sadly, but also affectionately. "She wasn't like anyone you'd ever meet. She didn't see the world in any kind of way that you'd call normal. When I asked who my father was, I got the divine angel story, and that was it. She never spoke of him, and really didn't like me asking about it. I thought I'd find out who he was in her journals, and Doyle was in there, but he was so much older than she was, my adolescent brain thought he couldn't possibly be my father, and . . ." She lifted a shoulder. "I stopped caring about it when I got older, because, frankly, it didn't matter."

"I guess I felt the same about him. I never thought of him as a father. Addie was my family. And Lord knows, I made it hard enough on her. I was pretty much angry at the whole world back then. Thank God she's so damn stubborn and stuck by me, or who the hell knows where I'd have ended up."

Sunny smiled. "You're lucky, then. And I guess Bailey is now, too. I'm glad to hear that. So, how did you come to know your mother lied about Doyle's paternity? Did he demand a paternity test or something?"

Sawyer shook his head. "No. He pretty much let Addie have her way about most things as long as he didn't have to do anything personally other than write a check or sign a document. He was too busy living life, seeing the world, whatever it was he was off doing. Living off his family's money, what there was left of it."

"So, how did you find out?"

"Addie had been suspicious all along, so she hired a guy to investigate my mother's past and eventually figured out what state and county I was born in, dug up my birth certificate. Doyle's name wasn't on it. Some other guy's name was listed. At that point,

Doyle had already legally adopted me, but Addie had a paternity test run anyway, because she couldn't know for sure that my mother hadn't lied about the paternity on the birth certificate, too." He shrugged. "She actually tracked my father down, but he'd died years before in a motorcycle accident. There was nothing to suggest he ever knew about me. I guess we'll never know that part for sure, but I'm definitely not Doyle's. Our best guess is that my mother apparently tagged Doyle when her new boyfriend put the pressure on because she knew he had money, knew how he was about fixing problems. I guess it hadn't occurred to her to do that sooner, or she probably would have."

"That's . . . God, Sawyer, that's awful. On all sides." She touched his arm, then immediately dropped her hand. "I'm so sorry. So, did Doyle know? About you not being his?"

He shook his head. "I don't know if Addie told him. He was my legal parent, but Addie was my actual family, in all ways that mattered. He wasn't around, so I don't guess it mattered all that much to him one way or the other."

"Didn't Doyle support you? Or her? Financially, I mean? They weren't married anymore, but she did take you in, so —"

He shrugged. "I honestly don't know what arrangement they had between them. She doesn't talk about Doyle, especially their married life. What she told you in the mill that day was the most I ever heard her say on the subject. And to be fair, though I know she stuck by me and we eventually became family to each other, I wasn't like Bailey. I was what they called a problem child. I counted myself lucky that I wasn't on the street."

Sunny gaped. "You can't honestly think that made it okay for your own mother to abandon you? And your father — at least he thought he was your father — to do more of the same? I mean, he knew Addie was taking care of you, but still. How much of a problem could you have been at — you said you were, what, nine when you came to Blue Hollow Falls?"

He just smiled. "I think the term *holy terror* would have been understating the case. Even at nine."

Her lips twitched a little. "That bad, huh?" She shook her head, then grew serious. "Well, with what you said about your mother's lack of parenting skills, and the uneven life you'd led to that point, you could be forgiven a lot. I mean —"

"Maybe. But you didn't go that route. To hear Addie tell it, you took care of your mama since you were little. You didn't become rebellious; you knuckled down and got it done."

Sunny looked down, clearly uncomfortable with the direction the conversation had taken.

"And Bailey, whose mother didn't even bother to find her a home first, just dumped her straight into the system and took off. And despite that, Bailey's been the model foster kid," he went on. "Not me."

Sunny looked up. She ignored the parts about her and Bailey, and said, "So, what turned it around for you? I mean, you're a war hero. To hear Addie tell it," she added with a short smile, when it was his turn to be uncomfortable.

"Addie likes her stories."

"So, the story about how you got the nickname Sergeant Angel isn't true?"

"When did you hear that? You took off right after we all met up for the first time. Addie said she hasn't seen hide nor hair of you since."

Sunny's cheeks turned a very becoming shade of pink, which he found himself enjoying more than he should. He bent down to catch her eye when she dipped her chin, and saw the guilt all over her face. His own face split into a wide grin. "Not so blasé about your new kin after all, huh? You Googled us, didn't you?"

She lifted her gaze then, tried for defiant, or at least dismissive. Failed miserably on both counts. To her credit, she laughed with him. "Guilty as charged, sir," she said, echoing his earlier words, even raising her right hand. "And I never said I wasn't curious. I just . . . wasn't sure what I was. I don't think it was all that unusual to do my own bit of research, see what more there might be to the story."

"What did you find out?"

"Not much. Nothing about Bailey. I found Addie's Web site." Her expression shifted then to one of sincere awe. "You're right, she is an amazing weaver. A real artisan. I was truly stunned by the beauty of her work. I had no idea."

"She talks a great game about everything and everyone else, but it's funny, she's not one to boast about her own talent."

"I looked up the guild she mentioned, too. Pretty cool, actually. You have some seriously talented folks there in the Hollow." She looked at him directly. "I think it's great, what you're doing with the old mill. On a bunch of different levels. It respects the history of the town, and helps launch Blue Hollow Falls in a new direction, all at the same time."

"Hold up, rewind," he said, not responding to her compliments. "Back to that research part. What exactly did you dig up about me?"

She merely gave him a rueful smile. "I can see why you were the youngest master sergeant ever, or something like that I think I read. You like ordering people around."

"I like keeping order. Call it childhood PTSD. Once I figured out that being on top of and ahead of things was far better than being behind and under things, I've worked hard to keep things on track and moving as smoothly as possible."

"Hence today's road trip."

"Hence the road trip," he agreed.

They were called over to the food truck for their order, and he realized they'd moved several yards away as the intensity of their conversation had increased. Sunny looked relieved to have an excuse to keep him from continuing to question her further, but the more he talked with her, got to know her, the more he wanted to know. In addition to being smart, sharp, and unafraid to say what was on her mind, she was also a little shy about some things, and far easier to make blush than he'd have guessed. There were some deeper vulnerabilities in there, too, and he'd be lying if he said he didn't want to poke and prod a bit, find out what other layers there were underneath that all-business, no-nonsense exterior.

He was interested and not a little turned on. And maybe it was because he did, in fact, like to run things, or maybe it was because she brought back a bit of that rebelliousness inside him that he'd been unable to control in his youth, but the Pandora's box question they'd both left alone was too tempting. He heard himself give voice to it before he could think better. "So, you thought I was your blood brother."

She'd taken a few steps toward the food truck, but paused and looked back at him, her expression guarded now. "An honest mistake, don't you think?"

He nodded. "I guess I thought you'd be relieved to hear we weren't actually related."

Now she definitely stiffened. He did, too, but not in the same way.

"Is it wrong for me to be relieved that I might have a little less responsibility to this supposed family dynamic I've been thrust into?"

He stepped closer, and saw the ways her pupils expanded. Yeah, when she'd looked like she wanted to take a bite out of him back there, kind of the same way she was looking at him right now, it definitely wasn't in a bad way. He'd stake his life on it. And he might be about to do just that. "Would it make you uncomfortable if I said I noticed you looked relieved in a way that had nothing to do with being responsible for anything? In fact, maybe the relief was specifically about the fact that you've been wanting to be a little . . . irresponsible?"

To her credit and his absolute pleasure, she locked her shoulders in a hard square and her expression went granite smooth. "Trust me when I say that I am never irresponsible. I wish I had that luxury. As you said, I wasn't as unaffected by finding out I had a family as I made it seem. But —"

She broke off abruptly when he walked up to her, stopping just shy of being in her personal space, but close enough that she had to tip her chin up to maintain steady eye contact. Which she did. Defiantly so. *Oh, the lady doth protest far too much.* And on confirming that truth, any chance he had to rein himself back in vanished on the spot. The smile slid slowly across his face, deepening to a grin when he noticed her throat work. "If I told you I'm relieved, too, and it has absolutely nothing whatsoever to do

159

with being unaffected . . . in fact, one might say, for the exact opposite reason . . ." He shifted to keep their gazes locked when she would have looked away. "Would that make it easier to admit?"

She lifted her chin higher, holding his gaze of her own will now. "Easier to admit what?" she asked boldly.

He reached up, caught another stray hair being buffeted around by the breeze, and wrapped it around the end of one finger before carefully tucking it behind her ear. His fingertips barely brushed the side of her neck as he let it go, but even that hint of a caress was like striking match to tinder, and the fire leapt straight into his belly. He knew the exact moment she realized that, as she was staring as intently into his eyes as he was into hers. Her pupils sprang wider still, absorbing almost all those golden iris rings. The pulse in her temple flickered, and her nostrils might have flared slightly — her reaction to him was that palpable. He was quite certain she was seeing every bit of the very same in him. Had he done what he wanted to do and tugged her up against his chest, she'd have had a whole lot more proof of the effect knowing they could do anything they damn well pleased with each other was having on him.

"Easier to admit that we wouldn't be breaking any laws of nature if we went with our instincts."

She stepped back then, turned away, and walked stiffly over to the food truck, where she scooped up the cardboard box holding their order.

*What in the hell are you doing, Hartwell?*

But rather than feel even an ounce of regret, he found himself grinning as he followed her back to the conservatory. In fact, he couldn't remember the last time he felt so damn good. He watched her stiff spine and the sway of her narrow hips with an entirely different set of thoughts running through his head than the ones that had been brewing there when he'd left the Hollow that morning. At least as they pertained to one Miss Sunshine Meadow Aquarius Morrison Goodwin.

Maybe the more things changed, the more they stayed the same. Maybe a person never really stopped being who they truly were, down deep inside. Maybe the best a man could hope for was to find a way to control the more troublesome parts. Or maybe it was simply the environment dragging him back. Part of him, anyway.

Because there he was, not back in Blue Hollow Falls for more than a minute, and already he was back to doing what he always did.

*Rousing a little rabble. Making a bit of trouble. Raising a lot of hell.*

And where Sunny Goodwin was concerned, damned if he didn't mind that at all, not one little bit.

# CHAPTER SEVEN

Sunny reminded herself she was merely doing what Addie Pearl and Sawyer had suggested she do. After all, it would be foolish not to make sure she'd legally covered herself. She was being wise. Mature.

She'd been telling herself some variation of that explanation since she'd left Old Town early that morning. Never mind she could have simply mailed the documents to Addie or Sawyer. She didn't have to hand them over personally.

She'd made an appointment with the estate lawyer the day after the surprise visit from the Blue Hollow Falls contingent. She'd done so mostly because it was the smart thing to do, but also, admittedly, because it had given her something to do during her non-work hours to keep her mind from incessantly replaying the last thing Sawyer had said to her by the food truck.

Epic fail there.

She shifted her thoughts willfully to Bailey. Sunny couldn't tell during their visit to the Botanic Garden if Bailey was any happier than she had been that day at the courthouse, but the interplay she'd seen between the young girl and Sawyer had looked like a step in the right direction.

Regardless of whatever Sunny's hormones wanted her to think about Sawyer, she did believe him when he said he'd stand by Bailey and that he was open to whatever kind of relationship they developed. When Sunny took everything he'd told her that day and coupled it with what she'd learned about him by doing her own digging, there was nothing to indicate he was anything other than what he appeared to be. A stand-up guy with a big heart who'd given himself in service to his country, and now to his hometown, and to his family, both old and new.

If Sunny were being honest, she'd admit she felt a bit guilty about that last part. There he was, being all big brotherly despite the fact that Addie had more or less dumped the girl in his orbit without conferring with him first, and he wasn't even biologically related to her. Sunny, on the other hand, was Bailey's actual half sister, and what was she doing? If anyone should be making an effort to help give the girl a sense of family, it should probably be her.

Since gaining her inheritance and a new family along with it, Sunny had excused herself from getting involved because of the distance thing. Addie and Sawyer were right there with Bailey, after all. But that *was* an excuse. One made more to soothe her own guilt than because she thought she had no role to play.

To that end, in addition to getting the paperwork properly signed while she was there, Sunny planned to work out a date for Bailey to come visit her in Old Town. It was a baby step, Sunny knew that, but she didn't know how else to begin. Heck, she wasn't even sure Bailey would want to come visit her. She had seemed interested enough to ask questions during the Botanic Garden tour, though, so Sunny hoped that might be a point in her favor.

She turned off the two-lane road that doubled as the highway in the mountainous part of the state and started up the narrower winding road that led higher into the mountains. She'd admittedly been looking forward to the chance to drive the corkscrew switchbacks along Big Stone Creek again, letting her little six-speed do what it was engineered to do, bobbing and weaving smoothly through the curves while she alternately downshifted and accelerated to get the most out of every bend. As she let herself go, let herself slide into the rhythm of car and road, she marveled at how much more colorful the forest had become in the three weeks since her last visit.

It was the middle of October now and the lower elevations were pushed almost to peak color. She knew that when leaves began to turn, the speed with which they went through the variations of their color spectrum, to when they finally fell, was impacted by a number of different factors, not the least of which was specific to the genetic makeup of each particular plant or tree. The unseasonably warm weather had slowed the transformation a bit, but at the lower elevations, the colors had already come in beautifully, and as she climbed higher and higher into the hills, she noted the color had crept up almost to the highest peaks now. How wonderful it must be, she thought, to watch the transformation up close and personal, like Addie and the other folks who lived in the Hollow got to do, year in and year out. The tapestry before her as she left the deep woods and entered the first high pasture was simply breathtaking. Once again, she felt her heart simply fill up with awe of the beauty of nature.

Of course, the second she plunged again into heavy forest where the view was restricted by the big oaks and soaring pines, her thoughts zipped right back to Sawyer. *Nothing new there!*

Yes, she'd been attracted from the moment she'd laid eyes on him, but, unlike the very flirty and charming Seth Brogan, she certainly hadn't seen any of that same sort of reaction from Sawyer. She'd done her best to hide the direction her thoughts had taken and had thought she'd been pretty successful. For his part, he hadn't seemed to be having that same struggle at all. And he'd known all along they weren't related.

The thing was, it had been bad enough when he'd been biologically verboten. Worse still was that moment when she'd learned he was fair game. It was like both of her X chromosomes had instantly burst into a happy dance. No waving aprons needed.

However, all that had been utter child's play as it turned out. Because things had gotten downright squirming-inside-her-clothes hot when Sawyer had made it clear his XY's were doing a little chromosome dance of their own.

Because she hadn't already been on fire

before that.

It was bad enough she'd read his service history and knew he was a war hero. He was also being an utterly adorable big brother to Bailey. Then he had to go all Taylor Swift dance mode at the food truck, and try as she might to feel embarrassed by his little hip-wiggling boogie, what she had been was amused. And charmed. The man did not give a flying fig what others thought of him, and for a girl sporting five names, that was an appealing attribute.

"And now you're heading straight back into the self-proclaimed bad boy's lion den for round three!" Except, she reminded herself, this time she'd come to put an end to all future rounds. Sawyer liked things to be controlled and in order? "Well, then, he should love this."

She had thought she'd take a little drive around, see if she could find the actual town of Blue Hollow Falls, but she'd waited too long to plug the little town into her GPS and hadn't had signal now for close to a half hour. So she went straight to the mill the way she'd come in before. Then almost wrecked her car as the mill came into view.

"Holy mother of muscles and sweat," she breathed as she somehow managed to swing into the same spot as before and cut the engine all while staring. There might have been a little drooling involved as well. *Stevie, you're going to be so mad at me.*

Stevie had offered to tag along for moral support, and because she was dying to get a look at the old mill — as well as another gander at Sawyer and high hopes for a Seth sighting as well. Sunny hadn't been sure how the meeting would go, though, and wanted to keep things simple. Plus, she'd yet to confide in Stevie about the whole food truck conversation, and she honestly didn't know how she was going to hold up to seeing Sawyer again. So she'd told Stevie they'd go together another time, but they'd both known that was an empty gesture, since Sunny had also honestly stated that she didn't know if or when she'd be going back to Blue Hollow Falls again.

"But I might be persuaded to make it a regular event if the scenery is going to look like that," she murmured. And she wasn't looking at the fall foliage. "It's like I died and went to lumberjack heaven."

There were three men up on the roof of the mill, and another half dozen scattered around on the grounds around it. Some were climbing up and down the scaffolding that now braced part of the outside wall, while others were running wheelbarrows back and forth filled with what she assumed were shingles. Or they were hoisting said shingles up the scaffold to the roof. All of that apparently required lots of glistening muscles to be bunching and flexing.

When she finally peeled her attention away from the man parade, she noted with some shock that a lot had happened in three weeks. The rusted, damaged tin panels that had once comprised the roof of the mill were gone. Only a small part of the wood frame was still exposed, and it appeared to have been largely rebuilt. The overall shape of the roof remained, as did the large cupola in the middle, but whereas it had been tin paneled before, the new roof had been fully reconstructed using . . . were those slate shingles? She snagged her phone and used the zoom on the camera. Yep. Blue slate shingles.

The former tin roofing, though showing deterioration, had been in keeping with the style and history of the mill, but the stone shingles lent it an entirely different look that was both rustic and beautiful. Set in the tableau of the fall foliage with the waters of Big Stone Creek rushing over the boulders next to it . . . simply gorgeous. She could see the place becoming a destination just for photographers alone. She imagined the setting with snow covering the banks and topping the low-stacked stone wall that surrounded the mill, maybe smoke curling from the two stone chimneys. It would have a distinct beauty in all four seasons.

Along with Addie, Sawyer, and the Bluebird Crafters Guild, Sunny had also Googled the mill itself, but there hadn't been much historic information available on it other than a brief newspaper story about the mill being shut down that had been reprinted as part of a bigger story on the history of silk production in the States. That had pulled her right down a rabbit hole where she'd ended up reading a great deal more about the history of silk production and silk mills in the British colonies. All fascinating stuff, particularly from a horticulture perspective. She'd read more about the *bombyx mori* moths and mulberry trees and thought how interesting it would be to actually explore the origins of silk production. She couldn't help but wonder if there might not be a better way to go about producing the desired result now, with all the advances that had been made in growth technology.

Sitting there now, seeing the mill coming to new life right before her eyes, she wished she could have seen the place as it had been originally, but she made a mental note to get Addie to send her photos of it when it was all completed. Or . . . maybe she'd bring Stevie back after all. Given she'd made that promise. Kill two birds.

Which brought her attention right back around to the men.

She'd spotted Seth as one of the workers on the roof immediately. His beard made him an easy one to ID. Sawyer was up there, too, along with another man she'd never seen before. Seth had on the same ancient fatigues, this time with a long sleeved green T-shirt and another heavier plaid shirt tied around his hips. His hair was in a single plait down his back today and between that, the beard, and those shoulders of his, he looked like some kind of Norse god as he tossed slate shingles up the steep incline of the roof to the other man, the one Sunny hadn't met. That man was catching and stacking them as if they were tossing around paper clips. He had dark hair that was a little on the shaggy side, and wore old tan canvas khakis and a blue Henley that hugged his lean muscled chest and ropy shoulder and arm muscles like a lover. But even with all that eye candy tempting her, once her attention snagged on Sawyer, she forgot all about the others.

He had on old worn jeans that snugly fit his thighs, which looked even bigger with the knee pads he had on. He was down to yet another filthy T-shirt that might have once been white, but Sunny didn't give a damn. He was kneeling on the roof, straddling the peak, hammering the shingles into place. Back in the city, the temperatures had steadily fallen in the past week, marking the end of the Indian summer they'd been experiencing, but had still hovered in the upper sixties to low seventies. Three hours south and west, but a few thousand feet higher in elevation, the thermometer reading on the dash of her car said it was a much brisker fifty-two degrees. That said, the sky was a blistering blue and the sun beamed directly down on the roof and the dark slate shingles Sawyer was nailing into place. All three men were sweating like it was the middle of July. Which made that old T-shirt cling to Sawyer's sculpted torso like a second skin.

From the safe confines of her car, she zoomed in with her phone camera and watched in guilt-free, rapt pleasure as he swung his hammer, driving in nails like a machine, one after the other, again and again. Her thoughts glided quite effortlessly to what he must be like in bed, pistoning those lean hips of his in that same methodical rhythm, muscles bunching, flexing, sweat glistening, as he drove himself into the warm, willing softness of her —

A rap on her window made her squeal and jump at the same time, and sent her phone flying into the passenger seat then bouncing down into the foot well. *What is it with people around here banging on the windows of my car?* Heart galloping, and her face not a little flushed, she turned and saw —

"Bailey?" Sunny pressed the ignition switch then quickly lowered her window. "Hey," she said, trying mightily to regroup as quickly as possible, but even she heard the breathless quality to her voice. "You startled me," she said with a laugh in a lame attempt to cover her reaction. "I was just coming to see you and Addie. I got caught up in all the changes to the mill. Wow, huh?"

The young girl looked over at the mill, and Sunny noticed her gaze went up to the three men doing the assembly line shingling of the roof. She looked back to Sunny, then to where her phone had landed, then back to Sunny, but her expression was, as always, unreadable. If she'd had any inkling what had been going through Sunny's mind, she didn't show that either. Sunny had to remind herself the girl was only ten years old. But looking into those bright but sober blue eyes, she wasn't so sure what Bailey might understand, even at such a tender age. Sunny certainly had been well ahead of the maturity curve when she'd been that young.

"I want to show you something," Bailey said. "Before you talk to Addie."

Surprised, and more than a little intrigued, Sunny nodded. "Okay, sure." She'd been about to tell Bailey she'd taken the following day off, so she had plenty of time before or after her meeting with Addie and Sawyer to go traipsing about with Bailey, but decided it was better to keep that bit of information to herself. If she needed a reason to cut and run, work was a handy excuse.

Opting to leave the paperwork in the car, and her purse along with it, she closed the window, grabbed her phone from the floor, and her key fob, then climbed out and clicked the lock button. "Where to?" she asked with a smile.

Bailey looked her up and down, her opinion of Sunny's choice of ankle-high black leather lace-up boots, black jeans, a thin, pearl gray sweater, and a deep red pea coat was neither approving nor disapproving. "Do you have gloves?"

"Gloves?" Sunny repeated. "It's a little chillier up here but I really didn't think — where are we going?"

Bailey motioned to the woods to the left of the lower lot. "Back that way. Not far, but it's colder in the trees. Mostly pine, so not a lot of light getting through."

Sunny followed her gesture, and recalled the last time she'd been here. It was the same direction she'd seen Sawyer and Bailey head off when they'd left the mill as she'd driven away. "Let me see what I've got." She moved to the back of her car and popped the hatch. Smiling, she came up with a pair of blue rubber gloves that were standard issue at work. "Well, it's better than nothing."

That got a hint of a smile from the girl. "Actually, those are good," she said. "You don't happen to have any clippers or anything, do you?"

Now Sunny frowned. "What kind of clippers?"

"Never mind. Come on."

"Wait, does Addie know where —"

"She knows," was all Bailey said before heading off in the direction she'd pointed to before.

Sunny closed the hatch and hit the lock button again, then happened to glance up to the roof of the mill and caught Sawyer looking straight down at her. How he'd heard her hatch slam shut over all the other ruckus, she couldn't be sure. *Maybe he just felt the scorch of your hot and steady stare.* She shushed her little voice and lifted her hand, waved. When he frowned slightly before waving back, she realized she was holding the blue gloves in her waving hand. *Aprons, gloves, what will you wave at the man next?* Certain other garments instantly came to mind, all of them made out of silk and lace, causing her to abruptly tuck the gloves into her jacket pocket and her prurient thoughts along with them.

Proving to herself that she was going to handle this situation with Sawyer in a mature, rational, and completely neutral manner, she gave him a friendly little salute, which earned her a wide grin in return, along with a hooting hello from the Norse god. *So much for being Switzerland.*

Ignoring the flush currently heating up her entire body, she hurried to catch up with Bailey. She swore she could feel Sawyer's gaze zeroing in on her retreating back. *Talk about scorching.*

She caught up with Bailey just as the young girl entered the woods. "Wow," Sunny said, as they entered the cool glade.

"It's beautiful in here." The undergrowth was gone here, as little to no sunlight made it through the canopy of high pine boughs. Beds of yellow pine needles, gray twigs, fat little charcoal brown pine cones, and fallen branches framed the trail that Sunny knew had likely been created by the deer in the area. They were creatures of habit and tended to follow the same course, changing only when forced change by fallen trees or shifts in water flow patterns of creeks and streams jammed with fallen foliage. She knew this because of her studies, not because she was the outdoorsy, hiker type. A fact that was becoming quickly and painfully clear; the little lace-up boots she wore were designed to look cute with her skinny jeans, but comfortable for hiking? Not so much.

The trees were a bit sparser the deeper they went, allowing the sun to cast beams of light through the high boughs, as if lighting their way. "Kind of magical," she added, as she trailed along behind Bailey. "When I was little, I started creating a garden in our tiny backyard in Alexandria. I liked to pretend there were fairies and elves living there. I even made a few little houses and some rustic patio furniture."

Bailey glanced back over her shoulder attentively, but didn't say anything to that.

They hiked on a few more silent minutes, and Sunny tried again. "You seemed to know a little about llamas. Have you worked with other farm animals? Or horses maybe? I wanted a horse like nothing else when I was younger, but we couldn't even have a dog or a cat, so I knew that was never happening." Not to mention there had been no budget for pets, but it wouldn't have mattered anyway.

Bailey went on a few steps, then slowed and waited for Sunny to catch up. "You never had a pet? Ever? Not even a fish or something? Are you allergic?" She said that last part with a tinge of disgust, as if allergies were a sign of weakness.

Sunny shook her head. "No, that wasn't it. My mom was pretty sick most of my life. All of it, really. One of her problems was respiratory, meaning —"

"I know what 'respiratory' means. She couldn't breathe right."

Sunny smiled. "Yep. So —"

"You could have had a fish. Or a dog that doesn't shed."

Sunny nodded. "Could have, but it was just better all around that we didn't." She didn't want to get into the particulars of some of her mother's mental flights of fancy. At least, that's how her mama had phrased them. Daisy Rose was often a delightful force of nature, but she had her issues, and not all of them were physical. So, even with the part-time care Sunny had eventually arranged while she was at school and, later on, at work, Sunny couldn't trust that her mother wouldn't get it in her head to set the fish free . . . or some other "live long and prosper" type thing she said her little voices occasionally coached her to do. Daisy Rose didn't believe in any of nature's wild creatures being kept in captivity, and Sunny often thought that included Daisy Rose herself.

To Sunny's surprise, Bailey nodded and said, "I get that."

Sunny wanted to ask her more, find out why she got that, get more of a feel for what Bailey's life had been like up to that point, but figured it was better to let Bailey reveal things at her own pace. On the other hand, maybe a direct approach would let Bailey know that Sunny might understand more than her young half sister thought she did. Sunny had grown up in one place with one parent, but neither of their childhoods had been what anyone would consider normal. "Addie told me a little about your file," Sunny told her, opting for the direct route.

"I'm sorry you had to move around so much. I guess that made it hard to have a pet."

Bailey shrugged, then turned and continued walking.

Sunny thought maybe her comment had been too frank, but then Bailey said, "I never thought about it. Not at first. None of the places I lived had any. It didn't come up."

Sunny knew there was a "but" in there somewhere, so she just said, "Yeah. I knew early on it wasn't going to happen for me, either, so I didn't let myself go there. Well, except about the horse, but, you know . . . horses. Hard not to want one of those." Bailey said nothing to that, so Sunny went on. "I think that was why I did the fairy gardens. I wasn't much of a doll or stuffed animal type person."

Bailey glanced back at that. "Me, either."

She didn't look or sound sad about that, like she'd shunned dolls and stuffed animals for fear of letting herself get attached to anything. She'd said it much like Sunny had, as if it was just how she was. "Well, I still have that backyard. I live in the same house I grew up in. The gardens I started as a kid are a bit more elaborate now, but the fairy places are still there. You know, if you'd

181

like to come see them, maybe hang out with me for a weekend or whatever, I'd like to do that. I was going to ask Addie today if we might work something out. If you're cool with that, I mean."

Bailey paused again, and Sunny almost bumped into her. She turned. "Really?"

Sunny looked down into those pretty blue eyes and saw not defiance or disbelief . . . but hope. And her heart teetered. "Really."

"I'll ask Addie," Bailey said, then immediately turned around and kept on walking, maybe a bit more determined than before.

Sunny smiled, and walked on behind her. *Baby steps.*

"I had a goat," Bailey said, almost in a rush, after another minute or two had passed in silence.

A more companionable silence now, Sunny had thought, and apparently she'd been right. "You did? At the farm you mean? Your last foster home?"

Bailey nodded, but kept trudging forward, her head a bit bowed now.

Sunny couldn't have said what made her do it, but she caught up to Bailey and put her hand on the girl's shoulder, gently halting her, then immediately let go, feeling that she didn't want to invade this girl's personal space unless invited to do so. Bailey had so little control over her life, Sunny wanted to respect what control she did have.

She waited for Bailey to turn around. When she did, the young girl's features were smooth. "It's okay," she told Sunny, as if guessing why Sunny had suddenly stopped her. "He's fine where he is. He belongs to them anyway."

"But he was yours, too?"

Bailey lifted a knobby shoulder and for the first time she looked exactly like the little girl she was. "I helped birth him. The Frasers — the family I was with — they raised pygmy goats. Little pains in the butts, really, they get into everything. But . . . you know . . . kind of cute, too."

"I bet," Sunny said, smiling. "You helped a mother goat with her baby? By yourself?"

Bailey shook her head. "No, Mrs. Fraser was doing the hard part, but she said I could help. I took care of the goats and she said when I proved myself, I could help with the babies."

"Wow, so I guess you did that. Good for you."

Bailey nodded. "It was totally gross," she said. "But, you know, pretty cool, too."

Sunny laughed. "My thoughts on birth exactly."

Bailey looked up sharply then. "Do you have kids?"

"Oh, no. No, I don't. But I had a friend when I was in college who had a cat she'd smuggled into her dorm room. I lived at home and commuted to school, but I happened to be there hanging out when the mama cat had kittens." Sunny wrinkled her nose. "You described it pretty much exactly how I remember it."

Bailey grinned then, and Sunny was struck again by how it transformed her face. She recalled hearing the giggle that Sawyer had somehow gotten out of her when they were walking along the Mall. She really hoped that this latest change in Bailey's young life would bring more reasons to laugh. A lot more.

They both turned up the trail again. Sunny could see brighter light ahead and thought maybe they were going to one of the high meadows. Maybe to see some ancient mulberry trees or something. After all of her reading on the subject, she'd actually be really interested in doing that. As the path widened, she and Bailey fell into step together, side by side, and Sunny wondered if maybe she shouldn't have checked with Addie or Sawyer personally before the two of them had taken off. What she knew of

Bailey's background led Sunny to believe the girl had been telling the truth when she'd claimed Addie knew about their hike, but they were going a bit farther than Sunny had expected.

Her thoughts went back to the goat, though, and the farm Bailey had been on before the inheritance had changed things. "Did you like the Frasers?"

Bailey nodded. "Yeah, they were okay."

"I'm sorry you had to leave like you did. Did you get the chance to go back and say good-bye to them? I mean, you went back to get your stuff and all, right?"

"We did that," Bailey told her. "Addie took me. We had to get papers signed. There was a lawyer, and we had to see Miss Jackson again."

"Oh," Sunny said, feeling suddenly and stupidly left out, realizing how much more there had been to Bailey's transition than she'd realized. "I'm sorry I didn't think to ask you that day you came to visit me."

"No problem," Bailey said, and Sunny wondered how often she'd said that in her life.

"So . . . did you get to see your goat?"

She thought she heard a little intake of breath, and Bailey just nodded. Sunny stopped her again, only this time, she left

185

her hand resting gently on Bailey's shoulder. "I'm really sorry, Bailey. I — I guess I haven't been very good about this. I just — it's all new to me, too. But I do want to try," and she realized as she said it, just how much she meant that.

"Your mom just died," Bailey said. "I'm sorry for that, by the way. But I know you don't want —"

Sunny crouched down. "It's not a matter of want. I didn't know what to even think about all of this. I've just been . . . trying to process everything, I guess. But that doesn't mean I don't want to know you, for us to know each other. I don't know what we can be to each other, or what you want us to be, but I'm open to figuring it out." She waited for Bailey to meet her eyes. "Cool?"

Bailey's eyes weren't watering, but that didn't mean they weren't swimming in emotion. Sunny felt her heart clutch tight in her chest when the young girl nodded. Bailey might play it like she was cool as a cucumber, and about a lot of things, probably she was. But at the heart of it all, she was just a kid. Sunny recalled that when she'd been Bailey's age and the truth of how her life was going to be really began to hit home . . . she'd toughened up a great deal, too. And yet, if someone had stepped into her world, like a Sawyer or maybe an older half sister . . . she'd have been hard-pressed not to let those walls crumble a little bit either. Hope was a hard thing to quash, and that wasn't a bad thing. Not at all.

"I can't pretend to know what it was like, living how you have so far," Sunny told her, deciding if the two of them were going to build anything, there had to be a solid foundation of honesty and trust. Without that, anything they constructed would be flimsy at best. "Just as most kids couldn't comprehend what my life was like, taking care of my mom the way I did. But I didn't care if they understood. I just cared that they wanted to be my friend, regardless of what my life was like."

"Yeah," Bailey said. "I get that."

Now Sunny's eyes were swimming in emotion. "I want to hug you, and tell you it's all going to be okay, and at the same time, I don't want you to get your hopes up about things I can't control. I wouldn't have wanted anyone telling me that when I was your age."

"You don't have to," she said, and Sunny let her hand fall away, respecting that this was a lot for Bailey, too. "I'm good. Addie is nice." She looked around, then back at Sunny. "It's good here."

"Did you have friends at school, where you were? Do you want them to come visit you here? Has Addie talked about school here?"

"The Frasers homeschooled. She had two older kids. It was okay."

"Will Addie homeschool you here then? Does Blue Hollow Falls even have a school?" She'd yet to see the town itself, but she couldn't imagine it was of any real size.

Bailey shook her head. "I had to go to the elementary school down in the valley — it's the closest one to here — and take some tests so they could figure out what grade to put me in. And we had to get the papers done first before she could enroll me."

"Oh," Sunny said, "well, that's good. I hope, anyway. You can meet kids your own age."

Bailey didn't say anything to that, which Sunny understood all too well. Making friends was dangerous, but much yearned for territory. And Sunny hadn't had to change schools every year, either.

"They said I could go in at a grade above my age, but Addie said it would be better for me to stay with kids my own age."

"What do you think?"

Bailey just shrugged.

"I didn't have a lot of friends when I was in grade school," Sunny confided. "I have a weird name and I was different. My mom was what they used to call a hippie, and I wasn't dressed like the other kids."

"What's a hippie?" Bailey looked interested once again, and maybe relieved not to be talking about herself.

"Well . . . I don't really know how to explain that. She lived on a —" Sunny broke off, thinking a commune wasn't something she wanted to try to explain to a ten-year-old. "A kind of mountain farming community. Everyone worked together and lived together and they grew and raised their own food and lived off the land. They tended to favor tie-dyed clothes and handmade things and . . . you know, I can't really explain it. But it was an alternate lifestyle that kids in the city definitely did not get."

"Your name's not weird," Bailey said.

Sunny smiled. "My full name is Sunshine Meadow Aquarius Morrison Goodwin."

That got a reaction out of the otherwise unflappable youngster. "Whoa. That's like a crazy bunch of names. Really?"

Sunny pulled her phone out of her coat pocket and opened the wallet side of the phone case. She slid out her driver's license. "Really," she said, handing it to Bailey.

Bailey took it and looked at the front. She looked back to Sunny. "Do all hippies have five names?"

Sunny laughed, shook her head. "My mother had six. She chose hers when she was eighteen. She chose mine, too."

"Why didn't you change yours then?"

"Oh, I planned on doing that, believe me. But by the time I got old enough, I had decided to own it instead. It's part of who I am, part of my heritage."

Bailey handed the license back, but didn't say anything. Then she blurted out, "My middle name is Danielle." She made a face. "I'm not a fan."

Sunny snorted out a surprised laugh at the attitude. "I'm not laughing at the name," she quickly added. "I think it's pretty. I do."

"It's kind of . . . foofy," Bailey said. "You know, like a frilly doll name."

"Well, if you wanted, you could go by Dani. But one thing I learned is that you get to go through almost your whole life once you're an adult without having to tell anyone your middle name." She smiled. "Even if you have three of them."

Bailey smiled a little at that, nodded.

"You know, that day you came to visit? My co-worker Stevie and I had just that day shared our middle names, and we've worked together and become really good friends now for well over a year."

"What's her middle name?"

"Aretha."

Bailey wrinkled her freckled nose. "Is that even a name?"

Sunny laughed. "Yes. It belongs to a really famous singer, actually."

"Well, she is a pretty good singer, so I guess that makes sense."

"You know, I guess it does," Sunny said, and pushed up to a stand. "I know this all has to be a lot to take in," Sunny told her. "But I think everyone is trying to do right by you. Addie and Sawyer definitely stepped up more than I did, but I will do better."

"It's okay," Bailey told her. "I'm —"

"Good," Sunny finished for her with a smile. "I know. You're also a kid who needs a family she can stay with until she figures out what she wants to do on her own. I think you have that family now, or at least the foundation for one. Doesn't mean it will be easy, or that starting all over again doesn't suck."

Bailey glanced at her then.

"You know you don't have to be okay, or good," Sunny said. "Not all the time." When Bailey frowned, as if confused, she added, "What I mean is, you can tell us when

191

you're not okay, when you're mad, or frustrated, or when you want to do something differently. You might not get what you want, but it's okay to speak up."

When Bailey didn't react to that pro or con, Sunny smiled and added, "Sawyer told me he was a holy terror as a kid — his words — and Addie hung on to him. I'm not saying go full-on holy terror, but you can go full-on Bailey, and be yourself. She'll hang on to you, too. We all will." Sunny had no idea what it was she was actually promising, only that she'd be true to her word in every way she could. For all that she'd finally found her freedom from family responsibility and wanted to revel in it, possibly forever, being Bailey's sister didn't feel like a burden to her. It felt like . . . a new beginning. A good one.

She tucked her license back in her wallet and fished out one of her business cards. "I know this is formal looking and all, but it has my e-mail and my cell phone number on it. So you can always get to me, no matter what."

Bailey took the card, looked at it, then back at Sunny. "Thanks," she said, and stuffed it in the back pocket of her jeans.

Sunny wasn't sure if Bailey was just being polite, or what she thought of the speech

192

Sunny had just made, and decided it didn't really matter at the moment. What mattered was she'd made sure Bailey knew she could reach out and had given her the tools to do so. *More baby steps.*

"We'd better go," Bailey said. "It's right up there."

Sunny tucked her phone back in her pocket and gave her a quick salute, much as she had Sawyer. "Lead on, Bailey Dani."

Bailey glanced up, the smirk on her lips almost a grin. "Right," she said, adding more quietly after she'd turned and gone a few steps, "Sunshine Meadow," the humor in her voice, clear as a bell.

Sunny hadn't thought about the plusses that might come with having family. She'd only fretted the minuses. For all that she'd worked so hard to maintain a positive attitude toward her caregiver role, she hadn't succeeded as well as she'd thought. Because, at that particular moment, she felt awash in happiness, and joy, and she was a little stunned by that. The prospect of befriending a smart-beyond-her-years, ten-year-old girl suddenly didn't seem so fraught with potential danger signs and lifestyle restrictions. In all of her pondering about what she should or shouldn't do where her newly discovered baby sister was concerned, never once had it occurred to her that Bailey might be giving something of equal or even greater value back to her.

They got to the edge of the woods just then and Sunny stepped behind Bailey out into a small clearing filled with overgrown wildflowers that the warmer than average fall weather had kept from going to seed far longer than usual. Bailey didn't say anything, but she didn't have to.

Sunny couldn't have spoken if she'd wanted to, because all the air had gone out of her on one stunned gasp. She took a small, almost stumbling step around Bailey and moved forward until she was standing in the middle of the hip-high meadow growth. It was both haunting and stunning, and for the second time in a row, this visit to Blue Hollow Falls had shown her something that left her utterly awestruck and speechless.

"It's amazing, isn't it?" Bailey said, her voice hushed, as if the structure in front of them warranted a certain reverence.

Sunny nodded, agreeing on the sentiment, and the tone in which Bailey had delivered it.

In front of them stood an enormous, horribly dilapidated and long abandoned, yet utterly stunning glass and wrought iron greenhouse.

"I thought you'd want to see it."

Sunny couldn't tear her gaze away long enough to even glance at Bailey, could only nod again, still dumbstruck. Somehow, past the lump that had instantly filled her throat the moment she'd laid eyes on the place, she managed to say, "It's unbelievable." She let her gaze run over every detail of the place, from the triple row of leaded green glass panes that comprised the walls of the two long wings, to the ornate iron filigree work that decorated the huge central atrium. "Look at you," she breathed, walking toward the green glass structure as if it was physically pulling her in.

Bailey ran ahead of her. "Follow me. I can show you where we can get in."

Sunny should have questioned that. The place was in terribly bad shape. But she couldn't shake the oddest sense of homecoming, though she'd never seen the place in her life.

Bailey went around the end of the right wing, then looked back and waved her hand, motioning Sunny to follow her.

Feeling as if she'd fallen into some kind of wild dream . . . Sunny did just that.

# CHAPTER EIGHT

Sawyer trotted down the wooded trail. He'd known the moment he'd seen Bailey lead Sunny into the woods exactly where they were headed.

"Bailey?" he called out as he finally jogged into the clearing. "Sunny?" He kept on across the small overgrown meadow, the spindly wildflowers brushing against his thighs as he looked around, but saw no sign of either of them. He hadn't let Bailey go inside when he'd shown her the old ruin, as he wasn't at all certain how sound the big structure was. Most of it was glass, and the last thing they needed was broken shards coming down on their heads. "Bailey! Sunny!" he called out again, but got no answer. "Dammit." He knew he wasn't wrong about their coming here, which meant they'd likely gone inside. He'd have thought Sunny, at least, would have shown more sense.

He had to pry the greenhouse door open. The metal door was heavily rusted and protested loudly as he urged the hinges to move. When they did, he gave the handle a pretty good tug to open the door a bit wider. The overgrowth in front of the door didn't help. Neither did the jumble of busted-up rocks that had once upon a time had been some kind of patterned stone patio in front of the entrance. Age had cracked the pavers and weeds had grown up tall and strong between the pieces. He didn't want to waste time clearing, so he put his shoulder in the gap and shoved the door another inch or two, enough for him to wedge his body sideways through the opening. The interior was even more over-grown than the exterior. A variety of plants both indigenous to the mountains and not — a few banana trees filled an entire interior corner — had gone renegade a long time ago and sprouted up into a thick, unruly jungle. Many of them were as tall or taller than he was, which made seeing anything more than a few feet away from where he stood all but impossible.

Just as he opened his mouth to call out for them again, there was a rustling next to him and a breathless Sunny suddenly ap-peared in front of him, having pushed through a few tall stalks so that she almost landed on top of him. She staggered back a step, but righted herself before he could reach out to help. Her hair was a mess and there was foliage sticking out from somewhere in the back, as well as clinging to various parts of her body, but she wasn't upset. In fact, she was beaming. Almost glowing. Her eyes were bright and her broad smile looked as if it was permanently etched on her flushed face. "Sawyer, oh thank God it's you," she said. "That squealing sound scared the bejeesus out of us. I was pretty sure that front door was rusted closed and thought maybe some kind of wildlife had gotten in."

He gestured to their surroundings. "I think it's a little late for that."

She swiped at the hair clinging to her face, still grinning. "I meant the four-legged kind."

"Oh, I wouldn't be too surprised if they are already in here." He looked down. "How do you feel about snakes?"

"Depends on what kind," she said easily, not remotely spooked by the idea. "A few healthy black snakes are never a bad thing. Keeps the rodent population to a minimum."

So much for making her aware of the

potential dangers. She needed to be more concerned about being inside this place, if not for herself, then at least for Bailey.

Sawyer glanced behind Sunny just in time to see the young girl step into the small clearing they'd made. On seeing him, she instantly smoothed her worried expression back to her typical "it's all good" countenance.

"Sorry," he said to them both, "I called your names out a couple times, but I guess you didn't hear me."

"What are you doing out here?" Sunny asked. "It's amazing, isn't it?" she went on, not waiting for him to reply.

"I saw you two go into the woods and I suspected this was where you were heading." He glanced at Bailey, then back to Sunny. "I figured it might be too tempting to leave alone, but I don't know if this place is very sound. It might not be a good idea to be in here."

"Actually, considering it may have been abandoned for decades, I'm surprised at how passable the central atrium section is. The west wing is partly caved in on the back side, so we didn't venture into that part."

"We came in from the back of the other side," Bailey told him, not appearing all that anxious about his disapproval. "The glass back there is completely gone, so it wasn't any problem."

"I went in first, checked it out," she assured him. Sunny gestured overhead where they could see the surrounding glass walls. "The busted panes here and there let the weather pass through, so the air pressure is the same inside and out." She turned and looked skyward up to the top of the huge soaring domed atrium that was the center of the structure. "Remember, this thing was built to withstand weather on the outside, but also to create its own weather conditions on the inside. The glass has actually held up pretty impressively. I'm not surprised we couldn't hear you. The panes are thick and heavy. Even more impressive is the ironwork frame." She pointed to the framework that extended into an intricate pattern up inside the dome. "Both impressive and enduring. You just don't see workmanship like this anymore." She turned in a small circle, her gaze still upward. "I mean, look at it, Sawyer. My goodness, just . . ." She let the words drift off as she turned in a slow circle again. "Look at it," she repeated in obvious awe. "She's absolutely stunning."

Sawyer didn't know what Sunny was seeing in her mind's eye, but it was something other than reality. Yes, the place was immense, like a big glass warehouse. With the Victorian style of the domed central atrium, the ironwork, the scrolled filigree on the exterior, and the green leaded glass panes that made up the structure, it certainly, at one time, had been quite an architectural showpiece. But that time had long since come and gone. He doubted with the rust and decay, not to mention the mold and God knew what else was growing in there, that it was even salvageable at this point.

But he hadn't missed the gleam in Sunny's eyes as she took in the place. Clearly, she was seeing it as it had once been. When he'd shown the old relic to Bailey, he hadn't stopped to think that given the passion Sunny obviously had for her work, the greenhouse could possibly be a big draw to her, where the mill had seemed more an albatross. Of course, back then he hadn't known much about Sunny at all, and he hadn't thought about the old ruin since that day he and Bailey had hiked out this way. Clearly, Bailey had been thinking about it.

At the moment, he wasn't sure if he regretted having shown the place to Bailey or not. The day they'd come out here, he'd just been trying to show the girl more of the property she'd inherited. The old greenhouse had seemed like a good distraction, something to divert her attention away from the major upheaval she'd gone through that day, as her young life had once again been turned on its head.

"What was this place?" Sunny asked. "It's too big to be someone's personal greenhouse. Was there another business out here? It seems tucked away fairly well for that, but if it's as old as the mill, or even in that ballpark, then maybe back then all of what is now old growth forest wasn't a factor." She turned to him. "Whoever owned it spent a pretty penny constructing it."

"Genevieve Buchleitner Hartwell. Third wife to the fourth Barthlomew Hartwell. He had it commissioned for her as a wedding present just after the turn of the nineteenth century."

Sunny's eyes widened. "Wow. Quite the gift."

Sawyer nodded. "That was near the end of the mill's heyday and despite a future that was already looking a bit dim where silk production was concerned, the Hartwells had become both prestigious and quite wealthy. By local standards, anyway. Bartholomew's ancestors had been wise enough to have invested their money over a much broader spectrum than silk production. A fact that remained true all the way down to Doyle, who apparently managed to blow through it all without contributing much back."

Sunny nodded but didn't seem all that interested in her father's contributions, or lack thereof, to the family history. "You said it was his third wife?"

"The story goes that after his second wife died in childbirth — the first having also passed on due to pneumonia — he traveled overseas in hopes of finding new ways to improve silk production and keep the main Hartwell business afloat. He failed in that respect, but ended up coming home with an Austrian wife instead. By all reports, it was a true love match, and the otherwise rather tightfisted Bartholomew shocked everyone by having this place built for her."

"Was she a botanist?"

Sawyer nodded. "It was quite a scandal. Both that she was educated and that she worked. The wife of someone of Bartholomew's standing was expected to do her duty to support his interests, not her own. So she was something of an outcast with the women in town." He smiled. "Not so much with the men. She was said to be smart, witty, and very beautiful. But also every bit as devoted to her husband as he was to her, forcing the locals to lust from afar."

"Sounds like a paragon," Sunny said, then smiled. "I wish I could have met her."

"Addie has a bunch of old journals and things. There's also a small library in town that has a whole section of historical memorabilia about the town and the mill. I'm positive there is more there about her, too."

Sunny looked upward again to the top of the atrium, then to the jungle that had filled the place. "What did she do with it? Surely with a place this size it was something more than pursuing her own work or research. This is more than one person could really utilize or maintain."

"I don't know," Sawyer said. "I never thought to ask." He looked around, too, trying to imagine it through Sunny's eyes. He was mostly aware of the dilapidation and the decay and the overwhelming scent of jungle foliage, not all of it still thriving.

She sighed. "I can't even imagine what I'd do with something like this." She looked at him, her gold eyes gleaming, and gave him a sardonic grin. "But I sure wouldn't mind trying."

The combination of joy, passion, and humor stirred his blood . . . and in turn that stirred some other parts of him he was better off not thinking about. Then it hit Sawyer that Sunny didn't know. Bailey hadn't told her, or maybe Bailey assumed she'd already understood.

Would Sunny feel a stronger connection to Blue Hollow Falls, too, once she realized that the old greenhouse was on mill property and therefore part of her inheritance? He'd thought about her a great deal in the week since their D.C. excursion. In fact, he'd spent far too much time thinking about her. With distance and the application of rational thought not fueled by hormones, his cocky insouciance that day by the food truck had faded. A more grounded, realistic viewpoint had taken its place. Ultimately, he'd decided that maybe she'd had the right idea when she'd simply walked away from what he'd been suggesting. Why complicate things? Wasn't it enough that he had a new stepsister on the premises? A mill to overhaul? A town to re-energize? Not to mention the fact that Sunny lived and worked over three hours away from the Hollow. It would be for the best all around if she went on about her business as planned, keeping her share of the mill tucked away on a shelf somewhere, off her mind and out of his hair.

"Do you think it can be fixed?"

Both Sunny and Sawyer looked at Bailey, who was holding the two of them in steady regard.

"The greenhouse?" Sawyer asked.

Bailey nodded, and Sunny said, "Maybe part of it. I don't know if it could all be saved. Those areas on the other end have fully collapsed. I'm not sure what caused the iron to give way there, maybe something fell on it at one point, but whatever the case, it also allowed the weather to get to that part in a far more destructive way. I'm not sure, but it's possible, given how the framework was constructed, that the loss to the structural integrity there would make the rest of it unsound." She sighed. "Sawyer is right about that part. We really shouldn't poke around more than we already have. Not without further examining it from the exterior at any rate."

"But you can't see the outside from the back," Bailey said. "It's almost totally overgrown."

"Which likely helped hold it up, too," Sunny told her. "That growth created a barricade of sorts." Sunny let out a sigh, clearly as disappointed by the verdict as Bailey, maybe more so. "I can't even imagine what it would cost to restore it, though, even if you could. Sanitation alone, with the mold and mildew . . ." She trailed off, shook her head. "On the other hand, it would feel so wrong to tear it down. But I guess that's not an issue, or it would have happened a long time ago." She looked at Bailey. "So, I guess it remains a relic."

"Would you do something with it if you could?" the young girl persisted.

"I . . ." Sunny let out a short laugh. "I don't know. Sure, yes, of course. But that's kind of like asking me would I like winning the lottery. Who wouldn't?"

"If I gave you my share, would that help?"

"Bailey —" Sawyer started, but Sunny responded at the same time. And what, really, would he have said? *Shh, don't tell her?*

"Your share of what? The mill?" Sunny hunched down so she was more on eye level with Bailey. "That's an incredibly kind offer. In fact, it's kind of funny, because that was something I planned to talk to you and Addie about. About putting my share in a trust for you, for when you're of age and can decide to do what you want with it."

Instead of Bailey's eyes widening in surprise, or pleasure, or gratitude, or any of those understandable reactions, a look of crestfallen disappointment flickered over her expression, before she quickly schooled it once again to one of careful indifference.

Sunny must have noticed, too, because she laid a blue-gloved hand on Bailey's arm. "It was so thoughtful and sweet of you to offer, honestly it was. And I love that you like this old place, too, and would want to restore it to its former glory, so much you'd give up one of the few things of value you have. I mean that. More than you know."

Sawyer didn't question Sunny's sincerity, and he appreciated that she was trying to do right by Bailey. Now, and for the girl's future. She'd caught him off guard with talk of a trust, but it spoke well of her. Very well, indeed. Apparently the two of them were on the same wavelength about how things should progress between them. That was good. A relief, really.

So why did he feel the sudden urge to rip a few of those banana trees up by their roots? Or something equally testosterone fueled and stupid?

"I'm afraid it would take a lot more than that to help this old place anyway," Sunny told her.

"It wasn't just the mill," Bailey said, but so quietly the words barely reached Sawyer's ears.

"What?" Sunny asked. She'd begun to straighten, but crouched down again to hear Bailey.

Bailey looked at her directly. "You're not coming back again." She didn't make it a question.

"I —" That had caught Sunny off guard.

Sawyer, too, but he found he was as curious to hear Sunny's response as Bailey might be.

"Why do you think that?" Sunny asked by way of reply.

"You're giving up your share of your inheritance." Bailey looked at her. "What if I don't want it?"

Sunny looked as taken aback by that comment as Sawyer must have. She hadn't tossed it in Sunny's face or anything. It was more like a sincere question.

"Well, then it will be your call to do with it whatever you want. That's why I want it in a trust. So you can decide when you're old enough to know more what you do want, what you don't."

"So you know you don't want it." Another statement, and more disappointment creeping past her normally stoic exterior.

"It's not that, Bailey. It's . . . I have a home. I have — I was trying to do something for you, give you a stronger foundation. I know we don't know each other and didn't even know we had a sister less than a month ago." She smiled, and lifted her shoulders. "Yet here we are, related." When Bailey said nothing, she added, "I didn't have an easy go of it when I was your age. Our father was kind enough, at least in my mother's case, to give her a place to live. I never knew the man, and I have a lot of mixed feelings about the other choices he made in his life, but that one thing he did saved my mom and me. A hundred times over. A thousand." She let her hand drop from Bailey's arm. "I don't have an empty house to give you, but I do have a share of a mill, and if it helps give you some stability, like our father gave me and my mom, then I want to do that. That's all there is to it. It doesn't mean I'm washing my hands of this place. Or you." She shifted on her feet as her legs got a little wobbly, but remained in a crouch. "I meant what I said before, when we were walking out here. I want you to come visit me. I do plan to be in your life, and I'm hoping you feel the same way about being in mine."

Bailey listened to everything Sunny said. Then she simply looked up at Sawyer, her expression sober once again. "She doesn't know, does she?"

"Know what?" Sunny asked.

Sawyer sighed.

"This greenhouse is part of your inheritance, too," Bailey and Sawyer said at the same time.

"It's on mill property," Sawyer said. "I think that's the share Bailey was trying to give you, with or without the mill part tacked on."

Bailey nodded. "You could have both, if it helped."

Sawyer wasn't sure if it was that bit of news, or if Sunny's legs finally gave out, but her eyes went wide, and so did her balance, sending her sprawling backward on her butt into the muck and dirt.

Sawyer's and Bailey's eyes caught, their mouths curved in almost exactly the same dry smile. Sawyer thought he might have snorted first, but maybe it was Bailey. In the end, all three of them erupted into gales of laughter.

"So," Bailey wanted to know, when they finally regained their wits, and both of them helped to pull Sunny up to her feet. "Is that a yes?"

# CHAPTER NINE

"Well, who did you think it'd belong to," Addie asked Sunny, as she used a pair of tongs to lift the fried chicken from the draining rack onto a big hammered pewter platter. Addie carried the platter over and set it on the heavy cedar plank table where meals were served in the great room of the small log cabin she, and now Bailey, called home.

Sunny carried over a pitcher of freshly brewed iced tea and a stack of hand-thrown glazed dinner plates, which Sawyer took and set on the woven mats that had already been laid out on the table. There was a long, hand-hewn bench seat on one side of the table, and a set of two mismatched bentwood chairs facing it from the other side. Tall backed armchairs, one upholstered with old gold brocade fabric and the other with an equally aged leaf and floral print fabric, both sporting colorfully quilted thick pads that plumped the seats up to table height, bookended the head and foot of the table. Addie took a seat in one, Sawyer the other. Both Sunny and Bailey took bench seats, as it afforded them the spectacular view through the big bay window that filled most of the one wall of the cabin.

"I don't think I've ever seen a bay window in a log cabin," Sunny said, then laughed. "Of course, I can probably count on one hand the number of log cabins I've seen, but it's a perfect showcase for that view." Addie's cabin was up on Hawk's Nest Ridge, affording her a view of the Hollow from the deep porch that ran along the front of the house, and a view out along the ridge and down the Blue Ridge chain from the side bay window. The colors were spectacular, and as Sunny looked, she could count at least four hawks making lazy swoops in the wind currents. "I can see where the ridge got its name."

Addie nodded. "Some great trails out there that take you right out along the ridge. The hawks nest in the tops of the trees, many of which top out at eye level with the rocky ridge, so you have a true bird's-eye view of them."

"Sounds amazing." Sunny smiled. She'd had no idea what to expect when Addie had invited her up for Sunday supper, as she called it, after they'd trekked back out of the woods and met up with her by the mill. But this homey log cabin, with its green tin panel roof, two dormer windows, deep porch, and the stone chimney framing it on the other side, was far more charming and beautiful than she could have imagined. "And this chicken smells unbelievable."

"Raise 'em myself," Addie said, beaming proudly.

Sunny might have faltered just a moment before she passed the blue-striped earthenware bowl of mashed potatoes to Bailey and accepted a smaller thrown pot full of corn from Sawyer. She really didn't want to think about where their dinner had come from, but she supposed that was part of mountain and farm living. Just not a part she wanted to be directly involved with, if she could help it. "And to answer your question," she said, "I guess I assumed that Doyle or his ancestors had sold that land or given it away a long time ago. It seemed like we'd been walking a lot farther than we had, I guess. I felt like it was at a much greater distance from the mill than it turned out to be when we hiked back out."

"Quite the property in its day," Addie told her. "Cyrus has a whole stack of photos down at the library if you want to take a look. Some newspaper articles, too."

"I would," Sunny said. "Thanks." Her mind had been spinning since Bailey and Sawyer had blurted out that she was now part owner of a century-plus Victorian-style greenhouse. It was, in so many ways, a lot more to take in than the fact that she owned part of a now-defunct silk mill. Of course, it wasn't any more valuable to her, in fact it was the opposite, since Sawyer was renovating the mill. The greenhouse was probably beyond hope. She ignored that *probably* part and focused on the meal. *Just when you thought you had a handle on this whole inheritance thing, boom.*

"Your home is amazing," she told Addie, who beamed.

"My granddaddy built the place." She hooted a laugh. "Didn't know the first thing about construction, neither. Thankfully, he had some friends who did, or this place would have likely come straight down on his head, first winter out."

"It looks beautifully made," Sunny told her, glancing around the great room once again.

"Oh, it's had its fair share of work over the years, but it's held up pretty good, all in all."

Sunny looked at Bailey. "Your bedroom is up there?" She pointed to the stairs that went up to a loft above the exposed beams that formed the structure of the interior. It was at least half the size of the main floor, tucked under slanted eaves and dormer windows, with a railing at the open edge.

Bailey nodded.

"I would have loved something like that as a kid," she said, quite sincerely, then winked at Bailey. "Would have been like living in my own fairy garden."

Bailey merely nodded, and dug into her mashed potatoes. She'd been even quieter than usual since Sunny had had to regretfully tell her that while the offer Bailey had made was wonderfully generous, the greenhouse wasn't likely a good salvage effort. As much as she'd hated to disappoint her newfound sibling, she knew in the long run it was better not to let Bailey build up any real hope on the matter.

Sunny sent a quick glance toward Sawyer and Addie, but they were eating as well, apparently not worried about Bailey's quietness. Perhaps she shouldn't either. It was just she couldn't get the peals of laughter they'd shared out in that greenhouse out of her head. Bailey's giggles had been so endearing and delightful, and when Bailey grinned? You just wanted to squeeze her. Sunny swallowed a small smile of her own and cracked open a warm biscuit before reaching for the apple butter Addie said she'd made herself from her own apple trees out back. Sunny was certain Bailey Dani wouldn't appreciate hearing how adorable and cute she was when she smiled and laughed. Before she had to head home, Sunny hoped the two of them could get back on the good footing they'd begun establishing on their hike out to the greenhouse.

They ate in companionable silence as Sunny continued to take in all the details of Addie's place. And there was a lot to take in. On the gorgeous stone fireplace was a mantel sporting a number of handmade items, the most fascinating of which, to Sunny's mind, was the beautiful mandolin and the handmade wooden stand it rested on. Sawyer hadn't been kidding about Addie not tooting her own horn when it came to her own work. She'd merely nodded and continued making supper when Sunny had oohed and aahed over the woven rugs that covered a good part of the hardwood floors, and some of the walls as well. Even the place mats they were eating off were a stunning rainbow of hand dyed hues, done in a variety of different fibers and textures. Every piece, from the rugs to the place mats, was a work of art, Sunny thought. She was especially fascinated by the plant-based dyes Addie said she'd used on some of her spun fibers.

Then there was the antique spinning wheel in the corner, which Addie said had belonged to her grandmother, who had taught her how to spin wool as a child, leading Addie to her life's calling, much as Sunny's early garden efforts had led to hers.

"I have a pie out on the porch sill," she told them as they finished up their last bites. "Has all the kinds of berries we got up here. Most grow wild on my property, the others I grew special, just for jamming and summer pies. You'll think you've died and gone to heaven, I guarantee it. Needs to cool a bit more."

As if on cue, Bailey sprang up and started clearing dishes. Addie smiled approvingly, but Sunny wasn't sure if it was Addie's rules, or something Bailey had simply done on her own. There was pride in Addie's gaze, too, along with sincere affection, and Sunny thought whatever the situation, Bailey was going to be better off having someone in her world who looked at her the way Addie did.

"Why don't we take a stroll," Addie said, pushing her chair back. "We can get the business chatter out of the way, and work up an appetite for that pie."

Sunny was definitely on board with that. Somehow she'd managed to spend the whole day in the Hollow. The sun was already heading toward the horizon line, which meant she'd be driving down out of the mountains after dark, but she really didn't care. Seeing that greenhouse — just seeing it — was worth a long day and a longer drive. Spending time with Bailey, starting a communication with her, had been worth it, too. "That's a great idea. Though I have no idea where I'm going to put a slice of anything at the moment. That dinner was delicious." She got up and helped Bailey by putting away the condiments and taking the place mats out for a good shake over the porch railing. "If you ever get tired of weaving," she said as she came back inside, "you could open a restaurant."

Addie and Sawyer had had their heads bent together, talking quietly about something, as she walked in. They glanced up, with Addie smiling casually at her while Sawyer got up and went over to position himself in front of the sink. "I wash, you dry?" he asked Bailey.

She nodded and took the dish towel from him.

Sunny watched the easy byplay among the three of them and felt her heart lurch a little. Bailey seemed to be fitting in as if she'd been in the Hollow forever. They made a nice little family, Sunny thought, and missed her mother more in that moment than she had since Daisy Rose had squeezed her hand, smiled, then let the last breath ease from her tired body.

Of course, Sunny knew it wasn't as simple as that. Bailey had to be going through a lot more than she was showing. She might have become an expert in rolling with the punches, but that didn't mean she wasn't still affected by them. Sunny worried about that, and found herself hoping Bailey would take her up on her offer to visit. The one-on-one time would give Sunny a chance to get to know her sister better, and also dig a little deeper, maybe, get a feel for what was going on behind that always-calm, but sharp and alert exterior.

More immediately pressing, Sunny also got the feeling that Sawyer and Addie were cooking up something that had to do with her. She wondered if that would be part of the business conversation on their little walk.

As it happened, she didn't have to wait that long to find out.

Addie had switched her regular walking stick for a heavier, taller one, prompting a little concern from Sunny regarding just what kind of walk they were taking, and if Sherpas would be required. She glanced at her footwear, which had been pretty much done in by the muck in the greenhouse. So she wasn't worried about that so much as she was at adding blisters to the ones already started on the back of one heel and the balls of both feet. Feet she had to stand on all day as part of her job.

Maybe Addie saw her wince, or maybe it had been the plan all along, but she paused, and leaned the cane back against the wall by the kitchen door. "You know," she said, all smiles, "why don't I take over dish duty and let Sawyer show you a bit of the area? You can discuss with him whatever is in those papers you brought, and when you get back, we'll all have ourselves some pie." She wiggled her iron gray eyebrows at Bailey. "Maybe with a scoop of that ice cream we churned earlier this week."

Sunny looked at Bailey. "Really? Like in an old hand-cranked churn?"

Bailey nodded and finished drying her plate and set it on the stack she was building on the island work station. "Hanford showed me how. He makes them out of old barrels and machine parts."

Hanford, Sunny thought as she nodded and smiled. Yet another name to add to the ever-growing list of craftsmen and women that Addie had mentioned just during this one shared meal. Everything from the hand-thrown stoneware pots Addie had cooked and baked dinner in, to the table they'd eaten it on, the bentwood chairs, and the bench she and Bailey had sat on, along with the plates they'd used, all had been made by this Hollow resident or that. "That's pretty cool. My mom had one that belonged to my grandfather, but it was electric and never did work right. The ice cream always came out like soup. Maybe you could show me the churn later. I've never actually seen a hand-cranked one."

Bailey nodded, then turned back to take another freshly rinsed plate from Sawyer. Addie bumped the side of Sawyer's leg with her hip to nudge him aside. "We've got this. You should drive her down around town a bit." She glanced over her shoulder at Sunny. "Those boots of yours look a bit worse for wear. You'll be wanting to get a sturdier pair for up here, especially with winter coming."

Sunny looked down at her boots, but before she could tell Addie that she already had a pair of nice snow boots, the old woman was talking to Sawyer again.

"Sunny said she hadn't found the town proper on her way in. You should show her how the roads all connect out here." She turned to Sunny. "With the sun setting, it will be pretty as a postcard. You'll see."

Sunny glanced up and caught Sawyer's gaze. He had a half smile on his face and a slight shoulder shrug that just said *You might as well go with it.*

Sunny nodded, knowing he was right, and thought *So much for my luck holding out.* Frankly, she couldn't believe she'd been fortunate enough to make it through an entire day with either Bailey, Addie, or both, providing a nice, safe human screen between her and Sawyer. Already her body was clamoring at the thought of the two of them spending any extended alone time together. She supposed it had been bound to happen at some point. She just wished that point had come a good bit later on. When she felt more confident about holding firm to her plan to pretend what he'd said by that food truck a week ago had never happened.

Instead of gaining confidence, however, the more time she spent with him, no matter how many people she kept between him and herself, the more jangled she felt. He hadn't done a single thing to so much as hint that he planned to push forward on that provocative little moment they'd shared. Quite the opposite, actually. From their time in the greenhouse, to their walk back to the mill, and all through getting dinner ready and eating it, he'd kept things easy, polite, and congenial. Not a flash of a knowing smile or even a tiny wink in her direction.

*See,* she'd told herself, *he's come to the same rational conclusion you have.* She was relieved that the only person she'd be struggling with was herself.

*Liar.*

Okay, okay, so she *wanted* to be relieved. Acknowledging the problem was half the battle, wasn't it?

Sawyer rinsed off his hands, then snagged the dish towel from Bailey like a magician snapping the cover off his latest trick, making her snort before she could stop herself. He dried his hands, handed it back to her with a flourish, then said to Addie, "Just leave the rest of these. I'll get them along with the dessert dishes later." He talked over

224

her reply. "You went to enough trouble making yet another wonderful meal. We'll handle the clean-up."

Bailey nodded in agreement.

"I'll be happy to chip in, too," Sunny said. Not because some part of herself ached to be part of their little family tableau. That wasn't it at all. It was just the polite thing to do.

*Still lying.*

She went to get her jacket. So what if she felt a little pang? She missed her mother. *Except you never had family moments like that with your mama. No one helped you with dinner or with the dishes afterward. This isn't missing your mama. This is yearning, plain and simple, for what you never had.* She shut that mental track down and decided she was ignoring her little voice for the remainder of the evening. She was free. Gloriously unfettered and positively, deliriously, thrillingly independent. That's all that mattered. "Is there anything we can get for you while we're in town?" she asked Addie. Then she smiled. "Assuming the town has things to be gotten?"

Addie let out a short cackle at that. "Oh, it won't be nothing like you're used to, I'm sure. Not one of those box stores or chain restaurants to be found. But we've got what we need to get by. And thanks for asking, but I think I'm all set."

Sunny had it on the tip of her tongue to ask if Bailey wanted to go with them, but she got the distinct impression that Addie wanted Sawyer to have some time alone with her. She could only hope Addie wasn't matchmaking, but Sunny doubted that. Addie was about as subtle as a Mack truck. If she'd had even the teeniest inkling of what had been discussed outside the Botanic Garden that day, Sunny was quite sure Addie would not have been shy about sharing her thoughts on the matter, pro or con.

Sunny was pretty sure it had more to do with Addie Pearl's Master Family Plan, as Sunny had come to think of it. That was something Sunny could handle. She wasn't opposed to Addie wanting to create some stability for Bailey. And as far as that went, Sunny was very open to finding ways to be part of that foundation, at least in a way that let her do so while living three hours away.

Sunny stepped outside when Sawyer held the door open for her. With the sun now edging the tops of the trees, the air had become downright brisk. She gave a little sigh. "This is the one part of the fall season I don't look forward to."

"Cold weather?" Sawyer asked as they walked over to his pickup.

She shook her head. "I don't mind the cold weather. That's my vacation time. Less outdoor gardening and yard work."

He nodded, smiled. "True. I hadn't thought of it that way."

"No, what I will miss is having the longer daylight hours. I like that it's still light outside when I leave work. Makes me feel there's part of the day left to explore. When I head to my car and it's already dark, all I'm thinking about is a hot shower and bed." As soon as the words were out of her mouth, she gave herself a mental head smack. *It's bad enough you can't keep your mind out of the gutter; no need to invite him to join you there.*

He must have seen something of this on her face as he opened the driver side door for her. Instead of taking advantage, however, he proved her earlier assumption to be a correct one. "It beats a cold drizzle and a tarp pretending to be a bed," he said wryly. *Move along, no sexual innuendo to see here.* "I'd have paid money for an early nightfall because that meant the skin-blistering day was over."

He held the door as she climbed in, then closed it behind her. No hand accidentally brushing against her leg, no pausing a moment to make direct eye contact all up close and personal like before as he closed the big, heavy truck door in her face. Nosiree. None of that. Which was good. Very good. Because that's the last thing she wanted. *Dear Lord, she was a lying liar who lied.*

Once he was in and had the engine rumbling, she said, "So, you served in the desert, I'm guessing."

He nodded. "I shouldn't complain about the heat. I also served in the mountains in Afghanistan. The winters were cold enough to freeze a witch's" — he caught himself, grinned — "broom."

"That would be uncomfortable," she said sardonically; then her tone sobered. "I can't imagine any part of what that must have been like." She looked directly at him. "Thank you for your service. I should have said that before. You know I looked you up online. There wasn't much there, and I guessed I missed the part about what branch you served under. But I saw a photo Addie had on the mantel. You were a green beret?"

"Army Special Forces," he said, then shot her a smile as he backed out of the small cleared dirt and gravel space between the house and the small outbuilding and chicken coop that sat partway down the slope of the side yard. "A green beret is a hat."

She let out a short laugh. "Got it. So I guess your tattoo has something to do with your service?"

He nodded. "Symbols from our badge."

"Bailey must know someone in the Army then. She recognized it that day we all first met. Have you asked her about it?"

He nodded. "Didn't get anything back, but there's something there to be sure. She started school this week down in the valley, so we haven't spent all that much time together since our field trip to the Botanic Garden. Have you worked there long?"

"Four years. I got the job not too long after I finished grad school."

"Launch pad or final destination?"

She lifted a shoulder. "Not sure. It was definitely a goal reached, and I love it there. But now that I'm not tied to the area, I've considered going back to school for my doctorate, possibly out of state. Or maybe doing some traveling, to study more in my specific field."

"Orchids?"

"Partly. Endangered plants is the broader scope. I was assigned to the orchids when I was hired, and have become fairly knowledgeable in that particular area, but I wouldn't limit myself just to studying them."

"And the Ph.D?"

"Not necessarily a long-held goal, but it would open a few more doors."

He started down the long, winding mountain road that led from Hawk's Nest Ridge into the Hollow, which was all still at a good elevation above the valley floor far below. "Are they doors you want to walk through?"

"What do you mean?"

"Would you pursue the doctorate because you want the knowledge, or would it purely be for career advancement?"

"Where did that come from?" she asked, not insulted, but genuinely curious.

He answered easily, comfortably. "My own experience, I guess. I was considered for further promotion a few times, but once I went much above master sergeant, I wouldn't have the direct experience of being in the field with my team."

"Some would say that, in your former line of work, that would be an advantage," she said with a smile.

He shared the smile. "True, but it meant I was a step removed from being on the front line of decision making for the men in my division. And any higher I might have gone would have been more steps removed. I didn't want that."

"Is this part of you wanting to control things and keep them running smoothly?"

He chuckled. "Definitely. And I realize I'd have had a broader control from the advanced vantage point, but that wasn't a goal I was after. My men and I had gone through a lot together, more than the layperson could ever comprehend. The kind of bond our missions created between us is deeper and stronger than anything there is, save perhaps between a parent and child."

He glanced at her, and those blue eyes of his raked over her body with such intensity, one would think they were discussing something far more intimate than his time putting his life on the line.

She felt like there should have been smoke rising from her clothes, but he had his gaze back on the road now, and he kept on talking as if he hadn't just visually frisked her. Maybe she'd misread it.

"I couldn't just hand them over to someone else," he said. "We started together from our first tour, most of us, anyway. I wanted to see it all the way through together."

"All of you did, what was it, five tours?" She shook her head. "You're right, I can't comprehend, even a little bit, what that would be like. Even to go once. And then to go back again. And again."

He shook his head. "Not all of us. Seth was with me through the last three, and we did have new additions. And some losses."

"I'm sorry," she said. "For those losses. That's even more beyond the scope of my comprehension. . . ." She let the words trail off and he simply nodded, but said nothing. "Was it that you couldn't imagine anyone doing for them what you did? Or you just weren't cut out for higher management? Not everyone wants to steer the ship. Some folks are meant to run it."

"It wasn't a matter of trusting another commanding officer. It was more like we'd risked it all for each other, so it was only right we saw it through as a team."

"Why did you enlist?"

He looked at her again. "What did Addie tell you?"

Sunny smiled, but didn't refute his assumption, though it was Addie who had talked to her about Sawyer, not the other way around. But she had listened, and she had been interested. "Just that you wanted to explore the world, see something bigger than the Hollow."

"She's right."

"Most kids just go away to college."

He smiled. "I wasn't most kids."

*I bet,* she thought. "Trouble with a capital

T, so you said."

"That, too. There was also a big part of me that wanted to be connected to something bigger than myself. Addie was my surrogate parent — still is — but otherwise the world seemed pretty disconnected from me. At least it did when I was younger."

"Hence all the acting out, trying to make the world connect to you? Just not in the right way."

He gave her a sideways glance, but he was smiling. "You sure your degree is in botany?"

"Horticulture," she said, then smiled. "And trust me, I'm the very last person to be psychoanalyzing anyone. That's Stevie's domain."

"She seems like a good person to be working with. She's a friend, too?"

Sunny nodded. "The best at both of those things, yes. She wanted to come with me today, see the mill."

"But?"

"I wanted to talk about the papers I had drawn up and I wanted —"

"To keep it business."

She surprised herself, and him, too, judging by his expression, when she said, "That, too."

"I know Addie is putting on the full court

press to make you feel you're a part of this new family dynamic she's creating," he said. "But it's not something you can force. I was telling her that when you came in from the porch."

"Ah. I wondered what you two were cooking up. I'm pretty sure sending you out as tour guide means she's not giving up on her mission."

"Her heart is in the right place, I can assure you that. But don't let her push you into doing anything you aren't willing or ready to do."

"I won't. I did want to talk to her about having Bailey come stay with me for a weekend, maybe when there's a school holiday, so we can get to know each other better. I asked Bailey about it on our trek out to the greenhouse, and she seemed interested. I know I can't be here like you and Addie are, but I do want her to know I want to be part of her life."

"If she said she wanted to come, then I'd believe she means it. She's not chatty, but I'm already learning that she always says what she means. And she clearly wanted you to see that greenhouse."

Sunny recalled, quite clearly, the disappointment on Bailey's face when she'd mentioned giving away her part of their inheritance. "I think maybe she's taking a page from Addie's family planning book." They shared a smile at that. "She's taken to you very quickly. I think that's a good sign."

"Of what?" he asked, as he slowed to take the tight corkscrew turns that led down to the first meadow.

"That she really is doing okay. With everything. I mean, she's a pro at not letting us see how any of this affects her, of remaining detached — well, no, not detached. But she sort of hovers above it all, observing, but not participating. Not really. And I can't blame her one bit; it's one of the healthier survival tactics she could have adopted."

Sawyer nodded, smiled. "Yes, I can second that from personal experience. The opposite experience."

Sunny shared his smile. "I do worry that she's bottling it all up, though. Keeping it all inside isn't a good thing. I mean, she should have at least one person she can confide in. That's my personal experience talking. So seeing her reaching out to you, trusting you, laughing with you, that's a really good thing to my mind."

"How did you deal with what you faced? So young, and taking care of a sick parent. I can't imagine the challenges you faced."

"It took me a good while to reach out, but I finally found a friend. It helped to talk. When my middle school guidance counselor found out what I was dealing with at home, she'd make the time to talk to me, and she had an uncanny way of getting me to open up and not make it seem like offering assistance. That basically saved my life during those years. I wasn't like other kids. They seemed so . . . I don't know. Carefree, I guess. And I had this weird name, and weird clothes." She looked at him. "My mom didn't believe in things like girls wearing pants, but they also had no business showing off their bare legs, so I was always in these long prairie skirts." She lifted her shoulders, let them drop. "Anyway, having that adult perspective, hearing another adult talk to me in ways that made sense to me, made me feel that I wasn't such an outsider, that maybe I was more like normal people than I thought I was."

"I guess I never thought about that part. You must have had to grow up pretty quickly. So it would make sense that with kids your own age . . . you didn't get each other."

"That changed as I got older. In a good way. Being eclectic and out there was considered way more cool later on. Plus, I'd

long since stopped caring what my classmates thought of me, and so maybe that
aloofness was more attractive than if I'd
been sullen, or shy. But knowing there was
someone I could turn to early on was a big
part of that happening. So much so I considered getting actual counseling and would
have if we could have afforded it." She
smiled briefly. "Instead I wiped out my local library on self-help books trying to find
ways to cope with everything."

"Did they help?"

She nodded. "Partly in the way I thought
they would, but they also helped me to
understand my mother better, which was
probably the bigger assist. And I learned
about the challenges caregivers face that
aren't so obvious, which ultimately led to
the most helpful part, which was realizing
that a lot of other people were out there,
doing exactly what I was doing. Enough of
them that there were whole books on the
subject. I wasn't alone."

"We're a lot alike in that regard," he said,
almost more to himself than to her, but she
responded to him anyway.

"Did you get help? For what you faced in
your tours overseas?"

He nodded. "Like you with your guidance
counselor, I had the great good fortune to

have a commander who looked out for the signs. I learned much later on that he had lost his own son to PTSD and his way of dealing with not being able to help his child was to pay extra attention to the signs of things affecting the men under his command." He shot her a grin. "He was a little less subtle than your counselor in how he went about offering his assistance, but then we were pretty stubborn about admitting we needed help, and even more hardheaded about accepting it."

"I'm so sorry about his son, but that was probably the best tribute he could have made in his memory. Does he know how much he helped you?"

Sawyer nodded again. "He does, yes. He made sure I continued to seek help once I got out, and I was smart enough, for once, to listen to him. I don't really want to think where I'd be right now if I hadn't."

They rode along in silence for a few minutes; then she asked, "Is that why you came back? Why you're rebuilding the town? Is that part of how you're making peace with yourself, by giving back to your hometown? Because there are those who would argue that you've already given more than enough."

"But it's not about that, is it?" he asked,

and she knew what he meant. "You had it exactly right. It's not about what I owe to anyone. It's about making peace within myself. Yes, I was defending my country, yes, I was following orders in service to my country, but that only washes so far."

She nodded, and they fell back into silence again, but it was a comfortable one. She was connecting with him in ways she hadn't expected. And it felt good. Maybe too good, but she didn't want to think about that right then. "You have every right to pursue whatever brings you peace," she said, more quietly now. "I said earlier that there wasn't much about you online. I did read the story about what happened on your last tour, though. The whole Sergeant Angel thing."

He sighed at that, but other than a quick glance out the side window away from her, he said nothing.

"What you did, running into a building you knew was targeted for bombing, because the insurgents discovered it was an underground school for educating young girls. Going in there, by yourself, getting them all out, even as the ordnance was already incoming . . ." She shook her head. "You earned that nickname, you know." She smiled then, but it was kind and compassionate, rather than teasing. "I'm sure all of those girls will think of you as their personal angel the rest of their days."

His expression remained flat, his attention focused forward. "It's what we're trained to do. I was lucky, very lucky, that day. That's all."

She probably shouldn't have probed, but it was a defining event in his life, and if they were going to get all personal, she wanted him to know she knew about it. "The president of our country personally awarded you a medal of honor. I think that pretty much says it all." She tried to lighten the mood with a dry smile and a sideways glance. "I bet you keep it in a drawer or something."

He didn't look at her, but the smile was back. "I sleep on a cot in a gutted mill. I don't exactly have it hanging on the wall."

"Addie has it, doesn't she?"

He nodded. "I'm surprised she hasn't shown that to you, too." Now it was his turn to shoot her a sideways glance. "You two have become a little chummier than I thought."

"Not really," she replied, relaxing a little, grateful her dip into his past hadn't gotten awkward. "I learned most of what I know when you all came to D.C., while we were walking around the Botanic Garden. You and Bailey were off exploring this and that and, well, Addie can be quite chatty."

Sawyer laughed, though it held a rueful note. "She's been working this whole thing even harder than I realized."

Sunny grinned. "I think you're right, that she means well. And I guess I do want to know about you, about Addie, about Bailey, and the town. It is part of my heritage, after all."

"Speaking of which, what are in those papers you brought with you? I know Addie told you to see a lawyer, but you know we're not —"

"You know I mentioned to Bailey on our greenhouse jaunt that I wanted to set up a trust for her, with my share of the mill." She looked at him. "Actually, I've already done that. My share of the mill has been set aside for her when she turns eighteen. I was going to make it twenty-one, but I thought Bailey more than most kids would probably know what she was about by the time she reached eighteen." She laughed. "Heck, she could probably make wiser decisions now than most folks twice her age. Or three times," she added, pointing at herself.

Sawyer laughed at that, too. "True." He glanced over at her again, his smile warm, and there was something that looked like admiration in his eyes. "That's a nice thing you did," he said. "She might not think so now, but I know in time she'll appreciate the gesture very much. Especially when she realizes that you didn't do it as a way to wash your hands of the mill or of her."

Sunny was still thinking about that, about Bailey's willingness to give up her share of her inheritance, if it meant Sunny might spend more time in the Hollow. "I was shocked when she offered me her share. I guess I should have put it together when she was so eager to show me the greenhouse in the first place. But she didn't really talk much on the hike out there and we were too busy exploring once we got inside."

"The day we went out there, the day she first got here, I was actually taking her up a trail that winds back to an overlook where you can see the top of the falls spilling down over the boulders, and get an aerial view of the mill and the whole area. I thought it might give her a different perspective, about her inheritance, and her new home. I didn't really think much about the greenhouse part of the hike, other than it might be a good distraction from what was a pretty crazy day, but she clearly did."

Sunny shook her head, unable to keep the smile from creasing her face. "I'll admit I can't stop thinking about it. The size, the scope, the artistry of the ironwork. It's beautiful, even in its decay. I'm so sorry it was abandoned for so long."

Sawyer drove out of the heavier forest through a series of open meadows separated by narrow creeks with a single-lane bridge spanning each one. "It's a miracle it was ever built in the first place. Can you imagine that undertaking back in that day and age, all the way up here?"

"Must have been true love," Sunny said with a sigh. "That's why the Taj Mahal exists, and look at the size of that."

"Have you ever been?" he asked.

"To the Taj Mahal? No, I haven't."

"In love," he clarified. "True or otherwise."

Surprised, she shifted to look at him. He'd asked casually enough, but given the soberness of a great deal of their conversation, she couldn't help but wonder if there was something more than natural curiosity prompting the question. "Once," she said, "or so I thought. Probably because it was the first time I felt it for real. I had crushes in high school, but I never pursued them, and was never really pursued."

"I find that hard to believe. Smart, pretty, good sense of humor."

She was even more surprised by the frankly delivered compliments. "Thank you, that's kind." Then she laughed. "But, to be honest, I was a pretty nerdy kid. Science geek, with a flakey hippie mom who dressed me funny. Although, to be fair, I'm sure most of the friends I had in high school stuck it out as my friend because they loved my mom." She laughed, and felt the tiniest bit of sheen come to her eyes. "She was Peter Pan, only with flowing skirts, bangle bracelets, and many, many scarves."

"I'm sorry I didn't have the chance to meet her."

Touched by his sincerity, she smiled and said, "She wasn't really that person by the end. Hadn't been in some time. But earlier, when I was in high school? Oh, she'd have loved you. You and Seth both." She let out another laugh, drier this time. "She was a shameless flirt, but also a harmless one. Back then she'd have charmed your socks off. I can guarantee that."

He wiggled his eyebrows. "Now I really wish I could have met her."

That made Sunny laugh again, and they settled into a comfortable silence as he drove through another long grove of pine trees, and then the little creek they'd been crisscrossing went under a bigger bridge and emptied into Big Stone Creek. At least, that's what the sign on the bridge indicated as they crossed over it.

"So, about that true love," he said, breaking the silence.

Her eyebrows lifted a bit at his persistence, but she said, "Sophomore year in college. I thought he was the one. I fell, he fell, I lost my virginity, and I thought maybe, just maybe, he would be willing to take on my not-so-simple life."

"Did you live on campus?"

"No, but he did. I was still a full-time caregiver, even with the part-time help we got from community services and my mama's church friends. I was a commuter."

"So, what happened?"

"Oh, he loved Daisy Rose, as did everyone, but when he was around long enough, he got to see it wasn't all singing camp songs and fluttering scarves. My mom had some pretty serious health issues and, as they progressed, not all of them were physical. She had a few fairly extreme . . . moments, as I called them, that he was unfortunate enough to witness. He bowed out pretty quickly after that." She lifted a shoulder. "It was just as well I found out sooner than later. I decided to focus on school, or even more on school. I went year-round and managed to get four years done in two and a half, then went straight into getting my graduate degree. I got that done by the time I was twenty-four. I've been at the USBG since I was twenty-five."

"If you stayed in D.C. for your doctorate, could you do that and keep your day job?"

"I'm not sure. I haven't had all that much time to consider it. Life is very different now." She glanced at him, smiled, but then looked away. "It must have been something of the same for you. I mean, looking at life through a new lens, when you got out, came home again. Nothing would look the same to you after your experiences. How could it?"

"That is true," he said, seeming surprised by her insight. "I guess I think of it as a process. I mean, it's apples and oranges in a lot of ways, my new world versus yours, but we're both looking at life in a new way. You take it one day at a time. Work on figuring out what you want, what you don't want. When what you do want takes some kind of shape, you take a hard look at how you can achieve it, then move on from there."

"You're still a man on a mission," she told him, smiling as she said it.

He let out a short laugh. "Yeah. I guess you can take the soldier out of the Army, but not the Army out of the man." He lifted a shoulder. "It's my training, I guess, to think about things as tasks to be accomplished, but it still holds me in good stead."

She nodded thoughtfully, liking that he was a man who spent time considering things, thinking them through. He paid attention not only to the world around him, but to his own world and what part he wanted to play in it. That was a rare thing, in her experience. It was one of the reasons she'd connected so quickly to Stevie. She was a thinker, too. So many people of her acquaintance just went through the motions, day in, day out. They didn't give thought to much of anything other than what to wear and what to cook for dinner, what television show to watch. Maybe it was the life she'd led, but Sunny spent a lot of time — too much, probably — contemplating the world around her, and how she fit into it. She'd thought a lot about what her role should be, what she wanted it to be, now that everything was different.

As if offering up proof that they were on the same wavelength, he said, "Then you find out you have this old mill and a whole family you knew nothing about and life flips what little bit you might have figured out right on its head, just for grins."

"Or restore a mill you thought was yours, then find out this whole family you knew nothing about not only exists but has co-opted a third of your home, and yeah, exactly," she added with a laugh. "You know," she added, sobering slightly, "I didn't really think about it that way until now. I guess this has probably thrown you as much as it has the rest of us."

He came to a stop when the road they were on ended at an intersection with a slightly bigger road, one that actually had lines painted on it, and paused to shift and look at her, hold her gaze for more than a blink. "One thing I learned, or have come to believe, is that things really do happen for a reason. It's such a cliché, yes, and yet maybe it's a cliché that came into being because so many people find truth in it. But the more important part, to me at any rate, is that a lot of those times, we think we know what that reason is, when, in fact, we're really only seeing what we want it to mean, or hope that it means. If we're smart, we spend a little time really looking at it from all sides, and learn what the real reason might be. I believe it's only then that you can really gain everything from whatever the change in circumstances has to offer."

"I know what you mean. Like when a

person is fired from a job and thinks, oh, that's an opportunity to look for a job they really love, when maybe, if they examined their disappointment in the loss, what getting fired really did for them was make them recognize they already had the job they wanted, but didn't work hard enough to keep it."

"Exactly." His lips twitched. "And sometimes we have to get hit over the head a few times before the real reason becomes clear. Or before we accept what fate is trying to hammer into us."

"A pretty profound realization, though," she said.

"I had a lot of time to think out there in the desert," he said dryly. He flashed another grin her way, only this time there was a lot more than casual, friendly interest in those gorgeous blue eyes of his. "And yet, even with all that time to think all those profound thoughts . . . here I am again, seeing what I want to see, and maybe actively working against what I'm supposed to be reaching for."

"And what is that?" she asked, all caught up in that sudden, abruptly focused gaze, only realizing when she heard the breathless note in her voice, that she'd spoken out loud.

"I keep thinking that complications equal bad, and smooth and easy equal good, and I generally opt for good. Complications in our missions weren't looked upon all that favorably. Or course, there, I had no choice. But in civilian life, I do. So what do I tackle? Restoring a two-hundred-year-old mill, which has been anything but problem-free. Complications galore. Yet, once all's said and done, it will turn out to be — I hope — one of the most rewarding things I do. As a civilian, anyway."

"And?"

He put the truck into park and flipped on the flashers, not that she'd seen a single other car on their entire drive down toward town. He shifted to look at her fully, then stunned her into complete stillness by reaching out and pushing her hair back from her cheek again, as he had that sunny afternoon in D.C. Only, this time he didn't stop there. He tucked the loose strand of hair behind her ear, then slid the side of his work-roughened thumb down along the side of her jaw. Her breath grew a little ragged, and her pulse rate leaped into a gallop. But she didn't lean away from his touch. It was only through great force of will that she didn't lean into it.

"You're complicated, Sunny. Doing anything about you, much less with you, would be beyond complicated. We spend a lot of time in the military learning how to keep ourselves from getting emotionally involved, to stay mission focused. So I tried to talk myself out of wanting you because complicated equals bad. But life doesn't work like a military mission. It's emotional and messy and rarely simple. At least so I'm told. Then I spend time with you again, and think . . . maybe I need to remind myself to look at this inheritance, and the fallout from it, from all sides, figure out what the reason it's happened really is." He let the edge of his thumb brush just the barest corner of her mouth, drawing a quick intake of breath from her, before letting his hand drop away. "And remind myself that sometimes, like with the mill, complicated is worth it . . . complicated can equal good."

He snagged her gaze then, and held on to it. But instead of leaning forward and doing something constructive, like kissing her, or ripping her clothes from her body, with his teeth . . . instead he did something far more devastating to her equilibrium. He picked up her hand and turned his palm upright, so he could fold his fingers through hers.

She looked from their joined hands, hers small and pale, his broad, callused, and deeply tanned, back up to his eyes. His smile was slow, and when it deepened, flashing white teeth and the wink of a dimple, the flicker in his eyes turned into a full-on flame.

"Really, really good," he said, a bit of a gravelly note entering his voice.

He gave her hand a slight squeeze, and rather than feel trapped, or pinned, she felt . . . safe.

"Maybe even the best thing that ever happened to me."

# CHAPTER TEN

*Nothing like diving from that frying pan in a full swan dive straight into the fire there, Hartwell.*

Sunny said nothing, just stared at him with those whiskey gold eyes of hers all wide and unblinking. And those lips he'd been trying like hell not to think about wanting to taste were parted now, and looking so damn soft that it made parts of his body anything but.

Another beat of silence played out, then another, without her saying a word. Yet she was staring at him in a way that used up every ounce of restraint he had to keep from reaching for her and dragging her into his lap.

When the silence pulsed on another beat, then another, for both of their sakes, he let her hand go, and opted to let his little declaration die its own natural death. He turned and put the truck back into gear, determined to keep his trap shut the rest of the way into town. He could spout all the profound crap he wanted, and examine this latest twist in his life until he was blind, but hadn't they just gotten done talking about her recent emancipation from a lifelong role as caregiver? *And* her talking about pursuing a possible doctorate? *And* how he'd told her she shouldn't let Addie steamroll her into playing any larger role than she wanted in this new, wacky family dynamic they had going on?

But it was okay for him to drop that truth bomb into her lap?

*Smooth, Hartwell. So, very, very smooth.*

Maybe he should do the really smart thing and drop her off on Seth's doorstep. His buddy had been drooling over Sunny since the first time she'd set foot in the Hollow. Given Seth could charm the smock off a nun, Sawyer would be doing all three of them a favor by letting Seth work said charm on Sunny and letting nature — as proven by Seth's one hundred percent success rate where women were concerned — take its lusty course. Then they could all get right the hell back to what they were doing. Problem solved.

Only the very idea of Seth Brogan laying so much as one fingertip on any part of

Sunny Goodwin didn't sit well with Sawyer. Not. Even. So, maybe he had to find a different solution.

He pointed out the post office, the small general mercantile, and Bo's, as they slowly drove through the old mountain town. Blue Hollow Falls covered a large area, from Hawk's Nest Ridge all the way down to Buck's Pass, but the town itself could only be described as tiny. Four blocks long and three wide with an ancient yellow traffic light in the middle that was only there because fifty years back a former mayor had thought it would make the town seem more advanced, and hopefully attract commercial growth. It hadn't worked, but rather than take it back down again, folks simply sat and waited for it to turn green, despite the fact that there wasn't enough traffic to require more than a stop sign, and even that would have been overkill. Venture so much as a yard beyond the four-by-three-block area, and you'd immediately be driving through cow pastures, crop fields, or deep woods.

"How does this road connect to the one the mill is on?" Sunny asked. The first words she'd spoken since his clumsy declaration.

He wasn't used to feeling clumsy — far from, in fact — and yet she made him feel like an untried, hormonal adolescent with two left feet just by smiling in his general direction. It would be funny if he wasn't so damn hard his teeth ached. "If we'd turned left at the traffic light back there, that road heads north out of town and winds up into the hills, eventually leading to Falls Road, which takes you in to the falls and the mill. You came in Falls Road from the state highway north of here. There used to be a little green sign on Falls Road where the route from town connects to it, but it came down in a storm a few years past and hasn't been put back up. Everyone out here knows what connects to what, so it hasn't been high on the list of things needing to get done."

"Will that disconnect — there not being an obvious route between the town and the mill — be an issue when you're drawing folks in, once it becomes a cultural center?"

"I don't think so. We'll have signage put back up there, and out on the state highway to direct folks, and we'll be doing lots of marketing in town, as well as online, which will probably be the fastest and easiest way to draw folks in. Will has discussed maybe even having a small storefront in town that can also sell products made by our artisans and crafters, sort of the boutique angle, but

I think that would be a good ways down the road, and only really worthwhile when and if the mill generates real growth in town due to tourist traffic."

"Will?"

"Wilson McCall. Jake's dad."

She nodded, but fell silent again.

He wanted to address the elephant that now sat between them in the cab of his truck, but since she'd clearly opted to let it lie, he knew better than to bring it up again. "There's a lot planned for the mill and its participants if we can pull this off. It's all part of a cohesive strategy we mapped out before I took on the renovation. I'd be happy to go over all of it with you."

"What?" she said, looking surprised by his offer, as if her thoughts had been elsewhere again.

"Well, it's part yours, or in trust for Bailey, but still, you should probably know what's being planned. I think you'll like how we've connected it all together." She said nothing to that, still looking a bit blank, so he plunged on, wanting back the easy camaraderie he'd gone and spoiled by pushing too hard, too fast. "We envision music festivals, winery tours, artisan showcases, classes, and, personally, I hope to eventually grow my microbrews to include a full pub menu.

My friend, Noah Tyler, runs an inn here, and another local couple is considering putting up cabin rentals. There's great fishing in Big Stone Creek, and down in the Hawksbill. I think there's potential for a little technical whitewater kayaking, as well as flat water canoe paddling. We already have hiking trails, a few that even intersect with the Appalachian Trail. The mill will be a way to bring all of this together and make Blue Hollow Falls a destination for folks wanting to explore a slice of mountain life."

"You have a microbrewery?"

"That's what you took from all that?" he said, chuckling. "Will have. It's something I've been interested in for a while. I toyed with it a bit when I was enlisted. Over time, it became the direction I was pretty sure I wanted to go once I got out. But the horse has to come before the cart."

"You said you have property here, too. Will you operate the brewery there or at the mill?"

"The mill. My property will be my next project." He glanced at her, saw she'd settled back in her seat, and relaxed a little himself. "It's up near the Ridge, down the chain a short way from Addie's place, as the crow flies. They look close on an aerial map, but it takes a bit of driving to get from one to the other since there aren't many roads up this way." He paused, then silently cursed himself even as he heard himself ask, "Would you like to see it?"

She didn't reject the offer outright. Instead, she looked out the windshield and up at the steadily darkening sky. "I had planned to drive home tonight."

"Do you have work tomorrow?"

"No, I took the day off, but —"

"Then stay." He pulled the truck over as they reached the other end of town and parked in front of a small brick building that had the town barber shop on the first floor and Danny Tremaine's tax service above it on the second floor. Both were closed for the night and the building was dark. He turned to her. "Listen, about what I said back there —"

"It's okay," she said quickly, then looked down at the hands she'd curled in her lap. A beat went by, and then she seemed to come to some kind of internal decision. When she looked up again, though, she kept her gaze aimed out the side window. "We're both adults. And . . ." She paused again, then let out a long, somewhat shaky breath and turned to face him, her expression resolute. "You're not mistaken, okay? Back at the food truck, when you assumed the attraction was mutual?" she explained. "It is." A hint of a dry smile curved her lips and she motioned at him with her hand. "I mean, have you seen you?"

He let out a surprised snort at that, but said, "Ditto," which made her blush, but he didn't say anything more. He was too busy waiting for the other shoe to drop, certain it was coming.

"I've gone over it in my head, too," she said. "More times than I care to admit. Weighed all the pros and the lengthy list of cons. And you're right, it does seem like a complication not worth pursuing. Not when the outcome, if it's not a good one, could upset more people than just you or me. Mostly, I'm worried about what it would do to Bailey. She's connected to you. Maybe it's the Army thing, or maybe it's because you're a genuinely nice guy who is trying to help those around him. Probably both. Whatever the case, she also seems invested in keeping me in her orbit. So the last thing we should be is cavalier about pursuing whatever" — she paused and made a small gesture between them — "whatever this is, and possibly get her hopes up about something, only to dash them later, or worse, make it awkward for us all to be around each other. She's had far too much disappointment and upheaval already. I don't know what role I'll ultimately play in her life. We all just found out about each other. But I do know what I don't want is to be a contributor to more disappointment."

When she didn't add anything further, he said, "Maybe it would be best if I get you back up to Addie's."

She surprised him by not sighing in relief. Instead, she shifted to look at him more fully. "I'm not rejecting this because of you. I'm —"

"I heard every word. And I get it. I even agree with it. With you. The problem is, the more you talk, the more you reveal about yourself, the more I admire you and like you. You're interesting and complex, you're a thinker and a ponderer. You're open-minded, but unafraid to state your own opinion. You don't leap before looking, before considering, but it doesn't mean you don't leap, or won't. All of those things are attractive to me. You are attractive to me." He leaned back in his seat and sighed. "I haven't even let myself consider that part of my life in . . . hell, I don't even know. What feels like forever. I wasn't looking. I'm not looking. And yet, boom, here you are."

She surprised him again by laughing, then tipped her head back and sighed again, this time more openly and with feeling. "Agreed. On all of that." She rolled her head to look at him. "But hey, at least we're keeping all this liking and admiring in the family, right?"

He choked out a laugh at that. "And if that isn't the most screwed-up part of it all." He shrugged. "What are you gonna do? Stuff happens, and like I said, then you have to sort through it and figure it out. That's all I'm trying to do." He glanced at her again. "I wasn't expecting you."

"Ditto," she said, holding his gaze, a smile still curving those lips.

He held hers right back for a long moment, then for another moment after that. Trying, and failing, not to let his gaze drift down to that mouth, and wonder what she'd taste like. Again. Sweet, spicy, and a few things he was sure he hadn't expected. Damn, but he wanted more. More with her, more of her.

"We're both adults here," he said, mostly because he needed to hear it, needed to heed it. "My life is here. Yours is hours away. We haven't actually started anything other than a friendship." He smiled then. "The beginning of a good one, I hope."

She nodded at that, but her expression otherwise had become harder to read, and it wasn't just the dwindling light.

"So, we do the smart thing. The wise thing," he concluded.

"For Bailey," she added.

"Right. Forge the friendship, support the kid, be there for Addie. Or I will, at least, on that last part. Try to keep her in check, anyway." He shot her a smile. "No promises there. And both of us will get on with the business of forging ahead with our life plan. The mill and microbrewery for me. Your doctorate and climbing the horticultural ladder of success for you."

"Sound plan."

"Indeed."

They both sat there, staring at each other.

She surprised him by speaking first, and echoing exactly what was going through his mind. "So, why does it feel like we're ignoring what the universe is taking great pains to tell us?" She laughed outright before he could respond.

"What?" he asked, when she just shook her head, but didn't continue.

"I can't believe I'm sitting here with someone I met less than a month ago spouting things about the universe's grand plan — utterly sincerely, mind you — and you're nodding like I'm making perfect sense." She leaned her head back again and sighed, but was still smiling. "Maybe we both went down the rabbit hole and this is some parallel universe. Or a really bizarre dream."

He chuckled, too. "It is a bit surreal. All of it, really. So why should this be any different?" *This,* he thought, as if there was actually something happening, when, in truth, nothing had happened. Of course, he was used to relationships beginning with the physical attraction taking center stage and the whole getting-to-know-you part happening sort of in the background, behind the cloud of pheromones that was usually dictating the pace at which things unfolded. Spending time around each other as they had, with the circumstances being what they were, had created a situation where they were learning a lot about each other in a short period of time, and the physical part had been shoved to the background, allowing them to get to know each other in an entirely different way. A way that was turning out to be a whole different kind of intoxicating.

"What about you?" she wanted to know. "I mean, you asked me earlier. Have you ever come close to putting a ring on it?"

He was a little surprised by her curiosity, but fair was fair. "No. Early on after I enlisted, I had a few relationships that showed promise, but as my career in the Army progressed and I made the choice to pursue Special Forces, it went from challenging to almost impossible to get a relationship to the serious stage. Even if I'd already been in a serious relationship, I think my career pursuits would have almost certainly ended it, and I wouldn't have blamed the woman for it. I truly was married to the job. My deployments weren't normal. I wouldn't have asked anyone to sit here at home and wonder or worry."

"I can't imagine you miss those missions, the danger of them, but do you miss being in the Army in general?"

"Parts of it, yes, but I knew about halfway through my third tour that I wasn't going to be career Army. And if I'd had any doubts about that, my last tour answered them for me. I'd done everything I'd personally set out to do, and given I wasn't interested in moving up the chain of command, I turned my sights in a different direction. A number of us bugged out at the same time. It was the right time to go. No regrets."

She nodded. "That's a really good thing."

Sawyer started up the engine again, and pulled away from the curb. He headed away from town, wondering if he'd still feel like he had no regrets after this night was over.

"Where are we going?"

"The moon will be up soon, and since you'll be crashing at Addie's tonight" — he paused, waited for her to nod yes to that, then continued — "I thought we might as well enjoy a moonlit ride in the country. I can text her and let her know not to hold dessert for us. I'll show you my property."

"It's dark."

"Actually, that's one of the reasons I bought it. You'll see."

She didn't object, so he drove on. The silence between them was comfortable again. The skies continued to deepen toward full dark as he wound farther up into the hills, and the sounds of birds chirping gave way to the buzzing of the tree frogs.

"So," he said, at length, "you're still thinking about that greenhouse, aren't you?"

She let out a short laugh. "Guilty. I was just thinking I'm both happy and sad to have seen it. Even if by some miracle it was salvageable, the renovation cost would be way above my pay grade. Beyond that, what the heck would I do with it even if I could?" She shook her head, then laughed. "The best way I can describe it is, even though the condition is deplorable, to a horticulturalist or even any lay gardener worth his or

266

her salt, that structure is like greenhouse porn."

He laughed outright. "I actually get that. I feel something of the same way about the mill and the setting. The stone and plank wood building, the metal waterwheel, the waterfalls. It's almost too good, too picturesque. At least, in my mind's eye it is."

"Exactly. I see that green glass and all that iron scrollwork and I can just picture how it looked in its heyday." She looked at him. "You're lucky, to be able to realize your vision. I hope everyone is grateful for the work you're putting in on their behalf."

"It's not entirely altruistic. My future will be there, too. And they're all pitching in, too, with labor, materials, or just donations. We all want this to work, to give us a home base, a foundation that will be stronger and more meaningful for everyone if we work on it together."

"Is that who those other men were I saw out there today? Some of the guild members?"

He nodded. "We've had to hire folks, too, to fill in the skill sets we don't have. Like Will, who is a stonemason. We'll have to get someone to help with the electrical, and the plumbing."

"What will you do when it's time for the

rest of the crafters to start moving in to their workshops? Will you start building on your property before then so you have a place to stay? Or will you go back with Addie?"

"Addie's cabin only has her bedroom and the loft, which is Bailey's room now, so the inn is full there. And that's fine. I don't want to move backward."

"Well, it would just be temporary, and it would probably thrill her. She offered me the fold-out couch for the night, so there's that, right?"

"Yes, and she's offered it, but I don't need a place. I have one." Just as he was saying this, they rounded a bend and hit the top of a hill where he slowed to a stop and cut his headlights. No one else would be coming out this way. No one except him.

"Oh, Sawyer," she gasped. "Oh, wow."

This particular view never failed to move him just like that. Like a punch to the soul. Here, the mountaintops formed almost a complete ring, creating what looked like a high elevation valley. In this case it was more of a deep pocket meadow. When the moon was up and anything more than a sliver, it cast a beautiful white glow over the little nook in the center of the mountain top ring. The complete lack of man-made light allowed for a spectacular view of the stars scattered across the night sky. They twinkled like cheerful, celestial confetti being sprinkled over one of the prettiest places he'd ever seen, and they put on that show just for him, every single night.

Each time he peaked this crest, his heart filled right up inside his chest. It was every bit as beautiful during the day, season in and season out. Sunshine, rain, snow; all lent their particular brand of beauty to this place he now called home.

"It's almost otherworldly," she said in a hushed tone. "In a stunningly beautiful way."

"I knew it was going to be my spot the moment I saw it."

"You bought land down there?"

"I did." All of it, in fact, though he didn't say so.

"I think driving into this, every day, or every night, would balance out even the worst of days." She glanced at him. "It's very secluded. Almost isolated."

He smiled. "Yet another selling point. I'll have all the camaraderie I want or need at the mill, and in town. For me, balance is key."

She studied him for a moment, and he could almost hear the wheels turning. He figured she was wondering if he had some

kind of lasting damage from his time overseas, if this was part of how he intended to
heal himself. She could have asked, given
the frank nature of their conversation so far,
but he liked that she was being respectful
enough not to. The answer to that, though,
was, yes and no. There was no denying he
felt some part of his soul settle every time
he drove into this pocket of the world — his
pocket of the world — but he suspected
he'd have felt that way even before he
enlisted. Wanting to be out here, up here,
was the culmination of all the parts of the
life he'd led up to this point. And who knew,
maybe it wouldn't be something he'd want
or need forever. The great thing was, it
didn't matter. If that time ever came, he'd
simply change course.

"I've always lived in the city," she said. "I
don't know if I could adapt to living such
an isolated life." She took in a deep breath,
and released it slowly. He saw her body
relax into her seat and a slow smile spread
across her face. "But looking at it right now,
I'd sure be tempted to try."

His smile deepened to a grin. "I'd never
thought about it that way, really. Living in
Blue Hollow Falls is already living 'out here'
as they call it. Rural, country, mountain life.
This is just taking it another step further.

But I knew this place was right when I saw it. Haven't regretted signing those papers for a moment since."

"How much land did you get? Have you decided where you'll build?"

"Actually, there is already a house, a few outbuildings, and even a small cabin in the back of the property, in the woods, beside a small creek that feeds into Big Stone. It was built back in the eighteen hundreds, probably by a trapper. The hunting cabin, not the main house."

"That's wild. Truly," she added, with a laugh. "So why sleep on a cot in the mill if you have a house?"

"It needs a lot of work and I wanted to get the mill well underway first, to give me some time to think about exactly what I want to do with the place. It was easier to just stay on site, get the renovation going. I really wanted to make fast progress before winter weather arrives."

"Mission man," she teased.

"Guilty," he echoed with a smile. "Would you like to see it? The house, I mean."

"Sure. We came this far. Though I don't know how much I'll be able to see, even with those gorgeous night-lights you have up there." She motioned to the sky.

"Just standing in the middle of the pocket

and looking skyward is worth the drive in."

She gestured with her hand. "Then on-ward we go."

He was glad he'd invited her now. They needed to find some way to move forward, and ending the evening after that awkward moment earlier might have let that unease grow. Just over the crest he turned onto a dirt and gravel lane that wound down into the heart of the pocket. It was, for all intents and purposes, his driveway.

"You're lucky the land was up for grabs," she said.

"It actually belonged to a farmer who was a good friend of Doyle's daddy, worked for Bart, Sr. when he was a kid, in fact. Sol Jenkins is his name. The land was handed down to him by his father, but he never married, never had kids of his own. He's ninety-two now, and last in the line. He's long since given up on farming due to his health and had moved down into the valley to a senior care facility quite a long time before I discovered this place. He tried to give the land to me, told me he was just happy to see it go to someone who'd take care of it, instead of its going to the state when he passed on. He'd wanted to donate it, but couldn't imagine who'd want it."

"That's . . . remarkable."

He gave her a quick smile. "More of that universe stuff we're supposed to pay attention to, I guess. I did buy the land from him, in a manner of speaking, all i's dotted and t's crossed, though he fought me on that score. Stubborn codger. Eventually, I made him a deal. He sold me the property for a dollar, for legal purposes. Then I had the property appraised, and told him I'd take care of his living and medical expenses with the money I'd have used to buy the place at the appraised rate. The balance of what is left when he passes will be donated to the charity of his choice."

"That's really lovely," she said, looking delighted. "Then the land he worked all his life will, in turn, take care of him, which is as it should be."

"I thought so."

She smiled. "You may not like that Sergeant Angel moniker, but when you do stuff like that, what do you expect?" She didn't give him time to push the compliment away, instead asking, "What charity did he choose?"

"Well, we argued a bit about that, too, but he won that particular battle." Sawyer slowed down so they could take a tight curve in the narrow drive as they descended the rest of the way to the bottom of the pocket. Then he glanced at her once the lane straightened out again. "His charity is the mill renovation. He said he couldn't ask for any better legacy than a chance for his hometown to have a new birth."

Sunny's face lit right up at that, and in the moonlight, he was once again struck by how beautiful she was, and in so much more than any conventional way.

"That's . . . amazing! Beyond perfect, really." Then her expression fell. "Oh, wait, though. So, if you're essentially mortgaging the work on the mill instead of this place, then how will you get the renovations done out here? And what about your microbrewery?"

"I'm doing okay. Enlisting in the Army isn't like working for a Fortune 500 company by any stretch, but if you're smart, you can do well enough." He grinned. "Easier to say when you haven't had to take care of anyone but yourself your whole adult life. But I knew I'd want to do something post-military, and the microbrewery was a dream of mine from pretty early on. The father of one of my Army buddies is an investment counselor." He shrugged. "That's worked out pretty well for me."

"The universe is paying back one of its angels," she said decisively. "I like it."

He just shook his head, but there was a smile to go with it. "Here we are," he said, as he pulled up in front of the house.

She turned from him and looked out for the first time as he parked the truck and turned off the engine. "Oh . . . Sawyer. Oh my goodness, look at it."

The house was much like Addie's but larger. Both were log cabins, with log-on-log frames where the logs crossed and extended out at the corners. Like Addie's, his also had a stacked stone foundation and a deep front porch, but in his case, the porch wrapped around three full sides of the place and had a hand-hewn, branch-style railing that ran along the edge. The tin panel roof was red, or had been at one point, and a wide stone fireplace occupied the middle of the back side, rather than the end, like at Addie's place. Even in the moonlight there was no missing that it needed a great deal of care. The porch sagged, the fireplace was crumbling, a good part of the porch railing was down or missing entirely, and the tin roof hadn't fared much better here than the one at the mill.

"I don't know what I expected, but it was nothing like this. It's big and rugged and fits so perfectly in this landscape."

"It needs a lot of TLC," he said, "and even

then, I may have to gut more than I can save. I haven't had all the testing done on it yet, but I wouldn't be surprised if it has some fairly serious issues. That's to be expected with something this old."

"How old is it? You said the old trapper's cabin was early eighteen hundreds?"

"Well, the first house built on this foundation was done about twenty or so years after the hunting cabin, around eighteen-seventy or thereabout. It burned down, struck by lightning. The rebuild was done after the turn of the twentieth century. It burned down, too. Forest fire got it and a bunch of acreage along with it. Sol's father inherited the burned-out shell and the property after his grandfather abandoned the area entirely. He came up here after he got out of the Navy, cleared a lot of the burned out area, tilled it, and farmed it, both crops and livestock. Eventually, he rebuilt the house. Same foundation. I haven't checked with the county on the last plans that were filed, but according to Sol, that would have been in the early to mid-thirties. So, not quite a hundred years old. Sol inherited the place and renovated it in the late sixties, put in modern appliances, indoor plumbing, upgraded the electricity. I don't think anything's been done to it since then."

"How long has it been empty? I mean, when did Sol move to the senior home?"

"It's been almost sixteen years now. He had a stroke in his mid-seventies. It wasn't much after that."

"Wow," Sunny breathed, looking back at the place. "What a heritage this property has had. How many acres is it all told?"

"Little over two hundred."

Her mouth dropped open at that. "Wow, so pretty much —"

"The whole pocket. Yes. It was all Jenkins's property. Always has been. I don't plan to sell any of it off. Some is high pasture, but more of it is woods, and rocks, and fairly rough terrain. Plus there's the creek." He nodded toward the house. "The well seems in decent shape, but I haven't tested the electricity yet. It's been turned off for years and I'll want it inspected before calling the utility company and flipping on any break-ers." He smiled. "Last thing I need is to burn the place down a third time." He looked back at the porch, the roof. "No central air and the heat is from a woodstove. There's also a fireplace, but the flue has been closed up for years and it's in pretty bad shape. Will's going to take a look at it, but there's a laundry list of more immediate concerns. There's the leaky roof and the havoc it has wreaked on the interior." He grinned. "Your basic dream house."

She didn't look at him, but simply nodded as he spoke. Her gaze was still on the house. "Oh, I hope you can get it all fixed up again. It's got so much character. What's the layout like on the inside?"

"A lot like Addie's actually. The main floor is mostly a great room that is both kitchen and living area, but there is also a bedroom in the back, and a full bath. The loft overhead was used mostly for storage, but could easily be an office or a second bedroom. I'd like to add on to the back, make the bedroom bigger, and expand the kitchen. I'd probably go ahead and extend the upper level out as well, make a full bedroom out of it and leave the front of the loft as an office."

"But you haven't given it any thought," she said with a dry smile, making a gesture with her hand, holding her finger and thumb close together. "Wee bit maybe."

His smile spread to a grin. "Maybe. Come on, you need to get out to get the full star show." The dark had grown deep enough now for the stars to really start twinkling into view.

They climbed out and Sunny immediately gasped and pointed upward. "Oh my goodness. You can see — that's the Milky Way."

"It is indeed," he said, looking at her, not at the stars.

"It's like a streak across the heavens, saturated with stars. That's . . . spectacular. I could lie on a blanket out here all night. The meteor showers would put on a spectacular show." She turned to him, animated and more beautiful than he'd ever seen her. "Did you come up here in August for the Perseids?" She didn't wait for an answer, but turned her attention skyward again.

He watched her watching the sky and thought her reaction was, in a word . . . perfect. He hadn't realized until that moment just how much of his heart he'd already invested in this place. It was only when he'd waited for her reaction and realized a part of him really wanted her to see it as he did, that he understood how much it had come to mean to him. Not that he needed her or anyone to validate his attraction to the place, he had no doubts there, but to just . . . to have someone share the excitement he felt.

It might have been her spontaneous response, her immediate understanding of why this spot moved him as it did. Or maybe it was how the moonlight danced in her eyes when she turned to him, her face alight with wonder. Probably it was all of that, and everything else that had been building up since Doyle had unwittingly sent their orbits on a collision course. But he didn't stop to think about any of that right then, much less question it. His actions in that moment weren't premeditated, or . . . anything really, but driven by an instinct he'd long since been trained to follow without question. It had saved his life many times over.

And when he reached for her, pulled her into his arms, and tipped her mouth up to his, lowered his lips to hers, and felt, heard, and tasted her sigh in pleasure and what sounded a lot like relief . . . he felt he'd saved himself all over again.

# CHAPTER ELEVEN

Being kissed by Sawyer Hartwell wasn't at all the way she'd dreamed it would be. And yes, she'd dreamed. Hot, sweaty, passionate dreams where the kisses were savage, leading right to clothes being torn, buttons sent flying, panties left in tatters. She'd expected him to be all soldier-on-a-mission, one where victory was determined by how quickly he could ratchet her up, then drive her straight over the edge.

She supposed she should have known Mr. Master Sergeant Special Forces would be far, far stealthier than that. And with his stealth, wreak far greater havoc on her body . . . and quite shockingly, her heart.

He laid claim; let there be no doubt about that. He was confident, but not forceful, skilled but not overly practiced, but his most decimating talent was that he paid attention . . . such close, close attention. If she gasped, he heard it, repeated what had caused it. If she sighed and parted her lips, he didn't immediately dive in. No, he made her sigh again, then again, until she was seeking his tongue, inviting him inside, all but begging his entry. If she relaxed into him, just a little maybe, he eased himself around her, steadying her, supporting her, inviting her to simply let go and don't you worry . . . I'll take care of the rest.

And oh . . . did he.

She wanted to be more in control, or at least share some part of deciding how this was going to go, where it was going to lead. But she was basically clinging to him, too busy being swept along on every ripple of sensation, shivering with ever-heightening awareness, moaning softly as he continued to explore her mouth like he'd discovered one of the Seven Wonders of the World. The pleasure she felt was intoxicating and all consuming. And they were just kissing.

He framed her face with those broad, strong palms of his, and angled her mouth so he could claim every last part of it. She was whimpering now, wanting his hands pressed to far more feverish places, exploring them the way his tongue was exploring the recesses of her mouth. As if reading her mind, and at this point, she was fairly convinced they were kinetically connected, he slid his hands to her shoulders, then down her arms. It wasn't until he lifted his head and gently set her a step back that she dazedly realized she'd all but entwined herself around him.

Feeling suddenly embarrassed by her very atypical display of clinging, wanton neediness she quickly lifted one hand to smooth her hair and the other to dry her damp lips. She turned away from him in hopes of gathering whatever remnants of her dignity might remain, only he caught her hand and gently tugged her back close. So close she had to look straight up to make eye contact. So close their bodies brushed, which only served to ignite her response to him like a match to fresh tinder. She tried to look away, to step back, but he kept her right there.

"We were both in it," he said quietly, speaking barely above a gruff whisper. He might as well have been stroking her skin with his tongue the way his words reverberated so clearly, so sharply inside of her. "Hell, you've been doing that to me since almost the moment I met you."

She realized when he broke off just how silent the air was. The absolute quiet was almost deafening in the complete absence of sound. No birds, no frogs . . . it was as if the universe had lifted its finger to its lips and shushed every living thing. Even the breeze had stilled. Rather than make her feel alone or isolated, she felt wrapped up in it like a cocoon, snug and at peace.

If only. Every nerve ending she possessed was still in full riot mode.

"Yes," she finally said, hating to break the silence, to put any more energy into the air. "But I don't normally go around —"

He tipped her chin up then, and what breath she had left caught right in her chest. His eyes were so beautiful, the intensity she saw there so palpable, it made her throat go tight. "You might not normally, and I might not normally, but *we* just did. It was honest, and . . ." He trailed off, and then his handsome face split into a wild, sexy grin that made her heart stutter. "Hotter than the desert at high noon." He laughed, and his eyes danced with merriment and not a little challenge. "There's no shame in that, Sunny."

"No," she said, taking it in, taking him in. And he was a lot to take in. "You — you're right," she said, then found herself just as suddenly smiling with him, and laughing. "It just went from zero to sixty like . . ." She trailed off, having no words for the effect he had on her.

"Look," he said suddenly, pointing up.

She glanced skyward and saw the celestial trail of a shooting star. She hummed in approval. "Like a shooting star," she murmured, more to herself, than to him. She didn't really want to think about what they might have just started. Especially coming right on the heels of agreeing to keep things at the friendship level. The reasons for that quite rationally achieved decision hadn't changed.

Then he was shifting her around so he could pull her into his arms with her back against his chest. He wrapped big arms around her and she wrapped hers over his as they both looked skyward, watching the stars continue winking to life. Standing there like that, fitting so perfectly in the shelter of his body, her head tipped back against his shoulder, felt too good, too delicious, to resist. So, for a moment anyway, she didn't. She relaxed and took in his warmth, breathed in the scent of his soap, of his freshly laundered shirt . . . of Sawyer.

She wasn't used to being with someone who was so much taller than she, so much bigger. If the quiet had made her feel cocooned, being held by him only amplified that sense further. He made her feel safe, cared for . . . cosseted. And she'd be lying if she said there wasn't a long-buried part of her that had yearned to feel that way for as long as she could remember. It was all the more soothing because she was no longer a child wanting to be held by her parent, and he wasn't offering simply an innocent hug or a comforting kiss to the cheek.

She didn't honestly know what he was offering her, but for that moment, this was far more than she'd anticipated ever having. She could have stood there, just like that, for as long as her legs were able. And at the same time, she wanted to squirm right out of her clothes and beg him to put his hands on her almost as badly as she wanted her next breath.

She was so damn confused and turned on and . . . confused.

"It can just be this," he said, once again dipping in to her thoughts.

She realized it was probably because his mind had followed a similar path. It was comforting to know she wasn't alone and, at the same time, made it that much harder to do what she knew — what they both knew — they had to do. "That would be the wise course of action," she agreed.

He leaned down and kissed the side of her neck, making her moan softly and instantly tip her chin to the side, allowing him greater access. "And this," he murmured.

"Yes," she breathed. "Definitely this."

He nudged her hair aside and kissed the nape of her neck, which sent little sparks of pulsing heat racing down her spine.

She felt him grin against her skin. "Sweet spot."

"Maybe," she managed, then immediately shivered in pleasure when he grazed his teeth over the same place.

He turned her to face him, said, "Hold on," then hiked her body up against his and held her there as if she was a featherweight, which she most definitely was not. He clamped one strong arm around her hips and used his free hand to release the catch on the tailgate at the foot of the truck.

It squealed and thumped down flat, making her cringe and laugh at the same time. "Sawyer —"

"It's dusty, but nothing that won't wash out," he said as he sat her on the lowered gate, then stepped into the vee of her legs, urging her to snug them around his thighs.

She'd like to say she took a moment to contemplate the wisdom of letting this go even a fraction further, but he was already leaning down to kiss her again and her arms were already so conveniently around his neck. Somehow her fingers found their way into the hair at the nape of his neck, and then his lips were once again a breath away from hers.

"Just this once," he murmured, almost more to himself than to her.

"Mmm," she agreed, her lips brushing his.

Then he was opening her mouth again, and it felt like her entire body was opening up to him when she took him inside. His fingers dug into her hips as he tugged her closer, and she gasped when the rigid result of all this foreplay pressed quite intently against the part of her that wanted it most. She curled her heels around the back of his thighs and kissed him back. Now it was his turn to groan and she felt his blunt fingertips dig almost reflexively into the softness of her hips as he struggled with the same wants and desires that were flooding every fiber of her being, begging her to give in to their demands. Everything they wanted was right there for the taking, for the having. Oh, she wanted to have him. Every broad shouldered, bunched bicep, rock hard and rigid inch of him.

There was a moment when she thought *Just take this, do this, have this — have him — then you'll be over it and you can stop wondering. No harm, no foul.*

Then she made the mistake of opening her eyes when he lifted his head to take a breath and found him looking so intently at her, all the same turmoil she was struggling with clearly there in his eyes for her to see. Perversely, it was his struggle, not hers, that snapped her back to reality. She leaned back just enough to hold his gaze more directly, then let her legs relax and her heels swing down again. "I don't know if I can do this just once," she said, as baldly honest as she'd ever been.

"Yeah," he said, his voice a sexy rumble now that made her curl her fingers inward to keep from grabbing him and pulling him right back where he'd been moments ago. "I was thinking the same thing."

Dear sweet goodness, she ached with wanting him, an ache made all the more painful for knowing he wanted the same damn thing and every bit as badly as she did.

"Sunny —"

"It's not just because of Bailey," she said quickly, before she caved, and took him with her. "Or my life being three hours and a hundred plus miles away from here. It's that I finally have the chance to go after what I want. And you're here doing the exact same thing. We're in a good place in life, each of us. So good." She pushed her hair from her face, her cheeks still heated, her lips feeling the effects of his kisses. "This is exciting and thrilling, and not a little intoxicating, but —"

"You don't gamble away the good for the momentary thrill," he finished for her.

She nodded, then let out a laugh that wasn't entirely a happy one. "And the fact that you keep getting inside my head and thinking exactly the same thing I'm thinking isn't helping."

"Sorry?" he said, his own smile a shade wry.

She shook her head, still smiling. She looked up at the sky, felt the punch of the grandeur splayed out above her, the enormity of it all, and felt so tiny and insignificant by comparison. With the entire universe on display, how bad could her problems be?

"Helps put things in perspective, doesn't it?" he said.

She nudged the side of his leg, giving him a sideways smile. "Get out of my head, Sawyer Hartwell."

He took her hands and helped her slide down from the truck gate. "It wasn't your head I was trying to get inside of," he teased, and reached around her to help dust off the back of her coat.

Purely out of self-preservation, she finally made herself step around the side of the truck and away from his touch. "I should probably be getting back to Addie's," she said by way of response. "I — I can go over everything with her tomorrow before heading out." She glanced at him, found him looking at her, and for once, his expression was unreadable. "If you'd like to be part of that, we could come to the mill maybe. Once Bailey is at school."

"You in a hurry to leave?"

"No," she said, surprising herself with that bit of truth. And not just because she wasn't quite done basking in the glow he so effortlessly created. "But I wasn't planning on spending that much time. Tomorrow is my only free day for the next week and I can't —"

He lifted a hand and sounded calm, steady, when he spoke. "Not a problem. If you and Addie wouldn't mind coming by the mill, I would like to hear the particulars of the trust. I'd also like to give you a set of the plans. You should have a record of what's being done. You can show them to your lawyer if you think that it means changing anything in the trust. I'll sign whatever needs signing, so you're covered, legally, in case anything unforeseen happens at the mill."

She nodded. "I appreciate that."

"I appreciate your not creating any obstacles to the renovation."

God, they were being so . . . rational, so responsible, so adult. It made her want to scream. It made her want to fling herself back into his arms and beg him to take her back to that mindless place that was all about feeling, and needing, and wanting . . . and leave all this responsible adulting stuff until later. Much, much later. She was so sick and tired of being responsible.

But that's what she did, wasn't it? That was her role. *Some things never do change.* "I have no interest in making things difficult," she told him truthfully. She just wished difficult didn't come with this particular territory. "Quite the opposite. I want to do right by Bailey, and otherwise I will stay out of your hair. You're doing a good thing. I'll also be honest and say I'm glad you don't expect or want anything from me where the renovation is concerned. Win-win." *See,* she told herself. *We can be friendly, do our business, get back to our lives.* "You know, maybe this was a good thing," she added, the words out before she could think them through first.

"This?"

292

She motioned between them. "Yes, this. Probably just as well we went there, briefly anyway, so we wouldn't always wonder about it."

Something flashed across his face, but in the shadows, she couldn't tell what. His expression was unreadable. "Probably," he agreed, but for once, he didn't sound like he was being completely forthright.

Well, that wasn't her concern. Or couldn't be, anyway. She had to look out for herself. And wasn't it grand that she only had herself to look out for, for a change? *Don't complicate that, Sunny. Revel in it.*

"So, I guess friends with benefits is out?" He immediately lifted his hand, laughing when her mouth dropped open. "Kidding." He waited a beat. "Mostly." He smiled then. "Too soon?"

She found herself smiling with him. She wished his teasing made her feel like things were back on track. Instead it made her want him like she wanted her next breath. "Actually, if I thought I could handle it . . ." Now it was her turn to laugh outright when his expression went momentarily slack. "Alas, I'm not cut out that way," she hurried on to say, quite sincere now. "Trust me, over the years, my social life would likely have been a lot more entertaining, not to mention my stress level greatly reduced, if I'd been able to get the hang of letting sex be just a physical thing." She lifted her hands in a helpless gesture and found herself being baldly honest with him again, thinking how funny it was that she'd been more open, more honest, more frank with him, than she'd ever been with anyone else. "But no, I pretty much suck at not getting emotionally involved."

"I can't fault you there," he said, smiling with her. "I also can't lie and say I didn't work at it maybe a little harder than you did." His grin returned, and she thought she caught that twinkle in his eyes when he added, "When I was on leave, sex was fairly high on the to-do list." The smile faded, and his tone sobered. "For me, the emotional entanglement part wasn't my Achilles' heel. But, what I found was that, after a time, the lack of it made the physical part less fulfilling." Now he lifted his hands, then let them drop to his sides again. "Going for any more than that didn't seem fair, though, knowing I was going right back to another mission, another tour."

She tilted her head, studied him.

His laugh was a little self-conscious, which was entirely endearing. Like he wasn't enough of that already. "What?" he asked, when her smile spread to a grin.

"Nothing. Just that I appreciate your candor. A lot of men — most, maybe — would have trotted out some sympathetic b.s. designed to lower my defenses. Your experience rings more true." She laughed. "And probably did an even better job without your even trying."

He wiggled his eyebrows and twirled an imaginary mustache. "She's on to my evil plan."

"Seems kind of cruel, then, really, you know?"

"Meaning?"

"You're no longer married to the Army. I'm no longer married to being a caregiver. And we still can't just jump." She sighed. "Well, we *could*, but . . ."

"I know. And yes, that whole universe thing. Like I said, sometimes it's the thing we can't have that makes us examine what we do want more closely, commit to it more firmly."

There was a long pause; then they both broke out laughing.

"Yeah, I wasn't buying that, either," he said. He closed the tailgate of the truck. "Come on. I'll get you back up to Addie's. We have an early start at the mill in the morning. I've got a bunch of guys showing up at the crack of crack."

"Did you finish the roof? I really like the look of that slate."

He nodded. "We did. And I dug up drawings and photographs of the mill, back from the beginning. Slate was used in one of the earlier incarnations. I'm guessing it got too expensive when times grew lean. But it will hold up longer than the tin, and it has the added benefit of not being so loud when the rain beats on it."

"Wise," she said. "I wondered if the stone was historically accurate. I liked the look of the tin panels, too, but the slate . . . it's just beautiful." Sunny paused before heading to the passenger side door, and held his gaze. "Thank you for bringing me here. For sharing this very special place with me. You know this is right for you, so you don't need to hear it from me. But . . ." She took a moment to scan the full vista, looking at the ring of shadowy mountain tops, then up to the moon that had finally risen above their smooth peaks. She let out a long, cleansing breath. "You're very fortunate to have found such a perfect fit."

"Yes," he said quietly, standing right behind her. "Yes, I have."

She thought she felt him lean down and brush a kiss against her hair, but it was probably the wind rustling a few strands. She didn't look back, afraid of what she might see. Or, more truthfully, what she might not.

# CHAPTER TWELVE

He never should have taken her up there. Sawyer banged a nail through the plywood into the floor joist with two heavy raps, then lined up the next one. He'd tried telling himself there was so much work to be done on the cabin, chances were by the time he moved in it would look, feel, *be* entirely different than it was now. It wasn't like she'd even set foot inside anyway. He banged the next nail home, lined up another.

Yet he knew that every time he reached that crest, he'd be hearing her swift intake of breath when she'd seen the high pocket meadow for the first time. When he pulled in and parked in front of the cabin late at night, he'd be remembering the delight that had crossed her face as she'd stepped out of his truck, and looked up at that ocean of a sky for the first time, marveling as she pointed to the Milky Way. He drove another nail home with a single swing.

"Somebody didn't get his Bo's coffee this morning."

Sawyer didn't bother looking up at Seth. One problem with working alongside someone who'd gone through the kinds of situations the two of them had gone through was that they could read each other with barely more than a glance. Sawyer wasn't interested in broadcasting this particular set of thoughts in Seth Brogan's direction. "I thought you were finishing up framing out the main floor bathrooms. Will's up on the roof completing the work on the cupola. He wants to get the scaffolding up on the chimneys by Wednesday. Looks like we're going right from Indian summer to early winter. Freeze warnings for next week."

"It's about damn time," Seth said. "I was up there with Will earlier. Felt like one of Hattie's grilled cheese sandwiches."

"I'll remind you that you said so when we're freezing our asses off in here getting the rest of the build-out done with no heat."

"Speaking of Hattie," Seth went on, "I'm calling in a lunch order shortly. I have to head to town to pick up that drywall tape we ordered. Sue called from the post office, said it was on the truck that just came in, said we might want to snag it now since it wouldn't go out on the mail truck for delivery here until Monday." He grinned. "I have to tell you, small-town living has its perks."

Sawyer banged in another nail and lined up the next. "Yes, it does. Nothing for me from Hattie's, thanks."

Seth poured himself a cup of water from one of the two big jugs they kept on site. This one was balanced against a corner beam up on the second floor where Sawyer was working. The floor had been framed out and he was putting down the plywood subflooring. "You know they make these things called nail guns now. We even have a few of them."

Sawyer made no response, just lined up his next nail. One good swing, then he lined up the next.

"Although you might be giving that gun a run for its money." He downed almost the entire cup of water in one swig, then dumped the remains on his head. "So, who put the bug up your ass?" He crumpled the cup against his thigh and made a two pointer into the paint bucket propped in the other corner. "Let me guess. Could it be a certain brunette botanist with a penchant for disintegrating greenhouses?"

"Horticulturalist," Sawyer replied, then added, "Bailey corrected me on that score."

"Ah. How is our youngest business partner doing? School going okay?"

"From what Addie tells me, she's having no problems with the schoolwork. But given she tested out at a grade level above her age group, that's not entirely a surprise."

"How about the social part?" Seth asked, crouching down and handing Sawyer more nails. "Making any friends? She's been going a few weeks now. That part going okay?"

Sawyer wiped the sweat from his forehead and looked up. "How should I know?"

"Because she's your shadow when she's not in school?"

"Maybe. But she's not much for talking, if you haven't noticed." Sawyer paused a moment, then took a breath. It wasn't Seth's fault he was in such a piss-poor mood. He had only himself to blame for that. He looked up at the man who was his closest friend. "Maybe you should try talking to her, see what you can get out of her. Women like you."

"Ah," Seth said, a grin spreading across his dirt-streaked face. "Now we're getting somewhere."

*No, it's the exact opposite of that,* Sawyer wanted to tell him. It had been eight days since Sunny had watched him sign the legal documents she'd brought with her, then said her good-byes to everyone and driven back out of the Hollow, and out of all of their lives. Eight days, and seven very long, sleepless nights. And he was getting exactly nowhere trying to forget what had happened out there under the stars that night.

"I heard Addie mention something about Bailey heading to D.C. to spend some time with our Miss Sunshine. When is that happening?"

"A few weeks from now. There's a school holiday for Veteran's Day. Three-day weekend."

"Maybe you should drive her up."

Sawyer banged in another nail, then looked up again. "And why is that?"

"Because you and Miss Sunshine apparently have some kind of unfinished business between you. And I think I speak for everyone here when I say we'd all be forever grateful if you could find some way to work it out."

Sawyer opened his mouth to tell his good friend exactly what he could go do to himself, only in some latent part of his sleep-deprived and, yes, dammit, sex-deprived brain, he recalled words of wisdom learned from his therapist. *Accept the help of friends.* Seth was a smart ass, but he was also the person Sawyer trusted the most.

He couldn't talk to Addie about the situation, because he was pretty damn sure Addie had sent him out with Sunny that night hoping exactly what had almost happened, would happen. She wanted her people around her, and she wanted them all to be happy, and in her mind, Sawyer and Sunny needed a whole lot more than family camaraderie to be truly happy.

"To be honest, if I knew how to work out our problems, I'd have driven up there myself by now."

If Seth seemed surprised by the sudden confession, he was wise enough not to let it show. "Maybe you should consider my solution then. You'll have Bailey there playing hall monitor, if you're worried about keeping your hands to yourself. Amongst other things."

"Very funny," Sawyer said, lining up another nail.

"Oh, for me it's all incredibly entertaining," Seth agreed. "I've known you a long time now, and I've never once seen you this wrapped. What I want to know is, what's stopping you? You're not blood related. Is it —" Seth broke off, grinned. "Did she shut you down? Is that it?" He hooted. "Well, well. Maybe I should give her a call myself then. I think we struck a little spark there, if you know what I mean."

"That's not it," Sawyer said tightly, thinking maybe it hadn't been such a good idea to confide in Seth after all. "Just the opposite, actually," he added, almost more to himself.

Hearing perhaps the honest uncertainty in his friend's tone, Seth looked sincerely concerned. "Well, that sounds like a good thing, man. A very good thing. So then what is the problem?"

Sawyer sat back on his haunches and spread his arms wide. "This. Everything." When Seth merely looked confused, Sawyer elaborated. "I'm rebuilding my hometown, and along with it, my life. She just broke free from a life sentence of caring for a very ill parent. One she loved deeply, so the loss and the freedom are kind of a double-edged sword. She's just now figuring out what she wants. But what she has is a job she loves and a thirst to grow more in her chosen field. Maybe a doctorate, who knows? And then we have Bailey — we both want only good things for her. And neither of us thinks it would be a good thing to get ourselves all tangled up, only to find there is no way to align our respective orbits. The fallout when things break apart would create all kinds of awkwardness, or worse, in what is supposed to be Bailey's brand-new, stable, forever home."

"So, you're both making this great sacrifice for Bailey's sake? Have you asked her about it?"

Sawyer's eyebrows shot up at that. "Did you just hear anything I said?"

Seth nodded, his expression even, his tone sage. "I heard everything you just said. And I think you and Sunny are using a ten-year-old kid as a lame excuse for being too chicken shit to take a chance on each other."

"What happens if —"

"What happens if Addie suddenly up and croaks?" Seth countered, rather heatedly, which stunned Sawyer into momentary silence. "What happens if you fall through the roof of that godforsaken cabin you bought while trying to rebuild it?" He crouched down on his haunches, too, and held Sawyer's now-stormy gaze solidly with his own. "What I'm saying is life offers no guarantees. Something you and I know a damn sight more about than most people. So if you and Miss Sunny Meadow decide you don't want to risk having a go at each other, fine. Then just say that. Don't lay it on life choices — which either one of you could change if you needed or wanted to. Would it be easy or simple? No. Would it require compromise on both your parts, maybe even a little sacrifice? Quite probably." He braced his arms on his knees and leaned a hair closer, his gaze intent as he added, "But whatever you do, don't lay it on Bailey. Because that little lady has bigger balls than the rest of us combined when it comes to taking her chances and muscling through. You're doing her a grave and rather insulting disservice if you think otherwise." With that, Seth straightened and strode over to the ladder that led down to the main floor. "I'm heading into town. Be back in a bit."

Sawyer wanted to order Seth to move his hard ass right back over to where he stood so Sawyer could respond. But one, Sawyer was no longer Seth's commanding officer and Seth no longer took orders from him. And two . . . Sawyer realized he had no response.

The only thing he did know for certain was that whatever it was the universe was trying to tell him by putting Sunshine Meadow Aquarius Morrison Goodwin squarely in his path, he quite clearly had yet to figure out what in the hell it was.

Sunny had her arms full of an overgrown pink calibrachoa that she'd just uprooted when her cell phone rang. She propped the phone on the rock border that surrounded this corner of her backyard garden and glanced to see who was calling. Stevie had said she'd call if she got done taking her mom to her eye doctor appointment in time for an afternoon movie. Sunny couldn't recall the last time she'd gone to a matinee. Probably not since college. But it wasn't Stevie. She recognized the area code as being the same as Addie's — who had gotten in the habit of calling her every other day or so, with this tidbit about Bailey, or that about the progress on the mill. But Addie was in her contact list now. This caller was not.

*Sawyer?* She carefully lowered the bundle of petunialike flowers and set the root ball next to the hole she'd dug for it, realizing it would have to be deeper, then slid her garden gloves off and snagged the phone before she could change her mind. "Hello?"

"Well, hey there, plant lady." It wasn't Sawyer.

"Hey, llama guy," she said, smiling easily while telling herself she was not disappointed. She hadn't spoken to Sawyer in over a week. Not since leaving Blue Hollow Falls. And she knew that was for the best. They really didn't have anything to talk about, and chatting for the sake of chatting would just make things worse. Because she enjoyed talking with him. Enormously. He made her laugh and he made her think. Their conversations were always interesting, insightful even. So no, it was a really good thing it wasn't Sawyer calling. She didn't need any more reasons to fall for him than the ones she already had. "What's going on?"

"Sorry to bother you on your day off."

"It's Tuesday. How did you know I was off?"

"I might have called your work number first."

"And how did you have —"

"I might just seem like your average llama-owning vintner," he interrupted, "but back in the day, when I was wearing a service uniform, I was actually known as the technology cyberoptics guy."

"Ah. So you're saying you hacked me. I feel a lot safer now."

"Actually, I just asked Addie."

She laughed, found herself grinning. "So, what's up? Everything okay out there in Hollowland?"

"Great, actually. Progress on the mill is flying now. Now that the roof is done and the interior framing finished, we're boot scooting right along."

"That's good news. I know from Addie that you all feel good about that progress with winter getting closer and closer. She told me Will is starting on the fireplace, and that's the last thing that is really weather sensitive."

"Ah, so you've been keeping in touch. That's good to hear."

She was still smiling, but definitely curious now. Seth might be an inveterate flirt and seem like a casual kind of guy, but to hear Addie tell it, he was also working every bit as hard as Sawyer on the mill, when he really didn't have to. His winery was still in the start-up stage, but it was and would always be separate from the Bluebird Crafters Guild. He'd be marketing his wine via the mill shop eventually, when he had wine, and it was true that creating a tourist destination out of Blue Hollow Falls would help his winery as well, but again, according to Addie, he was putting in additional long hours on his farm to accomplish things there that were also weather sensitive. So she'd been right about him being good friend material. "Yes, well, more Addie than me, I'm afraid. She likes to chat. She just discovered FaceTime, so that's been interesting."

Seth laughed. "You have me to blame for that I'm afraid. Now that we have her Web site up and running, she's become curious about all the other technologies out there."

"Yes," Sunny said, "she's pestering me to get an Instagram account so I can see the photos she's posting about the mill progress."

"You should," he told her. "You might surprise yourself. I'm sure folks would like to see photos of the work you're doing as well."

Sunny wanted to tell him she didn't have "folks." Well, other than Stevie, but she got to see firsthand the work Sunny was doing. "I'll think about it," she told him, not sure she would. "So, you're calling as Addie's technology pusher?"

"No, I'm calling to invite you to a party."

That stopped her cold. "Oh. I — uh, that's really nice of you, but —"

"Don't blow me off before you hear what the party is about."

"I wasn't going to —"

"You were, but that's okay. And don't worry, it's not like that."

"Like what?"

"I'm not asking you on a date."

"Oh. Okay," she said, relieved. He was sounding far too amused by her stuttering

310

reaction, though, so her guard was still up.

"Thanks," he said, chuckling. "My ego is lying on the ground now, whimpering, but don't you worry about that."

She laughed now. "I'm sorry. It's just — you caught me off guard. I'm elbow deep in replanting and — I am sorry."

"No worries. You can make it up to me later." He went on before she could form a reply to that one. "I'm calling as a fellow citizen of Blue Hollow Falls to invite you to our community party. Halloween is around the bend and we're going to throw a little open house shindig at the mill to celebrate. Actually, Halloween is just the excuse we're using. Everyone has been working hard for months now, and I thought it would be nice to give the guys and their family members a little break, have some fun before the weather turns brutal on us."

"Well, thank you for the invite. That's kind, especially considering I haven't done any of the hard work."

"You didn't stop the hard work. And you do own part of the place. Seems fitting to me."

"It's very thoughtful of you. I'll admit, I'm surprised Addie didn't mention it."

"Well, uh, maybe it slipped her mind."

Sunny's brows knitted together. "What are

you not telling me, Seth Brogan?"

"Wow. I'm glad you don't know my middle name or that would have been a scary mom flashback. Of course, no one could trot out the first-middle-last name, plus communion name if you were really in it, while simultaneously putting the fear of God into you, like my dear sainted mum." He'd said all of that with a dead-on Irish lilt.

Sunny laughed. "Sounds like a woman I'd like to meet."

"Lord help us all if you ever have the chance."

"Aw, don't be picking on your mother now."

"If Saint Mary Shannon Kathleen ever decides to wing her way east, I'd be the first one on the tarmac to meet her plane. But it's a fair warning I give ye, lass," he said, in full brogue now. "If you think Addie is a champion meddler, you've never met me mum."

"Ah, well, then. Maybe you have a point." She eased out of the crouch she'd been in, plopped herself down on the grass, and folded her legs. "And if you think you've distracted me from my earlier question, you would be sadly mistaken."

He chuckled. "Dammit."

"Exactly. So, let's start with you telling

me why Addie really hasn't mentioned this party to me. Is it because she doesn't know about it? And if so, why? Are you afraid she'd step in and take over the planning? Because that sounds like it would be a good thing. She's the head of the guild after all."

"Yes, she doesn't know about it. And no, it's not because I don't want her help. In fact, she'll be my next call."

"But I was your first call?" She tucked her feet farther under her legs and propped her elbows on her knees, heedless of the muck she was probably getting all over the back of her jeans. She'd never minded getting dirty. "So, tell me, what's really going on?"

"Will you come? Not this Saturday, but next."

She pursed her lips, trying to figure out what the game was here. "Does Sawyer know about the party?"

"He's not much of a party guy," Seth said, by way of response.

"But if it's a thank-you party for everyone who has pitched in and worked so hard, surely he'll be there."

"I imagine so, yes. Is that — will that be a problem?"

Now it was her turn to squirm a little. "Problem? No," she said, possibly too quickly. "Of course not. Why would it?" *Stop talking.*

The teasing humor was back in his voice when he said, "Great. Then we can expect to see you there? I'm sure Addie won't mind if you stay with her, but I have a spare room if needed."

"I'm sure you do," she said, giving it right back to him, grinning when he hooted. "But before I say yes, one last question."

"Ask me anything, plant lady."

"Does *anyone* else know about this little party you're planning?"

"Can I plead the Fifth on that one?"

"I think you just did."

"Sunny —"

"Why?" she asked. "That's all I want to know. What's the real plan here?"

"I really do want to do something for everyone who has been pitching in. Addie will love it, and I know that Sawyer will be on board. I'm not saying you should hold your breath about seeing him in costume, but —"

"Costume? I have to dress in costume?"

"What good is a Halloween party without costumes?"

"I could give you a list."

Seth laughed outright. "I can see why you and Sawyer get along so well."

"Who told you that?"

"My own two eyes," he said. "I was here when you came by last week to get those papers signed. A blind man might not have seen, but I'm not blind. And even a blind man would still have felt the heat."

Now she squirmed a little. "You're being —"

"Serious," he said, and actually sounded it as well. "I've also talked to Sawyer, so I know whereof I speak."

"And that's what prompted this party idea?"

"Yes."

His honesty surprised her, but she was glad to be getting to the root of it. "To what end? What is the desired result here?"

"To provide an opportunity for the two of you to get over whatever obstacles you've put up between yourselves. And, frankly, to give the rest of us back the guy we used to know and love. Because, at the moment, that guy would just as soon snap your head off as look at you."

"And that's my fault?"

"No, that's because he needs to get laid."

Her mouth dropped open, but no words came out.

"He also needs you. And since we're all adults here, I'll say that I was hoping you could kill both of those birds, if you know what I mean."

"I don't think you could be any clearer," she said, not sure if she should be pissed off, insulted, or admire the guy for doing something about the problem. Unlike her or Sawyer, who apparently were prepared to sit and endlessly stew in their own juices, as it were, rather than even attempt to find a solution. "And where, exactly, did you think this tryst was going to take place? On his cot there in the mill? On Addie's fold-out couch?"

"I — uh —" He broke off then, and she heard him cough to clear his throat.

She smiled, not unhappy to have made him choke a little. Fair was fair. "Seth, I appreciate that you're trying to help a friend. I might suggest you don't mention it to Sawyer, though. I'm thinking he might not take your suggestion quite in the spirit it was intended, which is how I plan to take it."

"Good, that's, ah — thanks. I wasn't trying to insult you. I've known Sawyer a long time, and he's . . ." He trailed off then, paused, and finally said, "You two should talk. That's all I was really trying to make happen."

"You could have just told me that."

"Maybe. But a social occasion where it isn't just about the two of you seems like the better plan. Relax a little, enjoy a little spiked punch, let your walls down a bit."

"Now I have walls?"

He laughed. "Other than the one I just ran into, you mean?"

She couldn't help it, she smiled. It was impossible to stay mad at him, or even be mad at him. "And then what?" she asked instead. "I mean, so I drive down, we socialize, walls are lowered, one thing leads to another, we reduce each other's frustration levels, and then? I drive three hours back to my home, to my life, and my work here that I love, and he continues working on building a life for himself and half of his hometown and . . . what does that do? What does that change? Other than create all kinds of new frustrations."

"Stop being so rational," he groused.

She laughed. "I know. It's such a pain when reality intrudes into fantasy. Listen, I know you're trying to do what you think is right by him, and by me. You and I don't know each other all that well, but I want you to know that I appreciate it. I think you're a good friend to have, Seth Brogan. I thought that about you when we first met."

"Thank you for not hanging up on me.

You're being a good friend, too. I probably could have gone about this better. I am just trying to help. I just think that choices aren't all carved in stone. Some are just that. Choices."

"Agreed. And one of my choices is not to get involved in a long-distance relationship. Another choice is not to further complicate what is already a fairly unconventional family dynamic."

"Did you ever stop to think that maybe the two of you being together would actually simplify it?"

She hadn't expected him to keep pushing, and she didn't want to consider that there might be something to what he was saying. She'd made up her mind, hadn't she? "That still doesn't resolve the long-distance part. Sawyer is where he belongs. With Addie, and now Bailey. He's home."

"Blue Hollow Falls is a pretty welcoming place," was all he said. "Folks welcomed me. It's my home now."

"My home is here. My work is here."

"Life is more than work, Sunny. Even if it's work you love. I'm a living testament to that. Why do you think I'm spending so much time helping with the reconstruct?"

"Have you ever been in love?"

That stopped him. But not for long. "I've

been in a lot of things," was all he said. "I've seen enough of the world, of people, to know what is truly important, where the real gratification comes from, what true contentment is, and why it's worth fighting for."

She hadn't expected such soulful, sincere wisdom from him. Who would have thought Seth Brogan was a thinker, too? So she spoke from her own place of absolute truth in response. He deserved that much. "I can't begin to imagine all that you have seen or done. You or Sawyer. I can only speak to my own life, my own experience. That's all any of us can do. And my truth, at this moment anyway, is that there is very little grounding me to what my world was almost nine months ago. Since then, I've felt very . . . untethered. And while there is good in that, freedom in that, there's also a lot that feels . . ." She trailed off, unsure if she could find the words to describe it.

"Sunny —"

"Like if I let go of any other part of me, I might just spin away," she said, pushing on, needing to get it out. Not so much for him, she realized, but for herself. "My home, my work . . . they ground me. I know what I'm about with them, what my role is, and I relish that. Cling to it, even. That might sound a little overly dramatic, and hearing myself say it . . . it kind of does. I'm not flighty and I'm not unhappy. I miss my mother. I do not miss taking care of her. I love what I do. I don't know what else I'd do. So, for now, I need to stick with that. And I know the rest will sort itself out. Because that's what time does. What having the freedom to choose does. And I have both now. So, that's what I choose, Seth."

There was a long pause, but the silence wasn't uncomfortable. It told her he was listening, and thinking about what she'd said. That made her not only want to hear his response; it made her care about it, too.

"Relationships always involve some kind of compromise," he said at length, his tone steady, measured, and most importantly, kind. "Sometimes one person has to give more than the other, but that's where the true strength lies. Knowing you can count on the other to be there when you need it, shift gears, even make sacrifices if necessary, because you'd do the same for them, and will probably need to at some point. You are right that what Sawyer is doing is for more than just his own future. So he's well and truly tethered at the moment. Happily so, but still, that's the way of it." He paused, as if he was debating saying the rest.

"It's okay," she told him quietly. "Go on."

"You're finally untethered. And it makes sense to not completely let go of what ties you have left. At least until you know what you'd be reaching for if you did. But you can't know what's worth letting go for if you don't open yourself up to what's out there. So, I guess what I'm saying is . . . think about whether Sawyer might be someone who's worth getting to know more about. Whether or not he turns out to be worth changing for, only you can decide. He was worth it for me."

He paused again, but she kept silent, letting him find his words, wanting to hear the rest. "My life, my roots, my ties, were all in Seattle," he said. "That's what felt safe when I got out of the service, and I couldn't really imagine going anywhere else. Like you, I felt very untethered. Sawyer convinced me to at least come out to Virginia and see what was what. He knew I'd dreamed of starting my own vineyard, but to me, that was pie in the sky. He pushed me, pretty hard, actually, to reach for it, because after all we'd done, all we'd survived, why the hell not? So, while it seemed like a big risk in some ways . . . I gave up a great job offer in the technology sector, something I knew I was good at, would do well at, even if I can't exactly call it a passion like yours. But it offered security, and familiarity, and had the added benefit of putting me back near my family again, my old friends."

He took a breath, then said, "In other ways, moving lock, stock, and wine barrel to Virginia wasn't a risk at all. I mean, it wasn't like I had to worry about stepping on a land mine, you know? I'd taken risks with my life. My actual *life.* Every day. And I was worried about moving to Virginia? That's what Sawyer made me see. And I'd trusted him with my life. More than once. So I trusted him again. And now I have an entirely different kind of freedom, one I really couldn't have imagined. I am doing something I am passionate about, even if there is zero security in it, and while I love my family, they can be suffocating, and I know they'd have talked me into keeping the secure job, even if I hated it. And I would have, especially after spending years risking my life in my last one. And the thing is, they're happy for me. Excited for me. They know I'm doing what I should be do-ing. But I wouldn't have known if I hadn't taken the chance to find out."

She had no words. His confession was as heartfelt a testimony as she was ever likely to get.

"So, just . . . think about it, Sunny, okay?

Party invite remains open." The teasing humor came back as he added, "Costume optional."

# CHAPTER THIRTEEN

"Absolutely not." Sawyer handed the red cape and blue tights back to Addie.

"Who better to be Superman than you?"

"I agreed to wear a costume. I'll take care of it." He leaned down and kissed her forehead. "Did you get Wonder Woman for yourself?"

She guffawed and swatted him on his behind as he stepped around her and walked over to the fridge. "I'm just glad to see you getting into the spirit."

He took a beer out of the fridge and popped the cap off the bottle. "I'm not a big fan of the dressing-up part, but the party is a great idea and definitely well earned. I'm glad Seth thought of it. I'd been thinking about a holiday party at Christmastime, but this makes more sense. The temperatures are more moderate and everyone's kids will have just as much fun."

"Nothing says we can't have a holiday

party, too."

He took a swig, enjoyed the cold rush of barley and hops, looking forward to working on his own brews again. He nodded after he'd swallowed. "True." He pointed the bottle toward her. "No candy, though."

Addie's shoulders slumped. "What kind of Halloween party doesn't include candy? The kids will be disappointed."

Sawyer didn't think it was the kids Addie was worried about. He happened to know that Addie didn't just have a sweet tooth, she had a mouth full of them. "We'll have mulled apple cider for everyone, and hard cider for the grown-ups, courtesy of Clyde Peterson's cidery. His wife said she'd do a caramel apple stand so the kids can dip their own apples. Seth said he'll do a bonfire out back so folks can make those marshmallow-chocolate-graham-cracker things. Trust me, there will be plenty of sugar."

Addie didn't look entirely appeased by that, but her excitement about the party won out. "Debbie Tibbett is doing a pumpkin carving table with the kids. Her pumpkins are a work of art every year, so that should be a treat."

"Given her wood carving skills, I can well imagine. We might want to make sure the kids have parental supervision working with the sharp tools, though."

Addie waved a hand. "Covered. Are you doing an IPA for the party?"

He shook his head. "Not enough time to brew any for this shindig. I haven't had any of my equipment hooked up since we started the renovation, so nothing is fermenting. And I don't have any stored. I will for the Christmas party."

"You should have said something. I'd have been happy to let you set up shop here. I could have made room downstairs in my studio."

"Thanks, that's generous of you, but I wasn't planning on starting up anything quite yet. In order to have some batches done for a holiday party, I'll need to get organized in the next few weeks, but by then we should have the electricity on at the mill and I can just set up there. I figure I might as well begin as I mean to go on."

Addie nodded. "Makes sense. I'm still waiting to hear back from Todd and Emily with their approval of how we've divided up the mill space. Todd is up in Canada somewhere taking pictures for his next series of prints. North American ducks, I think he said. Knowing him, he's well out of range of any communication. And Emily is at her folks' farm in Iowa helping out with her sister's kids now that the new one has arrived. They've got spotty cell service there at best and I don't have her sister's number. But I'm pretty sure they'll both be pleased with the setup. So if you want to go ahead and move your equipment in as soon as your section is done, I don't see why that would be a problem."

"That puts us at eight crafters on premises, including you and me. And what, six more off-site?"

Addie nodded. "Don't suppose Will has reconsidered joining us?"

Sawyer shook his head. "No. He said he's been focusing on work and helping Jake with school."

Addie sighed, but didn't seem surprised. "Personally, I say he's just dug himself into a hole since his wife passed on and doesn't know how to get himself out of it. I think if he could get that part of himself back, it would show him the way. Making music, either by playing it, or creating the vessel for playing it, soothes the soul."

Sawyer tended to agree with Addie, but he suspected Will's reluctance to resurrect that part of his life had to do with more than losing his wife. "There's only so much steering you can do, Addie. When he's ready, he'll find his way. I'd say he's taking care of the most important parts at the moment."

She nodded. "Jake is a good kid, and Will has definitely been an all-around godsend where the mill is concerned, I'll give you that. But doing well isn't the same as being well."

"Agreed. I'm keeping an eye out."

She patted his shoulder. "I knew you would." She took his empty beer bottle from his hand and put it in the recycling bin. "Don't suppose you've heard from our Sunny," she asked, casually enough, as she started pulling out the ingredients to make dinner.

Sawyer didn't come up to her cabin all that often these days, but Sunday supper had become something of a ritual, and one he happened to like. Having Bailey there now made it even better. Broadened the scope of the family, as well as the topics of conversation. Not that Bailey was particularly chatty, but she did offer the occasional keen observation, and had been known to ask the kind of questions that proved she was paying attention. She wasn't much for wanting the discussion to focus on her, but she seemed sincerely interested in the goings on in the Hollow.

"No, I haven't," he said in response to

Addie's query. "Should I have?" He knew he was being obtuse on purpose. Addie was up to something, and Sunny factored in somehow, he'd bet on it. He just wasn't sure what that "something" was. Yet.

"No, just wondering. I chat with her every few days. We FaceTalk."

"FaceTime," Sawyer corrected automatically. "Chat about what?"

Addie glanced over her shoulder. "What do you mean, 'about what'? All the things folks regularly talk about." She went back to chopping up green peppers and carrots. "She's been asked to do a special presentation at the conservatory on some of those rare orchids she works with. It's kind of a big deal, apparently. They want her to write a paper on her research. She said if it gets published, that would go a long way to helping her if she decides to go for her doctorate. The presentation is supposed to happen in November, right after Bailey visits with her. I told her I wanted to come up for it, but turns out that's the week I'm going down to that folk school in North Carolina to teach weaving classes. I'd get out of it, but they've already booked up all the slots. Wouldn't be right to reschedule at this late date." She glanced at him. "I meant to ask if you'd mind staying up here that week with

Bailey, while I'm gone."

Sawyer nodded. "Shouldn't be a problem."

Addie beamed. "Good. Sunny did say she'd take Bailey in to the conservatory and show her what they're planning to do for the presentation, if she wanted. I told her I couldn't imagine Bailey wouldn't want to see that and asked her to send me some pictures." She handed Sawyer a basket filled with ears of corn. "Shuck these, will you? Last batch of the season, I'm afraid."

Sawyer dutifully took the basket and headed over to the trash can, but didn't otherwise interrupt. He knew he didn't have to contribute much to the conversation. When Addie was on a roll, he'd long since learned it was best to simply nod and make the occasional grunt in agreement when necessary. He was admittedly surprised to hear that she and Sunny were in regular contact. He'd done a lot of thinking since Seth's little speech the previous week, but he'd yet to make any kind of decision on what, if any, action he might take. Hearing that Sunny was getting new opportunities at work and was probably seriously thinking about that Ph.D . . . well, he was happy for her, sincerely so. But that didn't exactly encourage any action on his part. And given the silence from her direction, he could only assume she hadn't changed her mind, either.

"I've tried to get the two to talk directly," Addie went on, scraping the peppers and carrots into the stew pot, then starting in on the potatoes. "Bailey and Sunny, I mean. And maybe they are and I just don't know about it. I've been a little distracted, what with the mill finally getting to the point where we can really start planning and trying to organize everyone. And now Seth's little shindig has got folks all excited." She paused for a moment, smiling as she took in a deep breath, then slowly letting it out again, her expression one of absolute joy. "I can't believe it's all coming together. Think of where we were just eight months back. And now Bailey is here. And we've got Sunny, too." She slid the potato chunks into the pot, then took the plate of corn from Sawyer. She was beaming with pleasure and pride.

Sawyer had taken note of the extra twinkle in her lavender eyes and the extra skip in her spry step over the past month. Addie Pearl was a nurturer at heart, so seeing her respective flocks come together, both at home and through the guild, had put her smack-dab in her happy place. And though the nurturing went hand in hand with the meddling and the poking, and prodding, no one deserved happiness more.

"Where's Bailey?" he asked, glancing up at the loft. "Is she out with the chickens?" Addie told him Bailey had simply taken on the care, feeding, and egg retrieval from the chicken coop. She was a natural with animals, to hear Addie tell it. Three out of Bailey's five foster homes had been on farms, so he supposed it was the one constant she'd had in her young life.

"No, she went with Seth after church."

His brows went up in honest surprise. "Seth? Why? Where?"

"Up to his farm, I guess. I didn't ask. They have some project or something they're working on. Thicker than thieves those two, lately."

"Since when?" He ignored the little prickle of jealousy. Hadn't he told Seth to talk to Bailey and see if he could get her to open up more? He just hadn't known Seth had taken him up on his request.

"Over this past week. Something to do with the party, I'm guessing, but I don't know for sure. I was just happy to see her getting involved, broadening her horizons. He'll have her up here by supper."

Addie was right — it was good that Bailey was making friends. He'd hoped she'd be doing that with kids her own age, but the fact was that her schoolmates all lived a fair piece apart. Beyond walking or even biking distance in most cases. That she was reaching out at all was a good sign. And he couldn't fault her instincts. Seth was a great ally and an even better friend. "I guess I shouldn't be surprised," he said with a smile. "What woman doesn't fall for Brogan's charms?"

Addie snapped a towel at him but she was grinning. "Look who's talkin'."

He snagged the towel from her, then draped it over her shoulder and dropped a fast kiss on her leathery cheek. "You might be a little biased."

"Maybe," she agreed, twinkle in full force, then smacked his hand when he reached for an apple from the bowl on the counter. "Don't ruin your dinner."

"Have you met me?" he asked, grinning around a big crunching bite.

"Just to make sure, there's a woodpile out back that needs splitting," she said with an arch look as he polished off the apple. She took the core from him when he was done and tossed it in the little plastic bucket she kept on her counter for compost material. "I'm not doing all this cooking only to hear you've no place to put it."

"Yes, ma'am," he said with a chuckle, and headed to the back door.

Sunny felt totally ridiculous. "It seemed like such a cute idea when I was standing in the costume shop." It wasn't quite dusk yet when she pulled in at the mill. Addie had been sending her pictures of the improvements, which were happening rapidly now that the roof was done and the interior had been fully framed out. At the moment, it looked wonderfully festive, with the strings of orange lights framing the roof, the big sliding door, and even the waterwheel. On closer inspection it appeared there were also tissue paper goblins and linen napkin ghosts haunting the pine trees closest to the mill, with wispy cobwebs strewn around the boughs. She could see pumpkins lining the walls, all carved and lit with candles. The carvings in the pumpkins were unbelievably complex and stunning. Little pieces of art, each one. There were also straw scarecrows and a big black iron kettle with something boiling inside it, sending steam wafting up into the gradually deepening night air. It was all rather charming and lifted her self-consciousness considerably.

*What would help even more is seeing someone else in costume. Anyone else. Soon.*

She opened her car door and wrestled her crinoline skirts out of the door, then stood and shook them out and back into shape. She pulled her white fleece shorty jacket closed in the front and zipped it up over her pale blue turtleneck. She would have checked her ankle-length pantaloons but she couldn't see them beneath the full skirt puffing out from her waist down. "We'll just have to hope they're hanging right," she muttered as she clicked her fob to unlock the Mini's hatch. She popped it open, slid out her little white bonnet, and tied it on. She'd put her hair in braided pigtails, and had to maneuver them so they worked with the blue gingham ribbons that tied the bonnet under her chin. Then she slid out the shepherd's hook, tied with a matching gingham bow, and propped it against the car.

A plaintive little bleat came from the large animal crate that she'd barely managed to wedge in the back, even with the back seat panels down and the front seats pulled forward as far as possible.

"I know, I feel the same way," she said, opening the door of the crate and attaching the leash to the tiny pink harness she'd wrangled the baby into earlier. "But trust me when I say you look about a million times cuter than I do, so buck up, little sweetie." Her heart melted all over again when the wooly black lamb looked up at her and bleated again, quite pitifully. "I know, I know," she murmured as she carefully urged the animal up and forward, then gathered her close so she could lift her from the crate and set her wobbly, impossibly long legs on the ground. "Let's take care of a little business first, shall we? Then I have one final indignity." She lifted out the big pink gingham bow she'd made to tie on the back of the harness.

The lamb just looked up at her, and bleated again. She laughed and rubbed its head. "I know," she crooned. "The things we do for family."

Once business was done and bow attached, her little lamb got decidedly friskier. Sunny walked over to the grass, away from the mill and the creek, and let the lamb race around a bit, while still tethered to the leash. "And to think I almost got two of you."

"My, my, if it isn't Little Miss Bo Peep," came a deep male voice behind her. "How fetching."

"Why, hello, Mr. Bro—" Sunny broke off halfway through her hello to Seth when she turned and actually saw him. "Oh . . . my."

336

He held out his arms and did a slow turn. He wore a metal panel skirt that came to midthigh, a breastplate, sturdy leather boots that came up past his calves. His hair was down, the first time she'd ever seen it that way. It was mostly a sun-bleached blond with a hint of auburn closer to the roots and far longer than she'd realized, hanging well past his shoulders. There were two thin, leather-thong tied braids hanging on either side of his temples. And his beard had also been woven into two pointed plaits. Added to all this was a Viking helmet, a shield strapped to a brawny forearm, and what looked like a giant hammer in his right hand. He grinned. "Too much?"

She realized her mouth was still hanging open and snapped it shut. It took her a moment longer to find words. She recalled thinking him some kind of Norse god when she'd first seen him. This was so . . . so much more than her paltry imagination could have ever conjured up. "Uh, Thor, I presume?"

"God of Thunder, at your service, Peep," he said, then swept into a metal jangling bow that she was desperately afraid might bind something it shouldn't, or worse, cut it off. She urged him to straighten with a quick wave of her hand.

"Impressive," she told him, noticing the face paint for the first time.

"Well, this is a party for a group of artists and craftsmen. You can't really half ass it, you know?" He motioned to her outfit. "Also impressive." Then he noticed the leash . . . and followed it to what was at the other end and made another bowing motion. "Not worthy," he said, chuckling, then crouched down to call the lamb over to him, causing Sunny to quickly avert her eyes before she found out what Thor wore under his metal skirt. Or what he didn't.

"What's your name, little fella?" Seth asked, giving the little lamb a scratch under the chin.

"No name," Sunny managed, keeping her gaze averted until Seth was upright once again. "It's — she's — a surprise."

Seth wiggled his eyebrows. "Kinky. I like it."

She rolled her eyes. "Seriously? Actually, I wanted to talk to you about it."

He kept the exaggerated leering grin. "I was so hoping you'd say that."

"Careful," she warned him. "I walk softly, but I carry a big hook."

He chuckled at that, and brandished his war hammer. "Well, in case you were worried, I'm not compensating."

She couldn't help it, she laughed. "Men," she said, shaking her head. "But I did want to talk to you about —"

She wasn't given a chance to finish, as Addie Pearl and Bailey had crossed the little dirt and gravel lot. Their costumes had Sunny grinning ear to ear. Addie was in a floor-length, flannel nightgown, with a silly gray wig on her head and a floppy, old-fashioned nightcap tied on with a big bow under her chin. Bailey had on her standard jeans and flannel shirt, but she had knee-high black boots on over her jeans, and sported a red, hooded cape. She had a basket on one arm, filled with some unseen goodies, covered with red-checkered linen.

"Hello, Little Red Riding Hood," Sunny said, delighted. She looked at Addie, "And Granny, my, what a big nightcap you have on."

Addie beamed. "Why, hello, Miss Bo Peep. It looks like all of Mother Goose's children are here this evening."

"Well, I hope you've been able to stay away from the big, bad —" Even as she said the words, they trailed off as she realized. "Oh . . . no." Her face lit up all over again, this time in pure glee. "You did not get him to — did you?"

"Did you what?"

She spun around to see a very tall wolf striding toward her. Even as her face split in an even broader grin, her pulse started drumming, and various erogenous zones all over her body began to pick up the beat. She'd never imagined herself jumping on the cosplay bandwagon, but at that moment, she might have been persuaded to consider it. He was in a full body fur suit, with a wolf mask complete with gleaming, wicked-looking pearly whites and a lascivious tongue licking out one side. There were big clawed hands and even bigger clawed feet. "My my, what big teeth you have," she quipped. The moment the words were out of her mouth, she realized that was the last opening she should have given him.

Fortunately, they had a small audience, though from the corner of her eye, she did catch Seth struggling mightily not to bust out laughing.

She immediately spun back to Addie. "I love it. What a great costume idea."

Addie beamed. "Actually, Bailey was the one who came up with it."

Sunny turned to Bailey and made a sweeping gesture at herself. "Proof, if we needed any more, that we share the same DNA."

That got a smile from the young girl and even a brief curtsy. She pointed at Sunny's leash. "What's on the other end of that?"

Sunny glanced at Addie, who gave her an almost imperceptible nod. Sunny took a short, calming breath, and sent up a prayer that she'd done the right thing. Addie seemed to think it was perfect, but Addie wasn't Bailey. And Bailey was still mostly an enigma to her.

Sunny turned around, but didn't see the — "Oh!" she said, as she felt something nibble at her pantaloons. "I — just a minute." She swished the layers of crinoline under her skirt aside, and out hustled the little black lamb, giving an annoyed bleat at having her snack interrupted.

Sunny heard a soft "Oh" and turned to see Bailey already sinking to her knees. She set her basket on the ground and flipped her hood back, then beckoned the lamb over. The lamb trotted right up and Bailey gave it a good head scratch, then rubbed its back. She kept her hand on the lamb's back as she looked up at Sunny, giggling when the baby tried to nibble on the ties to her cape. "What's her name?" she said, nudging the lamb away from the ties and scratching her under her chin.

"I don't know," Sunny told her. "I was thinking maybe you could help me with that."

Bailey's eyebrows shot straight up. "She's yours?"

Sunny shook her head and held out the handle to the leash. "I knew you missed your little goat. And, I'm sorry, I tried to find another pygmy goat, but D.C. isn't exactly teaming with livestock. A friend I work with, his family raises sheep on a farm in Maryland. She's a Herdwick. They're from the UK, they stay pretty small, and they do really well in rocky mountain terrain. So — what do you think?" She lifted a shoulder, looked at Addie, then back to Bailey. "I cleared it with Addie. She said that since her summer garden has been plowed under, the deer fence around it should hold this little one pretty easily, and you can use the shed for a make-do shelter. There should be plenty of time to get it all straight before the weather turns ugly."

Bailey just stared at her, saying nothing, her expression going carefully blank. But there was hope shining from those eyes like big, blue beacons.

Still, Sunny thought maybe she'd made a misstep. Maybe Bailey wasn't ready to let herself care for something, or get attached. "I — if you don't want her, that's okay. They will take her back, no worries at all. I just thought —"

Bailey launched herself from her crouched position and cleared the space between her and Sunny in a single bound. She wrapped her skinny arms around Sunny's waist, burying her face in Sunny's fleece jacket, hugging her as tightly as Sunny thought she'd ever been hugged.

Tears sprang instantly to Sunny's eyes and she instinctively clasped one hand to Bailey's head, and the other to her back and just held on. She caught Addie's gaze and the older woman merely nodded, a look of absolute contentment on her smiling face.

Bailey finally let go and looked up at Sunny. Her eyes weren't wet. In fact, they were as serious as Sunny had ever seen them. Fervently so. "I swear I will take the best care of her," she said, almost fiercely. "I promise."

"I know you will," Sunny said. She caught Thor turning sideways and possibly wiping a bit of dampness from his eyes. That made her smile; then a laugh bubbled up and she was dashing the tears from her own cheeks. "I had just been about to ask Seth if he'd be willing to help you with the animal enclosure when you all walked up. Since I don't know the first thing about it and he's got a llama and all. I should have called him up front, but somebody forced me to go hunting up a costume, and then there was the livestock wrangling, and . . ."

Seth turned back around, his eyes still overly bright. He had to clear his throat, but finally said, "Yes, sure." He looked at Bailey, and his grin was back. "We'll get it done up right." He made a fist and turned it toward Bailey.

She bumped him back, and they finished with the whole explosion-rain gesture. "Thank you, thank you," Bailey told Seth. "I've built pens before, so I can help."

"Indeed you will," Seth told her, and the two bent their heads together already in serious pen-planning mode. But not before Bailey knelt down and scooped up the lamb, who bleated, then tried to eat her hood. Bailey giggled again, gently scolded the lamb as she extricated the hood, then took the handle to the leash, and she, the lamb, and Seth all walked over to the grass together.

"A girl and her lamb," Sunny said, sighing a little. "And her Thor," she added with a laugh.

Addie smiled at that, and followed the trio, leaving Sunny alone with Sawyer.

Sunny felt a hand at the small of her back — a large wolf paw, to be more specific — as Sawyer stepped in behind her and bent down so the gleaming set of fake wolf teeth in the giant head of his costume was beside her ear. "I think someone just earned a pair of angel wings."

She dipped her chin at that, smiling, and felt a bit of warmth fill her cheeks. "Is this where I say it takes one to know one?" She slid a sideways look at him as he straightened and stepped up beside her, having to tip her head up to meet his eyes. "Is it hot in that thing?"

"You have no idea."

She thought she heard him chuckle, and she might have snickered herself. "Seth told me you weren't a costume guy. So I guess Bailey is a lot stealthier about getting her way than we gave her credit for."

"If so, she's being taught by the master." He nodded toward Seth, then shook his big wolf head.

"What?" she asked, when she heard him laugh and sigh at the same time.

"It's all falling into place now."

"What is?"

"The Master Plan. I knew Addie was up to something, and I was pretty sure Seth was, too. He and Bailey have been spending time together working on some project up at his farm. Addie has been talking to you, and I guess Seth has been talking to you."

Now it was her turn to shake her head. "You lost me."

"Can you help me with these?" He turned his hands palms up and she saw that there were elastic straps holding the clawed paws to the back of his own. She supposed so he could still use his hand to hold a drink or eat at the party. "Slide one off?"

She did. He used his free hand to slide the other paw off, leaving them both to dangle at his wrists, then reached around the back of his costume, fumbled for a moment. She heard what sounded like a zipper and a few snaps giving way. He lifted the head off the wolf suit. His hair was damp and clung to his scalp and his face was a bit flushed.

"You weren't kidding," she said. "Sauna in a suit."

"Pretty much." He glanced over to the mill. Addie, Bailey, the lamb, and Seth had made their way to where a group of other folks were gathering by the big sliding door. "Seth and Addie can probably handle things for a bit." He looked down at her. "Can we take a walk?"

She supposed she shouldn't have been surprised by the request. They hadn't talked since he'd signed the trust papers. Which, in essence, meant they really hadn't talked

346

since they'd kissed each other senseless under a starlit sky in one of the most beautiful settings she'd ever seen. "Yes," she said when she realized she hadn't answered him. She thought about her footwear. "Nothing too rugged, I'm afraid." She lifted her skirts to show him the black ballet flats she had on. "Bo Peep isn't exactly an all-terrain costume."

He chuckled. "Not to worry." He lifted one of his own costumed feet. "I'm not exactly equipped for a trail hike, either."

She laughed, then fished her key fob out of the little pocket that had been surreptitiously constructed in the side seam of her skirt and clicked the hatch button. "Why don't you stow that wolf head in here, so you don't have to carry it." She opened the door to the lamb's crate. "Perfect fit."

He managed to get it inside, with the muzzle facing out through the metal door when she closed it. "There is a horror movie script in this somewhere," she said, giving a little shudder as she closed the hatch.

"Well, I don't think you have to worry about anyone stealing your car, so there's that."

"True." She pocketed the fob again, then suddenly at a loss, she straightened her little jacket and wrapped her arms around her waist. It was quite chilly now that the sun was setting.

"I'd offer to trade costumes so you'd be warmer," he said. "But crinoline skirts are so last year."

She let out a bark of laughter at that. "I'm amazed you even know what crinolines are."

"Me, too," he said, "come to think of it." He started walking down the narrow road that led into the mill so they could stay on a paved surface. "I think I can blame Addie for making me watch *Gone with the Wind* with her when I was Bailey's age."

"Still scarred, are you?" she said dryly.

He slid her a smile. "She watched all of the *Planet of the Apes* movies with me, so I think we're square."

"I figured it would be pretty warm inside with all the people and the music and dancing going on, so I didn't bring anything heavier to wear. I'm looking forward to seeing how far along the interior has come, what with the second floor in now and all."

"I wish I could take you up there, but the subfloor isn't all in yet."

"No, that's fine." She wrapped her arms a bit tighter. "It is pretty brisk out here."

"There have been freeze warnings all week." He looked up at the sky. It was clear and the moon was up. "Hasn't happened yet, but from the feel of it, tonight might be the night. Let me know if it gets too cold for you and we'll head back and get you inside."

She nodded, and they walked on a bit. "So, what's this about a master plan?" she asked, going back to his earlier comment.

"Oh. Right. I didn't know you were coming," he said. "To the party."

She was sincerely surprised by that. "That's . . . odd. Addie knew, Seth knew." Then she paused, and thought about how the party had all come together, and said, "Oh. Right. That was probably Seth's doing."

"Yeah, I just figured that out."

"He's a good friend to you, but you already know that."

"I do. Which is why I won't kill him for meddling." He looked at her. "So, tell me what you know. About this little plan of his," he clarified.

Her eyes widened a bit at that, but he'd asked sincerely enough. "Well, Seth called me, about a week and a half ago, after . . . you know."

Sawyer merely nodded, saving her from having to be more specific.

"He . . . gave me some relationship advice."

Sawyer's steps slowed. "Okay," he said, sounding anything but.

She stopped then, and turned to him. "He had . . . deduced that things didn't exactly end on an easy note between us when I left here last time." She figured there was no reason not to be honest with him. "He encouraged me to rethink my decision about our relationship."

Sawyer looked away, didn't say anything, then rubbed his hand over his face and back over his still-damp hair. She might have heard him swear under his breath.

"I gathered that the two of you had talked, about . . . well, about us, but he didn't reveal any of what you said to him," she said. "And I don't blame you for talking to him. That's what best friends are for. I will say I think his heart was truly in the right place. I think he got the idea for the party as a way to bring us back in the same space, in a more relaxed, casual situation." She did not, however, think it was wise to tell him all of what Seth hoped would happen between them. "I told him I didn't know if I'd come. He said he was going forward with the party either way, and he hoped I'd reconsider."

Sawyer started walking again, slowly so she could easily keep pace.

He didn't say anything, but it wasn't awkward, and it wasn't tense. More like he was just taking the time to process it all. Plus, his big wolf feet were scuffing along the road, and she was using Bo Peep's shepherd's hook as a hiking stick, making it somewhat impossible for the atmosphere to be too intense.

"I talk to Addie — which I've been doing all along," Sunny went on. "She's made a habit of calling me, and . . . it's been a good way to get to know each other."

"She told me. I think that's a good thing, too."

"So, I told her I was coming. Mostly because I'd had the idea for the goat, which turned out to be a lamb, and I wanted to talk to her about it first, both to get her opinion and because she is Bailey's guardian. I wouldn't have just done that without —"

"I know," he said, quietly this time.

"So, I guess, with her knowing, I just assumed everyone knew."

He nodded, and kept walking along.

"You're probably feeling manipulated," she said, at length. "That wasn't my intent. I had no intent, actually. I just . . ."

He slowed again, then stopped and turned to face her. They were a fair distance away

351

from the mill now. Darkness was gathering quickly. She could still hear the hum of conversation and the occasional burst of laughter as the party swung into gear, but the sounds were muted. The music of fiddles playing and a banjo echoed through the cool evening air.

"Why did you come?" he asked her. "For Bailey?"

"I — she didn't know I was coming. I mean, I didn't know that until she walked up just now and was surprised to see me. But yes, seeing her was part of it. The lamb was a big part of it." She paused then, and looked down at her hands, which she'd twined together as she spoke. "I have thought about what Seth said, though. A lot, actually. But I didn't hear anything from you. So I had to think that maybe we'd made the right choice after all."

"Sunny —"

She did look at him now. "But there's Addie, and Bailey, and . . ." She let out a slow, measured breath. "This is part of my life now, Sawyer. They are part of my life now." She smiled briefly, and let out a little laugh. "Score one for Addie, I guess. She's made it happen." She forced herself to stop toying with her fingers and avoiding the main topic. She smoothed her palms over her skirt and looked at him directly. His gaze was on hers intently, no diffidence, no awkwardness. It was hard, as the shadows deepened, to read what was in his eyes, but there was no doubt of the intensity that charged the air between them. "I . . . I don't know how I will fit in here. Or how this place will fit in with me, I guess. Bailey is my half sister. I want to know her. She's coming to see me next month. And I guess . . . if I waited too long to come back, it would just have been more awkward. Or more . . . something." She lifted her hands, then let them fall by her sides. "So, I didn't come here tonight for you, but you were part of the reason why I came. If that makes sense."

He nodded, but his gaze never wavered. The moment spun out, then spun out a bit longer still.

She couldn't have put a name to all of the things she was feeling, but one of them was definitely lust. Hot, simmering, itchy-with-need wanting. And she silently begged him to do something, or say something, to help her put that back where it belonged. On some dusty shelf, where she could ignore it until it wasn't a thing any longer. Maybe she should have waited longer before coming back. Maybe more time would have helped. *Like what, a millennium?*

"Will you say something?" she finally said, as if the words were being pulled from her. "Please?"

She realized she was holding her breath, waiting for him to, at the very least, let her know in no uncertain terms that he wasn't particularly thrilled with all the behind-his-back machinations. She could have just contacted him directly, told him about Seth's plans, discussed this with him directly. Which, in that moment, seemed so obvious. But sitting at home in Alexandria, wondering what he was thinking, what he was doing, and not hearing anything . . . it hadn't seemed all that obvious.

"So . . . Seth convinced you to come," Sawyer said. "But he didn't change your mind?"

"What?"

"You're not here for me," he said, as if reiterating his question.

She shook her head, trying to figure out what he was getting at. "I just explained that I —"

"Would it make a difference if I told you that maybe he did change mine?"

354

# CHAPTER FOURTEEN

*What is it with you, the frying pan, and the fire?* He'd been around her less than twenty minutes, and every single one of the carefully constructed reasons he'd come up with for why he should ignore every last thing his closest friend had asked him to think about went, *poof,* right out the window. *Dammit, Seth!*

Sunny stared up into his eyes, her lips parted on a soft intake of breath, her own eyes unreadable in the encroaching darkness. "You . . . meaning what?"

"I don't know exactly," he said. "I'm not asking for — hell, I don't know what I'm asking or not asking." He raked his hand through damp hair, wishing like hell he could climb out of the rest of the damn wolf suit. Wishing like hell he could peel her out of that ridiculously chaste Bo Peep outfit, which still managed to turn him on. He was pretty sure she could wear a cloth sack and he'd still be raging hard. "I didn't plan on saying that. In fact, I've spent the past two weeks coming up with a long list of very good, very rationally thought out reasons why I should just leave it alone. Leave you alone. That's why I didn't contact you. I was trying to do what I thought was the right thing. But that doesn't mean I didn't want to." He looked up at the sky, as if there would be some kind of answer written in the stars, wishing the universe would just spell it all out for him. He looked back to her. "I didn't plan on you."

"So you've said."

There was a trace of pique in her voice, which snapped him out of his fugue state and put him squarely back in the moment. "When I'm not around you, I can — most of the time — find my way to thinking we made the right call. Okay, maybe 'most' is a stretch." His attempt at humor didn't make her smile. But then he hadn't been smiling when he'd said it. "Then I'm with you again, and I think only an idiot wouldn't do everything in his power to figure out how to make this work." He lifted his hands in the same helpless gesture she had just moments ago, then let them fall back to his sides. It was that or put them on her shoulders and tug her close, find out if less talking and more kissing would get them any closer to a solution.

When she still said nothing, he understood her plea for him to simply spit out what he was thinking. Now that he had, however, he realized that maybe she wasn't having the same difficulty ignoring the connection between them. Hadn't she just said she'd come back to find out how she could still fit in here without pursuing the thing between them? Had his pulse been thundering so loudly in his ears as he'd willed himself not to do what he'd wanted to do for pretty much every breathing, waking moment since she'd driven that damn car of hers out of the Hollow the last time that he couldn't clearly hear her rejecting this very thing?

Now he did laugh, but the joke was on him. "Be careful what you ask for, right? You asked me to tell you what I was thinking." He shook his head, wished he could find real humor in the situation. "I wish it was something easier. But we've been honest with each other this far."

She finally broke eye contact, and looked away. He saw her take in a slow, steadying breath. Heard her let it go, in a measured release. "I appreciate that," she said.

And with those oh-so-politely spoken three words, he felt like he'd just taken a bullet to the gut.

How had he let himself get into this situation, anyway? Twisting himself up like a pretzel for days on end, then pouring his heart out like a lovesick idiot. *Damn you, Seth, for making me think this was doable.* Only he knew the blame could only be laid at his own feet. Still, he might think twice before spilling his guts ever again. To anyone.

"Addie told me you were asked to do a special demonstration," he said, searching now for a toehold. They had to dig their way out of this hole. Or he did, anyway. "Congratulations on that. And something about getting a research paper published? I'm sure it was well earned."

"Thank you," she said quietly, almost absently, as if her thoughts hadn't quite made the shift to the new topic. She blinked then, and seemed to shake herself loose from wherever her thoughts had taken her. "I, uh, it's something I've worked toward for a long time. So, yes, it's . . . it's gratifying."

"That's good. Great." Silence followed. It was the first time the easy flow of conversation had ever stuttered between them, and that wasn't how he wanted to leave it. She was right; she had a right to be here, to find her place here, with Bailey, most definitely, but with Addie, too, and anyone else she chose to include in her new, widening life circle. He shouldn't be making that harder for her.

"You know," she said, quite suddenly, "I think" — she looked around, as if just now realizing how far they'd walked from where she'd parked — "I'm going to go. You know?" She smiled, seeming almost relieved. "That's probably for the best. I should have waited longer. Maybe. More time. We'll just — I mean, it was good, that we talked. Your candor — I —"

"Sunny."

She turned to go then, and his hand was on her arm before he could think better of it. The incongruity of the wolf paw dangling from his wrist and the gingham-bow-tied shepherd's hook in her hand should have been funny, but it wasn't any more surreal than any other part of this night.

She stopped, but didn't look back at him. "Could you, ah, could you tell Bailey I'm sorry I had to cut out?" Her voice was a little throatier now. "I'll call her. I should do that anyway. Addie's been asking me to. But I didn't know what to say. Now, with the lamb . . . I guess we have a place to start." She was rambling, talking too fast, sounding a little desperate.

He should let her go. But how would that solve anything? "I'm sorry, Sunny. I made this harder. I'm not sorry I was honest, because I think we should always know where we stand. But I don't want to make it more challenging for you to figure out how to fit Blue Hollow Falls into your life. And I definitely don't want to stand in the way of you and Bailey getting to know each other better. You went a long way toward that tonight. Seth was right about her. She's stronger and definitely braver than the rest of us. She sits back, stays quiet, looks at everything, but when she decides to leap, she leaps. I'm sure her coming to see you will bring the two of you that much closer."

Sunny nodded, but still didn't look at him. "Thanks," she said, and there was a bit of a rough quality to her voice. "I hope so, too."

"I won't get in the way of that. I heard you, loud and clear. Life goes on. We'll each move on with it. I'm . . . it's all okay, Sunny. We've started a solid friendship here, you and I. They don't roll around that often, so that means something to me." His hand tightened slightly on her arm in an effort to transmit his sincerity. "I hope at some point it won't be weird. For us, and for everyone else's sake."

She swore under her breath. And if that wasn't shocking enough, she spun on him then, and shocked him a whole lot further by letting her shepherd's hook clatter to the ground as she stepped right up into his personal space and grabbed his face between her two hands. "That would be a heck of a lot easier if you'd stop being so damn perfect for me." Then she kissed him.

His hands had fallen limply to his sides at her sudden burst of action. But they moved even before his brain could process what had just happened. His body didn't need to process anything. It knew just what the hell it wanted to do.

He slid one hand around her back, one behind her head, and hauled her right up against his body. Then he kissed her right back. Whenever his brain caught up, he could examine the wisdom of doing that. But in the meantime, he was going to kiss her. And be kissed by her. And he was going to enjoy every last damn moment of it.

There was no talking, no more words said. Their bodies seemed to have absolutely no problem finding a way to communicate. Because all those words they'd just used apparently amounted to nothing in the face of this.

It started like a rabid hunger, like they'd

better hurry up and get, give, everything they could, before rational thought bullied its way back in again and ended it. When that didn't happen, the kiss gentled and deepened. Her hands were still on his cheeks, but her fingertips relaxed, and then they moved, explored, and finally slid around the back of his neck to hold on, as he opened her mouth and took his time taking every last part of it.

There were no words, but there were gasps, and moans. Breaths were caught, groans vibrated in throats. There might have been a growl. And it might not have been his. But it could have been.

His rampaging heart slowed, then steadied . . . then swelled as the kiss shifted again, to one of caretaking, of nurturing, sliding them both closer and closer to the edge of that slippery slope, where they teetered, and teetered further, so close, so close to the precipice . . . in danger of tipping over. At least he was. Or maybe he'd already gone over, standing under the stars by his cabin, and he'd simply refused to acknowledge it then.

But his heart knew, even if his brain remained stubbornly fixated on what was rational. His heart knew.

They were ultimately interrupted by the

glare of headlights as a car came over the rise. They broke apart, but he continued to hold her as they stepped off the road into the gravel and grass. The car braked when they were caught in the headlights, then rolled slowly forward, coming to a stop beside them. The window lowered. Will tipped his head, smiled briefly. "Just wanted to make sure you weren't being attacked by the local wildlife, ma'am."

Sawyer's smile was equally sardonic. "Wilson McCall, this is Sunny Goodwin." He saw Will's son in the passenger seat and lifted a hand. "I believe you met his son, Jake, when you first came up here." He'd purposely blocked her from their view, giving her a moment to collect herself, smooth her hair, whatever was needed.

She stepped beside him now, all smiles, and lifted a hand in a short wave. She took in Will's costume, from the western hat to the badge pinned to his shirt, and said, "Pleasure to meet you, Sheriff McCall." She noted Jake's costume, and nodded, "Deputy Jake." The boy nodded, smiled shyly. "Thanks for the assist," she told Will. "But Bo Peep is pretty good at corralling wild animals. I'm fine."

"So I saw." Will smiled again, tipped his head with a short salute. "Enjoy your evening, ma'am," he said, in keeping with his character. He raised the window and they slowly rolled on toward the mill.

"Kind of quiet, like his son," Sunny said.

"Pretty much. But the man has a magic eye when it comes to putting rocks together. And you'll never meet anyone who works harder. His son seems to be more of the same."

"Jake's mom?" she asked. "Divorce?"

"No, she passed away when he was little. Will's mom helped out, then left them her property here when she passed. They moved to the Hollow full time not all that long ago."

"I'm so sorry to hear that. About his wife, Jake's mom, I mean. And Will's mother, too. That's a lot," she added, softly.

"I'm pretty sure that's just the tip of it," Sawyer said. When Sunny lifted a questioning gaze to him, he added, "I'm pretty sure he served. Not sure which branch, or where, or for how long, but . . ."

She put her hand on his arm. "It's good you're looking out for him. If anyone knows how, it would be you. Does Seth, is he — ?"

"Looking out for Will? We haven't spoken about it. I wouldn't be surprised, though. Or did you mean is Seth having issues from his time in?"

"The former, but both," she said, "now that you mention it. He seems pretty well adjusted — Seth, I mean. He talked to me briefly about his family back in Seattle. Sounds like they were pretty tight-knit."

Sawyer smiled at that. "Maybe too much so. He's one of six kids."

Her eyes widened. "Really? Where does he fall?"

"Right in the middle. One older brother, one older sister, three younger sisters. Bunch of nieces and nephews toddling around. Mostly nieces. His mom and dad own a good old-fashioned Irish pub. I think his mom also has like three sisters. So there are a bunch of cousins. They all live near each other, from what I understand."

"I feel a little claustrophobic just imagining it," she said with a laugh. "He said they all support his being out here, doing what he wants to do, so that's a good thing."

"Oh, I'm sure if he decided to go run a winery out there, they'd be on the next flight to help him pack and move. His mom might not be completely understanding about him needing to grow grapes in Virginia, when she thinks he could have a perfectly good vineyard in Washington State. But his dad gets it."

"His dad sounds like he's surrounded by

a whole lot of women," Sunny said with a laugh. "It's probably more likely he'd hop the next flight to come help his son here, just to get away for a bit."

Sawyer chuckled. "You're probably not far off on that. But to answer your other question, I think he's got himself straight. It's for him to say, not me. But that's part of why I encouraged him to come here, give it a go. He grew up in a big family full of very strong opinions. He went into the military because he wanted to serve his country, but also maybe because he wanted the order and regiment of it all, to cut through all the confusion of so many voices and find some focus. Afterward, I think he needed a clear drawing board, if you know what I mean. The autonomy to create his own space, put his own plans into action, without a lot of interference. He loves his family, they are very close, don't get me wrong —"

"No, I know what you're saying. He needed a place to breathe. He said you were a good friend, and he owes you a lot, for what you did for him."

They turned back to the mill and started walking again. Sawyer let out a short laugh. "I think he's gone into the wrong field. Sounds like he should have been a therapist."

She laughed with him. "After growing up in that huge extended family, I'm betting it was either be something of a therapist, or end up needing one." They continued walking, and she said, "So, you're not upset with him? For . . . well, for all of this? You know he meant well."

"I know," Sawyer said, recognizing they were going to have to address what they'd been doing back there, before Will's arrival had put an end to it. He'd rather not, though. He was tired of talking about it. He'd rather just . . . go with it. "We're fine. Even when he was under my command, he was always finding a way to do an end run, to get things going the way he saw them." He smiled. "So this shouldn't really have surprised me."

She shared his smile, nodded, but didn't say anything more.

She wasn't putting up any walls, or making any rash explanations, or worse, apologies, for planting that kiss on him. Or for staying in it when it had continued on, and turned into something else entirely. But that didn't mean she wouldn't when she'd had time to think about it more. So he opted to do an end run of his own.

"I started work on the cabin," he told her. Surprised, she said, "In all your spare time?" She laughed a little incredulously. "When do you sleep?"

He could have told her that sleep hadn't exactly been that easy to come by since they'd last parted ways, and work had given him an outlet. One where he could swing hammers and bang on things without anyone noticing, or offering unsolicited advice. Instead, he told her a different part of the truth. "It didn't take us as long to get the interior of the mill repaired and up to code. We ended up with some extra help and the frame out happened pretty fast."

"Ah, you lost your indoor camping facility."

"Something like that."

"I should have put that together with all the photos Addie has been sending me. I didn't even think about it. So . . . are you staying out at the cabin now? Does that mean you're able to salvage it?"

"I've had some tests run, inspections done, and yes, looks so. The roof needs to be entirely replaced. I've already had treatments done on the log frame, to protect it from wood-boring beetles and termites. That was the thing I thought would make or break it, but apparently Sol had been pretty good about maintaining that part. The logs were in surprisingly better shape than I thought they'd be. A good chunk of the interior flooring has to be replaced from water damage due to the leaky roof, but I've already torn up and replaced most of it, though I haven't sanded or stained and sealed it yet. The even bigger relief was that there weren't any of the mold issues I'd been afraid of. Tearing out the flooring took care of the little bit there was. The porch needs a lot of work. Will probably be easier and cheaper to just replace it. Same with the awning over it. The seals on the windows are shot, so those will come out. New triple panes are already on order. The wood-burning stove still works, but I'll put in a newer, more efficient model. And the list goes on. But yeah, it's all doable. And it honestly won't take all that long. Compared to everything we've done at the mill, it will be a cake walk."

"I'm really happy to hear that. It sounds like an exhausting amount of work, though, especially on top of everything else you're doing. And you have your brewery to start installing, too, at some point." She shook her head. "It's a lot."

"It is, but it's all good stuff. I don't mind the hard work. It's gratifying, seeing the place come together. There is no deadline, really, other than those dictated by the weather."

"Oh, I didn't think about that. Will you be able to get the roof done on the cabin before the snow starts?"

He nodded. "I'm sticking with the tin panels, so it's a relatively easy job. Not like attaching all those shingles. I've got it tarp covered for now, but that's the next order of business, as soon as the panels come in. Will is going to work on the stone foundation and the chimney. I'd like to get the stove replaced sooner than later. But the porch, and the planned additions on the back I told you about, those will have to wait until next spring most likely. And that's okay. I'll have my hands full enough with the mill. Our aim is to take the winter months to get the interior done, get all of us moved in; then come spring, we'll formally launch the place. Probably April, but nothing is set in stone yet. So I have time to work on both."

Sunny paused and turned to him. "You sound excited. Happy." She looked up into his eyes. "That's a really, really good thing. I'm glad for you."

He knew there was a "but" coming, only this time he didn't sit back and wait for it. "Let's go in," he said, nodding toward the mill, which was just a handful of yards away now. "Enjoy the party. I'll introduce you to

370

everyone you haven't met yet. Then I'd like to take you up to the cabin." He stepped in closer, until her chin tipped up so her gaze could lock with his. "The sunrises there are almost as breathtaking as the moonrises." Now he did wait, and his heart might have sped up a little. He tried not to think about what life would be like if he didn't find some way to keep her there. He shut that track down, because down that path lay rational thought and no easy solutions. Her life — the one she was just as happy about, just as excited about — wasn't here.

He waited for her to say all of those things. His heart might have stopped beating altogether when she tipped up on her toes and kissed him, and very softly said, "I think I'd like to see that. Very much."

# CHAPTER FIFTEEN

"Here, let me," Sunny said, helping Addie load the lamb's crate in the back of her Subaru. "And they sent along this to supplement her diet." She handed Addie a bag of grain feed. "She's nine weeks old. They weaned her at eight weeks because she was one of triplets and her mama was getting too skinny."

Bailey held the lamb even more closely. She was more than an armful, even at just two months of age, but the socialization of the past few hours had conked her out and she was fast asleep, her head drooping over Bailey's arm.

"She can sleep in the crate on the way home," Addie told her.

"Can I just —" Bailey looked at the lamb, then back to Addie. "It's not far. Can I hold her?"

Addie softened. Bailey wasn't one to ask for anything, and her heart was in her young eyes. "Sure. This once will be okay. But she's not sleeping in the house."

Bailey nodded, and carefully climbed into the backseat of the car, arms full.

Sunny smiled weakly when Addie turned to her after closing the hatch to the Subaru, all the supplies and crate now loaded safely inside. "Sorry?"

Addie shook her head. "Oh, don't you worry. I'm quite sure that child will be making a bed out in the shed for a night or two, until it gets good and cold. They'll come to terms with each other. Babies are cute, but they grow up. It will all sort itself out. They'll do well by each other, I'm sure."

"Seth said he has plenty of pasture if you end up needing it."

"Oh, I've got a fairly large cleared area down the side of the mountain behind my place. Used to farm it when my legs were better, but over the past half-dozen years, it's just gone to pasture. I'm sure the lamb will be more than happy to keep the overgrowth cut down to size. You got the perfect breed for the elevation and the terrain. Just needs the fencing repaired and we'll be set to go."

"I'll take care of that," Sawyer said, walking to the back of the car after helping to buckle Bailey into her seat. "I'll come up later on tomorrow."

Addie eyed the two of them, and Sunny was pretty sure she could see the sign over her head flashing "we're going to go have sex now" in big, bold neon letters. But all she said was, "That baby won't need much yet. You don't worry about the fencing. We'll get it all sorted out." She looked to Sunny. "When you think about it, send me the information on the farm you got her from."

"Oh, yes, sure. I know they'll be happy to answer any questions and —"

"Sheep are flock animals, so I'm thinking one or two more might be in order."

"Oh!" Sunny said. "I didn't even think about that. I — oh, gosh. This is going to turn out to be a bigger thing than maybe is good?"

Addie waved away her concern. "I'd have said so when you first brought it up if that were the case. I had thought to just add a few from a local farm here. I didn't know much about this smaller breed, but once you told me about it, I've done some reading and I think I'd like to get a few more of the same. Wool quality is a bit uneven, but the color variation is intriguing." She smiled. "I've already got some ideas brewing on that. Plenty of time, since we won't be shearing for a good bit yet." She reached out, took Sunny's hands in her own. "I'm quite sure Bailey won't mind tending to a few more. I think we'll both be enjoying this gift. Thank you."

Sunny nodded, then slid her hands free and leaned down to hug Addie. "Thank you. For taking her in." She leaned back, her eyes shiny. "And the sheep, too."

Addie cackled at that, waved a dismissive hand, but her eyes were a bit shiny, too. "It's what we do. Now, go on back to the party, both of you. This tired old lady is going to take those two sleepy lambs home."

"Good night, Addie," Sawyer said, leaning in and bussing her cheek. "Drive careful. Call me if you need anything."

"I'm sure we'll be more than fine," she said. She made no mention whatsoever about Sunny using her fold-out bed later that night. Instead she just climbed in and started up the engine, leaving Sunny and Sawyer to step out of the way as she backed out, gave them a short wave, then headed off down Falls Road.

"I should have thought about the herd thing," Sunny said, trying not to let the heat of embarrassment flame her cheeks anew. She was grateful to Addie for not making things awkward. "I'll help her with getting the others out here. If I can fit them in my car, that is. I can always rent an SUV."

He turned her to face him. "Or I could drive up, and we'll go get them together. Plenty of room in my truck."

Her heart instantly leapt at that idea, which was both thrilling and not a little alarming. She needed time to think. And at the same time, she didn't want to think at all. She just wanted to do. "That's a lot of driving. You don't have to —"

"I want to. And I suspect we'll both be doing some of that. Fair's fair. I'd like to see your home if you're comfortable with that."

She looked into his handsome face. He was smiling, his tone confident, but what she saw in his eyes was hope. She didn't want to think about that, either, or what the future would look like once this night was over. Her body was a roiling mass of nerves, some anticipatory, some excited, some just . . . nervous. She wanted to simply live in that moment, enjoy the night as it happened. What they did or decided to do afterward could wait, at least until morning, couldn't it? "Are we going back to the party?" she asked.

"Not unless you'd like to. I've said my good-byes."

"I'm — no, I've said mine, too. I just met

everyone, and Addie and Bailey are gone now, so —" She was talking too fast, the nerves showing, and he must have heard it, too, because he tugged her closer.

"We don't have to go up to the cabin tonight. And even if we do, nothing has to happen beyond . . . whatever we want to happen."

She took the front of his wolf suit in her hands, balled them into fists, and pulled him closer still. "I'm pretty sure if it doesn't happen, I'm going to climb right out of my skin. Fair warning."

He let out a surprised laugh at that, but the hope in those eyes turned to a gleam of hunger. *Big Bad Wolf, indeed.* "Well, Miss Bo Peep, your chariot awaits."

"Should I follow you up?"

He shook his head. "Your car will be fine here. I'll bring you back down for it tomorrow."

"Good," she breathed, not really wanting to be apart from him, or give herself any time whatsoever to talk herself out of this.

"Good," he agreed, then leaned down and kissed her. "I like that you say what you mean," he murmured against her lips. He nibbled his way along the side of her jaw and nipped her earlobe. "And want what you want."

"I'm a big fan of wanting at the moment," she breathed, as she tipped her head to the side and allowed him to continue his slow, devastating kisses to the tender skin at the base of her neck. "Are you wearing something decent under that fur suit?" The wolf head was sitting on top of her car at the moment, but he still had the rest of the fur suit on.

"Why, Miss Peep," he said, his teeth grazing the pulse point beneath her ear. "Is that how you got your name?"

She moaned when he kissed her there, then gasped, just a little, when he nipped her earlobe.

"I'll show you mine if you show me yours," he said, nudging open the collar of her little fleece jacket. "Just what does Bo Peep wear under all of those layers of crinoline, hmm?"

She let out a baleful little laugh as she mentally pictured what she was actually wearing.

He lifted his head, his lips curved in a wry smile. "That sexy, huh?"

"Dead sexy," she said. "Emphasis on *dead.*"

He shocked her by scooping her up, skirts and all, and carrying her to his truck, which was parked a few yards away. "Why don't you let me be the judge of that?"

"Sawyer — you can't. I'm —" She clung to his neck, mortified. She'd never been bodily scooped up in her life. At five-foot-eight, she was hardly scoopable. But she quickly realized that his height advantage was just that . . . an advantage. And a really, really nice one. She might not be scoopable to most mere mortal men, but for Sawyer Hartwell, it was no big thing.

"Oh, I believe I can," he said, propping her backside on one bent knee so he could open the passenger door. He easily lifted her up and onto the seat. "Watch your head."

When she automatically ducked, he caught her mouth in a short, soul-searing kiss that left her breathless until he leaned back, then pulled the seat belt across her hips.

"We're going to have fun," he said, then closed the door.

"I — I think that might be the understatement of the century," she said faintly. Then let her head drop back on the headrest and closed her eyes. *Don't think. Just do.* "Yes," she said. "No thinking. Only doing."

She heard a thump that was probably Sawyer depositing the wolf head in the back of the truck. When he climbed into the cab of the truck a minute later, he was wearing a gray microfiber T-shirt that clung to his shoulders and abs like a second skin over a pair of black biker shorts. He had Tevas on his bare feet.

"The wolf feet make driving a bit problematic," he explained, noticing her once-over. "I changed in the mill when I got here."

"I — yeah." She tried, and epically failed, to stop looking at him. All the parts of him. "Aren't you — won't you get cold?"

"Cold's a good thing at the moment," he said, backing the truck out and turning toward the road. Then he turned to her with a fast grin and a wink. "As long as you keep looking at me like that, I don't think there will be any chill issues."

"I . . . I think I can manage that," she said, wondering if she might actually be drooling. *Dear Lord, have mercy.*

She could feel the heat of the grin he shot her way, before he turned on to Falls Road and drove on past the mill, then up higher into the hills.

It was a winding, twisting drive. Neither one of them bothered with any attempt at small talk. They'd talked quite enough.

She didn't think she could be blamed for not taking the time to look up at the wonders of the universe when he finally pulled to a stop in front of his cabin about twenty minutes later. She did notice the tarp he'd mentioned, now covering the roof. It wasn't until he cautioned her on where to cross the porch to the door, to avoid the weakened spots, that she even thought to ask, "Are you still sleeping on that cot?" She'd never had the opportunity to go camping, but she was already mentally figuring out how to put together a makeshift bed on the floor, maybe in front of the wood-burning stove he'd mentioned, when he opened the door and ushered her inside. There, in the middle of the great room, sat the one and only piece of furniture. "Oh. Well, okay then."

A sea of mattress, and a box spring to go with it, sat on a handmade platform frame in the middle of the room, moonlight spilling across the tousled sheets and rumpled comforter.

"I decided I've spent enough nights of my life on cots, or worse," he said, walking over to the windowsill on the right and lighting an oil lantern. He set that one back down and went over and lit another on the mantel over the fireplace. The cabin was softly illuminated in a deep yellow glow. "Once I got the roof wrapped, I went and got this out of storage." He grinned. "I just didn't take into account the size of the door leading to the back bedroom."

She looked at the narrow doorway to the

back room. "Ah. Yes. Will it even fit back there anyway?"

He smiled. "It will when I'm done building the add-on. I'm not sure what I'll do in the meantime, but for now . . . I'm not complaining."

"Me, either," she murmured, looking again at the bed, thinking it was the size of a small playground. Then smiled, thinking that might be an appropriate description. It was nice and toasty inside the cabin, and as she looked around, she spied the potbelly woodstove in the far corner, an orange glow emanating from behind the little grill panel door on the front.

"Sorry it's not tidier," he said, glancing at the bed. "I didn't expect company. The sheets are clean," he said, then motioned to himself. "But I am not. I'm going to grab a quick shower out back."

"Out . . . back?"

"Don't worry, there is indoor plumbing. Toilet works fine, as does the sink. But the showerhead broke off and I haven't replaced it since I'm going to gut the bathroom and start over when I expand."

"So, you're going to rinse off in the garden hose or . . . ?"

He laughed. "Kind of. Sol had an outdoor shower, which, in fact, runs off the garden hose. For now, anyway. I hooked up a heat-on-demand unit, runs off a little propane tank. Handy. At least until we get our first freeze. But I'll have it piped into the house system by then. I'll be right back."

She nodded dumbly, trying to imagine the rig, then stood in the middle of the cabin's main room, listening as he rummaged in the room off the back of the great room — the bedroom, she surmised. A door squealed open, and slapped shut. She assumed it led to either the backyard, or a back porch, she didn't know which. What she did know was that imagining him outside, stripped down to the skin, standing under a shower, under the stars . . . *Have some serious mercy.*

She felt a little overheated herself and took off her little fleece shorty jacket, then went ahead and unzipped the skirt and unhooked the waistband that all the crinoline layers were attached to, and let them crumple to the floor, so she could step out. She kicked off her ballet flats, then looked down at the ankle-length white pantaloons and the pale blue turtleneck and thought maybe she should stop there. Because the ratty gray college gym shorts and tank top she wore underneath . . . not really designed to drive a man to his knees.

But then, she hadn't really considered that

this was where she'd end the evening. Or maybe, some part of her had considered it, and the shorts and tank combination had been her version of underarmor. "Because nothing says 'come take me' like ancient gray cotton."

"I don't know," he said, from right behind her. "I think you should let me be the judge of that."

She hadn't heard him come in, and didn't dare turn around to see what he was, or wasn't wearing.

"Do you want to shower?" he asked, cupping his broad palms over her shoulders, then sliding them down her arms as he moved in closer, until her body was pressed back against his. His chest was bare, and still damp. He had something on though, probably a towel, wrapped around his hips.

"I — maybe I should," she managed, thinking he'd have to show her how to use it, but those words stuck in her throat. Because he had lifted the hem of her turtleneck and was pulling it, and with it her arms, upward, so he could slide it up and off. He tossed it over on top of the skirt pile, then fingered the skinny straps of her tank top. She wasn't wearing a bra, mostly because she didn't need one. Sad to say. It had been a good long while since she'd been naked in front of someone, and she'd forgotten about all the body anxiety issues that went along with disrobing. *Too late now.*

But then he was cupping her breasts, covering them with his big hands, and urging her to lean back into his body, and it suddenly didn't matter. He nudged aside one braided ponytail, and pressed a hot kiss to the side of her neck, making her shiver. Then he nibbled along the edge of her shoulder, before slowly dragging the thin tank strap over and down . . . with his teeth. And if that wasn't enough to make remaining upright a challenge, he'd splayed his fingers over her breasts, then moved them together again, catching her now-rigid nipples between them. He gently rubbed them, still covered in soft cotton, the sensations so exquisite she arched her back, pressing them more firmly against his touch.

Her moan when he gently bit the other side of her neck wasn't soft, it was deep and guttural, and she let her head drop back against his shoulder. "All the better to eat you with," he murmured, then slid the other strap over and off her shoulder.

She shuddered, hard, when he slowly dragged the tank down over her arms, rubbing the cotton snugly over her nipples, one deliciously agonizing inch at a time.

Some distant part of her thought she should probably be participating, doing more than just standing there, but she couldn't seem to make any part of her move. She felt languorous, as if her entire body was as heavy lidded as her eyes.

When he got the tank to her waist, he slid his fingers around the waistband of her pantaloons until he found the cotton ties that held them up. He tugged one tie, slowly, so slowly, urging the waistband looser, until she wanted to yank them out of his hands and yank the things off herself, then beg him to put his hands back on her. Anywhere on her.

But his arms were wrapped around hers, holding them by her sides, and he was doing ridiculously delicious things to the nape of her neck again, first with this teeth, then with his tongue, then his teeth again. And she forgot her urgency with the ties, because it was too hard to feel and think at the same time. She went with feeling. Waves upon waves of the most tantalizing feelings, rushing through her, cascading over her skin, shivering down her spine.

And then her pantaloons fell slack to the floor, in a puddle of soft white cambric. He shifted them so she could step out, moving the two of them closer to the bed. He stopped, and rolled down the wide elastic band that held up her thin cotton gym shorts. Then rolled it down again, and again, until he was satisfied there was nothing underneath them. He slid the sides of his thumbs along just inside the waistband, out to her hip bones, and she held her breath, expecting him to hook them and drag the shorts off. Hoping, maybe, too.

Instead he turned her in his arms so she faced him. He was shirtless, and he was . . . magnificent. But not perfect. There were scars. More than one. In fact, it looked like he'd been sent to do battle with no armor at all. He had a thick white towel wrapped and tucked in at his waist, but her gaze wasn't drawn downward, and her thoughts had shifted quite abruptly from his sublime seduction to tracing her fingers lightly over a puckered, circular scar just below his right collarbone. It was old, the skin shiny now. She moved to the long slash of a scar that bisected his ribs on the left side. It was old, too, judging by the color. There were others, some small, some not so small. Some smooth and surgically healed, others jagged, left to heal on their own.

She knew her eyes were wide when she lifted her gaze to his, and she didn't want him to feel self-conscious, though she doubted he was the type to care. But seeing the scars brought home in a different way the danger he'd willingly put himself in — and these were just the visible scars. "Thank you," she said, feeling humbled. "For . . . your service. Sawyer . . ." Her gaze went back to his shoulder. "That's . . . from a bullet. Right?"

He nodded, then tipped her chin until she looked at him directly. "It's okay. Aw, Sunny," he murmured, when her eyes glassed over. "That's done. I'm okay." He framed her face with his hands. "You are very sweet, to feel what you're feeling. It speaks well of you. A lot of men weren't so lucky as me. I'm fortunate. Focus on that. I do."

She sniffled, and wiped at her eyes with the back of her hand. "Right. Yes."

He pulled her against him and just held her. She wrapped her arms around him, hugged him, a little fiercely. But her emotions were fierce in that moment.

He eased her away from him so he could look at her again. "You know one of the best reasons we do what we do?"

She shook her head.

"So we can come home and do this." He kissed her. There was heat, and there was comfort, all wrapped up together, and she thought she should be the one giving comfort. "And this," he said, pulling the elastics off the ends of her braids, then loosening up the strands so he could rake his fingers through them and shake them out. Then he sank his fingers into her hair and pulled her mouth up to his again. He edged her back, until she sank down on the side of the bed. He followed her down, angling his body half over hers, never breaking the kiss.

"This is the freedom we fight for, Sunny," he said, turning to his side, pulling her with him. "Freedom to live where we want," he said, kissing her cheek, her temple, her chin. "Freedom to do what we want." He nipped at her lip, as he reached down to help her shimmy her shorts over her hips, kissing her as he helped her push them down her thighs, until she could kick them off. His towel came free when he rolled her to her back and moved his body over hers. His face was buried in her neck, and she was already moving under him, gripping his shoulders, when he murmured, "Loving who we want."

Her heart stuttered even as it lurched, and she decided she'd think about that later, too. Because hearing him say those words, even though he probably meant nothing more than lovemaking, hadn't scared her. No, it had thrilled her. *Thrilled her.* Down deep in some place she'd yet to connect to inside herself.

Her mind felt as if it had scattered into a million little thoughts and feelings and emotions. But then he was working his way down her body, and it was exactly what she wanted him to be doing. It was exactly what she wanted to be doing. Oddly enough, it was something Seth had told her that echoed through her mind, even as her body arched up almost violently when Sawyer closed his lips around one nipple.

Seth had said she couldn't decide what she wanted until she had enough information to make an educated decision.

So she shoved all of her doubts and indecision and even the tantalizing prospect of what it would be like, to be loved by Sawyer Hartwell . . . all of that went to the wayside. And she focused on letting herself learn more. About him. And maybe herself along with it.

Then she'd decide what came next.

# CHAPTER SIXTEEN

He should have put more wood in the stove last night. It was decidedly brisk inside the cabin that morning. He'd turned the oil lamps off sometime after three A.M., but hadn't thought to load the stove. He'd been . . . distracted by other things. Wonderfully delicious, sensual, delectable things.

Sawyer rolled over and found Sunny sprawled on her back next to him. Her hair was a brown tangle on the pillow, more in a car wreck victim kind of way than a sexy bed head kind of way, and what little makeup she wore was still there, but no longer where it had started out. The sheet, blanket, and duvet were pulled up to her chin, where she held on to them in two tightly clenched fists, as if someone might steal them from her at any moment. And rather than having that angelic expression of peaceful sleep, she was snoring. Not too loudly, but steadily nonetheless.

He decided right then and there it must be love, because to him, every part of that was adorable.

He shifted as quietly as possible to the edge of the bed, intent on adding more wood to the stove, then a quick trip to the bathroom and his toothbrush.

He'd barely rolled an inch, when she murmured, "Sawyer?" and reached out blindly for him. Her eyes were still closed and he was pretty sure she was still asleep. He lay back down and her hand landed on his arm. She curled her fingers into his bicep, smiled, then scooted closer and snuggled farther down under the covers. A moment later, she was snoring again.

He wasn't sure about anything at the moment, not how they'd make this work, or how he'd keep from barring the door so she'd never leave. Definitely not how he would sleep in this bed ever again without remembering every last second of what they'd done in it last night. What he was sure about was that he liked that she'd instinctively reached for him, even in sleep, and that knowing he was beside her comforted her.

He leaned down and kissed the small bit of forehead that was peeking out above the edge of the covers. "I'll be right back," he whispered.

She mumbled something, but didn't say anything more when he slid her hand off his arm and slipped from the bed.

He was halfway through brushing his teeth, trying to decide how best to start the morning, when he heard her call out his name. And she was definitely not asleep.

"Sawyer! Did you see?"

He couldn't tell if she sounded alarmed or excited. He quickly rinsed and wiped his mouth, then at the last second, for her sense of modesty, not his, he snagged a towel off the rack and wrapped it around his hips. He walked back out to the great room. "See what?" he asked.

He smiled when he saw she was sitting up in the middle of the bed now, sheet, blanket, and duvet pooled around her hips, completely unconcerned with her nakedness. *So much for worrying about offending her delicate sense of modesty.* He approved of her morning-after bedside manner. Heartily.

"That," she said, pointing to the cabin's side window, which faced the foot of the bed.

He reluctantly shifted his gaze away from her and looked outside. His mouth went slack.

"It snowed," she said, sounding a little

sleepy and a lot stunned. "Like . . . a lot."

"I can see that."

Her head swiveled toward him, eyes gleaming and alert now. "Oh, no! What about the lamb? And Bailey?"

"I'm sure they're both fine, but we can call to check on them in a bit. It's just past dawn. Still pretty early." Though, likely, Addie was already up.

She looked upward. "Good thing you wrapped the roof."

He nodded, thinking he was happy they were protected from the snow coming into the cabin, but he wasn't so sure about the roof holding up under the weight of all that precipitation piled on top of it. He supposed it had been handling snowfall for many years, and the tarp would assist in the weight distribution, but he'd climb up and check on it later, nonetheless.

His more immediate concern was how this latest curveball from the universe would affect the course of that day. And the next.

"Is that normal up here? This much snow on the first day of November?"

"It's a little early, but it's been known to happen. I'm just surprised I missed the weather report. I didn't even know there was a chance." He looked from the window to her and the corner of his mouth lifted.

"But I have been a little preoccupied."

The most becoming shade of pink stained her cheeks and she finally gathered the sheet up to cover herself. That was adorable, too.

"You said you had men coming in early to help at the mill today."

"I'll get in touch with Will. He lives closest to the mill," he told her. "He or Seth can direct the work happening there this morning." He walked closer to the window. "Though I'm not so sure much will get done."

The wind was howling a bit, but the sun was just peeking over the tops of the mountains and the sky was clear, so hopefully the dig out wouldn't be too bad. "We're at higher elevation here," he said, "so the mill might not have been as affected. The valley probably didn't get much of anything. That's usually how snow season starts up here."

He looked at the bed of his truck, but with the wind, it was hard to get a depth reading. "Uh-oh."

"What 'uh-oh'?" she asked, scrambling from the bed, then grabbing the duvet and pulling it around her like a cloak as she tiptoed over to him. "Brr. It's chilly in here."

"I forgot to re-load the stove last night. I just put more wood in, so it will warm up pretty fast now."

She stood next to him facing the window. "Oh," she gasped. "Will you look at that. It's gorgeous," she breathed. "It looks like a Currier and Ives painting out there. All you need is a horse-drawn sleigh."

"Wait till you see the view off the back porch."

"What was the uh-oh?" she asked, bouncing a little, probably due to bare feet on the chilly wood floor.

He pointed to the front of the cabin, where his truck was parked.

She followed his gesture, frowning, then covered her mouth as a spurt of laughter came out. "Oh, no."

The open bed of the pickup was largely filled with snow, blown into drifts against the rear window by the wind. In the middle sat the wolf head from his costume. It had an . . . interesting vibe now.

"You've gone from Big Bad Wolf to Indomitable Snowman."

"The rest of the costume is back there, too."

She shook her head. "I'm sorry." She slid a hand out from her blanket and patted his back. "But look at it this way. Next year you have two costume options."

"Those crinolines are looking better every

moment," he said, looking down into her smiling eyes. He'd been worried about how the "morning after" would go. Maybe he should thank Mom Nature for the timely distraction. "What about you? Anyone you need to call?"

She looked confused for a moment, then her expression cleared. "Oh! No. Well, not immediately anyway. I'm off today. I mean, I have things I'd like to get done. The presentation is coming up and I'll be putting in longer than usual hours, and now there's the paper." She waved a hand. "But it's not the end of the world if I get back later tonight."

He glanced outside, then back at her. "We don't exactly have county plowing up this way."

She looked back outside, and her expression fell. "Oh."

"Oh."

"So, how do you get in and out of here? I mean, I'm assuming this will be a regular event for the next few months."

"I put a big plow on the front of my truck. But at the moment, it's sitting behind the mill. They were calling for a freeze warning, but like I said, I didn't see anything about a storm. It can happen like that, though. Sometimes the snow hangs up on the other side of the range and it's clear as a bell here while they're getting hammered." He nodded toward the window. "And sometimes the hammer swings this way."

"So, what happens? I mean, I can probably scrape a little extra time off, but — do we have to wait for it to melt?"

He shifted his body so she was between him and the window. She turned to face him and he walked her back until the blanket pressed against the glass. "How much scrape time are we talking?"

She didn't laugh and push him away, as he'd half expected her to. Instead she surprised him with a slow, seductive smile, and let the duvet drop to the windowsill, then slide to the floor. "Why do you ask?"

She really was perfect for him. He scooped her up, making her squeal. His needless modesty towel dropped to the floor as he carried her over and deposited her on the bed. He followed her down, climbing directly on top of her. He braced himself on his forearms while she squirmed under him. The gleaming gold irises of her eyes were being quickly swallowed up by the rapidly expanding pupils and her lips were already parted.

"Being as it's so early and all," he began, leaning down and nipping the side of her neck, making her gasp, "we probably should wait a bit," he went on, drawing the tip of his tongue along her collarbone, then sliding his body down as he took the trail south. "We can call in the troops to get us out of here." He slid down between her legs. "A little later," he breathed, before parting her and sliding his tongue over her.

"Yes. Later." She groaned, arching off the bed as she gathered a fist full of sheet in one hand, and a fist full of his hair in the other.

He chuckled, which made her shudder against his tongue. He did love a woman who knew what she wanted and wasn't afraid to go after it.

He'd learned many of her body's secrets the night before, and a few more in the wee hours of this morning. He intended to build on that knowledge right now, and slid a finger inside of her as he suckled her into his mouth.

She came instantly, and she wasn't quiet about it. He liked that about her, too. Having a cabin in the middle of nowhere was going to come in handy, he thought. Key word there being *come.*

He slid out of her, and worked his way back up her body. She was already grabbing his shoulders, digging her nails into his skin as she urged his body up and over hers. Something about that aggressiveness had him going from rigid to diamond hard. He grappled off the side of the bed for the string of condom packets that had oh-so-mercifully still been buried deep in his gear bag. He might have actually pouted when he saw they were down to the last two. He tore one off with his teeth, and thought, *Oh well, there are other things we can do.* The outdoor shower came to mind. Nothing like a steamy outdoor shower for two in the middle of a snow day. He'd pour hot water on the damn hose to thaw it out if he had to.

"Sawyer," she urged.

"Demanding little shepherdess, you are," he said, taking care of the condom, then kissing his way back up her body. "I like that about you." He paused to spend some quality time on her nipples. Her breasts were small, but her lovely plump nipples more than made up for it.

She squirmed and shuddered, and begged him a little. Then she apparently got tired of waiting, because she hooked her ankle over his and surprised him by flipping him over on his back.

He didn't try all that hard to stop her. "You have a mean hook there, Peep," he said with a grin. Then she straddled him and slid down over him . . . and his eyes threatened to roll right back into his head.

She leaned down and bit his earlobe as she moved on top of him. "My, my," she whispered in his ear. "I see everything is big on this bad wolf."

He would have laughed with her but she was too busy driving him screaming right to the edge, and with only one condom left, he wanted this time to last. He turned the tables, rolling her to her back. "This big bad wolf is going to be a spent wolf if we don't slow it down."

She made an exaggerated pout, then proved she'd been paying attention to his body last night as well, and crossed her ankles behind his back, pulling him in deeper . . . then tilting up, and — oh, God, deeper still — then clenching those sweet, amazing muscles of hers and —

His growl was deep, guttural, and supremely heartfelt as he shuddered through his release. When he slumped over her, barely catching his weight on his forearms, he found he had absolutely nothing to complain about.

She lifted her head and nipped his chin. "It's kind of sexy when you lose control." She beamed, seeming quite pleased. "I'm not unhappy I can do that to you."

He could have told her she'd had him on the edge while sprawled on her back, snoring like a buzz saw, but the mischievous twinkle in her eye told him he might want to be careful letting her know just how far she'd already wrapped him up. He kissed her nose. "Then it's a mutual admiration society." Her cheeks turned pink again and the incongruity of that made him laugh.

Her eyes widened, which just made his chuckles deepen. She snagged a pillow and swatted him with it. "Off of me, beast."

"*Beast* is it now," he said, sliding off of her, but rolling her back to him when she tried to move away. He pulled her back tight against his chest, realizing the tactical error there when she merely pressed her sweet, sweet fanny right against his rapidly recovering . . . beast.

They squirmed and laughed, and there might have been a few more pillow swats, but eventually she gave up, breathless, and lay limp in his arms. She flung an arm dramatically over her face and turned her head away. "You win. Have your wicked, wicked way with me." She slid her arm up just enough to open one eye and look at him. "Really wicked." Then closed it again, and assumed her much aggrieved, supplicant pose.

If he hadn't already figured out he was more than half in love with her, he knew it at that moment. They'd had a fair share of deep and serious conversations in the time they'd known each other, and he liked how her mind worked, how she saw the world. They'd also never gone more than a few minutes without shared laughter, even amidst the harder topics. It had been that combination that had drawn him in. Now they added a physical conversation to the mix, as intimate a conversation as two people could have, and at times, it had been just as deep and serious . . . at others, light and playful. And all of it had been as exactly right, as natural, as what had gone before. He didn't want to lose that. He didn't want to lose her.

"Sawyer?"

He realized he'd gathered her tightly against him. Too tightly, perhaps, as she pushed gently at the arm he'd banded around her waist.

He turned her toward him instead, then tucked her into the shadow of his body as he drew his fingers down the side of her face, smiling as he wiped away a smudge of mascara that was now down below her cheekbone. "Next year, I'm thinking Indomitable Snowman for me. Raccoon for you." He leaned in, kissed her mouth when it formed an indignant "O" before she could swat him again.

He continued kissing her until the fist she'd pressed against his back relaxed, then slid gently around to cup the nape of his neck. They continued to kiss, unhurried, exploring, simply enjoying each other. In some ways, that felt more intimate than the way they'd been joined just minutes ago.

He lifted his head, waited for her to open her eyes. Her lips curved when her gaze met his. The words were right there, on the tip of his tongue. It was only because some distant part of his brain was still tied to a shred of reality that he held them back.

"Hi," she said quietly, her voice slightly hoarse, from lovemaking, from laughing. Her expression grew more serious as she reached up to lightly trace his face with her fingertips. And everything she was feeling, the affection, the confusion, the lust, the sense of connection, was all laid bare for him to see.

He understood exactly how she felt.

His lips parted and he knew he'd lost any ability to not tell her, but before he could utter the words that would irrevocably change things — for better or for worse —

his phone rang. It was loud and jangling, the ringtone he'd assigned to Seth.

They both startled at the sudden barrage of sound and he instantly rolled to his back and reached down to the floor, groping for his phone, knowing the moment was shot to hell, and wondering if he should kill Seth, or kiss him. As signs went, at this point, whatever it was the universe was trying to tell him, he really wished it would just spit it the hell out already.

He found the phone, clicked if off, but it buzzed right back to life again. Still Seth. He looked at the screen and saw there had been texts coming in while they'd been . . . otherwise engaged. The last one read "911."

Sawyer immediately sat straight up and answered it. "What's wrong?"

His grave tone had Sunny scrambling to sit up next to him, her expression full of concern.

"Hello, friends and neighbors, this is your friendly early warning service," Seth said, quite jovially.

Hearing that, a large part of Sawyer immediately relaxed. *Thank God.* Nothing had happened to anyone or anything he cared about. The remaining part of him scowled at the unwanted intrusion and thought *not yet anyway.* "Warning about what?"

"A contingent of well-meaning folk should be arriving with snowplows any —"

"Shit." Even as Seth spoke, Sawyer heard the sounds of heavy engines and loud scraping noises coming from a short distance away.

"I know this because they've already been here to dig me out. I couldn't think of a prudent way to ask them to leave you and your lovely houseguest snowbound. I'm sure they think she's up at Addie's, given how you all lit out of the party at the same time last night."

"Yeah," Sawyer said, rubbing a hand over his face.

"I tried to be discreet and text. But when those went unanswered, I went with phoneus-interruptus. Sorry if I interrupted anything," he said with a chuckle. "But better me interrupting than —"

"Got it. Thanks."

"Anytime. Please extend my hearty morning hellos to —"

Sawyer hung up on his friend's overly amused self, then looked at Sunny, whose attention had already shifted to the window and the noise that was drawing ever closer. Not exactly the way he'd hoped this interlude would end. "Seth says hi. We need to get dressed."

# Chapter Seventeen

"Do you know the only thing more mortifying than dressing up in a Bo Peep costume?" Sunny asked as she and Stevie continued carefully packing a selection of rare and endangered orchids for transport to the conservatory. "Wearing a Bo Peep costume while doing the walk of shame. In front of half the town."

To her credit, Stevie gave her a consoling look . . . before bursting out laughing. "Oh, I'm sorry," she said, unable to stop. "But the visual alone . . ." She waved a gloved hand in front of her, and covered her mouth with the other, but the spluttering laughter didn't stop.

Sunny couldn't blame her, and ended up having to squelch a snicker or two herself.

"So, then what happened?" she asked. "How did the two of you leave things?"

Sunny had told Stevie about the party, about Bailey's reaction to the lamb, which

Stevie had known about beforehand, and about ending the evening with a drive up to Sawyer's partially renovated cabin. She hadn't gone into any great detail about the night itself, other than to say that it had been quite possibly the best night of her entire life, had left her even more conflicted about what she should do, but that she had absolutely no regrets. Every part of which was true.

"He drove me down to the mill, to my car. They hadn't gotten quite as much snow there as we did up at the cabin, but there was still a good five or six inches. It's funny, but up there where they are used to that kind of snowfall, it was like no big deal."

Stevie nodded. "Here we got little more than a dusting and it's a total media freak out." She smiled, then sighed. "I bet it was pretty."

"Utterly breathtaking," Sunny said with a sigh, wishing she'd thought to take a photo on her phone to share with her friend. And maybe to have for herself as well. A keepsake. Just in case. "He really does have a beautiful spot in the world. When we were driving out, I was thinking that waking up to that every morning, all year round, has to help him put all the ugliness of war into at least a little perspective."

"Probably why he bought it," Stevie said, carefully wrapping batting around the next planter.

Sunny nodded as she took the Dragon's Mouth orchid from Stevie and cautiously stowed it in the large travel container.

"So, what now? What next?"

Sunny wiped the bare wrist above her gloved hand across her forehead. Nerves regarding the upcoming presentation, along with the humid conditions in the greenhouse were causing beads of perspiration to pop up. At least that was the convenient excuse. "I don't know," she said, honestly. "He'd mentioned earlier that he'd be willing to come here to help me transport the other two lambs Addie said she was going to get. He wants to see the town house, see where I live." She lifted a shoulder, smiled weakly. "So, I guess we're starting a long-distance relationship."

"You don't look overly enthusiastic about that. Isn't that what you want?"

Sunny stopped what she was doing, and looked at her best friend. "I honestly don't know. Sawyer belongs in Blue Hollow Falls. His life is there. Not just his work. That's the smaller part of it, actually. It's so much bigger than that. He belongs there, it's where he should be, and where he needs to be. For so many reasons. I mean, even look-ing at it as objectively as I can, big picture, once Addie's gone and Bailey has grown up, who knows . . . maybe he'd want some-thing else for himself. But for the long-term foreseeable future, he's exactly where he should be. I would never want him to change that."

"So . . . ?"

"So, that means I end up in a long-distance relationship. I don't want that, but I also don't want to stop seeing him." She looked at her friend. "So, what choice do I have?"

Stevie smiled and shook her head as she went back to work.

"What?" Sunny asked, seeing that Stevie clearly had a definite opinion on the matter, given the look on her face.

Stevie glanced up, but didn't stop what she was doing. They had to get the orchids transported by noon so they could do all the unpacking at the conservatory before the end of the day. "We all have choices," was what she said, kindly, but pointedly all the same.

"So, what, I give up everything and move to the mountains to be with him . . . and do what?" She lifted her hands. "My work is here. And I know it's 'just a job,' " she said, making air quotes, "but it's not just a job to me. It's work that I love and am passionate about. I also happen to think it's important work. Collectively, we're helping to preserve and promote the ongoing survival of the better part of two hundred species of orchids. I'm just now starting to make headway with my work on germination, . . . aaand I'm preaching to the choir," she said, trailing off as Stevie simply smiled and nodded. Sunny let out a heavy sigh. "I care about what I do and I want to do it here, but even if I was willing to change employers, Blue Hollow Falls is not commuting distance to anything having to do with my work, my studies. Heck, I'd just as soon commute to here and back, but then I wouldn't have any time left to spend with Sawyer."

"So, you have thought about it," Stevie said, sounding satisfied. "That's good."

"No, good would be finding a solution that would let me have my cake and eat it, too."

Stevie handed her the Showy Lady's Slipper she'd finished wrapping up and smiled. "Well, then, I'd say that right there is your starting point."

"Thanks, Hattie," Sawyer said when the

older woman slid his platter of lost bread and eggs over easy in front of him.

Henrietta Beauchamp was a tall woman, with an ample bosom and a posterior to match. Advanced age had not seemed to affect her posture or her belief that women simply weren't seen in public "without their face on." Her pale, wrinkled cheeks always sported a faint sheen of translucent powder, with a hint of blush — she called it rouge — adding a bit of color to her high cheekbones. The lipstick of choice was always some shade of red, and even the most talented artist would say that her penciled-on eyebrows were a work of art. He had no idea what her natural hair looked like or even if she had any at this point, but the wig she favored most often was Lucille Ball red in color and style, including the starched little scarf tied around the middle.

Despite the fact that she owned the place, she wore a traditional waitress uniform, the style dated sometime back in the fifties. The color of the shift style dress changed, but there was always a white apron tied over it, the kind with a pocket on the front to hold her ever-present order book. A book he'd never once seen her actually use while taking an order, along with the pencil that was perennially tucked behind her ear. There was a matching white kerchief, starched and folded into neat little points, tucked into the bosom pocket. She wore thick hose and thicker soled nurse's shoes, also circa 1950, and a no-nonsense, wind-up Timex watch strapped around her age-spotted wrist that was probably as old as she was.

She refilled his coffee, and nodded to the heavy white plate stacked high with the freshly toasted, golden brown, Cajun version of French bread. "Need more syrup to go with that, *cher*?" she asked, setting a little porcelain pitcher full of maple syrup next to the plate.

"No, ma'am," he said, opening up the linen napkin and spreading it on his lap. Miss Hattie believed in dining room manners, and he'd long since learned that if he didn't know the proper use of table linen, she'd be happy to give him a demonstration. "I believe this will do the job just fine, thank you."

"Mmm-hmm," she said, clearly disagreeing.

He looked up and saw pity in her dark brown eyes. "I'm good," he assured her.

"Far be it from me to offer advice where it's not appreciated," she said, which indicated she was about to do that very thing. "But all the maple syrup in the world isn't going to replace the kind of sugar you're missin'."

Good thing he hadn't taken a bite yet, or he'd have surely choked on it. "I — appreciate that," he finally managed. "But I'm fine." He smiled. "Truly."

She made a little noise that let him know what she thought about that, and moved on to fill the coffee mugs of her other regular morning patrons.

Sawyer had no more breathed a sigh of relief and taken the first bite of perfectly cooked egg, when Bailey slid in to the booth seat across from him, looking quite serious. He couldn't hide his surprise, but he swallowed the bite, smoothed his expression, then casually said, "Shouldn't you be in school right about now?"

"School is boring," she said, then folded her arms on the table, continuing to stare at him with serious regard.

"And yet," he said, taking a sip of coffee, trying to figure out the best way to handle this, "they kind of get a little upset when students just up and head out."

"Did you ever play hooky?"

He'd just started to wipe his mouth with a napkin, and tried to cover the sudden cough with a clearing of his throat. "Well, I

don't know that that has anything to do with
—"

"I *had* to talk to you," she said, her blue eyes radiating urgency. "I'm ahead in all my schoolwork and we were just having some dumb assembly today. I'm not missing anything important. I swear."

"How did you even get back up here from the valley?"

"Seth came and got me." She put her hand to her forehead, clearly playacting, yet remaining soberly serious. "I wasn't feeling well."

"Right." Sawyer glanced out through the window and saw a smiling Seth leaning against the side of his Range Rover. He lifted his hand in a short wave.

Sawyer did not wave back, but looked back at Bailey. "You should probably tell me what's going on." He put his knife and fork down carefully on the edge of his plate. "Now."

Bailey sat up straighter at that, and her calm demeanor flickered briefly. She glanced out the window at Seth, then back to Sawyer. "We have to show you something."

"We? And it couldn't wait until after school?"

She shook her head. "I'm afraid you're

going to screw this up."

He frowned. "Screw what up?"

She lifted her hands from the table, then let them fall to her lap. "Everything." She'd said it with the kind of heartfelt emotion only a ten-year-old-going-on-thirty could muster.

Given Seth was standing outside and therefore also involved in whatever this little drama was about, and Sawyer knew Seth wouldn't have encouraged Bailey to do something irresponsible that would get her into trouble, he opted to sit there calmly and listen to what Bailey had to say. "Can you be more specific?"

He assumed this must have something to do with the lamb, maybe the snow, though who the hell knew what that could be, exactly. He also knew from her past history that Bailey was far more a rule follower than a rule breaker, so this was definitely out of character. Still, despite her wise-beyond-her-years, solemn exterior, she was still just a little kid, and as such, potentially given to overexaggerated worry.

"It would be better if we just show you." She looked at his plate of food, then at him, as if asking him to decide which was more important.

He sighed, and considered whether he

should ask for a to-go box. He hated to waste food. Hattie was a step ahead of him, though, and arrived with a carryout container for the French toast and a small plastic container for the syrup. "Here you go." She slapped his tab on the table and gave Bailey a look.

To her credit, Bailey smiled angelically as if she did that all the time. "Hi, Hattie," she said with a little wave.

Hattie just nodded. "All kinds of trouble when that one comes of age," she told Sawyer under her breath. "Mark my words, cher." Then she strode off.

Bailey had already poured the syrup in the clear plastic container and snapped on the lid, then busied herself with transferring the toast to the other container while Sawyer got out his wallet and pulled a few bills out to cover his tab. She added a few foil-wrapped packets of butter, then tossed in a few jelly packets.

She looked at him and wrinkled her nose. "You don't want to save the rest of the egg, do you?"

He'd broken the yoke with his single bite of the delicious, brown sugar–laden breakfast he rarely allowed himself to have. He refused to admit that Hattie might have had a point about why he'd chosen that particular morning to indulge. He shook his head. "Don't worry about it." He slid out of the booth. "Come on. You can show me what needs showing, then Seth can take you back down to school by the lunch bell."

She made a face at that, but one look at him had her grabbing the to-go box and sliding out of the booth without another word. He didn't know if it was her attempt to hedge her bets, or just the urgency she clearly felt, but she took his hand and all but dragged him along in her wake.

He remembered the first time she'd reached for his hand, and knew that whatever this was about, he was likely going to give in on it. She had that effect on him. *Looks like you're a sucker for all the pretty faces in your life.*

He probably shouldn't have smiled at that thought, but he did. His night with Sunny might not have ended as he'd hoped, but he'd come to the decision that it was a good thing he hadn't blurted out anything that morning. She'd headed on back to the city yesterday morning after they'd been plowed out and had texted him later that she'd arrived home safely. Fortunately, D.C. hadn't been as affected by the surprise storm. He'd texted back that he was looking forward to his trip to see her, and she'd responded that she was, too.

So, their aborted morning hadn't been an ending. Things were just beginning. And he'd spent most of the next twenty-four hours telling himself he was good with that.

He wiped all expression from his face when they reached the parking lot. Seth had parked his Land Rover next to Sawyer's truck and was wise enough to hurry things along and avoid any protracted discussion. "Good morning," he said to Sawyer, then nodded to the to-go box that Bailey held in her hand. "Beignets?"

She shook her head. "Lost bread."

Seth closed his eyes in sincere reverence. "Also a good choice." He shifted his weight off his Land Rover and said, "Think I have time to run in and grab a cup of —" He took one look at Sawyer's expression and clapped his hands together. "Okay, then, on the road we go."

"On the road to where, exactly?"

"I didn't tell him that part yet," Bailey explained.

"Oh," Seth said, but regrouped quickly. "Okay. Back up to the mill," he told Sawyer.

"Shotgun," Bailey said, and scooted around to the passenger side of Seth's truck.

*Smart move,* Sawyer wanted to tell her, but pointed to his truck and said, "In there, kiddo." She'd managed to get what she wanted, but he thought a little more conversation might be in order, if for no other reason than he didn't want her to think this was the new status quo.

One thing was for certain, Bailey was definitely coming out of her shell. He just hoped that whatever it was she was emerging into would be to her benefit. She was too smart by half, and twice as sharp as most kids her age.

They drove through town in silence, but when he took the turn at the light and headed up toward Falls Road, he glanced her way, and caught her looking at his tattoo again. She glanced away.

He drove another mile or so, then said, "You want to talk about it?"

She didn't pretend she didn't know what he meant. "I knew someone who was in Special Forces," she said. "He had a tattoo kind of like that. It had more stuff on it, though."

"Was he a teacher?" he asked.

She shook her head. "My second foster dad."

That sat Sawyer back. So many directions that could go, he thought, praying like hell it wasn't a bad one. "Good guy?" he said, trying to find the right way in.

420

"The best," she said, with a heartfelt sigh.

Sawyer relaxed. "I'm glad to hear that." He glanced over at her, relieved to see that her expression was one of fondness, not pensiveness, or worse. "What happened?"

"His wife died right after they took me in." She quickly added, "I didn't know her. She was already in the hospital. And I was little then."

"Did he have kids of his own?"

She nodded. "One. He was a grown-up, though. He was in the Army, too."

"So he was an older man, then?"

"Like a grandpa," she said. "Maybe not as old as Miss Addie though."

He smiled at that. "Did his wife dying mean you couldn't stay?"

"No, I stayed. I was there longer than anywhere else. I think he would have adopted me. But he had P.D. . . ."

"PTSD?"

She nodded. "Yeah. That. He had bad dreams. And sometimes he thought I was in the Army, too."

Sawyer frowned now. "Did he ever —"

"He never hurt me," she said, immediately and not a little fiercely. "He loved me." She turned away then, and from the corner of his eye, he saw her work to get her composure back under her control.

He wished she hadn't had the kind of life that made her so good at that particular skill. "Good," he said. "Sounds like he tried to do the best by you."

"He did. But then . . . it got worse, and he —" She broke off, frowned hard, and looked out the passenger side window.

"Where is he now?" Sawyer asked, hoping that was the easiest way for her to tell him the last part.

"In a hospital," she said. "Where they take care of soldiers with P . . . D . . . you know."

"I do. I'm glad he's getting help. I'm very sorry he couldn't keep taking care of you."

"They didn't want him to. After his wife died, social services came," she added. "But he said since I was doing okay, didn't it make more sense to leave me where I was, and so they did. But after he went to the hospital . . ." She let that trail off, and Sawyer didn't press her further. "I got to go see him once. But he didn't know who I was anymore. They explained to me that . . . inside his head . . . he was in the war all the time. So, it didn't mean he didn't care about me." She paused, then shrugged. "I read him a storybook. It was one he used to read to me. *Goodnight Moon.* I don't know if he got it." She looked away again. "I didn't go back."

"I'm sorry for that," he said, his heart breaking for her. "I'm glad he's somewhere where he's getting help from people who know how to take care of him. I'm sure he'd have done right by you if he could."

She nodded. "I think so, too."

Sawyer understood now why she'd believed she could trust him so quickly. Certain kinds of triggers could get implemented at a very young age. That Special Forces tattoo had been one for her. He was just thankful that this particular trigger had served her well.

"Do you have bad dreams sometimes?" she asked, after they'd driven a few more minutes in silence.

He glanced at her. "No. I — I talked to someone. When I got out of the Army. It helped me. A lot. So I don't have bad dreams."

"No PD —" She just waved a hand, and that made him smile.

"No."

"Good," she said, then sat back, looking both relieved and happy.

Sawyer spent the rest of the drive to the mill trying to unknot the lump that seemed to have permanently formed in his throat. Bailey was a pretty special little girl. And, right or wrong, he was no longer as inclined to be upset with her for her little adventure today.

He turned onto the narrow service road that went down to the lower lot behind the mill. The bigger construction equipment they'd needed early on was gone now, and the materials they were currently working with were mostly all stored inside. Which was a good thing, given everything was still blanketed in a few inches of snow, despite the return to warmer, sunnier weather that day and the day before. Another day or two more of sunshine and the snow would all be gone.

Sawyer backed in so his door was next to Seth's when they both climbed out. "What's this all about?" he asked his friend, keeping his voice quiet.

"You'll see," Seth said, but his tone was straightforward, not teasing, and he nodded toward the trail behind the mill.

Confused, having assumed whatever it was had something to do with the mill, Sawyer looked at the trail, then back to Seth. "What the hell?"

"I talked to Sunny last night," Bailey said.

Both men turned to find her standing right behind them. "Okay," Sawyer said. "I'm glad you two are talking." Which was true. He realized then that maybe he should have called her himself, instead of simply responding to her text in kind. He suddenly felt like a dorky adolescent who wasn't confident enough about what he wanted to simply up and go after it. He'd been trying not to be any more aggressive about those wants than he already had been, as well as be respectful enough to give Sunny space and time to make up her own mind. He'd been quite content knowing she hadn't spent the three-hour-plus, post-storm drive home talking herself out of a future with him, and was still expecting they'd spend an upcoming weekend together. One step at a time. That was the best way to move things forward.

*Liar. You post-adolescent dork.* He should have called her. Leave it to the ten-year-old to point out the obvious.

"She said she didn't know when she was coming out here next," Bailey went on.

Sawyer snapped out of his thoughts, looked back at Bailey, who seemed more than a bit perturbed about that. "Ah. Well, that's because I'm going to drive out to see her."

"When?" she wanted to know.

"I . . . uh . . . I don't know yet." He was about to tell her about the lamb transport aspect of his trip north, but then wondered if Addie had mentioned that to Bailey yet or if it was some kind of surprise. He looked at Seth, but got no help there. "You're going up to see her in a few weeks, right? For the school holiday weekend?"

Bailey just sighed and looked at Seth. "See? I told you."

Seth nodded, lifted a shoulder in a short shrug, like *What are you gonna do?* "Yep. I thought he might have pulled it together, but . . . you were right."

"*He's* about to get in his truck and head back down to Hattie's for a fresh order of . . . everything on the menu," Sawyer told them, his patience for this little game nearing an end.

"Well, come on this way," Seth said, all Mr. Magnanimous. He turned and followed Bailey out from between the two vehicles, "Let's go see what there is to see. Then I'll come down and join you on that protein and carb load bandwagon." He clapped Sawyer on the back and grinned. "We're probably going to need it."

Will pulled up just then and got out of his SUV. "Good," he said matter-of-factly, "you got him here."

Sawyer thought he probably looked downright comical when his head swiveled from Will, back to Seth and Bailey, then back to

426

Will. "You're in on this?"

Will just closed the door of his vehicle and pulled on a pair of heavy work gloves. "Oh, I think we're all going to be in on this if we have a hope of pulling it off." In his usual quiet style, he simply turned and headed across the lot, then on across the snow-covered grass toward the opening where the trail led into the woods.

Bailey trotted ahead and fell in step behind him. Seth gestured to Sawyer to go ahead of him. "Go with it, man," he advised his friend, his smile sincere. "Trust me. It's all a good thing."

# Chapter Eighteen

"It's beautiful, Sunny," Sawyer said, stepping through the French doors at the rear of her town house and into the keyhole garden. "It's pretty incredible what you've been able to do in such a small space."

"You should see it in the spring when everything is blooming."

He walked out from under the tent awning that covered the small, flagstone patio and fingered the ends of the multitudinous scarves that were tied to each of the support poles, some silk, some cotton, some woven, most all of them bleached heavily by years of exposure to the sun.

"My mother had a thing for scarves," Sunny said, humor and honest affection lacing her words. "I guess I've gotten used to them, because I couldn't take them down."

"I think they're kind of festive," Sawyer said, meaning it.

"Oh, no," Sunny said, "this is festive." She

reached back inside the door and flipped a light switch. It was late Friday afternoon, and being early November, that meant dusk was fast encroaching. The shadows were deep enough that the twinkling lights filling every nook and cranny of the backyard were quite easy to see.

"Wow," Sawyer said, stepping off the patio, out from under the awning. Strand upon strand of small white party lights had been wrapped in and around the branches of the short dogwood that filled the back corner. They also outlined the edge of the six-foot-tall, board-over-board privacy wall that bordered the three sides of the tiny yard, and were wrapped around the support posts of the awning, and the edges of the awning itself. "That is very festive."

"I'm only sorry you're not getting the full musical accompaniment to go with it."

He arched a brow at that. "Should I be afraid to ask?"

"Very," she said, smiling and pointing back under the awning to the tall speakers that framed the doorway. "My friends used to call it Woodstock South. But at least old Mr. Bennett next door doesn't scowl at me any longer when we take our trash out at the same time, so I have that going for me now."

"Sounds like your mom believed in putting a lot of life in her life."

"She did that," Sunny said, smiling as he walked back toward her, happy he was here. And a lot less nervous about it now that he was.

He'd called her the night after she'd returned home from the Halloween party, and they'd talked for several hours. The topics had been as wide-ranging as all of their conversations. Sprinkled with topics of importance, some that were silly and innocuous, all of them entertaining. Five days later, it had become something of an evening ritual between them. She'd text him hello when she got up in the morning, as he'd already been awake and working for a few hours at that point, and he'd call her when they were both ready to turn in. There were the very occasional texts sent during the day, mostly photos showing something one of them thought the other might like to see, but they seemed to have tacitly agreed not to intrude too much into each other's workday.

She might be a little more sleep deprived than she'd like to be, but with the uninterrupted time at work, it seemed like a minor sacrifice to make. The only downside was that every minute they spent talking had made her miss him that much more. She still heard from Addie regularly, and now she and Bailey were talking, too, and she was enjoying getting all three perspectives about what was going on at the mill in particular, and the Hollow in general. Having met most of the other guild members and their families at the Halloween party, she felt she was really becoming a part of the town and its goings-on. And she liked it. She liked it a lot. *Who knew?*

In fact, it had highlighted just how cut off she was from the people in her own little world. Mr. Bennett was actually the only neighbor she knew by name, and they were hardly acquaintances, let alone friends. She'd lived in her house her entire life and that was the sum total of her involvement in the neighborhood. She could put the blame on city living and the high turnover that happened in the neighborhoods there, hers included. But she knew it was also due to her not making any effort to reach out. Stevie's family lived in the Adams Morgan area, right in the city, and they were having block parties every other week it seemed. It hadn't happened that way for her in Old Town, and yet, she hadn't been in the Hollow but a few times, and already felt like she knew everyone there.

"Bailey told me about your fairy gardens," Sawyer said, sliding his arms around her from behind, then turning her to face him. "I'm sure the wee folk enjoy the party lights."

"Mmm," she said, sliding her arms around his neck, her body singing to life at his touch. "I hope so." She was amazed they hadn't torn each other's clothes off and gone at it right in her foyer the moment he'd arrived. Their evening conversations hadn't been entirely centered on local gossip and revealing childhood stories. Some of them, in fact, had gotten downright . . . heated. And in a very good way.

She'd worked herself up into quite a state of nervous anticipation. She knew things would be good between them when they were finally together again, but she'd had some qualms about having him in her home, mostly because he'd be the first man she'd ever invited there. She still went to bed in the room she'd slept in since child-hood, though she'd long since had it redone to reflect the adult who lived in it now.

Her mother's room was simply her moth-er's room and she couldn't imagine moving in there, particularly since by the end it had far more resembled a hospital room, com-plete with adjustable bed and racks for holding various bags of intravenous fluids and oxygen tanks.

She didn't think she'd ever be comfortable claiming it for her own. She thought she might turn it into her office, with built-in library shelves to store all of her rapidly expanding research materials.

"Where are your thoughts?" he asked, kissing her forehead, then nudging her mouth up to his.

"On you," she said. "On having you here. It's not something I've done before."

"I know," he said, because she had told him that already. "If it's not comfortable, I told you I'd be happy to book a room and —"

"Don't be silly," she said. "It's fine." She stretched up to kiss him again, thrilled beyond measure that she could simply and finally do that. She thought she might be doing it often over the next few days. Bank them for the next time they were apart. "It really is," she told him when he eyed her skeptically. She fingered the collar of the pale blue chambray button-down he wore. "This might be the first time I've seen you in something other than sweaty T-shirts or fur."

"Yeah, I get that a lot."

She laughed, and he caught her in a soul-searing kiss before she'd finished. By the time he lifted his head, more than her ability to breathe had been compromised. Her knees were feeling a bit wobbly as well.

"I missed you, Bo Peep."

She smiled and flushed and felt basically pretty damn good all over. "You should know, I've had to return it to the rental shop," she said with mock gravity, placing her hand over his heart. "So, if you had some kinky ideas about pantaloons and a shepherd hook —"

He covered her hand with his own and matched her mock gravity. "As sexy as that outfit was, what with the millions of impenetrable layers of crinoline and the turtleneck that covered every inch of your torso, as it happens, the only ideas I had, kinky or otherwise, require zero costumes. In fact, I was thinking a clothing-optional weekend would simplify matters entirely."

Her eyebrows lifted. "Wow, well, how very . . . thoughtful of you. Thrifty, too. Think of all the laundry soap I'll save."

"I try," he said, humbly. "And seeing as your work is all about conservation, we could shower together, too." He leaned down to kiss the corners of her mouth. "Save on water."

She sighed and leaned against him, wondering how she'd gone a whole week without this, conveniently refusing to think about how much harder that was going to be after this weekend was over. She felt young and silly — it had been a week, for goodness' sake, not a year — but maybe that's what it felt like when you were falling head over heels. And falling felt pretty damn good as it turned out. When it wasn't terrifying, anyway.

He was spending that night with her, all of Saturday and Saturday night, then they were picking up the lambs in Maryland Sunday morning, and heading on down to Blue Hollow Falls that afternoon. She'd stay with him at the cabin that night, and drive straight to D.C. very early Monday morning, putting in an hour or two at the end of the day to make up the difference if she was late due to city traffic, which was pretty much guaranteed.

It had initially been planned that he would just pick the lambs up and head home Sunday afternoon. But when she'd commented that she'd miss seeing Bailey's face when the two new arrivals were introduced, he'd offered that alternative idea. Though she might be kicking herself come the crack of dawn on Monday, right now it meant another night together, so she was all for it.

The truth was, in addition to seeing Bailey, she wanted to be back in the Hollow, too. She was already trying to figure out how she could fit in a quick little trek out to the greenhouse. She'd promised Stevie she'd take some photos. And she wanted to see it again, take more time, just . . . more.

But that was Sunday. Right now they had a whole night ahead of them, followed by a whole day. Just the two of them. It felt like a glorious vacation to her, filled with endless possibilities. "There might be a flaw in your water conservation theory," she said, starting to unbutton the front of his shirt.

"Oh?" he said, looking down at what she was doing, and making not a single effort to stop her. "Why is that?"

She gazed up into his blue eyes, thinking they looked even more brilliant against the blue of his shirt, his dark hair, and the tan he'd likely have all winter from spending so much of the summer and fall out of doors. "You're assuming we'd only be in the shower the normal length of time."

"Ah," he said. "You may have a point."

She'd unbuttoned his shirt halfway down his chest, revealing a snowy white, perfectly clean T-shirt. She'd been about to tease him about that, but he was nudging her away just far enough so he could reach down and grab the hem of the button up and the tee and pull them both over his head.

"Well, hello there," she said. She wanted to rub her hands all over that magnificent chest. Then take a bite out of it. That's how good he looked.

"You make your living doing research," he said, "so I thought you'd probably want to test your theory out." He lifted his arms. "I'm simply a willing test study subject."

She stepped back into his arms, almost closing her eyes in bliss as she breathed in the scent of him again. "I was thinking . . ."

"Go on," he said, rubbing his hands up along her spine, tucking her more snugly against him.

"Well, it wouldn't really be a proper conservation test if we don't actually need a shower."

His eyebrows lifted in consideration. "See, that's why you're the scientist."

"Botanist."

"Tomato, potahto."

She giggled. "So, do you have any ideas on how we could get a little perspiration going? Maybe you could help me in the garden with some repotting," she said, all chaste and innocent. "Or we could water the —"

"So, your bedroom would be . . . ?"

"Top of the stairs, on the left," she answered immediately.

A second later she was head down over the back of his shoulder, with one of his strong arms clamped over the back of her thighs, while her hands grappled at his waist for a handhold.

"I'd have carried you the traditional way, but it's a narrow staircase."

Her squeal of surprise had changed to a squeal of something else entirely when his hands slid up her bare calves, under the tea-length skirt she'd been wearing. *Old habits die hard.* She thought her mother would be thrilled to know her daughter tended to favor skirts over trousers, even when given a choice.

*Choices.*

She'd been exploring a few of those over the past week, but hadn't told him about any of it yet. It was too soon. And a part of her wanted to see what it would be like when they were together again. See if it was as wonderful as she'd remembered, or if she'd painted over their time together with a fantasy brush.

At the moment, staring at his very fine backside while he drew his fingertips farther and farther up the inside of her thigh, she was thinking maybe she'd downplayed just how wonderful it had been. Of course, that might be because all the blood rushing to her head was making her dizzy.

She whooped out a laugh when he slid her over his shoulder and deposited her on her bed with a bounce. She was already reaching for him as he followed her down.

In the decadently wanton hours that had followed . . . and extended through Saturday, and last night . . . before starting up again as the sun had come up that morning, Sunny learned a little more about Sawyer, and a lot more about herself.

She learned he was picky about his toothpaste, but thought body soap doubled perfectly well as shampoo. She learned he eschewed chocolate and sweets, not because they weren't good for him, but because he had absolutely zero self-control around them. As evidenced by the now-empty container of leftover chocolate frosting that had been sitting in her fridge since she'd made cupcakes for Stevie's birthday. Although, to be fair, it had served an additional use as a foreplay condiment. She'd never be able to look at cupcake toppings again without blushing.

She'd learned that he didn't make his bed — something she already knew from that night at the cabin — but that he never left clothes lying on the floor. Well, he might have initially left them there, mostly because they'd been yanked off in the heat of — *so much heat* — but he routinely picked them up, his and hers, whenever he next left the bed.

She learned he would help with anything she asked him to do in the kitchen, but should never be left to his own devices on dinner prep. He had very different ideas from her as to the kinds of things that belonged together in the same pan. If it was a leftover, if was fair game. Conversely, he also made the fluffiest, tastiest scrambled eggs she'd ever eaten. Who knew using a food processor to whip eggs would create something so delicious? And he liked his toast one shade this side of burnt, which was exactly how she liked hers. Raspberry jam for her. Apple butter for him. He'd brought her a homemade jar of the sweet, brown spread, a gift from Addie, then gone through half of it himself. He'd promised her her own jar on his next trip.

About herself she'd learned that she liked having someone around who could open the raspberry jam jar without running it under scalding hot water for ten minutes, then threatening to smash it with a hammer.

She'd learned that showers for two were, indeed, significantly more entertaining than showering alone, but she'd been right in assuming her water bill would not be getting any lower. And she was perfectly fine with that.

She'd learned that while the utter peace and quiet she'd come to treasure over the past nine or so months was still a balm to her soul, hearing him use his lovely baritone to sing eighties pop tunes was the perfect soundtrack when the silence started to feel oppressive rather than restorative. That he easily and quite wittily made up lyrics for the words he didn't know, many of them delightfully bawdy, added tremendously to her enjoyment.

Most shocking of all, she also learned that after less than forty-eight hours of having him under her roof, she wasn't sure she'd ever be as comfortable banging around in the place by herself again. Her mother had been larger than life and such a huge presence, in ways both good and bad, for so long, Sunny had honestly been concerned about her ability to live with anyone else, ever again. The soundtrack that had been life with her mother haunted the house, echoing from every room, every corner. She didn't think any number of years would ever completely silence that echo.

She smiled now, thinking that after only two days with Sawyer, the kitchen would forever echo a terrible rendition of the Back Street Boys' "I Want It That Way." In the shower, it would be Elton John's "I'm Still Standing," which would also forever make her blush. And in the backyard, her mother's sanctuary, her own sanctuary, it would be Frank Sinatra's "It Had to Be You," which he'd sung to her as they'd danced under the fairy lights. For that gift alone, she could have loved him forever.

But living with someone was about far more than singing down the ghosts of her past. She didn't think she ever wanted to give up the sublime and treasured gift of being able to set her own schedule to suit her own needs, doing what she wanted, when she wanted, whether it be at six o'clock in the evening, or three o'clock in the morning. She didn't have to set her clock to anyone's medication schedule, or sleep with one eye open in case a medical machine buzzer went off.

She was at the kitchen counter, staring out the window into the backyard, rinsing off the last of their breakfast dishes so they could get on the road to Maryland, when he came up behind her and slid his arms around her waist. He had a habit of doing that, one she hoped he'd never break. He leaned down and nudged her hair aside to kiss the nape of her neck, in that spot he already knew she loved most. It made her shiver in delight.

"The bags are packed and in the back of the Cooper." He kissed her there again and she could feel him grin against her now-heated skin. "I even made the bed."

"Racking up those brownie points," she teased, smiling. "I approve."

"I was hoping you could show me the brownie point redemption catalog later so I could pick out my prize."

She laughed and leaned in to the warmth of him. Her eyes drifted closed and she thought, *Then again, maybe even the biggest sacrifices were worth it.*

# Chapter Nineteen

"Did you tell her?" Bailey asked. She'd come out of Addie's cabin and was heading across the yard before they'd even parked his truck.

Sawyer climbed out, gave her a little shake of his head, and saw her breathe a little sigh of relief.

"Tell me what?" Sunny asked, as she hopped down from the passenger side.

"Nice," Bailey said, pointing down at her hiking boots.

Sunny smiled and pointed one toe, turning the ankle-high leather boot one way, then the other. "Thanks. I figure I should be ready for anything up here at this point."

"They won't last one winter up here," she said. "You need something waterproof."

Sunny's smile drooped. "Huh. Well, maybe when you come visit me, we can go boot shopping."

Sawyer watched the two and thought what

a difference six weeks had made, for both Bailey and Sunny. Bailey was still Bailey, and he noted she remained quiet and watchful when she was around most folks, but with him, Addie, Seth, and now Sunny, she'd clearly opted to start sharing her observations rather than keep them all inside her head.

"Hey, Bailey," Sawyer said, motioning her over to the back of the truck. They'd gone to the mill first and left Sunny's car there. Since they had to go right by it on the way to his cabin, and because they'd already spent most of the day in separate cars, they'd opted to take the trip up to Addie's in his truck. He lowered the tailgate and opened the door to the cap he'd put on the back after the last snow. "Can you help me with this?"

She came right over. "With what?" Her face lit up and he liked that she was also starting to be as open about revealing her emotions as she was about her thoughts. It made her seem more like a kid, even if she was still ten going on thirty. "Did you get the mesh wire to put around the rest of the pasture fencing?"

He nodded. "I did. And Seth is going to bring over more board fencing he had left over, too, so we can make the space even bigger. He motioned into the bed of the truck.

Bailey peeked inside, then saw the two crates. Her mouth dropped open and her eyebrows climbed halfway up her tanned little foreheard.

"Addie thought that since sheep are flock animals, it would be better for — what did you name her again?"

Bailey was still staring, slack-jawed, into the back of the truck. "Peep." She finally tore her gaze away and looked at Sawyer. "Sunny said she was a triplet. Are these the other two?"

"One is her sister, but the other female isn't related. Distant cousin, maybe." The third lamb had been a male, and Sawyer didn't want to get into a discussion on breeding or the differences in male/female sheep relationships. Although, on second thought, given all the farms she'd lived on, he suspected Bailey could probably tell him a thing or three about that. She was at least one live goat birth ahead of him, at any rate.

"Addie knows?" she asked, and he could see she was banking her hope against any possibility that this might not actually be happening.

"It was her idea," Sunny said, walking over. "I guess I should have thought of it when I got Peep." She grinned at Bailey. "I like the name."

Bailey nodded, but looked pleased that Sunny liked her idea. "I think I'll call that one Red," she said, pointing to the other triplet. "And since that one's a girl, too, it can't be Wolfie. Or Thor. Since she's older . . ." She looked at Sawyer and a mischievous light twinkled in her eyes. "How about Grandma?"

"I like it," Sawyer said, though he planned on letting Bailey tell Addie about her naming strategy.

"Addie said she's already got plans for the wool when it comes time to shear them," Sunny told her. "Apparently, they turn more gray and red when they get older." She laughed. "Which actually makes their names that much more perfect." She put her hand up to high-five Bailey, but instead she opted to give Sunny a quick hug.

"Thank you," she told Sunny. Then she turned to Sawyer, and hugged him full out. "Thanks, Sawyer. Thanks for going to get them." She looked up at him, put her hand up next to her mouth, and whispered, "And thanks for getting her here." She pointed surreptitiously to Sunny.

Sawyer could see Sunny's ears prick up at that, but he smiled over Bailey's head and shrugged, as if to say, "crazy kids." But he could tell Sunny knew something was up.

"My pleasure, kiddo," he said, and gave her braid a tug. "Go ahead and hop up in there and help move the crates to the gate."

The next two hours were spent unloading, then getting the critters down the hill and to the fenced-in former-garden-turned-paddock area. Fortunately, the sun had been shining and temperatures had been up in the fifties all week, so the better part of the snow had melted. It made for a muddy, mucky mess, but it was far easier to traverse the downhill path that way than in the slippery, icy snow.

Peep began bleating the moment she laid eyes on the other two lambs. Sawyer didn't know if sheep siblings could recognize one another, and there was a fair amount of head butting and general trouncing of each other going on, but nobody was getting hurt, so he thought things would work out okay. Seth showed up in the middle of it all, and he and Sawyer spent another hour shoring up the fence so it would be sturdy enough for when the sheep got bigger, and adding the taller mesh around the rest of the wood fencing so they could have a larger grazing area.

Bailey took Sunny over to the old stone crofter's hut that had been built right into the side of the mountain, just at the edge of the small pasture. Addie had used the place for storage and a potting shed back when she'd had her vegetable garden there. Sawyer was working on the fencing just outside the open doorway, and he shamelessly listened in, curious whether Bailey would spill the beans, but not otherwise intruding on their time alone.

Bailey showed Sunny how Will and Hanford — he of oak barrel ice cream churn fame — had spent time earlier in the week gutting out the interior of the croft and patching up some of the stonework to turn it into a makeshift stable.

"This is amazing," Sunny said, looking around. "Perfect, really. Will they all be okay in here together?"

Bailey nodded. "The goats did fine that way, except when they were pregnant or just had babies. I've been reading about these kinds of sheep. They should be fine." She was quiet for a few moments while Sunny scoped out the place more closely, then asked, "Are you staying?"

Sunny nodded. "Tonight? Yep. I'm going to have to leave really early though, to get in to the city before it's too awfully late, so

I don't think I'll see you tomorrow."

"Oh," Bailey said, sounding a little deflated.

"But you're coming to see me in, what, five days? Addie and I worked it out to meet halfway on Friday after I get done working."

"She told me," Bailey said, politely enough, but there was no real enthusiasm either.

Sunny must have heard it, too, because she asked, "Do you still want to come?" sounding sincerely surprised by the apparent shift. There was another pause, and then she said, "*Oh,* you're worried about the lambs, aren't you?" She laughed. "I wish I could say you can just bring them with you, but I really don't have anywhere for them to stay. I think they'd do a pretty good number on my garden."

"Maybe you could bring me back on Sunday, and stay over to Monday. It's a holiday, so you won't have to get up so early. I could ask Sawyer if it's okay for you to stay with him."

Sawyer might have choked a little on that last part and hoped he didn't give himself away, as he was now about a hair's breadth from the open side window, no longer even trying to look like he wasn't listening in.

"I'm sure he won't mind," Bailey went on.

"Well, I —"

"He likes you," Bailey blurted out. "A lot."

He heard Sunny's soft laugh; then she said, "Well, that's a good thing. I like him a lot, too. But, unfortunately, I've got some work to do at the conservatory that weekend for the presentation later the following week. I was sort of hoping you'd come and help me with it."

"I can do that," Bailey said, her polite tone back. Her enthusiasm meter was still around zero, however.

"I thought you were kind of excited to come," Sunny said, her tone one of sincere curiosity. "It's okay if you'd rather stay here. I know I'd probably feel the same if I had new little four-legged charges. I know it might sound funny, but how you feel about your lamb — lambs now — is how I feel about my orchids."

"But they're just plants," Bailey said and Sawyer smiled, because she'd sounded just like Sunny. Not accusatory, but sincerely curious.

"Plants are living things, too," Sunny said. "Not in the way animals are, but they need air, and they need food, and the right kind of temperature in order to survive."

"I guess I never thought of it that way."

There was a pause; then she said, "So, you really love them. Your orchids?"

"I do," Sunny said.

Sawyer could almost hear Bailey's heart sink and his own took a bit of a hit as well.

Then Sunny said, "If you'd like, I could show you how to grow some. There are some species of North American orchids that grow wild in mountain areas like this. We could probably get some Showy Lady's Slippers to grow on Addie's property, not too far from the house."

"Are they rare?"

"Some are, but I was thinking of starting off with something a little hardier."

"That would be cool," Bailey said, sounding sincere, but like she was still mulling it over. "When could we do that? You'd come up here to help, right?"

"I would, and we could do it as soon as the temperatures are right."

"Not in the winter, then."

There was another pause and Sawyer assumed Sunny was shaking her head no.

Then Bailey said, "You grow them all year in your greenhouses at work though, right?"

"We control the environment there, so yes. We can start yours there, then transplant them."

"Okay, cool," she said. "We should check

452

on Sawyer and Seth. They're probably done." There was a definite spark in her voice now, and while Sunny might think it was about her orchid growing offer, Sawyer suspected it had a different source entirely.

He quickly moved away from the window and was staple-gunning mesh to a fence post when Bailey came around the corner of the croft.

"Sunny said she has to leave early tomorrow, so we need to go down to the mill now," Bailey told him. She moved closer, and looked over her shoulder to see if Sunny had followed her. "I don't think we can wait," she said in a whisper. She glanced over her shoulder again, but Sunny had walked across to where the lambs were scrambling around and was laughing at their antics. Bailey sighed in relief, then looked back to Sawyer and said, "It's all going to work out. I told her how much you liked her, and she said she liked you a lot, too. But we have to show her so she knows it will all work out."

Sawyer's heart had been yanked in so many directions since the two sisters had come into his life. He wondered if they had any idea how similar they were. Caretakers by nature, whether of flora or fauna, and survivors, both of them, sturdy and strong, but with hearts that were still very tender.

He finished stapling the last of the mesh and scooped up the leftover. "I think we can manage it. Hold up," he said when Bailey looked like she was about to run off to tell Sunny and Seth they were leaving. "Bailey —" He started, then paused, because she'd turned back to him, and gone was that guarded ten-year-old who kept herself carefully apart. All the hope in the world was shining out of those big baby blues, and he wanted like hell to promise her the moon and the stars for being so damn brave. He wanted to tell her that it had in some part been her willingness to put herself out there with her newfound Blue Hollow Falls family that had pushed him to do the same with Sunny.

Instead, he was as honest as he could be. "What you've done, and Seth, Will, too —"

"You've helped, too," she said, and he could see her bracing herself, pulling back behind that carefully guarded wall. He hated that.

"I have, and that's because I think it's a really great thing you did, are doing. It shows how gigantic your heart is. Big enough to fit all of us inside, those lambs over there, and who knows what else. I know you can't comprehend what a good thing that is, but it shows what kind of person you are."

"You're going to tell me it won't work. She won't stay."

"I'm going to tell you that we can't make her stay. That's not the same thing. Some people sit around and moan that life isn't giving them what they want. You didn't do that. You got up and figured out a solution. That's damn impressive." He didn't apologize for the swear word, because she'd earned the accolade. "But it's not a guarantee. That's all I'm saying here. She'll love you more for it, there's not a single doubt in my mind. But the rest . . . it's complicated."

Bailey didn't reply. She wasn't pouting or anything, but her expression could only be described as stubborn. Privately, Sawyer thought that trait would likely end up serving her just as well as the others he'd mentioned. Maybe more. She didn't like hearing something couldn't be done. Most of the world's biggest successes were motivated by that very same trait.

"I'm on your side," he told her, walking over and putting a hand on her shoulder when she turned back to watch Sunny and Seth laughing over the lambs. "I want her here, too."

Bailey looked up at him. "You really do?"

"I can make you one promise that I know I can keep."

"What is that?"

"That I will always be honest with you." He crouched down so they were at the same eye level and gently held on to both of her arms so she faced him. She held his gaze as directly as anyone he'd ever met. She'd put half the men in his unit to shame with her ability to maintain eye contact. He smiled at that. "I will do my best to give Sunny every reason there is to want to figure out a solution that will have her spending as much time in Blue Hollow Falls as she can. And I think she wants that, too. Not just for me, but for you, for Addie. Her biggest concern when we decided to —" He faltered for a moment.

"Start dating?"

"Yes," he said, relieved. Sometimes adults could so overcomplicate things. "She worried that if we decided at some point we didn't want to date anymore, it might make things awkward for you. She didn't want that to happen."

"Me, either," Bailey said, quite bluntly. Equally bluntly, she added, "But you live here and she's my sister, so it's not like we couldn't get over it if something happened."

Sawyer laughed out loud at that, causing Sunny and Seth to look their way, both smiling.

He sent them a little wave, then looked back at Bailey. "Well, see, that's what Seth said."

"He's a good friend," she said. "He has my back."

Sawyer chuckled. "Mine, too. And you couldn't ask for a better person on your six."

Her eyes brightened. "I know what that means. Seth told me it's like if there is a huge clock lying flat on top of your head, and the twelve is in front of you, then the six is in back of you. So, having your back means he has your six o'clock."

Sawyer grinned. "Exactly."

She studied him with focused regard. "So, do you think you'll ever stop liking Sunny?"

Sawyer glanced over at Sunny, who glanced up just then, as if feeling his gaze on her, and immediately smiled. "I don't think so," he said.

"Good. Then we just have to get her to say yes," Bailey said, as if it was so obvious she didn't get why the adults were being so lame. She grabbed his hand, pulled up. "So, let's go. We're burning daylight."

"Did you get that from Seth, too?" he

said, chuckling and letting her drag him along.

She shook her head. "Mr. Will says it. A lot."

Sawyer nodded, smiled. "Sounds about right."

"I'll go up and make sure it's okay with Miss Addie," she said, all bottled energy now. "I'll meet you at the truck." She started to take off, then ran over to the lambs first. She entered the enclosure and went over to them, breaking them apart with absolute confidence that she wasn't going to get nipped or bopped by an errant hoof, then proceeded to hug each lamb and give them all stern instructions on their expected behavior until she returned.

"I know I'd listen to her," Seth said, coming to stand next to Sawyer.

Sunny and Sawyer both nodded, then watched as Bailey left the paddock, careful to exit through the double panel they'd set up to keep the sheep from inadvertently escaping when anyone entered or exited. And to their collective shock, all three lambs trotted over to the gate after she'd closed it, then wandered over to the water trough and began calmly sipping away, as if they'd been doing that the entire time.

"She's the sheep whisperer," Sunny said.

"Come on," Bailey called out, already halfway up the steep trail that led to the house.

"And half mountain goat," Sawyer added.

"Where are we going?" Sunny asked, as they began the climb back up the hill. "Does this have anything to do with whatever nefarious plans have been going on behind my back?" She laughed when both Seth and Sawyer instantly pasted on innocent expressions. "You're about as subtle as Addie."

Sawyer winced. "That transparent?"

"Like glass."

"Well, the suspense will be over shortly," Seth said, then jogged ahead and on up to the top like it was nothing more than a Sunday stroll in the park.

"You can see why the two of them get along so well," Sawyer said, holding Sunny's hand to help her over the slick, muddier parts.

"So, you're not going to tell me? Not even a little hint?" She leaned in and batted her eyelashes.

"You drive a tough bargain," he said, dropping a fast kiss on her mouth. "But I think I'm more afraid of the ten-year-old in this instance."

Sunny laughed. "Good instincts."

"They've kept me alive this long." He led

Sunny the rest of the way up the hill, wishing he had half of Bailey's moxie. And trying like hell to keep the same hope from filling him that he'd seen filling her innocent, young baby blues.

# CHAPTER TWENTY

Addie had been elbow deep down in her studio, prepping materials for her upcoming classes in North Carolina, so she'd opted to stay at her cabin. The rest of them caravanned down to the mill. Sunny was beyond curious about the surprise they'd apparently all been cooking up. She honestly hadn't a clue. Privately, her real hope was that whatever it was wouldn't take all that much time to show her, so she could make all the appropriate noises, and still have time to head to the woods and out to the greenhouse before the sun started to set.

They pulled in around the back of the mill. The snow was all but gone there. She was looking forward to seeing the mill blanketed in snow, like Sawyer's property had been. Sawyer had told her that in cold winters, a good part of the falls would actually freeze over, looking almost as if they'd frozen in motion. She was fascinated by that and would love to see it, but she wasn't otherwise rooting for a heavy winter. The clearer the roads remained, the easier it would be for her and Sawyer to see each other.

She was already not looking forward to going home alone in the morning. *Buck up, ya big baby.* She'd been giving herself variations of the "you could have worse problems" pep talks during the entire drive down earlier that day. But time felt like it was already racing by, and she wasn't ready to leave him yet. Truth be told, she wasn't ready to leave everyone else, either.

She climbed out of the truck as Seth pulled in with Bailey riding shotgun in his Land Rover. She wasn't sure what to make of Bailey's sudden lack of interest in coming to see her the following three-day weekend, but hoped it had more to do with the lambs than anything personal that might have suddenly turned her off. Sunny had planned all kinds of what she hoped would be fun outings for the two of them, and yes, there was work to be done, but she'd been hoping to make that fun for Bailey, too. She supposed she should have thought the whole lamb thing through a bit more. Of course Bailey wouldn't want to leave them so soon.

But there was no lack of enthusiasm now, she noted, as Bailey was all but dragging Seth by the hand. "Come on," she urged.

Sunny started walking toward the back door to the mill, looking forward to seeing firsthand what had been done during the past week. She was amazed at how quickly it all seemed to be coming together now. Sawyer and Addie had been sending her photos, and now that the space had all been framed out and the subfloors and drywall were up, the whole layout was quite clear to see. Looking at those photos, she could hardly believe it was the same cavernous relic she'd walked into that first day. It felt like a full lifetime ago now.

But Bailey wasn't tugging Seth toward the mill. The two of them started off across what was now more mud than grass toward — she stopped dead in her tracks and looked back at Sawyer, trying like hell not to think what she was instantly thinking.

He must have read something of the cascade of thoughts and hope and curiosity and . . . hope that crossed her face. He came around the front of his truck and took her hand. "Come on," he said.

"You realize I might die at least five times in the next five minutes if you don't tell me what —"

463

He turned in front of her so she neatly walked straight into his chest, cupped her cheek, and kissed her until she calmed down. Calm being a relative term, but he'd successfully diverted her attention at any rate.

He lifted his mouth from hers and said, "It's Bailey's surprise. I'm just along for the ride."

Sunny calmed down then, because, well, Bailey was amazing, but she was only ten years old. So, whatever this was, it wasn't likely to be about the one thing Sunny knew lay down this path. Her greenhouse.

Well, Bailey's greenhouse, and Addie's and Sawyer's, as they all technically owned a piece of it. But in her heart, it would always be her greenhouse. She couldn't help it.

The trail felt like it went on even longer this time, and she had the sudden thought maybe they were actually going to that overlook Sawyer had mentioned way back the first time they'd come out this way, the one he'd taken Bailey up to see her first day in the Hollow.

But just before they got to the clearing, Bailey turned around, and ran back to her and Sawyer. "Close your eyes," she instructed Sunny, sounding intensely serious and wound tighter than a drum, all at the same time. She took Sunny's hand in her own, and waited until Sunny complied.

"But —"

Sawyer took Sunny's other hand, leaned in, and whispered, "Have faith."

Sunny nodded, and tried to block out every wish she'd ever wished about the greenhouse, and there had been far too many of those made, usually when she was lying in bed at night, unable to sleep, too busy thinking about the amazing twists and turns her life had taken since that pretty fall day in Turtle Springs.

They led her slowly forward so she didn't trip over any tree roots or rocks. She could feel the sun on her face the moment they left the thick stand of pine trees.

"Okay," Bailey said, her voice almost painfully tight. "Open them."

As she said this, she was all but squeezing the life out of Sunny's hand. A moment later, both of Sunny's hands were covering her mouth, her gasp the single sound filling the air.

"We only just started," Bailey hurried to say.

Somehow Sunny managed to tear her gaze away from the greenhouse, and the grounds surrounding it, to look down at Bailey, whose little face was creased with more anxiety than any ten-year-old should ever be feeling.

"You did this?" Sunny managed, still in shock. "But . . . how?"

"I had help," she said, still anxious.

"Oh . . . my . . ." Sunny might have stumbled forward a step, but Sawyer took her elbow. She felt something damp on her cheeks and brushed at them, only to realize that they were tears.

"She's crying," Bailey whispered fiercely to Sawyer.

Sunny pulled herself together then, and sank to her knees, heedless of the mud and muck and pulled Bailey into her arms, almost hugging the life out of her. "I don't know how you did this, but you are the most amazing girl I've ever met."

Bailey held Sunny's shoulders and looked her square in the face, making sure she didn't misunderstand. "So . . . you like it?"

"Like it?" Sunny sat back and laughed in shock. "It's . . ." She trailed off again and looked past Bailey to the greenhouse and, with Sawyer's help, slowly got to her feet. With her hand on Bailey's shoulder, they both turned to survey the area. The land around the greenhouse had been completely cleared, and all the vines and weeds and growth that had covered the front of the building had been removed. That alone made such a tremendous difference, she almost didn't recognize the place.

The oversized front door had been scrubbed clean as much as it could be and was hanging correctly on what appeared to be new hinges. The glass panes on the front of the atrium appeared to have been scrubbed as well. She could see inside better there than through the panes on the west and east wings that jutted out to either side. The scroll trim that bordered the front of the atrium peak had been cleaned and whatever white paint had remained, along with all the mold, scale, and Lord knew what else had been scraped off and stripped down to the wrought iron. It gave the place an entirely different look. More . . . regal, less folly.

"We haven't gotten to the rest of the glass on the front. Some of it needs to be replaced." Bailey glanced at Sawyer, her expression still worried, then said, "Probably more than some."

Sunny dragged her gaze away again and looked down at Bailey. "I've never seen anything more beautiful in my entire life."

Bailey's wiry frame relaxed and her face split into a wide grin as she let herself begin to believe her plan was going to work out the way she wanted it to. "Seth and I started to clear out stuff from the inside, but then I wasn't sure if you wanted to keep any of it. The plants, I mean." She started pulling Sunny forward. "We took out a lot of the dead stuff, and most of the tables and stuff are rotted."

"I — I don't understand," Sunny said, trotting along behind her now. She cast a glance back at Seth. "You helped her with this?"

He nodded. "She's not just the lamb whisperer," he said, chuckling. "I think she's had the better part of half the town up here at one point or the other. We all pitched in, but it's a worthy cause."

"But —" Sunny finally slowed as they reached the door, and gently tugged Bailey back around to look at her. "Why?"

"So you'd have a place here, too," Bailey said, as if it was the most obvious thing in the world.

Sunny looked helplessly at Sawyer, who finally spoke up. "Seth had a builder friend of his come give it a look before they did anything. Bailey had the idea, but Seth wasn't sure the structural integrity hadn't been compromised by the part in the back that's caved in. Apparently, that part is a total loss, but the contractor said it could just be cut out and a new back wall installed closer in. So the two sides will be different sizes. He admitted he didn't know anything about how greenhouses worked, so, I don't know if that matters, but he said the overall structure would be stable and functional in a general sense."

Sunny was still trying to process everything, but one big chunk of reality managed to stomp right through all the pretty fairy-tales-do-come-true part. "That's going to cost — all of this is going to —"

Sawyer tugged her close and gave her a hug. "That's okay. At the moment, the only cost has been sweat equity and a few door hinges. The equity was donated." He grinned. "The hinges however, those are gonna cost you."

"Addie gives me an allowance for chores," Bailey said. "I can chip in."

Sunny laughed and said, "Oh, sweetie, if anyone owes anyone anything, it's me to you." She smiled. "But it was very kind of you to offer." She looked at Seth and Sawyer. "I don't know how to thank you, or everyone else who pitched in. I know you're all already working overtime on the mill, so I don't know how . . ." She trailed off and looked up at the atrium again. It was still a long way from being functional. A very, very long way. But there was promise now, and hope. She reached out and laid her hand on the front door, as if she was making a silent promise to the place that it was in good hands now. Just as she was.

She didn't realize she was crying again until she heard Bailey whisper as much to Sawyer. Apparently, to Bailey, there were no tears in reconstruction.

"It's a worthy cause," Seth said. "We figure when the boss man is happy, we're all happy. And what makes him happy, is making you happy. Simple math really." His smile deepened and she saw there were indeed dimples underneath that beard. "It's what small towns do, Sunny. Everyone pitches in. Like plowing you all out of the cabin. You'll have plenty of opportunity to pay it back when someone else is in need. It's like they say in *The Lion King*. It's the circle of life." He lifted his arms skyward, as if he was raising up baby Simba.

Sunny laughed even as the tears continued to trickle down her cheeks. "Well, that's beyond all possible kindness," she told him. "But I can't expect or even ask for any more, and this is still —"

"Shh," Sawyer said. "Let's go inside." He leaned closer. "The universe is talking," he whispered. "Just listen for a bit. See where it takes us."

"About that," she said, dashing her tears away, smiling up into his beautiful face. "It's been talking to me for a while now. I have . . . there's something we need to talk about."

# CHAPTER TWENTY-ONE

After walking through the interior of the greenhouse, which was now navigable thanks to the removal of much of the dead plant life and the heaps of mostly disintegrated wood tables, Seth and Bailey said their good-byes so Seth could take her back up to Addie's. There was still weekend homework to be done and lambs to be fed and put to bed.

Sunny and Sawyer stayed behind, basically because she couldn't yet tear herself away. She'd taken dozens, maybe even hundreds of photos with the camera on her phone. Only the failing light kept her from taking even more. The work that had been done was merely the tip of a glacier-sized iceberg, but the instant gratification of being able to see a goodly part of the entire greenhouse interior from anywhere they chose to stand, as well as being able to see clearly out through the front wall of the atrium, as the setting sun turned the scrubbed glass panes from green to gold, proved they'd chosen the best tip to start with.

"So . . . now that we're alone, what has the universe been whispering to you," Sawyer asked her, tugging her back into his arms and propping his chin on the top of her head.

He'd had a moment of panic when she'd first said they needed to talk, because those words did not usually bode well. But the moment had passed almost as quickly as it had come, because whatever it was, he felt confident that it was something she intended for them to deal with together.

And, frankly, that was the only part that mattered to him.

"You have a Seth," she said, amusement in her tone, which also helped to calm him.

She didn't sound nervous. How bad could this be?

"I have a Stevie."

"We are blessed with good friends," he agreed.

"Opinionated good friends who like to prod their good friends into what they are certain is the correct direction."

"Speaking for mine," Sawyer said, "this would be true. But then, his success rate makes it hard to quibble." He leaned down and pressed a kiss to her temple.

She sighed a little and snuggled back against him. "Stevie's batting average isn't so bad, either."

"I knew I liked her."

Sunny laughed. "Well, when I was possibly being a teensy tiny bit whiny about the whole long-distance relationship thing and how I didn't have much choice if I wanted to continue seeing you, she might have tossed it in my face that maybe the key word there was *choice,* and perhaps I should start thinking if there might be a third option. One that took care of the long-distance part, and left the relationship part intact."

He'd been comfortably humming along, letting her talk, happy to have her in his arms, happy that she seemed happy, excited even, fairly confident wherever she was going with this was going to be a good thing. He hadn't expected that it might be an amazing thing.

He turned her around in his arms. "And . . . did the magical third option appear?"

She smiled and the anticipation and downright glee in her eyes made his heart speed right up. "I'm . . . not sure yet. That's why I didn't say anything. But, actually, while we were exploring in here, it occurred to me that Bailey's gift might be an even bigger one than she realizes."

"I'm liking where this is going. Everyone is winning."

Sunny's tone might be saying caution, caution, but her eyes were saying yes, yes. "You know I told you that the orchid program I'm part of is a joint effort on the part of many linked botanic garden facilities around the country, all working together to try to save the native orchid species of North America."

"You did. I had no idea there were so many kinds indigenous to our country. They seem too exotic for that."

"Well, it's a shrinking number as we reduce their natural habitat. The paper I was asked to write is actually about new advances we've made in learning about the relationship between the ability of tiny orchid seeds to germinate in the wild and their reliance of these special little fungal critters."

"Would that be the technical term?"

She nudged him with her elbow. "Mycor-rhizal fungus, smarty pants."

"Sounds kind of sexual and gross all at the same time."

She grinned. "Actually, the sex lives of

orchids are rather wanton."

He nibbled on her ear, making her squirm. "Sounds like late-night phone call fodder to me."

She nudged him again, but he just wiggled his hips against her. She swatted at him, but she was laughing. "I'm trying to tell you something."

"I can't help it. All this orchid porn talk is making me hot."

"Actually, that might be the sexiest thing you could possibly say to a horticulturalist."

"Well, then hurry up so I can lure you up to my cabin with my own special brand of myochorri — actually, you know what. I just realized using any term that includes the word *fungus* is really not going to get me where I hope to go."

"Again, know your audience." She looked back at him and wiggled her eyebrows.

"Kinky," he said. "I like it." He made a face. "Maybe."

"*So,*" she said, emphasizing the word, "I contacted the director who oversees the whole North American orchid preservation program and explained my situation, and told him that it was possible I might be able to get exclusive use of a rather large privately owned greenhouse facility." She turned in his arms now and faced him. "I thought even if I could save the atrium, maybe part of one wing, it would still be substantial square footage. Or worst case, tear it down and build a new facility on the same property — though that would have pretty much broken my heart." She saw the confused look on his face and hurried to clarify. "One of the biggest problems we face is finding facilities that meet our specific needs and with enough space to even be worth setting up a research program. Even though the greenhouses we do work with can handle plant varieties that aren't native to their specific location, the more diverse locations we have, the better."

"And I'm guessing a mountain-based facility would be a good get?"

She nodded, but lifted a hand to stall any premature celebrating. "All of this costs money, of course. The kind of money I don't have. Even if I sold the town house —"

"Sunny," he began, his expression immediately changing to one of concern.

"I'd been thinking about it anyway, even before we met. I don't need all that space, and besides . . ." She lifted a hand. "I don't want to bury my memories of my mother along with her. I couldn't anyway — they will always be with me. But I thought I might not mind burying some of the ghosts of the past, if you know what I mean. I just . . . every time I thought about actually doing it, I couldn't imagine still living in the same area and knowing there were strangers living in my house." She shrugged. "I know that sounds weird, but —"

"It doesn't sound weird at all," he said.

"But that's not the solution to the money problem anyway," she said. "There are grants available, and charitable foundations who also underwrite various research facilities. The director agreed with me that we might have a leg up on getting one awarded to us based on the unique elements I already mentioned." She looked up into his face. "So . . . I applied for one. In fact, I applied for several. Just to hedge our bet."

"So . . . what does that mean, exactly?"

"It means if we win one or more, I would leave the USBG and work independently with the national orchid preservation group. The restoration would be underwritten, and some percentage of the research. I'll always have to be scrounging after funding, but that's more or less the nature of most research anyway. And with a facility this size, especially if Seth's friend is right and we can preserve most of the square footage, it's likely that others in my field will come up and work here, too. I couldn't do it all on my own."

"That's . . . incredible. I can't believe you've kept this a secret."

She motioned to their surroundings. "Really?" she said dryly.

He chuckled. "Touché."

"If it happens, it's not going to be for some time," she warned him. "I'll need to stay with the USBG until we get an answer. Which is fine because I still have the paper to write."

"What about the doctorate?"

"Well, if I do choose to pursue that at some point, the work here would go a long way toward forming the basis for my thesis. I thought a lot about what you asked. Was I going for the education or the career advancement? I realized I'd only been thinking about it for the latter. But with this new path . . . I don't know. I'm thinking maybe it will be something I want on a deeper level. That's distant future though."

"And . . . if the grant doesn't come through?"

She pressed her palm to his cheek, then let her fingertips trace down along his chin. "Then I'll find another one, and another one, and I'll keep applying until I get one. There is no better solution, and, quite honestly, it's a really fabulous proposal." She let her hands slide to his shoulders. "It was surprising, really, how it all fell into place. It won't earn me much and, as I said, I'll constantly be beating the bush for funding." She smiled. "And Bailey and I will have to revisit that whole donating-her-share-of-the-greenhouse thing, and I'll need to talk to you and Addie as well, because we'll have to secure the property separate from the mill."

"Something tells me that will be the easiest part of this whole endeavor."

She grinned. "I was also thinking that, while we're waiting to find out about the proposals, you and I will have some time to explore our relationship, before getting too ahead of ourselves." She toyed with the hair at the nape of his neck and stepped more fully into his arms. "But if that goes well, then when the time does come, I'll put the town house on the market and invest whatever I get for it in getting a place of my own . . . or in getting that cabin of yours up to snuff. Maybe throw a little at the trapper's cabin. I've always wanted my very own potting shed."

"Sunny," he said, utterly abashed. "You don't need to —"

"Doyle gave that house to my mother, and

to me. So, in a way, it's also part of our inheritance. I mean, if part of that mill is mine, then it's only right that part of the town house should be yours."

He just shook his head, humbled and filled with admiration for her. "So, now I have something to tell you."

Her eyes widened slightly, but she didn't look overly worried.

"That first morning I woke up with you, you were lying on your back, hair every which way, mascara in very fetching streaks on your cheeks, and did you know you snore?"

"You sweet talker, you," she said wryly.

He slid his hand under her hair, stroked a fingertip along the nape of her neck, enjoying the little shiver that went through her. He loved discovering her sweet spots. He loved that he was going to have the chance to find the rest of them. "I watched you sleeping that morning," he said quietly, lowering his mouth closer to hers. "And every part of me was thinking the same thing."

"Run, run for the hills?" she said, but there was a breathless element there now, and her gaze was locked on his.

He smiled. "If the phone hadn't rung, and the snowplow cavalry hadn't arrived, I doubt I could have kept it to myself. But now I'm glad I did."

"Oh?" she said, looking worried for the first time.

"Because this is the perfect spot to tell you."

She didn't say anything then; she just gazed into his eyes. And he'd never been so sure of anything in his life. "Sunshine Meadow Aquarius Morrison Goodwin . . . I love you."

He watched as emotion filled her eyes and she closed the distance between his mouth and hers and gave him possibly the very best kiss he'd ever gotten, because along with it came the words, "Oh, thank God."

He chuckled against her lips. *Only Sunny.*

"I was really hoping I wouldn't have to be keeping that a secret, too," she said. "Master Sergeant Sawyer Angel Hartwell, I love you right back." Then she grabbed his face with both hands, and claimed him for her very own.

*Thank you, Universe,* he thought. *It's about damn time.*

# EPILOGUE

Over Sawyer's protests, Addie carried the heavy pewter tray loaded with the turkey over to the dining room table. "I've managed to get every Thanksgiving turkey to this table from the time I was no taller than Bailey there. The November I can't manage it is the November that finds me already six feet under."

Sunny and Bailey shared a pained look behind Addie's back, then grinned as they dutifully carried over the marshmallow yam casserole, green beans, and hot buttered rolls and set them on the table before everyone took their seats.

Sawyer had the job of slicing the majestic bird, but he paused, carving knife and long-tined fork held aloft. "I thought we should all take a moment to say one thing that we are thankful for this year."

Addie beamed. "That's a wonderful idea. I'll start."

Sawyer lowered his utensils and nodded her way. "The floor is yours. Or the table, as it were."

Addie smiled and reached out to pat him on the arm, then looked at them all. "While it's true that D. Bart had a tendency to bring far more problems along with him than pleasures, the one thing he did do quite well was bringing the four of us together. I don't know that I've ever felt so thankful about anything in my life, save for the fact that I'm drawing breath long enough to see it happen." She shook out her linen napkin and laid it across her lap, but she wasn't done yet. "It's not often I reflect back on the years that are behind me. I'm one who believes it's a great deal more fun to look ahead and wonder what comes next." She smiled. "That said, I'll admit that I had been feeling a bit pressured by Father Time to get busy forming the guild and seeing the work on the mill through to fruition before the good Lord saw fit to call me home." She took a moment to look at each of their faces. "But I sit here now and look at the life, and the vitality, and the love that surrounds me every day, right here in my own home, and I know that it's true, that even at this point in my life, the best days are yet ahead of me."

"Here, here," Sawyer said, and Sunny and Bailey both cheered. Then they all lifted their water glasses in a toast.

"Ditto," Sawyer, Sunny, and Bailey said at the same time as they clinked their glasses together, then laughed to the point that they couldn't take their respective sips.

The meal was consumed with great gusto as stories were shared and laughter continued to be the keynote of the day.

Sunny and Bailey were clearing the dishes as Sawyer worked on storing the leftovers. Addie was wiping down the table and shaking out the place mats, and had just proposed a hike down to feed some scraps to the lambs, in hopes of working up an appetite for her pecan pie when the phone rang.

It was Sawyer's cell phone, which he found sitting on a wicker stool by the front door. It was Seth. "Hey, happy Thanksgiving."

"Same," he said, sounding quite jovial.

"You still in Seattle?"

"No, I opted out this go-around."

Sawyer frowned. "Everything okay?"

"Excellent, as it happens. I just decided to take some R&R for myself while everyone else was preoccupied with turkey and pie. I had a little project I really wanted to get done. You and the tribe feel like a short road trip?"

"Road trip? Um . . . I guess, sure." He looked up to find the other three had stopped what they were doing and were listening in. He lifted his shoulders, having no more idea than they did. "Where to?"

"Come on down to the mill. Bring the whole gang."

Sawyer shared Seth's request with the others and a few minutes later Addie and Bailey were heading down in her Subaru, followed by Sawyer and Sunny in his pickup. They'd just continue on up to his cabin from there.

The answer to what Seth's little project had been about was answered before they even got close enough to park.

"Sawyer, look!" Sunny was pointing, but Sawyer had already slowed the truck so he could get a good look himself.

"The waterwheel . . . it's working!"

And apparently, Sawyer wasn't the only one Seth had contacted. The lower lot, the upper lot, and the sides of the road were all filled with cars and trucks, and even a tractor or two.

"The whole town is here," Sunny said, as they parked and climbed out.

Bailey raced over to them. "Oh my goodness, do you see it?" She didn't wait for an answer, but grabbed Sunny's hand in one of hers, and Sawyer's in her other. "Come on!"

Sawyer looked over his shoulder at Addie, who merely lifted her walking stick and shooed them on ahead, a big smile on her weathered face.

They all joined the rest of the folks who had gathered on the banks of Big Stone Creek. Seth had climbed up on an overturned wine cask and he lifted his hands, gathering everyone's attention.

"So, I was talking to my dear auld mum the other day, about Thanksgiving, and family, and what it meant to me. Now, I love my mum, and my dad, and all my siblings and cousins and nieces and nephews. But when I thought about what home meant to me, what family meant to me, the first thing that came to my mind was all of you. You all welcomed me here, you took me in, and you made me feel like a part of this town I now call home." He gestured to the mill. "And look. Look what we did here together!"

A loud cheer went up from the whole crowd, filling the chilly, late-November air.

Seth looked out at the sea of smiling faces. "There are new faces in the crowd this year.

And you've been just as wonderful in welcoming them." He tipped an imaginary hat toward Sunny and Bailey. The crowd turned to look at them, some nodding, some clapping, and a few others lifting their hands in a show of solidarity.

"And who knows what is in store for us in the next year," Seth said, then shot a suggestive look at Sawyer and Sunny and wiggled his eyebrows. That caused a titter of laughter to run through the crowd, which quickly changed to cheers and more than a few whistles when they collectively turned in time to see Sawyer bending Sunny over his arm and kissing her soundly on the lips.

Bailey, who was standing right next to them, had covered her eyes. Addie put her hand on Bailey's shoulder and beamed from ear to ear.

"Happy Thanksgiving, everyone!" he shouted.

There was laughter, and more than a few hugs. Parents warned children not to race too close to the water's edge. Others went over to ask Seth how he'd gotten the ancient wheel to run again, discussing mechanics and bearings and engine parts. Someone brought a fiddle, another a mandolin, and music once again filled the Hollow.

*And the universe looked down, nodding in*

satisfaction that its message had been duly received. The focus shifted then to a new story about to unfold . . . and orbits were once again spun into motion. Some would miss. Others would collide.

What was in store in the coming year? Indeed, Mr. Seth Brogan was about to find out.

He only had to listen. . . .

# AUTHOR'S NOTE

Turtle Springs, Hawksbill Valley, Big Stone Creek, and Blue Hollow Falls exist only in my imagination (and yours now, too, I hope!). However, the words used in the place names I chose for this book, as well as the some of the names of the people who populate my little mountain town, all originate in this lovely part of the Blue Ridge Mountains that I call home.

The history of silk production in the United States mentioned in the early part of the story, along with the origination of American silk mills, is based in fact. While most of those mills are now defunct or long gone, there are still a few in operation, even to this day.

In *Blue Hollow Falls,* Sunny Goodwin is a horticulturalist with the United States Botanic Garden. While I did take a bit of literary license with some of the elements surrounding Sunny's job and the operation of both the conservatory and the production facility, both the USBG conservatory and the production facility are quite real. (You can even follow them both on Facebook!) The Care for the Rare program is also real. You can learn more about that program here: www.bgci.org/usa/carefortherare

And, lastly, there are indeed approximately 200 species of orchids that are native to North America. It is also true that many of them are threatened or endangered due to loss of natural habitat. The germination research mentioned in the story is part of actual research currently being conducted by the also very real North American Orchid Conservation Center. To learn more about the work they are doing, you can check them out here: www.northamericanorchid center.org (It's worth a visit, if for no other reason than to see the amazing and awe-inspiring photos of some of the world's most beautiful flowers. And yes . . . that crack Sunny made about their sex lives? Totally true! You can read more about that there, too.)

Oh, wait, there is one more thing! If you want to see how adorable a real Herdwick baby lamb is, go here and scroll: www.herdy .co.uk/blog/all-about-herdwicks/21/post (I knew I'd found my sheep breed when they compared a Herdwick ram to Russell Crowe in *Gladiator*!)

Thank you for spending time with me in my beautiful mountains here in southwestern Virginia. I hope you'll drop by for another visit!

# ABOUT THE AUTHOR

*USA Today* bestselling author of the Bachelors of Blueberry Cove series, **Donna Kauffman** has been gratified to see her books get rave reviews in venues ranging from *Kirkus Reviews* and *Library Journal* to *Entertainment Weekly* and *Cosmopolitan*. She lives in the beautiful Blue Ridge Mountains in western Virginia, where she is presently applying her crafty DIY skills to decorating her new mountainside abode. When she isn't busy trying to keep the bears from hanging out in her flower and vegetable garden all day and night, she loves to hear from readers! You can contact her through her website at www.donnakauffman .com.

The employees of Thorndike Press hope you have enjoyed this Large Print book. All our Thorndike, Wheeler, and Kennebec Large Print titles are designed for easy reading, and all our books are made to last. Other Thorndike Press Large Print books are available at your library, through selected bookstores, or directly from us.

For information about titles, please call:
(800) 223-1244

or visit our website at:
gale.com/thorndike

To share your comments, please write:
Publisher
Thorndike Press
10 Water St., Suite 310
Waterville, ME 04901